Praise for *Amaz...*

An Instant *New Yo...*
A *Today* Read with J...
An Indie Next Pick for September 2023
One of the *Washington Post*'s "10 Best Feel-Good Books of 2023"

"The most hilarious, feel-good book of the year . . . You will laugh on the first page and you will keep laughing until you're crying on the last page."
—Jenna Bush Hager, *Today*

"Grace Adams is also the latest in a series of brilliant, beautiful and privileged protagonists (Amy Dunne, Bernadette Fox, Barbie) undone by the challenges of modern womanhood."
—*The New York Times Book Review*

"With this hilarious debut novel, Fran Littlewood delivers a fantastic ode to female rage and how it (wildly!) plays out over the course of a single day." **—*Real Simple***

"A gripping story of joy, grief, stress, worry, love at first sight, parenting . . . frank, nuanced, and evocative." **—*Kirkus Reviews***

"Hugely enjoyable. Compelling, funny, and poignant. I devoured it."
—Paula Hawkins, #1 *New York Times* bestselling author of *The Girl on the Train*

"I just adored this beautiful debut novel! Funny, moving, and at times absolutely heartbreaking, it had me captivated until the very last page. An unforgettable read." **—Liane Moriarty, *New York Times* bestselling author of *Big Little Lies***

"From the first hot minute when Grace Adams, stalled in traffic, stuck in her car, simply opens the door and walks away from it all—into her day, the single day that gathers all her days up to this tipping point at the middle, she had me. How life in the middle of our lives breaks us open—and apart—and then open again. I finished her story on a plane above the country, so full, and in tears. 'Ma'am?' my seatmate asked, 'are you ok?' 'Oh, yes,' I answered. And gave him this book."

—**Sarah Blake**, *New York Times* **bestselling author of**
The Postmistress **and** *The Guest Book*

"*Amazing Grace Adams* is an exacting and brilliantly structured novel about love, grief, hope lost and then found again. I rooted for Grace from the first sentence." —**Mary Beth Keane**, *New York Times* **bestselling author of** *Ask Again, Yes*

"Fran Littlewood has written a magnificent novel. Grace Adams is every woman—filled with promise, trepidatious in love and, eventually, a besotted mother. *Amazing Grace Adams* is a fully realized story of catastrophe and joy, grief and love, and the hidden chambers of the human heart that carry the best and worst of our experience. A stunning debut."

—**Adriana Trigiani, bestselling author of** *The Good Left Undone*

"I can't remember the last time I read a novel with such unbridled enthusiasm. *Amazing Grace Adams* is a raw, uproariously hilarious portrait of parenthood, love, and family; it's also a profound examination of the way language can both save us and fail us when we need it the most. I'd walk across London on the hottest day of the year with Fran Littlewood—hell, I'd walk anywhere with her. I'm begging you: read this book."

—**Grant Ginder, author of** *Let's Not Do That Again*
and *The People We Hate at the Wedding*

"I devoured it. Vivid, visceral, and incredibly emotional. I laughed and sobbed." —**Tim Minchin, Tony Award nominee,**
Matilda the Musical **and** *Groundhog Day the Musical*

Amazing
Grace Adams

A Novel

Fran Littlewood

A HOLT PAPERBACK

HENRY HOLT AND COMPANY

NEW YORK

Holt Paperbacks
Henry Holt and Company
Publishers since 1866
120 Broadway
New York, New York 10271
www.henryholt.com

A Holt Paperback® and 🅗® are registered trademarks of
Macmillan Publishing Group, LLC.

Published in the United Kingdom by Michael Joseph. Michael Joseph is part
of the Penguin Random House group of companies.

The Library of Congress has cataloged the hardcover edition as follows:

Names: Littlewood, Fran, author.
Title: Amazing Grace Adams / Fran Littlewood.
Description: First U.S. Edition | New York : Henry Holt and Company, 2023.
Identifiers: LCCN 2022052737 (print) | LCCN 2022052738 (ebook) |
    ISBN 9781250334152 (hardcover) | ISBN 9781250907608 (Canadian edition) |
    ISBN 9781250857026 (ebook)
Subjects: Domestic fiction. | Novels.
Classification: LCC PR6112.I885 A83 2023 (print) | LCC PR6112.I885 (ebook) |
    DDC 823/.92
LC record available at https://lccn.loc.gov/2022052737
LC ebook record available at ttps://lccn.loc.gov/2022052738

ISBN 9781250857002 (trade paperback)

Our books may be purchased in bulk for promotional, educational, or
business use. Please contact your local bookseller or the Macmillan Corporate
and Premium Sales Department at (800) 221-7945, extension 5442,
or by e-mail at MacmillanSpecialMarkets@macmillan.com.

Originally published in hardcover in the United States in 2023
by Henry Holt and Company

First Holt Paperbacks Edition 2024

Designed by Meryl Sussman Levavi

Printed in the United States of America

1   3   5   7   9   10   8   6   4   2

This is a work of fiction. All of the characters, organizations, and events portrayed
in this novel either are products of the author's imagination or are used fictitiously.

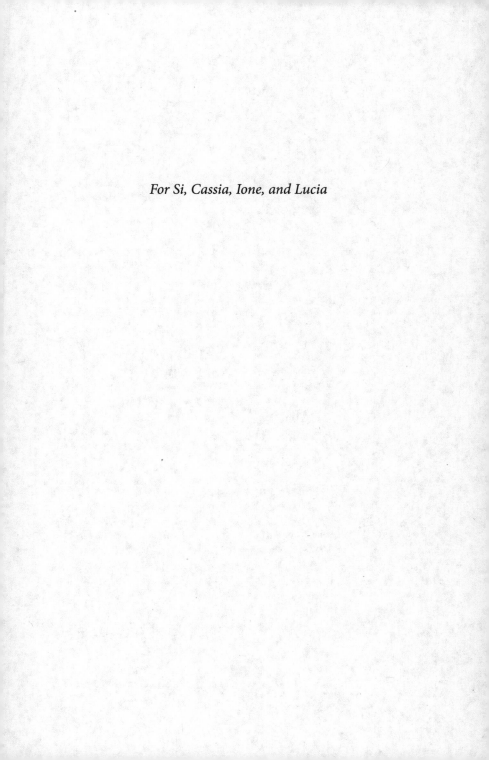

For Si, Cassia, Ione, and Lucia

How I raged, and woke to hear the rain.

<small>VIRGINIA WOOLF</small>

Amazing
Grace Adams

Now

GRACE IS HOT. There's the sun, like boiled breath, on the roof of her car, but it's more than that. This feeling that from nowhere she's been set on fire from the inside out. Between her breasts a line of sweat is tracking a slow, itchy S, and she wants to jam a hand under the neck of her shirt and wipe it away. It's gridlock, though, and she's hemmed in on all sides, and there's the man in the Audi, whose car window is level with hers. He's staring at her like she's the distraction he needs in this. Screw you, she thinks. Screw you, screw you, screw you.

"If you're feeling hot out there today," the woman on the radio is saying, "according to the latest report from climate think tank Autonomy, it's only going to get hotter . . ."

Grace revs the engine to drown out the words and her eyes find the clock on the dashboard: 12:23. Can that be right? She checks her phone on the passenger seat. Shit. She's late. Really late. There's the *Love Island* cake to pick up, the one she's had specially made. The cake she can't afford but is staking everything on. One, two, three, four . . . She begins the CBT count that doesn't work—the half-remembered one from the online course she abandoned after the first few sessions—then takes a deep breath in through her nose. Now her jeans are sticking to her thighs. Grace fiddles with the vents, stabs yet again at the button for the air-con she knows isn't working. It's the cheap heat in the synthetic fabric that's making it all worse and she spreads her knees as wide as they'll go, trying to get some nonexistent air between her legs.

On the passenger seat her phone goes and she starts. Lotte? The thought is automatic, that it might be her. But even as she's leaning across to check she already knows. Instead there's the shock of a jowly face frowning from the screen, and it's a moment before she recognizes herself, understands that Cate is trying to FaceTime her again. Grace shrinks back against the driver's door. She doesn't want to answer, and although she's pretty sure she can't be seen—Lotte has laughed at her about this a hundred times—still she has the sense that her sister is somehow watching her. Grace knows already what Cate is phoning to say: she's left a vomit of messages over the past fortnight that somehow manage to be both compassionate and accusatory. *Mum called me to say she's been trying to get in touch, Grace. She's worried about you. Dad too. It isn't really fair on them to . . . Listen, call me and let me know you're okay. I mean, not okay but . . . We're all worried, Grace . . .*

There's the blast of a horn behind her and she twists in her seat. Like it's aimed at her. The traffic is solid, stretching back as far as she can see along the skinny road that runs from the foot of Muswell Hill all the way to the Emirates Stadium. The kind of road that would be better suited to a sleepy village, or medieval times, but that's clotted chaotically with work vans and city buses and delivery drivers and SUVs. "Really?" she says, into the void of the car. "Really, arsehole? You want us to do what exactly?"

The sides of the car are closing in on her and she can smell burned plastic. How are they not moving yet? Sitting here like this it's reminding her of something—a book, a TV show, a screenplay . . . she can't remember. She can barely remember her own name these days. Slumping in the seat, she tries to bring to mind the things she hasn't been able to recall recently. But, of course, she can't. It would almost be funny if it wasn't so terrifying. Like a part of her brain dropped out when she was looking the other way.

Her phone starts to ring again, and someone is leaning into their horn. The man is still staring at her, the heat in the car . . . and something is trapped and buzzing in here with her now. A fat black fly vibrating against the windows. Sweat pops at her temple and she's slapping herself because the fly is dive-bombing her, ricocheting frenetically around the car's interior.

Suddenly a face appears at the rear window of the car in front. A little girl with a grubby doll clutched in her hand is staring at Grace, unsmiling. She can hear the hiccuping beat of a track on the radio, the bone-judder of drilling from the roadworks ahead. And the fly is on her cheek now, on her arm, in her hair, and the traffic still isn't moving, and time is jumping forward in units that aren't as they should be, and she can't be late, not today, there's just no question.

And that's it. She's had it.

Thick fumes catch in her throat as Grace steps from the car, gripping her phone, and jamming her credit card and a twenty-pound note into her back pocket. It's all she needs. She doesn't want to lug her bag around in this heat—she's wearing the wrong clothes as it is: too-tight denim that makes her legs feel as if they're melting. Grace slams shut the door, points her key and—*ca-chunk*—the doors are locked. And she's walking away, picking a path along the white lines in the middle of the road, when there's a shout behind her.

"Hey, love. Love! What d'you think you're doing?"

She stops and turns.

It's the man in the Audi. He has his window down and he's raising his voice above the blast of horns starting up. She registers the threat in the pulse of the engines around her, the angry atonal soundscape, but she has the strange sense that she's somewhere beyond it, that it's separate from her.

"You're not seriously . . ." The man is yelling now, gesturing wildly so that she can see the sweat patches under his arms. "You need to get back in your car! You can't leave it there!"

Grace can taste the metal heat coming off the vehicles wedged either side of her as she smiles at him. With her mouth, not her eyes.

"Deal with it," she whispers.

Four Months Earlier

Northmere Park School
London N8 6TJ
nps@haringey.sch.uk

Dear Parent or Carer of Lotte Adams Kerr,
It has come to our attention that Lotte's attendance has dipped below 70 percent this term and that many of these absences remain "unauthorized." This is significantly below the Ofsted targets set out in our school-parent agreement and as such is extremely concerning.

At this worrying level, Lotte's absenteeism will be having a serious impact on their learning and achievements. As you know, research shows that for every nineteen days of school missed, a student can expect to see their GCSE results fall by a grade.

We would like to request you contact the school to make an urgent appointment with Lotte's tutor, as well as their head of year to discuss the matter as soon as possible. At this time no external agencies are involved. However, we do have a duty to report the repeated or prolonged absence of any pupil.

Yours faithfully,
John Power, Head Teacher

LEANING AGAINST THE kitchen counter, Grace reads the letter twice and still she can't process it. She frowns, checks the envelope. She can only assume there has been an administrative error, that they have sent the letter to the wrong person. Even so, she can feel a tightening in her lungs, as if she can't quite catch a full breath.

"Lotte!" she calls. She knows, though, that her daughter will be in her bedroom with her headphones on, that there's no way she'll hear her. She glances at her laptop on the table. Up on-screen there's the shitty Japanese romance she's in the middle of translating—or, rather, that she's in the middle of *not* translating. She doesn't want to think about how far past the deadline she is. She doesn't want to think about what will happen if she doesn't get her act together on this, because she can't afford to mess up the translation-agency work. Quite literally. The laughable amount she earns from her other job—her anything-to-get-her-out-of-the-house job, teaching French to uninterested under-twelves at Stanhope Primary— would barely cover her gas bill.

Grace takes her phone from the side and—because this is the way they do things now—texts her daughter, who is less than ten meters away from where she stands, up a floor, through a couple of walls. Waits. Nothing.

"Lotte!" she tries again, louder this time, and she feels the familiar itch of irritation in her gut. Then she screws up the letter and throws it hard across the room toward the overflow that's pooled around the recycling bin.

Grace knocks but doesn't wait before she enters the room. Lotte is sitting on her bed and immediately slams down the lid of her laptop. Her expression is at once hostile and vulnerable. She has dyed her hair pink again and it looks so pretty on her, that color, like spun candy floss, and Grace is struck by how beautiful she has become, her perfect-wild daughter. How, if she could, she would just stand there drinking her in. She's wearing shorts and a green top that's more of a bandage really, barely covering her breasts. Those braless breasts that seem held up by magic. *Aren't you freezing?* Grace wants to ask. Because she has become a cliché. She has become her own mother.

"What?" Lotte says, lifting her headphones from one ear. "I'm in the middle of something." And Grace can tell it's taking everything she's got to keep her tone just the right side of politeness. That is, the newly low bar of mutually accepted "politeness."

Grace opens her mouth to answer, but finds she has to pause because she feels suddenly as though she may not be able to get the words out without her voice splitting. She skates her eyes around the room, like she's looking for clues. There's the honey-and-sweat smell of dirty laundry, a knocked-over plant that has spilled most of its earth underneath the window. Posters on the wall of the girl from *Stranger Things*, the guy from *Sherlock*, the bright-painted *matryoshka* in the middle of the bookshelf, a tangle of hoop earrings, and the little brass Buddha on the bedside table. Grace's mind skids from one object to the next as if they might hold the answers to where her baby went. To who this strange new person is.

"What?" Lotte asks again, and she isn't trying to disguise her impatience anymore. And then, under her breath, "Jesus."

The word winds Grace, just a little, but she lets it go, fixes her eyes on her child's. They have the same eyes, she knows: everyone tells them this. The same deep-set dark blue eyes. Eyes that could undo a person, Ben used to tell her.

"I've had a letter from the school that doesn't make sense," Grace says.

2002

Sitting there with her foldout table, pens lined up, she's asking herself why on earth she has come. There's the jump of nerves in her stomach and she feels as if she's back in college. Twenty-eight years old and it's like she's eighteen again. Strung above the stage is a PVC banner, a yellow background dotted with line-drawn illustrations of various global landmarks—the Taj Mahal, the Eiffel Tower, St Basil's Cathedral, and, picked out in bold green lettering, the words "Polyglot of the Year 2002." A geek convention, Marc calls it—*called* it, Grace corrects herself, because he's in the past now; they are no longer together. "A *genius* convention, I think you'll find," she'd told him, as she stuck the application form to the fridge and raised her middle finger with her back still to him.

A few seats along from her she sees the man in the black sweater with the holes at the wrists, the one she noticed at Registration. He's younger than her, she guesses, maybe by a couple of years. But he's the only normal person here. As she's thinking this, he leans toward her like somehow she's leaked her train of thought.

"Excuse me, hi . . ."

Up close he has extraordinarily hollow cheeks, and an L-shaped jaw—you could measure a 90-degree angle by it. His hair is going in several different directions at once, but his brown eyes are on her.

"Do you have a pen?" he asks.

Grace looks down at her stash on the foldout table and wonders for a moment if he's joking. She has ballpoints in blue, black, and red; a set of highlighters; and three HB pencils. Suddenly she feels like a ridiculous swot. "I do seem to," she says. "Take your pick."

He smiles at her, stretches farther across the seats, and eyes her table. He's taking his time doing this and again she gets the sense that maybe he's making fun of her.

"I'll go blue Bic," he says eventually.

"The classic." She takes it from the desk, hands it to him. "I approve."

He laughs and thanks her. Then he taps the pen twice against the palm of his hand, like he's testing it. He has beautiful fingers, she notices. Long with square nails cut short.

He leans back in his seat and immediately forward again as though something has spiked his back. "I'm Ben, by the way."

"Grace." She feels the heat rise in her cheeks when she says her name.

A screech of feedback from the sound system saves her. There's a man onstage now, fiddling with the microphone. He's deeply tanned in a linen suit and looks like something out of *A Year in Provence*. He taps the mic once, twice, clears his throat.

"Welcome, all," the man says, and presses his palms together in prayer. "And congratulations on making it this far. I'm David Turner and *you* are some of the best linguists in the country."

Grace glances back at the man in the black jumper. He raises his eyebrows just a little; she opens her eyes too wide in return.

". . . which means you've all been selected on the strength of your videotaped entries," David Turner is saying, "and I don't mind telling you the standard this year is *sky*-high. We've got participants here aged from twenty-three to seventy-four and from all corners of the UK, which I think you'll agree is fantastic. So, okay, there'll be introductory talks this morning and we have some incredibly exciting speakers lined up. The real fun starts this afternoon!" He power-punches the air and laughter scatters the room. "I know you're all keen to crack on, so it only remains for me to wish you . . ." He pauses and winks. Grace definitely sees him wink. ". . . *Bonne chance, buena suerte, viel erfolg, udachi, held og lykke*, et cetera, et cetera, et cetera!"

Grace turns to the man in the black jumper and winks stagily. "Good luck," she tells him.

"You too." He winks back, his face straight.

Lunch is served in the cafeteria. It's outside term time and the campus is eerily empty. Grace isn't hungry but opts for a jacket potato the size of a brick and some dying salad, waits for the woman in the queue behind her so that she has someone to sit with. Soon they are surrounded at their canteen table by—well—*geeks*. The talk turns to conjugations and Cyrillic and Klingon and, she can't help herself, she's hoovering it up. She's lost in language but, even so, she's aware that from time to time the man in the black jumper with the holes in the sleeves is looking her way from across the canteen.

The afternoon passes in a head rush of linguistic sparring and she's in her element—she's on fire. She's killing it in French, Spanish, Japanese, Russian, Dutch. There's pronunciation against the clock—a speed read of a hundred phrases in ten minutes, simultaneous interpretation, and critical discussion of unseen questions with just sixty seconds to respond. They attempt to learn Romanian in an hour. Grace is gone and her brain, her body are channeling the words. She has studied and studied for this. She has put in her ten thousand hours, but it's easy for her. It's as if the words, the sentences, the language structures were there all along, lurking in her cerebral cortex, and she just needed to excavate them. She guesses the same must be true of the other competitors because the man in the linen suit—David—is right: they're all fierce. Every year for the past three she has almost entered the contest, but something always stopped her, a sense that maybe she wouldn't be good enough. She even filled in the forms last year, but in the end didn't send them. Now that she's here, she can't believe she talked herself out of it. And suddenly she wants this. She wants, more than anything, to win.

When she arrives in the student union bar where the prize-giving will be held, he is already seated. It smells of stale smoke and disinfectant, and it's like Pavlov's dogs: Grace immediately wants a drink. She hesitates and the man, Ben, beckons her over, makes room so that she can sit down. Then he takes her blue ballpoint from his pocket and hands it to her. "Thanks," he says. "My secret charm. *Le Bic bleu . . .*"

"Ha," she says. "I hope it worked." The pen is warm where it's been in his hand and she has a sudden urge to bring it to her face, to inhale the place where his fingers have been.

There's wine on the table and she fills her glass, offers the bottle to him. "I feel like we should be drinking snakebite and black."

"Totally. Or warm lager slops."

Around them the tables are filling. She waves at the recruitment consultant from Cambridge, the one she sat with at lunch. David Turner is setting himself up at the front of the room and there's a silver trophy on the bar behind him.

"So how did you go?" Ben asks.

"Pretty good, I think," she says. "You?"

"Yeah." He nods.

"*Yeah?*" She laughs. "What does that mean?"

"*Okaaay* . . . we're a bit behind time so let's get started." David Turner is raising his voice above the chatter. "Thanks again, everyone, for taking part. I'm proud to say . . ."

She's trying to concentrate on the announcement, but Grace is sure she can feel Ben looking at her, the heat of his stare on the side of her face. She can smell him too, this close to her. A raw white smell that makes her think of winter.

". . . and so I'll jump straight in now with third place." David Turner shades his eyes with his hands and looks out into the room. Now he has her attention. Grace holds herself still.

"Ariel Jones, are you here somewhere?"

They're facing forward and clapping, both of them, as the slight man with the ill-advised moustache accepts his prize, and maybe it's the wine that's gone straight to her head but she has the strange sensation that she has been in this moment before.

". . . and our runner-up with a score of 163 and winning a hundred-pound Foyles book token . . ." David Turner consults his piece of paper, ". . . is Ben Kerr. Well done!"

The man in the black jumper glances at her as he stands, pulls a fast, surprised face before he moves to the front of the room to accept his prize. There's a quickening in her that she doesn't understand. Her palms are throbbing from all the clapping and she's pleased for him, she is. He seems like a nice guy, but at the same time she doesn't like to think that he has scored higher than her in this thing. And she has no idea why this matters to her so much, what she's trying to prove, because it's just a dumb little competition and . . .

". . . taking the title of Polyglot of the Year, with an incredible 164 points—that's just one point, ladies and gentlemen, separating our winner from our esteemed runner-up . . . it's Grace Adams. Many, many congratulations, Grace. We salute you!"

It's a moment before she processes that David Turner has announced her name. Across the student union bar, people are swiveling in their seats.

"Up you come, Grace," David Turner calls.

And as she gets to her feet all eyes are on her. Because she's won, she's bloody well gone and won it. She tries and fails to keep a poker face as she moves toward the bar. This day has filled her up, she realizes. It has made her happy. And it's the first time she's felt this way since Marc—since *she and Marc*—decided they were done. Since long before then, in fact.

Someone hands her a glass of champagne and she's presented with the silver trophy. There's an envelope too, but her hands are full and she can't take it.

"Well, I can tell you," David Turner flexes the envelope, "that, courtesy of our great friends at Language Matters, you've won a weekend break for two at the beautiful Kerensa Hotel in Cornwall . . ."

Grace has no idea how long it is before the crowd around her dissipates. She has smiled and smiled and drunk and drunk, and her face is aching with the effort of it all, and suddenly it's just her and the man in the black sweater, holes at the wrists, standing together at the bar.

"I knew it would be you." He's leaning his body close to hers so that they're almost touching. "The minute I saw all those pens lined up, like a little stationery army, I knew I'd lost it. A single point, though." He clicks his tongue. "Snapping at your heels."

She pours red wine from a bottle on the bar into her champagne glass. "And, dammit, if only your prize had been an M&S voucher. You know you need to buy yourself a new jumper, right?"

"Nice one, Grace," he says.

And there's something in the way he uses her name like that—like he knows her. It makes her stomach go liquid.

"So a weekend at a chichi hotel . . . that's pretty nice."

"Yeah. The thing is I can't go."

"What? Why not?"

"I have no one to go with." Grace sets her glass on the bar. "Okay, now

I'm hearing how that sounds, but I broke up with my boyfriend a month ago. Everyone else is . . . It's getting to that age, you know . . ." She trails off; she doesn't want to think about it.

"That sucks, I'm sorry."

"Well, yeah." She shrugs. "Although it would've sucked more if we'd stayed together. I don't want children and it turns out that was a deal breaker." At least, that was what Marc had made out. But thinking back to that awful evening at the Ethiopian restaurant in Kentish Town, Grace knows that had she said she was desperate to start a family that would have been the wrong answer too. *I'm sorry, hon*, he'd told her, as he held her gaze across the small table. *I love you but I don't think I can do this anymore.* He'd said it like he was a vet counseling her to have a sick pet put down. They'd been eating injera flatbread with meat stew, and she'd fought the instinct to lean across the table and smear the food across his too-concerned face. Anything to stop the falling-in feeling at her chest.

She'd had a lucky escape, she knows, even if it doesn't feel that way, because there'd been others while they were living together. She suspects this; she knows it in the root of her. He wasn't even that careful about it but she chose not to see it. She was addicted to him, stupidly, and in the end he just wasn't that into her, so that was three years wasted.

Next to her Ben clears his throat.

"Sorry." She blinks. "I have absolutely no fucking idea why I just told you that."

"It's been a long day?" he suggests, and she laughs.

"It's been a long day," she agrees. "And I'm quite drunk."

"Who would've thought it would be such a rave?"

They look at each other then, and she finds she doesn't want to look away. There's an unsteadiness in the air around them. Like the equilibrium has been suddenly knocked out of whack.

"We could split the prize." The words are out of her mouth before her brain has a chance to catch up. "I mean, look, there was only one point in it. It was me, but it could've been you." She takes her envelope from the bar, waves it at him. "Do you want to come with me?"

As soon as she's said it she can't believe she has. She wants to take it back but at the same time she doesn't. A part of her is thinking, *Game on.*

The man in the black sweater pulls a hand through his hair, studies her. "Okay," he says, after a pause. "Why not?"

"Okay," she repeats, and she's nodding, like she's trying to interpret what he's just said.

"I mean, I'd rather take the trophy but if all you're offering is the other . . ."

And they're both laughing now at this crazy thing they're proposing. A fizzing, mad, on-the-edge kind of laughter because the two of them know in that moment that they'll do it. They know—with the exquisite certainty of a regular verb—that it will happen.

Now

GRACE HAS THE car keys still bunched in her hand, the flame-throwing sun on the back of her neck, when she realizes she'll walk there. There's the growl of the stopped traffic a street away, car horns going like it's carnival day, and the release of just walking, walking on her own two feet after the suffocating fug of the car, is immense. It's liberating. She's cutting through the alleyway between the jerk chicken place and the hardware shop, which will spit her out onto the main drag. Despite the graffiti on the walls, tangled weeds, and a musty-sweet smell of scorched piss, she's thinking with a clarity that has evaded her for days, weeks, longer even. She will walk from here to there, to Ben's flat across North London, to deliver the cake to her daughter for her sixteenth birthday. That is what she will do. No problem.

She just needs to pick it up, the two-hundred-pound offering that feels like a bribe. It's the invitation she has not received and she will arrive with it, triumphant, as though she is the curse in a twisted fairy tale, the bad witch. "No!" The word bolts from her, there in the alleyway, like she's some crazy woman talking to herself. That is not how it will go. It is an act of love, this cake, and Lotte will see that. She will. And she will forgive her.

Four Months Earlier

1. $(x + 2)(3x - 12) =$
2. Solve for x and y:
   $$3x + 7y = 14$$
   $$6y - 6x = -19$$
3. Solve for x:
   $$24x(14 + 2x) = 45$$
4. XXX + L = *I nearly came just looking at you today . . .*

"LOTTE?"

She's holding the torn-off piece of worksheet as she comes into the bathroom. Lotte is naked in front of the mirror, striping deodorant under her arms. Her daughter's eyes meet hers in the mirror, a question mark in the dip of her eyebrows; her body is perfect, like she's been freshly sculpted by angels. Grace crumples the note, pushes it into the pocket of her jeans. It isn't the moment.

"Oh, for God's sake, put them away," she says instead, her voice all faux-disapproval. "Come on, we've talked about this. I don't need it at my age." As she approaches, Lotte is shaking her head, rolling her eyes at Grace's reflection.

"How are they so ridiculously pert?"

"Stop, *Mother* . . ."

"Are they even real?" She makes as if to poke at Lotte's boob, retracts her finger like it has bounced off. "I *mean* . . ."

They are both laughing as Lotte swats her away.

"Don't touch me, you crazy woman." She's got her mad face on but her eyes are smiling still. "You are so inappropriate. How are you even allowed to be in charge of a class of primary-school kids?"

"Not in charge, in fact, *so . . .*" Grace scrunches her lips.

Lotte scoops her towel from the floor, her phone from the sink. "Yes. Good," she says, as she backs out of the room. "Thank God."

Don't go, Grace thinks, standing there like she's stranded. There's the soapy-damp smell of her child's sublime skin, a buzz in the air where she's just been.

"I'm starting the new season of *Parks and Rec* tonight," Grace blurts, although she can already hear footsteps receding on the stairs. "If you want to watch?"

"Maybe."

Grace can tell from Lotte's voice that she's distracted, probably back on Instagram already. And she knows that "maybe" means "no." She waits a beat, two. Then there's the soft click of the bedroom door shutting that feels like a punch.

She takes the note from her pocket, scans the words again. *I nearly came just looking at you today.* It doesn't lose its ability to shock, this scrap of printout. She has a hard time reconciling the fact that someone has sent this to her daughter, to her fifteen-year-old child. She doesn't know how to raise it. I was going through your blazer and . . . *What?* What can she possibly say? I'm worried about you. You know you can talk to me. I feel like there are things you're keeping in, and I don't want to pry but I do want you to know I'm here. She looks at her reflection in the mirror. Yes, all of those things, Grace, she tells herself. But, Christ, it all sounds like something from a bad soap and she is so damn tired. Suddenly something about her face strikes her, and she moves closer to the washbasin so that she can see herself better.

What the fuck has happened to her lips?

They are vanishing. She screws her mouth in several different directions. It's like the top part of her upper lip has disappeared. Overnight. So that where it was pink before it is now white, but with the little vertical lip lines still there so that, *abracadabra*, it has become one big wrinkle. But it can't have happened overnight. Can it? In which case how can she not have noticed this before?

A thump of bass starts up, coming through the ceiling from Lotte's room. And standing there, staring at her stupid disappearing mouth, she pictures her daughter there moments ago, considers the fucking terrible timing of it all. How, just at the point that she—that all the mothers—are drying up from the inside out (or from the outside in, who could possibly call it?), the daughters are busting out all over with the exact same firm, ripe potency they are losing. And maybe the worst part is they don't even know it.

And then she's thinking again about the scrawled note, the explicit porny tone of it, and about the letter she's ignored. The letter from school that Lotte agreed didn't make sense. It's more than a week now since it arrived. There's been a follow-up email too. She will call the school tomorrow, she will. It's just that doing this all herself now, with work and the house and the translation and . . . The guilt starts to creep in. The guilt and also, of course, The Guilt. She snaps the thought shut: she won't go there.

2002

THEY HAVE ARRANGED to meet on the beach at 7 p.m. He's come on the train because he knows the final third of the journey is supposed to be pretty stunning, but he barely noticed it. He hasn't got past page five of *No Logo*, didn't finish the sandwich he'd bought at Warwick Parkway for lunch, didn't even get the notes for his PhD thesis out of his bag. Images from the convention keep flashing through his mind. Images of her. Hair knotted messily at the crown of her head, her dark jacket rolled up at the sleeves like she meant business. How smart she was, how fierce, how funny, how beautiful. Not raised on gymkhanas and gin cocktails, not written in the code his family would understand. A language nerd like him. But he's asking himself, as he makes his way along the coast road that smells of salt and rubbish and hot stone, whether he will even recognize her when he gets there. He hasn't told anyone he's doing this, not his housemate Isaac, not his brothers, no one. It feels like something he needs to keep private, a mad secret he doesn't want to share.

She's sitting in the sand with her knees drawn up, staring out at the sea. She's the only person on the beach so he knows at once that it's her—the thought passes through his head that really he would have known her anywhere. There's a weird mesmerizing light, a hyperreal glow that's turning everything pink at the edges. His mouth is dry. He kicks off his trainers, wobbles precariously as he peels the socks from his feet, and he's steeling himself, about to call out to her, when she twists toward him. Her cheeks are flushed and with the sun on her face she looks like that actress, the clever one with the red hair. Julianne Moore.

Dumping his bag in the sand, he walks toward her.

"Oh, hi, you came," she says, shading her eyes. "What's your name again?" And she smiles, quick and wide.

"Very droll."

"Droll." She nods. "A good word."

"A good word," he agrees, and comes to sit beside her. Not too close.

Instead of asking him how his journey was or making any kind of small talk, she points to the left of the beach, out toward the horizon. "Over there. Look," she says, as though they are midway through a conversation, and he follows her gaze.

It takes him a moment to find it but then he sees what she's seeing—something that looks like it could be a rock or a buoy. It's dark and sleek, bobbing up and down a fair distance out.

"A seal?" he asks. "A dolphin . . . a *shark*?"

She nudges her elbow into his side. Lightly, so that she almost doesn't touch him. But, still, it's as if she has set an electric pulse running the length of him. "A surfer, you idiot. He's been out there since before I got here, making it look so damn easy."

"Do you surf?" he asks, and he feels the awkward shape of the words on his tongue, his overenunciation of the too-formal question.

"I have done. Not for a long time, though."

She doesn't elaborate and she doesn't ask him the question in return. They sit in silence as they stare out to sea. Ben presses his feet into the sand, trying to root himself. There's the grittiness between his toes, the skip of his chest, and he isn't sure whether it's nerves or excitement. He isn't sure what this is, what the two of them are doing here, why they have come, but he can feel the pull of her next to him. Like their flesh is fused, although they're inches apart. And he wonders, Is she feeling it too? He would like to reach out and turn her gaze from the sea. He'd like to look into those dark, laughing eyes and ask her what this thing is. He wants to lay himself bare, to strip away the veneer and acknowledge how bizarre it is—the fact they barely know each other and yet they are doing this. He wants to open her up, to gain access to her.

Instead he finds himself asking, "Did you check in already?"

"Yup," she says. "I booked us in for dinner at nine if that works. Or we could just get chips or . . . Wait." She's up on her haunches, her face a frown, and she's slanting her upper body forward, looking down across the beach and out to sea. Her entire countenance has changed.

"What?" he says. "Grace?"

"The surfer," she murmurs, like she's talking to herself not him.

Ben follows her line of sight. There's the gray-green of the water but he can't see the dark shape against the waves now. He scans the surface, waiting for him to reemerge.

"I don't . . . Something's not right." In one movement she pushes herself up to standing, takes her phone from her pocket, drops it onto the sand. Then she's running toward the sea, away from him. The sand is thick, like brown sugar, this far back on the beach but she's moving through it like it's been tide-washed. For a moment he sits there, stunned, like what the fuck is going on? Is she mad, this woman he barely knows? But then he gets to his feet, too, because he's looking but still he can't locate the sleek black body in the waves. Everything is pink-filtered, and there's the low stain of evening sunshine that's making him feel it's all unreal, like he's in a film.

By the time he gets there she's cutting a line through the water, out beyond the buoys where the sea is dark and ripple-pitted. He can see the surfer again now, farther out, and he starts to wade into the sea, taking big strides so that within seconds his jeans are clamped to his legs. The freeze of it makes him gasp and he's keeping on but she's so far away from him already that there's no way, there's just no way. He's up to his waist when he stops. His head is all over the place, he can't think. He needs to call the coastguard, that's what he must do. Heart banging in his throat, he turns.

"We have people on the . . . less than five minutes to get to you."

Down here on the wet sand there's one bar on his phone and the woman at the other end keeps cutting in and out.

"Okay," he says, although he isn't really following: he can't concentrate.

"Does it look like it could be a riptide?" the voice at the end of the line asks.

"I mean, I don't know," he says hopelessly.

"And can you see them still?"

He can. He can.

". . . four minutes away . . . That's the . . ." the voice says. "Keep them in sight and stay on the line."

And now that he looks, he thinks that maybe she's moving closer. He squints. The light is starting to dip and it's difficult to make out but he thinks that perhaps he can see the surfboard and two figures against it. He covers the mouthpiece with his hand.

"Grace!" he shouts. "Grace!"

If she hears him there's nothing. She doesn't respond.

"I need to go back in," he tells the woman on the phone.

". . . more help to us . . . stay on the line . . ."

There's the sore itch of salt against his thighs and saliva catching against the back of his tongue. He can't just stand here doing nothing.

"I'd ask you . . . give it a moment, please, sir."

A tremor is moving up through him now. The shock of the water, the chill of his fear, because what if something happens to her out there? What would he do? He knows her name, her phone number, a handful of disparate facts about who she is. She speaks five languages, he imagines himself telling a compassionate police officer. Japanese is the one she likes best. She has an ex who dumped her; she doesn't want children; her favorite pen is a blue Bic. That's pretty much all he's got. He checks the horizon, searching the dark, shifting expanse. Nothing. Who would he even contact as her next of kin? Pushing the thought from his mind, he starts to move once again toward the water because, whatever the woman on the phone is telling him, he wants to get Grace out of there. He needs her to be okay. He wants to have this weekend just as they planned.

And then there's the sound of sirens and Ben turns to see the coastguard driving toward him down the beach. Relief punches him and he throws up his arms, like he's surrendering, starts to wave them dementedly above his head. "Over here!" he shouts, although they're coming straight for him. "Quick! Over here!"

They have them out of the water so fast that it's as if there was never any danger at all. The surfer—a woman with brown hair straggling like snakes—is bleeding at the temple but he can see that she's conscious, and they're loading her onto a stretcher, stanching the wound, checking her over for concussion. He watches uselessly while a paramedic takes Grace to one side.

"You can stop waving that bloody piece of tinfoil at me," he hears her say. "I was only in there five minutes."

The paramedic beckons him over, hands him the silver blanket she says she doesn't want. "You need to get her out of these clothes," the paramedic tells him, and he lists the symptoms of hypothermia, tells Ben to dial 999 if he has any concerns. And then that's it. The vehicle drives off and they're left alone.

They stand there, shocked. She's in a white shirt that's rucked up around the neck and sticking to her body so that he can see her bra through it, patches of apricot skin. Her blue jeans have turned black and shiny.

"What are you? Fucking Superwoman?" His voice comes out wheezy and she's smiling. But it's a strange, twisted smile and he realizes she's about to cry.

"Hey . . ." he says, and he moves toward her, pushes the hair from her face. Salt crystals dot the bridge of her nose, her forehead, accenting the freckles there. "It's okay, it's all okay. But you're really cold, Grace. You need to get dry."

Up close like this there's the force of her. A feeling in him he can't explain but that's wrenched his gut, like the hidden dip in an unfamiliar road. He only understands that he needs to know her, this bright, strange, reckless woman, who fills him up and terrifies him. He needs to know every part of her.

Her hot breath is on his skin as she reaches up, catches his hand that's still in her hair. And then her mouth is on his and there's the salt and rust taste of her, a slipping-away feeling in him that goes on and on until suddenly she's pulling back.

"Jesus, Ben." She plucks at her wet clothes, her hair. "I feel like we're in some kind of bad eighties porn movie."

And he's laughing but he's so damn hard he doesn't know what to do with it. He licks the taste of her from his lips, clears his throat.

"Let's go." She starts to walk away up the beach. "I need to change. You too," she adds, and she points over her shoulder to the tidemark on his T-shirt where everything goes dark just below his navel.

The hotel is carved into the top of the cliff overlooking the sea and she has relented and is wearing the space blanket around her shoulders by the time they get there. There are expensive cars parked outside, and in the foyer he takes in velvet sofas and an Eames Lounge Chair, a huge starburst clock on the wall. No one is at the desk and he's relieved they don't have to explain themselves as they head straight to her room on the second floor.

When she fits her key card into the lock there's an intimacy that ambushes him. It's the whole hotel-room thing, the seedy connotation of it, and he's sure she must feel it too.

"So . . . not only do you speak as many languages as Cleobloodypatra, you also appear to be athlete fit?" He's scrambling to keep it light as they enter the room.

"It's true. I am pretty cool." She has her back to him, flicking on the lights, but he can hear the smile in her voice. "Also, I grew up by the sea. In Brighton. I did my lifeguard training, everybody does. Christ, I'm freezing, I can hardly—"

"Grace," he cuts in, suddenly serious. "I should've come in after you."

She turns toward him. She's hugging her arms around her torso, like she's holding herself in, but even so there's a wild look about her, something altered. Then she fixes her eyes on his and he feels a charge go through him. Neither says anything and he's aware of the quiet tick of a radiator, or a clock in the room. And he knows what this is. Now he knows for sure why they have come. She's looking straight at him and there's a power in her so that he can't pull away his gaze as she unbuttons him, pushes down her own jeans. And then he's lifting her up against the wall, asking her *Is this okay?* and she's tipping back her head, closing her eyes. Her body is cold and damp and soft. There's sand in the creases of her thighs and at the backs of her knees and he is biting down on his lip so hard he can taste blood.

They order room service. There's warm pumpkin bread and crayfish with aioli, artichoke hearts in spiced truffle oil. A waxed vintage cheddar, charcoal biscuits, kalamata olives. Peppered cherries and marzipan and bitter chocolate mousse in smoked-glass jars. The room has a sea view and they sit on the bed watching the night-black water and wearing the white toweling robes they found hanging on the back of the bathroom door. And they eat like they're afraid the food will run out.

"This all feels very unreal," he says, licking chocolate from the back of a cold spoon.

"What? The enchanted food?" She has a cherry in her mouth and as she speaks some of the juice dribbles down her chin and onto the white robe. "Shit." She laughs, then wipes her face with her sleeve, smearing crimson across it.

"Nice." Ben shakes his head, smiling.

"Oh, they bleach all this stuff after you've worn it once anyhow." She lifts her shoulders, lets them drop. Then, "What feels unreal?"

He pauses. He would like to tell her how insanely beautiful she is. Sitting there, cross-legged on the bed, the aftershock of sex still in her cheeks. How she is unlike anyone, any woman, he's ever met.

"What?" she asks again.

"This." He pulls a hand through his hair. "You. Everything. That whole crazy thing on the beach—did that even happen?"

"You mean the whole saving-a-woman-from-drowning thing? Child's play," she shrugs, "for someone who taught herself the Spanish subjunctive aged twelve."

When she grins, he takes her shoulders and pushes her back against the headboard. Pins her there, laughing, before her dark eyes turn serious and he presses his mouth on hers again.

Now

Forty-five is the unhappiest age you can be, according to a new study from the US's National Bureau of Economic Research. 45.2 to be precise. So says former Bank of England economist Anthony Blanche, who analyzed data from 132 different countries across the world.

In the UK, the study drew on research from the Annual Population Survey, which posed the question: Overall, how satisfied are you with your life nowadays? Respondents reported that from the age of 40 onward happiness nosedived.

As SHE TURNS onto the high street Grace snorts, thinking about the *Guardian Online* report she'd read the week before. Two months to the day after her forty-fifth birthday, in fact. It was one of those *Truman Show* moments when she'd felt like some omnipotent being somewhere was watching her, studying her, laughing at her. Like she was a daddy longlegs having its legs picked off one by one. A human experiment pretty much down to her last leg.

The crazy bonfire heat is blazing through her as she moves past the nail bar, the Oxfam, the Japanese deli, and now her vagina is itching too—she can't pretend it isn't. It's been itching for the past two minutes. Scratch that. Her vagina has been itching for the past two years. *Everything* has been itching. No, she thinks, no, because she can't use another Monistat this month, she cannot. She has already exceeded her six-month quota by a factor of . . . She has no idea. More than is medically advisable anyhow. Considerably more. *It's that age* . . . her mum had said to her obliquely, when she'd cracked one day and called for advice. *It's all downhill downstairs from here on in, and everywhere else for that matter* . . .

It strikes Grace as she glances in at the window of the new coffee place, the one where Harry Styles reportedly gets his daily fix, how miserable *everyone* looks—that age or not. Young, old, male, female, Black, white, brown . . . all of them hatchet-faced and wilting under the acid hot sun, stress seeping from every pore and spreading, like an infection. Like the way a smile given by the checkout girl at Tesco is supposed to travel in a feel-good way from one person to the next to the next. Except the exact opposite of that.

The traffic is a throbbing metal mass and there's a fumy taste in her mouth that's making her feel queasy. A fair-haired woman is blocking the narrow pavement up ahead, patches of red on her cheeks and on her chest where the neck of her T-shirt is sagging. She's probably in her thirties, but to Grace looks nowhere near old enough to have one child in the buggy, another strapped to her front in a complicated-looking sling. Co-op bags hang from the handles of the buggy and Grace can see they are banging into the woman's legs. The toddler is reaching upward, his hand a fat little star. His head is tipped back and he's staring at the sky.

A memory swoops, snares her. And she is standing in the middle of the park, a heavy-soft parcel of baby on her hip as she points up at a tree struck by sunshine. *Look at the leaves,* she's saying. *Look.* But she's talking as much to herself as the child in her arms because how has she not noticed this before? It's like she's never looked. Like she's gorging on the wonder of it for the first time, as though her baby is teaching her how to see. Her neck is stretched back, and above her head fragile leaves, the color of bright limes, etch a dazzling, fragmented ceiling. It is beautiful, vital, otherworldly—the beginning of something she can barely grasp but that feels like hope—and she is dizzy with it.

And then her mind shifts sideways and she's remembering, she's remembering . . . and it's too late, she's seen it: she has glimpsed the dark rip in the fabric of things. Putting out a hand, she steadies herself for a moment against the wall of the health-food shop because it's all too much. The heat and the rush and the thoughts in her head. What is she doing? She should give up, go home, abandon this ridiculous quest. She waits for a gap in the flow of people and then she turns, walks back the way she's come.

She's got as far as the cook shop when she stops suddenly. Someone—a man in a too-tight suit—bangs into her from behind, swears under his breath, turns to glare as he passes her. But she barely registers him. *Come on*, Grace, she thinks. And she clenches her fists, steels herself. The fact is there's no choice: she knows she has to do this and she pivots on her heel. She just needs to put one foot in front of the other and she'll get there.

When her phone goes she reaches for it automatically, answers before her brain has had time to stop her.

"Grace, I've been trying to get hold of you."

Paul. It's Paul.

"Grace?"

Fuck.

"Paul, hi. I'm so sorry, I've been meaning to call. I mean, obviously I have . . ." She pictures him sitting in his hot, cramped office near Fleet Street, the thirsty, Jurassic-looking fern in the corner, the walls lined with books.

"Grace, I've had to give the Yamamoto translation to someone else. We were two months past the deadline on it and I can't keep making excuses . . ."

There's no preamble and Paul is measuring out his words, like he's reading from a script. Her heart starts to go in her chest as she turns off the main drag onto a residential street.

". . . and I know things have been tough for you this past . . . well, it's been a long time now, I mean, since . . . since . . ." he falters, ". . . and the thing is, Grace, I have to think of the business. I'm sorry but I'm going to have to let you go."

He says the last bit in a rush and the cliché of it almost makes her burst out laughing. Or maybe it's the shock of his words that's giving her the strange looping feeling inside.

"Listen, Paul . . ." she begins, but what can she say? That she needs this job. That she needs it for her self-esteem as much as the money because two months ago the head teacher at Stanhope Primary, where she's worked for the past three years, decided she would not be renewing her part-time contract. Grace had to stop herself allowing an odd, trapped-in smile to invade her face then too, while the head addressed her as "Madame Adams" and waffled about cuts to the language budget, when they both knew it had nothing to do with the cuts.

She pinches the skin between her eyebrows, tries again: "This is terrible timing, Paul. I have to tell you that. The worst—"

But he cuts across her. He isn't listening. He has his lines, the things he needs to get out. ". . . so I'm really sorry, Grace. You've been with us such a long time—twenty years, isn't it?—and it goes without saying you're wonderful at what you do, our best freelancer by a long, long way, and I'm sure you'll pick up stuff elsewhere, but I can't . . ." Paul trails off. "I know you know that."

No, Grace thinks. No, she does not know that. But she doesn't want to hear any more. She wants to make this stop. Paul is in the middle of saying something about paying her double for the work she's completed so far, when she jabs the little red phone icon on her screen and hangs up.

"Cheer up, love, no one died."

Grace jerks her head up. There's a man in the front garden just ahead of her steadying a ladder against a square Edwardian house, another—balding and sunburned—on the top rung, holding a long squeegee mop and leering at her. Brown soapy water is running down the window he's in the middle of cleaning. Grace feels her scalp tighten.

There's the deliberate pause, the heavy, swaggery stare.

"Go on, give us a smile."

She can feel damp patches under her arms and between her legs where she's sure the sweat will be showing through. She's nearly level with them and she's searching for the perfect comeback but there's no answer to give, she knows this. And she's about to set her face, put on the glassy stare she keeps close to the surface for these moments, when the man calls, "What? Don't tell me. You're one of them feminazis." He's looking at his mate now, not her, pulling his face into a grimace of comic-disgust, and he raises his voice for the punchline: "You lot need to take a chill pill and get a leg wax, ain't it?"

Something splinters in her. It's like she hears the snap.

Okay, you know what? she thinks. *Not today.*

She plants her feet, leans in toward him as though she's about to confide something. "*Que te den,*" she says, and her voice is clear and steady. "*Usero. Vas te faire enculer. Poshel na khuy. Rot op.* That's 'Go fuck yourself' in five different languages." She crosses the fingers on both hands and holds them up and out toward him, scrunches her face in mock concern.

He's glancing at his mate, grinning still but there's a looseness around his mouth, his eyes, and she can see she's unseated him—humiliated him—like he wishes he was on the ground and not up the ladder in full view. Then she releases her forefingers and punches the air with her two middle digits, before she turns and walks away.

"You crazy bitch!"

His words are a kidney blow, but Grace sets her shoulders, walks on, and she's halfway down the street when the adrenaline hits. It's pumping through her and she knows she should feel elated at what she's just done, liberated. But she can't shake the residue of his thinly veiled anger, his aggression that she knows he'll be telling the other guy was *just bants.*

She's forced to dip her head to pass under the low-hanging branch of a plane tree, and as the leaves brush her hair it's as though someone has reached in and scooped out her insides. She can't believe she has a child who turns sixteen today; a child who won't see her. It's as if she gave birth, blinked, and now here she is, forty-five years old, her uterus shriveling, her life falling apart around her. Ben's flat is all the way across north London—it's the other side of Swiss Cottage—and the party, a barbecue in the garden, is due to start at 4 p.m. She has to get the cake there before the guests arrive: she wants to present it to Lotte and she does not need an audience for that. Checking the time on her phone she winces—1:08 p.m. She is barely fifteen minutes' walk away from her house and she's been going almost an hour. How has this happened? Where has the time gone?

She will get there, whatever it takes, and she will make Lotte see. She will show her how fiercely she loves her. She will bring her daughter home.

Four Months Earlier

Hola . . . Haven't written in ages I know and not much time because ten to midnight, but phat zero out of 10 day today and need to vent. Didn't see T which is not cool but also maybe good job because skin is fucking AWFUL and I am UGLY. Period still hasn't come and my face is busting out all over like it's going to blow and Leyla called me out in front of the Populars for having foundation in my hairline. Like hahaha you bitch. But—coincidentally—v. funny in Biology because doing the menstrual cycle AGAIN and Mr. Laghari did that manspreading thing he does, sitting on his desk at the front of class like he is SO chill with it and Vee chucked a tampon from the back of the class and Mr. Laghari was like, I think you dropped something, Vee, which on reflection was pretty cool of him tbf but I am off point here because don't want to write this next bit but can't not . . . Letter from school came today and Mum now knows—but also doesn't. Shit shit shit. What do I do????

GRACE CAN'T TELL Lotte what she knows. Because to do so she would have to tell her she's read her diary. But she is angry, worried, confused, bursting with the weight of it as they wait on the blue plastic chairs outside the head teacher's office. It's raining outside and there's a bucket a little way down the corridor and a drip from the ceiling that's like water torture. The whole place has the worn prefab look of somewhere that might collapse in a storm. The anxiety of it tugs at her every time she comes here—this piss-poor lack of investment—her mind shooting forward to fallen ceilings, windows, walls . . . students, *her child*, bloodied, battered, dead. A grid of young smiling faces plastered across the evening news.

"Hello, Lotte, Mrs. Adams."

She jerks her head up. The head teacher has popped his door at last and he's standing there slim, long-nosed, with a neutral expression on his face.

"Sorry to have kept you waiting." He adjusts his tie, doesn't quite make eye contact. "Come in."

Lotte goes first, all caved-in shoulders, and Grace follows reluctantly because there's the sense that she, too, is about to get a bollocking. The office is neat and gray, and in the air, the sweet stale after-smell of packed lunch. Gesturing to a pair of low padded chairs, the head teacher invites them to sit, then settles himself at the other side of his desk in his much higher executive chair. Grace feels something ignite in her gut. It's a power move. A power move by John Power. He is literally looking down on them and she feels shrunken, belittled, instantly on the offensive.

"So, Lotte," he presses his palms together, sets them on his desk, "what's going on?"

Next to her Lotte shrugs. Grace feels the movement of the air on her skin, as if all her senses have been amplified.

"What d'you mean?" her daughter mumbles.

John Power smiles a smile that isn't a smile at all. "Your attendance is below seventy percent, Lotte. Your mum has told us over the phone that you haven't been off sick. What's going on?"

There's silence and Grace starts to speak into it, but John Power holds up a hand to stop her. He may as well have shushed her.

She is not your kid, she wants to say.

"Lotte?" He drags out the *e* accusingly.

"I don't know what you're talking about." Her daughter directs the words into her lap.

The head teacher shuffles through some papers on his desk. "This," he holds up a graph, "charts your attendance, Lotte. If you haven't been sick, then you've clearly been bunking off, so I'll ask you again, what's going on?"

Sitting there looking at the chart—the absences there in black and white—Grace is suddenly mortified that she hasn't had the conversation with her child. Not properly. That she has waited until now. She doesn't know what she was thinking.

"I haven't been bunking off." Lotte starts to cry.

"Listen." Grace is forward on her stupid low seat. Her instinct is to defend her daughter, to protect her—even though she's read her diary, she knows she isn't telling the truth. It's pretty obvious to all concerned that she isn't. She wants to ask what she's hiding, what's so bad she can't say.

"Look, I don't know if you're aware but Lotte's dad and I separated nine months ago." She rests a hand in the middle of Lotte's back, feels the clammy heat of her through her nylon blazer. "Obviously it's been a difficult time for all of us and . . ." She trails off, she can hear the shame she's trying to keep out of her voice.

Before she's finished speaking John Power is nodding. His cheeks are shaded with color now and she sees in his face that he is recalculating, panicking a little, changing tack.

"Right, okay, so I have to tell you that we have an excellent counseling program in school, as well as a mentor scheme, which I think needs to be something we take a—"

"I don't need a fucking counselor!" From nowhere Lotte is on her feet and shouting. "I'm not one of your dumb anxiety kids." She flicks paired fingers in the air as she spits out the word *anxiety*.

"Lotte, hold on . . ." Grace gets up, takes her daughter's elbow. She has never heard her swear out loud before. There's a feeling in her like her lungs might burst. This is not the girl who gets good school reports, does her homework, is polite to teachers. This is not the child she knows. She wishes suddenly that Ben was here, that she didn't have to do this alone. She hasn't told him about the letter from school, the follow-up emails. She'd felt somehow that it was her mess to clear up. She'd wanted to show herself she could do this without him, that she could cope.

"Mrs. Adams, I'm afraid this kind of language is not okay and Lotte knows that." John Power stands, looming over his desk. The scent of cheap men's shower gel comes off him and Grace feels nauseated.

Lotte wrenches her elbow free. There's the shock of cold against Grace's palm where her child has broken away from her.

"What am I? *Ten?* Don't patronize me!" Lotte screams. "Screw your stupid rules, screw your shit show of a school." She's across the office in three strides, yanks open the door, and slams out.

2002

THE PRODUCER FROM the TV studio has the press cuttings set out on the
conference table in front of him. It's disconcerting to see herself like that,
drenched in accolades and sexism both. A brainy page-three girl minus the
tits. Anodyne quotes attributed to her, things she's pretty sure she didn't
say. *I'm delighted . . . this is a dream come true . . .* She's pleased, of course
she is. She's almost famous! But at the same time part of her wants to
screw up the coverage and toss it into the bin.

"So, Grace," the producer, Ed, is saying, "we've got a proposition for you."

She glances from the press cuttings to him. He's in his forties maybe, with thick dark hair, a large forehead, teeth that have been overwhitened. Over his shoulder there's the glass wall of his office and beyond it well-dressed people at workstations, pretending not to look at her.

"Okay." She swallows.

"We're launching a new show. It's a *Countdown* kind of thing but more contemporary." He takes a sip of water. "We've got pretty much everything in place so we're ready to go and we had someone lined up, but then," he gestures to the newspaper articles spread out between them, "we saw you. We'd like you to be our Carol Voderman, y'know our sharp-as-hell numbers expert—except for foreign language not maths. Sorry, that's just an irresistible pitch. I mean, basically, you'd be our equivalent of Dictionary Corner. A spiced-up multilingual Dictionary Corner. So, pretty fun, nothing too *big*." He throws his arms out wide, like he's holding a giant box. "But a commitment—weekly, twice weekly, we're not a hundred percent sure yet. We'd do test screenings, et cetera, but all of that's pretty much a formality. Your face fits. You've got the gig if you want it." He drums his fingers on the table. "What d'you reckon? You interested?"

There's a fizzing in her stomach that's making her feel a little sick. She pictures herself in her damp basement flat in Chalk Farm, picking her way—line by solitary line—through the translation of yet another low-rent thriller with a high female body count. Or, worse, forcing her way through a Japanese engineering manual. "I thought maybe you were going to ask me to take part in a documentary or something," she says. "This is, well, I mean, sure, I'm interested. I think."

"Good." He smiles, like, *Of course you're interested*. There's a bit of food caught in the top of one of his too-white teeth. "Now for the boring part. The detail."

While he's taking her through the proposal her mind splits. Half of her is playing catch-up. Is this happening? Could she really do it? The other half is trying to process what he's saying. And then he's pushing himself up out of his seat: he's got another meeting.

"Think it over." The producer gathers up the press cuttings. "Obviously we're on a bit of a tight deadline, so I'll need a decision by, say, ten tomorrow morning?"

Grace panics. Like, what if this chance slips away from her? "I mean, I'd be crazy to say no."

"So is that a yes?" He raises his eyebrows at her.

"Well, I guess . . ." She laughs.

"Great." He pumps her hand. "We'll get some contracts drawn up and I'll be in touch."

They're at the door when he turns. "Oh, just one thing." He says it like it's an afterthought, but there's something stagey—self-conscious—in the way he clicks his fingers, scrunches his cheeks as though he's just remembered. "Your age. I mean, it's *that* age, isn't it? You're not going to go off and have a baby on us, are you?"

"Oh, God, no," Grace answers, on an emphatic out-breath. "I don't want children. Not my thing."

His face relaxes. "I'm so glad you said that, Grace. The last woman I interviewed tore a strip off me when I asked her the same question." He plants his hands on his hips, shakes his head with incredulity. Then he pulls open the door, gestures for her to go first.

Something's troubling her as she comes down the front steps of the building out onto the street. It's what the producer said about her having a baby. Or, rather, *not* having a baby. A sense she's been caught out. She wasn't trying to say the right thing, it's just fact. But somehow she feels as if she's colluded with him and in doing so she's betrayed the other woman—the one who came before her—and all the women who will come after. That standing there in his glass office, smelling the sour coffee on his breath, she inadvertently made herself a cheap agent of the patriarchy.

There's a Starbucks opposite and Grace buys herself a peppermint tea. She's in the middle of Soho, and the place is packed with tourists and shoppers and creatives, and she can't think of a worse place to be because her head is spinning with everything that's just happened. She finds a seat at the window, squashed in next to a group of Italian teenagers, and takes out her phone. There are two new messages. Pressing the phone to her ear, she strains to hear. The first is a voicemail from her sister, Cate: "So what did Mike TV have to say? Does he want to exploit you? I bet he does. Going to bed now, it's one in the morning here, but call me tomorrow. Kisses."

She's still rolling her eyes, smiling, when the second message starts up:

"Hey, Grace, it's Ben Kerr. I'm in London next week. Be nice to meet up? Call me."

At the sound of his voice she is back there, in the hotel room, his body pressed against hers and the hot sharp taste of him. Grace flips her phone shut. She won't go there. The fact is she already owes Ben Kerr a call, she knows this. She hasn't responded to his last voicemail and they've only spoken once since Cornwall: she'd let him know she'd gotten back okay. Staring through the coffee-shop window, she feels like her head might explode through the glass, showering the beautiful chaos outside with the flesh-and-blood mess of her mind. She likes him, she does. He's smart, he's sexy, he loves language like she does. He made her laugh; he made her feel how she hasn't felt in a long time. The way he studied her face, like he was trying to read her, as if he wanted to know her. She thinks of the shape of him under her fingers, the hard muscle and sinew that surprised her, the trail of dark hair from his navel, the way his pupils went liquid when he came . . . Grace slams the thought shut. There are so many reasons not to get involved. She's fresh out of a shitty relationship. He lives a hundred miles away. And now this. She squints at the building across the road. This crazy job offer. The truth is, she can't do it. She can't allow herself to contact him. Now just isn't the right time.

Now

HER EYES ARE sweating. She really believes this, that she has become one big leaking sweat gland, sweating from places where she used not to sweat. It wouldn't surprise her to find her nails perspiring, her teeth. Grace glances at her reflection as she passes the cut-price bookshop, the kids' hairdresser, the butcher, expecting to see herself shiny. There is no part of her left immune to the crazy supernatural heat. *I am an old boiler*, she thinks. Because this is surely where the phrase comes from. She mops her face with her palm and it comes away slick but she keeps walking. There's the bakery up ahead—she can almost see it around the curve in the road—and she pictures the cake that's waiting for her there, in the shape of a villa complete with swimming pool. There'll be a row of double beds, a firepit, suntan oil, everybody's favorite *Love Island* sweethearts, Dani Dyer and Jack Fincham, perched on top, her in a neon bikini, him in matching Speedos. It will be their in-joke—hers and Lotte's—that will bind them again.

Outside the chemist a lipsticked woman thrusts a leaflet into her path.

"Ten percent off all suncream. The best anti-aging product you can buy," she says, with a fixed smile.

Grace shakes her head, a scratch of irritation in her gut. But a thought strikes her and she stops. The prescription in her bag for a hormone patch that's been in there for three months. A prescription it took her a year to get since she doesn't go to the doctor because, well, everything fits the symptoms of cancer. Or death full stop.

"The offer's for today only . . ." The woman tries again but the leaflet is limp in her hand, like she's given up on Grace, on the job, on life. Grace glances through the window. She'll be in and out, it'll add barely two minutes to her journey, and today is the start of something, or maybe the end of something, she can't tell which but either way it is a monumental shift. She can feel it.

"Sorry, excuse me." Grace moves past the woman, steps inside. The air-con hits her like bliss.

There's a queue stretching from the counter all the way along an aisle of insanely expensive skin-care products. It's too long, she knows this, but the cool air is a balm to her soul and she joins the back of the line; she'll give it five minutes. On the shelf next to her a wicker basket is stuffed with facecloths and she picks one up, wipes her hands on it surreptitiously. Then she brings it to her chest and does the same, edging it down into the clammy crack between her breasts, sighs out in relief. But someone at her shoulder is standing too close. Grace replaces the cloth, half turns toward the woman, who's maybe a couple of years older than her. She's immaculately bronzed and with a glossy brown blowout, and she's staring straight ahead, eyes on the counter. Grace feels something in her speed up. *Why so close?* she wants to say.

The mosquito buzz of piped Muzak is in her ears, and if she could swat it away, she would. The same goes for the woman, who's still too close behind her, attempting to edge her way in front. Grace is trying to make her mind a blank. Trying not to think about the fact she's just lost her job, trying not to think about where she should be. The fact that what she is doing—or, rather, not doing—is starting to look like self-sabotage. Checking the time on her phone, she feels a flicker of panic. But the queue is moving: she's jumped forward all the way from Clarins to Vichy in the past minute. The woman behind her leans past Grace, plucks something from the shelf, examines it, puts it back. In doing this she has moved forward, just a little, so that they are now almost abreast. Grace feels her pulse pick up. Braces her shoulder to block her. There's the smell of unwashed hair coming off the man in front but she inches closer to him, as close as she can go, there's no choice. The woman moves forward too.

It's all Grace can think about. This woman at her shoulder. Her body is stiff with the unnatural position she's adopted in trying to hold her off and she is consumed with hatred. But something else too: an abject despair because it's just so unnecessary, this impatience. This pointless pushiness that puts everyone on edge, that feels like it's going to push them *over* the edge. However long it takes she will not leave now. She will win this standoff. She will get served first.

"Yes, please." The man behind the counter is gesturing in their direction. He has an official-looking lanyard around his neck and his eyes are on the other woman's face.

Before Grace can gather herself the woman steps forward.

"Sorry, excuse me." Grace waggles a hand at the man behind the counter. "I was first. I'm first."

The woman turns. Her eyebrows are a puzzled *V*. She pulls a face that makes Grace think of Lotte. An exaggerated mystified look that suggests *Jeez, where's your self-control?*

The man behind the counter aims a hostile smile at Grace. She can see from his lanyard that his name is Chris. "I'll be with you in just a minute, okay," he tells her.

"Wait, no," Grace says. And now she steps in front of the woman, barging into her with the side of her body as she moves past. "No, that is not okay. I'm in a rush. I've been queuing for ten minutes and I've been ahead of this woman the whole time." She turns to the woman. She can feel that her eyes are crazy. "I've been ahead of you. You know that, we both know that. What's your problem?"

"As I said," the lanyard man interjects, "I'm in the middle of serving this lady and I will be with you in just a minute, madam." He says it like he's saying *little madam*. "And if that's not okay with you, then you are very welcome to leave."

He turns back to the other woman, shoots up his eyebrows. "*Okaaay*, how can I help?"

Grace feels herself rise up, like a scream.

All thought is gone as she slams down her arm on the countertop, drags it fast across the surface, scooping boxes of cough sweets, plastic hair bobbles, organic lip salves, energy bars, a display stand of reading glasses, silver snore rings, a Macmillan charity collecting tin, and sweeps them violently, majestically to the floor. There's the shock of broken glass, a smell like cough syrup, and Grace is buzzing, like someone has just plugged her into the mains. She's aware of the queue of people stretching away from her, aghast, the woman in her peripheral vision backing off. "Hey, what the . . . ?" she hears someone say.

Behind the counter the man with the lanyard has stepped back so that he is pressed up against the rows of toxic pharmaceuticals that aren't allowed on the shop floor. The ones you could too easily kill yourself with. Grace fixes her eyes on him, and when she speaks, the words come out soft, steady.

"Chris, I'm glad we had this little talk. Remember, every good conversation starts with a good listener."

Four Months Earlier

GRACE PUSHES OPEN the door to Lotte's bedroom. She has half an hour. Half an hour before her daughter gets home from school and she has to stop. Twenty minutes, really, if she's going to clear out of here and have everything back to normal. Already she thinks Lotte must have figured out that she'd found her diary, because when Grace checked the hiding place again—squinting down the back of the radiator—it was gone, and she couldn't find it anywhere. The blind is down still and the room is in half-light but she won't pull it—she knows she mustn't leave any trace of herself. Lotte's laptop is in the middle of the floor, half covered by a flung pair of jeans, and she retrieves it carefully, sits down cross-legged where she is, and flips open the lid.

Check the history, Cate had said, when Grace called her in LA, waking her up in the middle of the night. *And if there's nothing there get yourself a fake Instagram profile and check her posts.* The password request is on screen and Grace has a sick feeling inside . . . *And screw the ethics*, she hears Cate's voice in her head. *This is your kid. Have you really not done this before? Christ, Grace. Sara and me pretty much spent two years straight checking Dylan's posts through the Skunk End Times.*

Grace starts to type. h–a–r–r–y–p–o–t–t–e–r. As she's tapping the keys, a rare clear memory strikes. She sees her little girl at the kitchen table, all white-blond hair and squeezed up against Ben in that easy, lazy way, like her limbs are a part of him and his a part of her; there's no distinction. Her feet don't touch the floor and she's bent over the computer, her tongue poking into her cheek in concentration, her clever eyes bright with the heady task of setting up her own log-in.

The gray rectangle in the center of the screen judders. The password's incorrect. Of course it is. Like Lotte wouldn't have changed it in all this time—especially if she's got something to hide. Grace tries again. 1–2–3–4. The narrow box judders. 4–3–2–1. Nothing. She tries Lotte's birth date. Digits for the month first, then spelled out. Still not right. She'll be locked out if she goes on like this. She tries again. l–e–s–l–i–e–k–n–o–p–e. The gray box shakes. Hovering her fingers over the keys, Grace squeezes her eyes shut. Then, in a rush, before she has time to overthink it, she starts to type a long-buried series of letters. She isn't really expecting anything, but there's the sudden glare of the screen, and something catches in her as it comes to life.

Grace loads Safari and clicks on the history tab. There's TikTok and Depop and Tumblr and Reddit and Netflix and Discord and YouTube and . . . everything she would expect to see. She scrolls down and down, further through the list and back in time, but there's nothing, nothing at all that alerts her. The dawning relief of it is huge, it's enormous, even though she has no idea what she expected to find. *Yes, she has.* The toxic things she has barely allowed herself to imagine. Self-harming sites and "thinspiration" pages, soft porn, hardcore porn, religious cults, worse. It is everything you know your child would never do. Except would they?

From the shelf she feels the glossy-dark eyes of the *matryoshka* on her. She remembers the flicker of warning when Ben gave it to her. More than a decade ago now and still she recalls the shadowed sense of dread that came from nowhere. Grace checks the time at the corner of the screen and her heart speeds up a little: she's been in here ten minutes already, she doesn't have long. She tracks the cursor down the page and still there's nothing—it's all fashion and makeup and TV shows and music and *What is she doing*? Grace slams down the lid of the laptop. The sound in the silence shocks her and her stomach contracts. She can't do this. It's an intrusion. An invasion of privacy Lotte doesn't deserve.

Her mind jumps and she's back there. Running, running along the road outside Lotte's school. The sky is pewter and up ahead Lotte is leaning against the car, her blazer hoicked over her head against the rain. Grace is so relieved to see her there—to see that she hasn't run off, that she's waiting despite what's happened in John Power's office—that she forgets to be angry. Instead she takes her child and holds her, and she isn't sure whether it's rain or tears spattered like diamonds across her daughter's cheekbones, lips, jaw, but she pulls her sleeve over her hand, wipes them away, and Lotte lets her do it. "Well, that's some fresh language you've got going on," Grace murmurs. "Where did you get that potty mouth?" And Lotte looks at her like, *Hmm, I wonder?* They both start to laugh then, and if she wasn't crying before, Lotte is now, tears running down her face.

Her child begins to talk in a language Grace doesn't understand about Instagram and airing and *left on seen*, "which means you haven't read someone's message even though they can see that you're online, or you've read it but you haven't replied, which is basically like telling someone to eff off . . ." And Grace is trying to grasp the vernacular, trying to wrap her head around these strange new social rules, and she's telling her daughter it's just not a thing, that you don't have to get back to people straight away and is she being bullied, when Lotte's voice cuts across hers: "You don't understand. It's like blanking someone in the middle of a conversation and there's no escape from it, not at school, not at home, not at three o'clock in the morning, and it's fricking with my head but you can't tell Sir because he's an arsehole and it'll make things worse for me, Mum—it'll make something where there's nothing—and it's not that bad, it's honestly not."

Standing there in the street with the rain dragging at their clothes, painting them dark, Lotte looks up into her face with those eyes that could undo a person and tells her, yes, that is why she's been skipping school, she just needed a break, and she's sorry she didn't say—she didn't know how—but she isn't being bullied, she isn't, and she promises she'll stop bunking off, she will. And Grace wants to believe her but she knows. She sees it, she smells it, she feels it in the pit of her. Because there's that look on her child's face—the guarded look she knows so well: she's known it since Lotte was two years old. There's something more that she's not saying. Her daughter is lying to her.

In the half-light of the bedroom Grace snatches up her phone. Picturing Lotte's face like that, rain-washed and shut down, is the push she needs to do this. The reason—the excuse—to betray her trust. She hears Cate's voice in her head: *You'll have to register in a name she won't recognize, something cool, Grace. Okay? Not, like, agentmum.* Her sister laughed as she said it, but Grace isn't laughing now as she clicks on the app store, downloads Instagram.

Less than three minutes later she's searching for her daughter, typing in the letters of the name they took weeks, months to choose, she and Ben. The name that is stamped on her heart. Hitting return, Grace sits back—and, *ping*, there she is. Lotte Adams Kerr. A public account and a profile picture that makes her look like she's twenty-five. And here right in front of her is her child's secret life, a life she knows nothing about. At the top of the page there's a photo of Lotte at King's Cross, standing in the light tunnel. There's the crazy rainbow backdrop and her daughter jutting her chin forward, her arms spread wide. She's crossing her eyes but still she looks stupidly beautiful. Beneath the picture is a trail of comments and Grace scans them greedily.

jivan.s Prettyyyy 🖤🖤

    lotteadamskerr_ @jivan.s look who's talkin ;)

leyla.nicol_ you gorgeous x 🖤 🖤

    lotteadamskerr_ @leyla.nicol love you lysm x

parisxnc omg cute imma go there this weekend take me some photossss bruh

    lotteadamskerr_ @parisxnc lol don't care ;) imma come with you xx

k.a.di Posting but not answering my DMs. I see you. I see you I see you I see you I see you I see you I see you I see you I see you . . .

    bee.macf For real bitch? Airing again??????

k.a.di I see you I see you I see you I see you I see you I see you

    ava.d WHALE. jk . . . maybe just a bad angle for you. Don't you dare block me bitch

k.a.di I see you I see you I see you I see you I

Grace feels a hand reach down her throat and crush her airway.

2003

BEN ISN'T WORKING. He's at his desk in the house at the bottom end of town and he's staring out across the overgrown back garden, through the gap at the side of the house beyond. He can see the weir from here. He can hear it too, the hypnotic gush of water that's making him sleepy and thirsty all at once. Pushing his papers to one side, he gives up the pretense. The words in front of him have become meaningless squiggles, much like the tribal dialect he's supposed to be writing about. The lecture he's preparing—the lecture he has to deliver tomorrow that's helping fund his PhD—will have to wait. He needs to take a break.

In the kitchen he takes a pint glass from the cupboard, fills it at the tap. The lunch things are still on the table, the breakfast dishes stacked haphazardly on the side. He takes the butter, the cheese, the orange juice, all of them unsettlingly warm to the touch, puts them back in the fridge. Then he moves through to the lounge, flops down on the sofa, and grabs the remote control. Sod it, he thinks, as he flicks on the TV. He'll deal with the rest later.

It's four o'clock in the afternoon, the dead zone of television viewing, and he isn't holding out much hope as he switches through the channels. And he's still chuckling at an opaque advert for incontinence pads, wishing someone was here to share the gag with him, when suddenly she's there. Grace Adams is on the screen and in his lounge. Ben folds forward over his knees, bringing himself closer to the TV. He's checking for some kind of doppelgänger because it can't be her, can it? She's wearing bright crimson lipstick and a short green dress and it's like someone has polished her skin to a shine. In her hand there's a kind of baton and she's pointing at a German word—*TORSCHLUSSPANIK*—written outsize on a large whiteboard next to her. Ben knows the word, he knows, too, that it is almost untranslatable, and he cranks up the sound on the TV as she starts to speak.

". . . so this magnificent German word literally translated means 'gate-shut panic.' It dates to the Middle Ages when citizens would race back to the city gates before they closed at night so's not to be left vulnerable outside. You can break the word down into three smaller words—*Tor*, meaning 'gate,' *schluss* from the verb 'to close,' and *panik*, which is, of course, as it sounds. But what *Torschlusspanik* is intended to describe is that anxious, claustrophobic feeling that avenues and opportunities are shutting down. The notion that you haven't done very much with your life, that you've missed the boat, that you've left it too late. Probably the closest term we have in English is 'midlife crisis' . . ."

The woman who looks like Grace lets the final sentence hang. Then she turns to the host—a man in his fifties who has the appearance of someone who hasn't yet read the recent World Health Organization stats on the global obesity crisis—and gives him a slow wink. There are laughs from the studio audience and it is such a lame, lame joke but Ben can't help it: he's laughing too. And it is her, of course it is. There's her voice that's like cinnamon-flavored smoke, her quick, wide smile, her dark, dark eyes that might undo you. But still it feels as though his mind is playing tricks on him because it's completely nuts that she's there on this afternoon show, presenting—of all things—obscure language to the masses. "What are you? *Fucking Superwoman?*" he murmurs.

And he wonders if she thinks of it too, of them. He sees her pens lined up on the foldout desk, her hair the color of October. The pink Cornish light, her hot breath on his skin, sand in the bright, bleached hotel sheets. The way she made him laugh out loud and messed with his head all at once. And he wants to ignore it but it's tugging at him still, somewhere deep-rooted. The fact that he fell hard for her—that he's *fallen* hard for her—even though she blew him off, a humiliation he's tried to bury. That he called her not once but twice and she didn't get back to him. And sitting there, staring at her face on screen, he still doesn't get why she never returned his calls, because he's not stupid: he knows there was a potency in whatever passed between them. That it was more than a one-night stand, a dirty weekend away. Something he struggles to describe in language. There's a word for it in Japanese, a word he's sure Grace would know, a word she could feature on this TV show of hers and maybe he should call her up and suggest it. *Haragei*. Those nuanced, nonverbal cues that fill the gaps in language. Things unspoken but weighted. Facial expressions and gestures and postures, the length of a silence. So perhaps, perhaps, he eyes the screen, this TV job is the reason why he didn't hear from her again, or it is at least *a* reason why.

Ben barely registers the front door opening and banging shut. Then Isaac is in the room behind him, dumping his bag with a thud on the floor—and Ben starts, as if he's been caught watching porn.

"Wow, she's hot . . ." His housemate nods at the screen, and he makes a *tsssssss* sound through his teeth to demonstrate the point. "Jesus, man," he calls, as he moves through to the kitchen. "Could you not tidy up a bit? Or have you only just got up?"

Ben grips the sofa, flinches at the nails-down-a-blackboard feel of the chenille against his fingers. Even though this is a joke between them— that he is the feckless postgrad student, Isaac the MBA suit—he isn't finding it funny because he can't get past what Isaac said when he came into the room. And he's fighting the urge to go after him, to seize him around the throat, and that isn't like him at all, it isn't what he's about, but he can't stand the way his housemate tossed out that comment about Grace, as though she were public property to be picked over.

On screen the jowly host is behind his desk, extending his arm with a flourish. ". . . and thank you to our AMAZING Grace Adams," he's saying, as the camera swivels toward her. Grace smiles, faux-curtsies, and it's as though she's looking directly at him, there in his lounge, eyeing him. Then the camera pans back from the set, out through the shadowed studio audience. And Ben feels himself start to get hard to the sound of row after row of pensioners clapping politely while the credits roll.

"D'you want a brew, mate?" Isaac calls from the kitchen.

But Ben is already out of his seat and up the stairs. Her cinnamon voice is in his head as he slams open the door to his room . . . *It's the anxious feeling that opportunities are shutting down . . . that you've missed the boat* . . . His phone is on the desk and he snatches it up, and he's all set to dial her number when he stops. Because there are so many reasons why he shouldn't do this. Or maybe there's just one. He doesn't want to humiliate himself again. No matter how much he wants to talk to her, to see her, to taste her, it isn't worth that. His fingers are trembling as he puts down his phone.

Now

HE CAN SEE it's Grace who's calling because her name comes up before the screen goes blank. She's called and hung up, called and hung up about five times now, and he's exasperated and a little concerned. There's the food to prep and he's trying to decide how much beer to put in the fridge to chill, how much is acceptable for a bunch of fifteen- and sixteen-year-old kids versus how much they'll expect to drink. It isn't usually him who decides this stuff, it's Grace and . . . His phone rings again, goes dead.

Ben leans against the sink, mops his brow with the tea towel he's holding. It's so damn hot in here. He's done nothing with the place since he moved in and every single wall is brilliant white. Sharp sunshine blares through the floor-to-ceiling windows and it's like the brightness in the space is burning through to his retinas. On the side, his phone goes again. He ignores it, takes a beer from the box next to the sink, stacks it in the fridge. But this time Grace doesn't ring off and he's swearing under his breath, scrambling to get to his mobile before the answerphone kicks in.

"Ben?" Her voice is loud in his ear—she's almost shouting—and he can hear that she's outside, somewhere busy. "It's Grace . . ."

I know, he wants to say, because it's bizarre that she introduces herself like this. They were married for more than a decade, for heaven's sake. They still *are* married, he thinks.

"I'm going to be late," she's saying now.

"Late for what?" he asks, but he's got that cold warning feeling inside.

"I've had a couple of holdups but I'm just about to pick up the cake and . . ."

"What are you talking about, Grace?"

". . . I'll still be with you well before four."

"Wait. What?"

"I'm bringing the cake, Ben."

She says it like it should mean something to him, as though they've discussed this.

"You can't come here, Grace."

There's silence on the line. He can hear traffic in the background, the impatient blast of car horns.

"But you told me about the party and—"

"I told you because you asked. Jesus." He shuts his eyes, tips his head back.

"Look, I've ordered this cake. It's a big, big cake. Two tiers, fluorescent piping, her name in gold icing. A *Love Island* theme. Miniature modeled characters, hearts and bikinis and suntan oil, all that. Super-tacky but also kind of cool . . . It's our thing, mine and Lotte's, and she's going to love it. I mean she's going to love to hate it, I just need to get it to her—"

"Grace—"

"—and, Jesus Christ, it shouldn't be that hard to get a cake from A to fucking B but I've just been kicked out of the chemist by a bloody security guard . . ."

She's acting like she's mad. Her voice is loud, distorting a little down the line, and he's lost the thread of what she's saying when Lotte appears in the doorway. His daughter has changed for the party already and the sight of her stops his heart. She's barefoot and wearing a silver dress. Her pink hair is twisted on top of her head and she's so beautiful—she's so like Grace—he almost can't bear it.

Who is it? Lotte mouths, and he shakes his head, like, no one you know. But he can't meet her eyes as he does it. Pressing the phone to his chest, he whispers to her, "Just give me a minute, Lotte, okay?" And she gives him the thumbs-up, turns, and leaves the room.

"Is that her?" Grace is saying. "Is she there? Is it Lotte? Let me talk to her."

"She won't want to, hon, I'm sorry." Too late he clamps his mouth shut:

the word has already slithered out from between his lips. *Hon*. It feels like a transgression, like he's said the wrong thing because this isn't them anymore. His head is as hot as the sunshine slashing through his tall, wide windows. And even though she can't see him there—even though she probably hasn't noticed he's said it at all—he is blushing like a teenager. "Sorry," he tells her again.

The dishwasher starts to beep, little stabs of sound, and Ben crosses the kitchen, yanks the door open. Steam blasts him.

"It's her sixteenth birthday." Grace is speaking slowly now, articulating every word. "Her sixteenth. How can I not be there? This is it. There won't be another. I've already missed so much. What kind of mother does that make me if I'm not around for . . ."

He can hear the catch in her voice, her breath on the line. "I promised Lotte." He says it softly, like that way maybe he hasn't really said it at all.

"Listen, I'm just bringing the cake. That's all. But there is something else."

There's the sound of her inhaling, a hard rush of air in through her nose, like she's steeling herself.

"I'm having to walk to you because I've . . . The thing is, the car . . . I think maybe I've done something stupid, Ben . . ."

"What? Grace, what are you talking about? You can't . . ."

But the line's gone dead—or she's hung up, he can't tell which.

Four Months Earlier

There are a number of signs that you may be perimenopausal. These symptoms usually present from some time in your early to mid-forties and may include:

*Anxiety and stress	*Bladder incontinence
*Breast tenderness	*Irregular pounding heartbeat
*Body odor changes	*Depression
*Difficulty concentrating	*Weight gain
*Overwhelming fatigue	*Gastrointestinal problems
*Uncontrollable crying	*Hot flashes
*Vaginal dryness	*Irregular menstrual cycle
*Feelings of sadness/desolation	*Mood swings
*Itchy skin	*Joint pain
*Loss of libido	*Memory lapses
*Night sweats	*Osteoporosis
*Sleep disorders	*Tingling extremities
*Headaches	*Hair changes: increased facial hair, but thinning hair elsewhere

GRACE IS FULLY dressed and lying in bed with a migraine. Exhaustion is rooted in the core of her and she's been like this for the past three hours. She has her eyes shut, two fingers jammed into the muscle at the top of her neck where it meets her skull, trying to relieve the pain there. She had a glass of wine last night. One! And now this. This outsize headache that is her punishment. Grace pictures the article torn from a magazine that she keeps in her top drawer, the list of symptoms her friend Natasha passed to her and they laughed about hysterically because, really, what else was there to do? *It's like a bad joke. I thought we had until we were at least fifty*, Natasha said. Natasha is one of the handful of people who will actually talk about this stuff. About the near-comedic deterioration of their itching bodies, their cloudy minds. But the fact is Natasha is a yoga teacher: she has the face of a thirty-year-old, the body of a contortionist. Grace does not.

There's light coming in through the gap in the curtains. It's penetrating her eyelids and she turns—carefully—onto her side. She hoped she'd be feeling better by now because it's one of her teaching days. But she can't do it, she can't go in. There's no way. She called the school office first thing and left a message with the cheerless receptionist, warning her she most likely wouldn't make it. Again. She doesn't want to think about how many times she's been late recently, or not turned up at all. She dreams about giving it up, this job that is more about crowd control than creating a generation of bright young linguists. But she can't, of course she can't. Not now that Ben has gone. She needs the money, what little there is of it, and she needs the distraction.

Anxiety has lodged in the fabric of her body, an uneasy flickering that won't go away. She thinks back to the previous afternoon, to the slam of the door, the *thunk* of Lotte's school bag in the hall. She sees her daughter standing disheveled in her uniform as though she's walked twenty miles to get there. "Leyla's mum's been in touch." Grace has her cover story all lined up: she knows she has to get the words out, that she must say it all before she changes her mind. "She sent me a screenshot of something she saw on your Instagram." Midway through tugging off her tie, Lotte glances up. Gives her a look, like, *What the fuck?* "She was worried, Lotte. I'm worried." She wants to say, *Because I know you're lying to me.* "It's bullying, sweetheart. Those people. You need to block them."

Her daughter laughs wildly. As though Grace has said something so outlandish, so stupid, so naive she can't contain her disdain. "You can't block people, Mum. And you can't hide the fact you're online because everyone knows you're hiding it—they can see you've turned off your activity status, and that makes you a psychopath, okay? Like literally everyone thinks you're a psychopath if you do that . . . The stuff up there, on Instagram, it's just the way people talk. It looks worse than it is. And anyway they're jealous because—" She stops like she's been slapped. Color floods her cheeks.

"They're jealous why?" Grace asks.

Lotte presses her lips together, holds her stare for a little too long. "I don't mean jealous, I . . . Honestly, Mum, it's fine. It's nothing. *Really.*" She bends her head to kick off her shoes so that she's hiding her face. There's the unfamiliar smell on her, the outdoors smell she brings in that always feels other. *Tell me the truth*, Grace wants to say.

"Mum, I would tell you," Lotte murmurs, as if she's read her mind.

On the pillow next to her the phone goes. Grace pushes herself up onto her elbow to check the screen. Inside her head something dips and swerves as though she's going to faint or vomit. It's Cate. It must be 6 a.m. in LA— early even for her.

"Hey!" Her sister's voice is all jumpy and hoarse, and Grace can tell straight away that she's running. She pictures her on the treadmill in the den of the house in Los Feliz, all blond and sweaty and lean.

"Hi, how are you?" she says. It hurts her head to talk.

"Ben called," Cate pants. "Look, shit, I'm sorry, Grace, I think I landed you in it, y'know, about Lotte skipping school . . ."

Her sister starts to speak in small bursts of words, and Grace holds the phone a little way from her ear because she already knows what Cate is going to say and she doesn't want to have to engage with it. Now that she's half sitting up like this, something uncomfortable is pressing into the top of her thigh. She's wearing her jeans still and it's in the back pocket. Shifting her weight to one side, she pulls out a balled-up scrap of paper, smooths it out. *XXX + L = I nearly came just looking at you today . . .* The words vibrate as she reads them and she has the urge to rip the paper to pieces. She can't believe she's forgotten this: another cryptic piece of the shifted parallel existence Grace no longer plays a part in.

"So did you find anything, then?" her sister is asking. "On Insta?" She says the word like she's put quotation marks around it.

Grace tells her briefly, speaking quietly into the phone, trying to hold her head still. ". . . and the thing is she's been through so much already with the separation and with everything . . ." She pauses. For a moment she thinks she might not be able to go on. "I just want to fix it, Cate. But I know if I push too hard she'll push back. I know I can't force her to tell me. She's sixteen in a few months. Legal, for God's sake! She'll be able to smoke, have sex, get married, leave home, take two flipping acetamino-phen instead of one, the whole damn shebang, and I just feel like there's so much she's keeping in. Too many secrets. I don't know how to find her anymore and—"

"Woah!" Cate breaks in. "Steady on, Columbo. Listen, Grace, it is what it is. It's the process. It's just what they do, and here's the thing, maybe we don't understand them—even you, language nerd. I mean, they speak in bloody acronyms most of the time. LOL! And they're a salty lot. Maybe Lotte's right, maybe we are just too past it to get it. Christ, that's a real buzzkill." She snorts down the phone.

Grace knows Cate is just trying to reassure her, but it pisses her off, this implication she's being neurotic or—the worst of all slurs—*overprotective*. The suggestion that she's making something out of nothing. The fact is Cate and Sara's kid ended up in rehab. He's now working shifts as a barista in West Hollywood at the age of twenty-six.

Her sister is still talking but Grace cuts in: "I've got a migraine, Cate," she says. "I need to go." As soon as she's said it she feels bad because she knows she's been blunt, she knows Cate is just trying to help. "But thanks for giving me the heads-up about Ben," she adds. "And, look, it's not your fault you landed me in it, okay?"

As soon as she's hung up, the phone starts to ring again. It's Ben.

She pinches her fingers to the bridge of her nose, picks up.

"Why didn't you tell me, Grace?"

"Well, hi there, how've you been?"

"You can't keep this stuff from me. She's my daughter too."

Grace moves her hand to her forehead, presses her palm against the skin there. "Let's not forget, Ben, *you* left *me*."

"That's not fair. You know it's not."

There's the plant on the side that's dying and Grace feels suddenly crazily thirsty. The words scratch her throat as she starts to explain about the absences, the meeting with John Power—nothing Cate hasn't already said. She doesn't tell him about what she's found online. She doesn't want to think about it.

"Jesus . . ." Ben says when she's finished. "This just feels like it's come from nowhere, right? What are we going to do?"

"Listen, Ben." She closes her eyes, leans her head back on the pillow. "I've got this horrible headache. I'm supposed to be at work. I can't talk about it right now."

When he answers his voice has softened. "Call me back, then," he says. "Okay?"

Something in his intonation gets her, and from nowhere she's picturing him here in their bedroom, his body above hers. The fresh white smell of him and his arms either side of her, the ligaments pulled taut. His pupils have spread like ink blots, like he's high, and he doesn't take his eyes from her face as he pushes himself into her. And she wants to reach out and touch him but she knows she can't.

"Grace?"

"Yes. Sorry." Her voice comes out staccato, guiltily. "Look, it's basically all sorted. Honestly, you don't need to worry. I'm dealing with it—I've dealt with it." She's talking too fast and, hearing the words coming out of her mouth, she almost wants to laugh because she sounds like Lotte. Like mother like daughter.

2003

GRACE IS STANDING on set next to the outsize whiteboard. Her feet in the stupidly high shoes are aching already and she's feeling like she's about to burst out of her dress. The lights are up in the auditorium and Ed, the executive producer, is sitting in the middle row, legs splayed and tongue out. No, his tongue isn't actually out, but he's staring at her in such a way that it might as well be. Crossing one leg in front of the other, she tugs at her hem. Is it just her or are they supplying her with outfits that are getting steadily tighter and shorter?

She's in the *Sun* again today, a quarter-page photo of her under the headline "Polyglotty Hotty." The scoop? That she was wearing a red dress yesterday. Oh, and that she may or may not have gone up a dress size since starting the show. *Curvaceous Grace Adams sizzled in scarlet on ITV's flagship afternoon show yesterday.* There's an entire panel devoted to speculation about her weight, a "dietary expert" arguing that stress—*like the kind we get when we start a new job*—can cause overeating and therefore weight gain. A "high-profile" fashion designer warning that the wrong dress can bump a size-ten woman up to a size sixteen. *Never underestimate the power of good tailoring, ladies . . .*

"Ignore it all." Cate had been on the line first thing from Los Angeles. "They just want an excuse to run your picture. Take it as a compliment."

Patrick Blake, a.k.a. The Diva, hasn't shown yet. The show's host likes to make an entrance—even at rehearsals, it's all the same to him—and she's checking that she's got the card with her word of the day on it, her marker pens all lined up in front of the whiteboard, when Ben Kerr slams into her thoughts. The black sweater with the holes in the wrists, his body not quite leaning into hers at the student union bar. *I knew it would be you*, she hears him say. *The minute I saw all those pens lined up, like a little stationery army. I knew I'd lost it . . .*

The voice of one of the assistant producers, Marie, comes over her earpiece. "Word up, Grace." She laughs. "His Nibs is on his way apparently, but you're all set, yeah? You've got your crazy-arse saying or phrase? Give it to me again?"

Grace uncrosses her legs, tips forward a little on the five-inch heels as she plants her feet. "So, today's untranslatable word is *hüzün*. It's an enigmatic Turkish word that has an Arabic root and it describes a spiritual anguish. The gloomy feeling that everything is in decline and that the situation—often political in nature—will probably get gradually worse. But this isn't about a personal sense of darkness or persecution. There's— oxymoronically—a shared joy or magic in having this word to remind us that our misfortune, our dark mood, is largely collective. We're together in this as the curtain comes crashing down . . . so huzzah for *hüzün*!" Grace laughs. "The closest word we have to the mysterious *hüzün* in English is probably 'melancholy.' And, finally, Turkish author Orhan Pamuk described the concept exquisitely as 'the emotion that a child might feel while looking through a steamy window.'"

"Okay, cool, great."

Behind Grace, there's a commotion as Patrick Blake comes onto set. Moving past the whiteboard he holds out a fist—not entirely ironically— for her to bump.

"Oh, just BTW, Grace," Marie's voice is in her ear again, "you do know the camera adds, like, ten pounds, yeah?"

Before she's had a chance to process what the producer has just said, there's the click of Marie's mic going dead. Marie, her supposed friend. They spent the evening together in a wine bar just last week. Grace stands there stunned, straining to keep the smile on her face because she's up here flood-lit in the heat of the lights, in full view of the entire crew. So Marie has read the coverage. Of course she has—they all will have. Her hand goes to the bulge of her stomach. It's warts-and-all tight, this dress. Yes, there are lumps and bumps—she's not a bloody supermodel. She'd like to see Marie rocking this. Grace stops the thought. Because the fact is Marie is stick thin. Without doubt Marie has an eating disorder. Marie *would* rock this dress. Unlike Grace who has zero control when it comes to food. None. Even less recently. It is one of her few comforts—pretty much the only one right now. She sucks in her stomach, considers what she might pick up from Budgens on her way home for tea tonight. They do those really nice Indian ready meals. She likes the prawn one, the korma with the creamy sauce, and she could get a naan to go with it, some plain yogurt, a bar of Green & Black's . . . Grace gags. It's come from nowhere, this feeling, and she clamps a hand over her mouth, waits for the nausea to pass.

"Are you all right?" Patrick Blake is leaning forward from behind his desk. The makeup artist Sangeeta is blotting powder onto the rolls of his chin, but she doesn't look up.

Grace has an acid taste at the back of her throat and she swallows, nods. "Fine." She smiles. "I'm absolutely fine, thanks."

"Okay, wagons roll!" Ed calls from the auditorium.

Twenty minutes later it's a wrap and someone's been to Costa, bought coffee. It's just what Grace needs because she hasn't been sleeping well. Maybe the tabloids are right—maybe the stress is getting to her. Taking a sip from her paper cup, she nearly spits it out because it tastes too strong, like there are five shots in there and, really, she'd rather have a glass of water. But she needs the caffeine, feels like she's going to fall where she's standing without it. She rips open a packet of sugar, stirs it in.

"Sweet tooth?" Ed winks, as he walks past her.

She has barely got the cup to her lips when the surge of nausea comes again. Leaning back against the whiteboard, she inhales deeply. Then she places the full cup carefully on the shelf next to her marker pens, leaves it there, and hopes no one will notice.

Now

HER MOBILE IS ringing as she rounds the bend in the road and at last she is in sight of the baker's. She's within spitting distance of the cake. The phone is hot in her hand. It's Ben calling her back, calling on a loop, and she doesn't want to pick up. She has said everything she has to say to him.

The clock tower is behind her but she won't turn to check the time: she thinks it might tip her over the edge to see how late it is. The traffic is gridlocked still. Humming, glinting metal stretching in every direction and the taste of gray air on her tongue.

And then she spots her up ahead, coming down the hill past the green-grocer. Freja. It's definitely her, with her silver bucket bag, her dentist-white Birkenstocks. The school mum she tries to avoid.

Grace can't pretend to be on her phone because it's ringing still. Putting her head down, she moves to the inside edge of the pavement, so that her arm is almost scraping the gray brick wall of the YMCA. The street is busy and there's a chance she can make it past without being spotted. And then a miracle happens. The ringing stops. When it doesn't start up again Grace puts the phone to her ear, talks into the mouthpiece.

"Yes," she says to no one. "Right, yes, okay . . ."

"Grace!" Freja has seen her and is waving madly.

Grace forces a smile. Then she points to the phone and scrunches her nose, mimes regret.

"Yes," she says again, into the mouthpiece, an earnest expression on her face. "That's right, yes."

She's maybe three feet away from Freja now, and she's smiling, nodding as if she's agreeing with something the person at the other end of the line has just said, when her phone starts to ring.

Blood burns from her solar plexus to the crown of her head. It's as if her entire body is blushing. Pulling a quizzical face, she takes the phone from her ear, holds it out in front of her as though it's some kind of extraterrestrial being with a life force all its own.

Freja stops in her path.

"Bizarre," Grace says. "I just got cut off and then this . . . ?"

Freja reaches out, clamps her arm. "How *are* you, Grace?"

It's that question already. Freja is straight to it.

"I'm good, thanks, yeah . . ."

Now the sympathetic eyes. Grace can't bear it. It's a wonder Freja can emote with her facial features at all, she thinks, registering her too-shiny skin, the fact that she appears to have been ironed from her forehead to her chin. *Mokita*. The Papua New Guinean word pops into her mind. *A truth everybody knows but nobody speaks.* There's no equivalent in English, but it's Botox in a nutshell—the wide-open secret that isn't discussed. The big pretense that no one is cheating, that their post-forty beauty is all about good genes and great moisturizer, that they are *winning* aging. Grace would like to win aging: she would like to cheat too. But the most she can afford is a fringe down to her eyebrows that she maintains disastrously, between hair appointments, with a pair of kitchen scissors.

Freja gives her arm a squeeze before releasing her grip. "You know, I'm so pleased to see you because we've got the international food evening coming up and we need volunteers. It's always a good one. Were you there last year, when Yasmin got *quite* drunk? Wait, let me show you the pics . . ." She takes her mobile from her pocket, starts to swipe through photos. "Oh, hang on, this is funny . . ." She holds out the screen as if she's accidentally stumbled on something. "It's the climate thing . . . the art competition at school? You know, the we're-all-dancing-on-top-of-a-volcano-but-please-make-a-nice-piece-of-art-instead-of-going-on-the-Greta-Friday-strikes-or-you'll-get-a-behavior-point thing?" She rolls her eyes, laughs.

Grace shakes her head. No, she does not know about the art competition at school. But she does know about Freja's carbon footprint. She also knows what's coming: she has been Freja-ed a thousand times before.

"This is Olivia's entry." Freja waves a hand over the screen, like, *pfff*, why are we even looking at this?

Grace glances at the phone. The sun is glaring off it and she can't see the picture at all.

". . . and Ms. Zaine—you know, head of art? Well, it's ridiculous, really, because obviously you probably have to be eighteen to enter the Summer Exhibition . . ."

Fragments of words, sentences reach her. Something about GCSE results day, Camden School for Girls, a fortnight in Vietnam. But Grace is somewhere else. She hears a door slammed shut, the cold, hard ring of a slap. There's the smell of spirits and sweat and too-sweet perfume. Tears on Lotte's face, dirt on her hands, her top. Flesh against flesh.

". . . some mummy-daughter time . . ." Freja is saying, ". . . at the Topshop nail bar . . ."

My daughter does not want to live with me, Grace thinks. *She will not even see me. It is her sixteenth birthday today and she doesn't want me there.*

Bloody hell, Grace. From nowhere her mum's voice crashes into her head. The words that came at her down the line when she called to tell her she was pregnant with Lotte. Admonishing, as though she'd spilled red wine on the carpet or reversed the car into a lamppost. *It's hard enough, you know, without . . . I mean, have you really thought about this? Do you know what you're getting yourself into?* Then her memory unspools further and she's coming into her parents' bedroom, clutching in her hand the ballpoint-drawn card she's been making for the past twenty minutes at the table downstairs. She's drawn a vase with tall flowers in it, sunflowers because she knows they're her mummy's favorite, and she's pleased with what she's drawn, proud. She's worked hard to get the vase just right. She's even added some shading because she's nine now and they've been learning about it in art at school.

The lights are off in the room, the curtains drawn, but she can make out a long humped shape in the bed. The side where her daddy sleeps is flat, undisturbed. *Dear Mummy,* she's written in the card, and she's spelled out the word *Dear* in bubble writing. *Get well soon.* Her tummy feels all knotted up inside as she tiptoes across the rug, feels the tickle of the wool against her bare feet. "I made you a card, Mummy," she whispers, unsure whether she is awake or asleep because she doesn't quite want to look. She tries to prop the card on the bedside table, but it's made of paper and keeps slipping down. "I'm sorry, Gracie." The voice makes her start. It sounds thin, faraway, not right. "I'm just not feeling well, darling."

She leaves the paper card collapsed, like it has jelly legs, against the alarm clock and comes to sit on the edge of the bed. Her mummy's eyes are only half-open, like it hurts her to look out, and her face is wet. She doesn't look like herself. Grace springs up and pulls a tissue from the box on the bedside table. Then she starts to dab at the tears. "Don't cry, Mummy," she says, and she's trying to keep her voice from wobbling, even though her heart is going too fast and she can feel it pumping in her tongue.

Downstairs there's the sound of the lounge door opening, a blast of TV news, Cate's voice asking how long until tea because she's so hungry. Then her dad is calling her name and she thinks he'll be cross if he finds her in here. She places the balled-up tissue carefully on the pillow. "I love you, Mummy," she says. She wants to lean in and kiss her cheek, the soft part that smells like home. But she's too shy or afraid to do it, and she leaves the room as quietly as she came in.

Freja is still talking but Grace isn't hearing a word. Her mind flashes to the car she's abandoned five hundred meters back down the road, the man up the ladder, the woman in the chemist, her boss on the phone, the crushing heat, and before she knows what she's doing Grace starts to walk away. She's aware, in some blurred part of her, that Freja is scrutinizing her, frowning, as she leaves the woman standing on the pavement and doesn't look back. There's a whizzing feeling in her—around her—that seems to stir the dead air in the street. Such potency in a simple act. Quietly, calmly, she has taken the bolt cutters to social convention. She has set herself free.

Four Months Earlier

GRACE IS CLEANING her teeth in the bathroom. She's only just had breakfast, even though it's eleven in the morning on a Saturday, because she's actually slept. Not through the night—that would be miraculous, alarming even, like she'd been drugged with Rohypnol or Nyquil. But she's had a decent night's sleep, a decent week in fact. There have been no more absences, no more letters, no more emails, no calls from the school, and she's starting to think maybe Cate was right: maybe they just don't get the dialect of youth. Maybe it's true and Lotte is fine: she isn't being bullied. Grace has even managed to negotiate a call from Paul. He phoned the day before about the Japanese romance, and although she might have fudged things a little, she's going to throw herself into the toe-curling prose starting Monday. She's feeling like things are pulling together, slowly, slowly.

She's spitting toothpaste into the washbasin when the doorbell rings. "Lotte!" she calls, without any hope that her daughter might actually answer the door. She's upstairs practicing TikTok dances. Grace knows this because the ceiling is shaking as if she's about to come through it, and she can hear the distorted yelp of music from Lotte's mobile, which is turned up to full volume. She's belting out the words too—she has a beautiful voice. She's musical. Grace has no idea where she gets this from—it isn't down to her or Ben. In the past, Lotte has tried to teach her these dances—she choreographs her own steps too—and she's a good, patient teacher, but Grace can't grasp them at all. The two of them always end up collapsed in laughter on the kitchen floor. *You're getting better, Mum, honestly*. Grace hears Lotte's voice in her head, fat with stifled giggles, but sweetly, earnestly trying to encourage her. And then her own reply, *Oh, no, please don't pity me, that's the worst, my life at this point is over . . .*

The bell goes again. Dragging a hand across her foamy mouth, she heads downstairs. On the doormat there's the local paper—another headline about health care closures. Averting her eyes, she opens the door.

"You need to sign for this one." The deliveryman is holding out his electronic pad and she squiggles the screen with a fingernail, takes what he's proffering and thanks him. It's a brown envelope, official-looking, A4-sized, and with a cardboard back, like it might hold a certificate or photograph. There's a tightening in her as she shuts the door, moves down the hall to the kitchen.

The table is covered with books and sticky notes, mugs trailing herbal-teabag strings, the jade glass vase filled with browning sunflowers gone crunchy at the edges—and it oppresses her instantly. Her zen is gone. Leaning her back against the sink, she runs her finger under the gluey flap of the envelope, pulls out a wad of stapled paper, a document. Her eyes leap ahead of her conscious mind, swallowing the information there in one gulp.

HM Courts & Tribunals Service D8
Application for a divorce, dissolution or (judicial) separation.

Section 1
Your application
(known as petition in divorce and judicial separation)

1.1 What application do you wish to make?

Someone—Ben—has ticked the box that says: "Divorce on the ground that the marriage has broken down irretrievably."

Grace feels suddenly untethered, as though she might float from where she is standing, through the ceiling, past the roof of her house, and up into the sky. Because it has come from nowhere, this document, these divorce papers. There has been no warning, no conversation at all. Her husband has started divorce proceedings without telling her. Grace places her hand on her breastbone. Her breathing isn't right and she's trying to smooth the air in and out of her lungs. Strange, formal words jump out at her as she scans the page.

> Section 2
> About you (the applicant / petitioner)
>
> 2.1 Your current name
> First name(s): Benjamin Samuel Talbot
> Last name: Kerr

There's a second document that's separate from the first and she pulls it out from underneath the top sheaf, scans the heading.

> D8OB: Statement in support of divorce / dissolution/ (judicial) separation—**unreasonable behavior.**
> Section 1(2)(b) Matrimonial Causes Act 1973
> Section 44(5)(a) Civil Partnership Act 2004
>
> If completing this form by hand, please use black ink and BLOCK CAPITAL LETTERS and tick the boxes that apply.

Unreasonable behavior? Grace kicks the cupboard under the sink. She can't believe what she's reading. Why has Ben done it? And like this? It's barely a week since he was on the phone accusing her of withholding information from him. She can hear his voice in her head: *Why didn't you tell me, Grace? You can't keep this stuff from me, she's my daughter too . . .* Does he not see the hypocrisy in this? What was he thinking? Then a thought blasts her. Has he met someone else?

Lotte swings into the kitchen, singing. Grace hasn't heard her come down the stairs and she feels suddenly trapped, tries to arrange her face into a smile. But her daughter barely glances at her before she has her head in the fridge assessing the contents, pulling out a carton of orange juice. Grace's fingers clutching the papers are trembling. The edge of the sink is cutting into her back where she's pressing against it, holding herself up because she's light-headed. That low-blood-sugar feeling like she hasn't eaten in too long.

"What's that?" Lotte says, over her shoulder.

And it strikes Grace how they notice everything and nothing, these selective, narcissistic young adults. Everything you don't want them to see. Grace opens her mouth to answer but the words lodge in her throat. She can't find the language to explain to her daughter what this is: she has no idea what to say. And then, from nowhere, something like nausea is rising in her and she realizes she is crying.

Lotte shuts the fridge, moves across the kitchen toward her. "What, Mum?" she's saying, and there's fear in her eyes. "What is it?"

"No, no, it's fine . . ." Grace's voice is a scrape. "Sorry, sweetheart, I'm being so stupid." She's still crying, she can't seem to stop, and she's so dismayed at herself, so appalled, because this is not what mothers do. She should be keeping it together for her child. "Sorry," she says again, and she presses her lips together, waits a beat, two beats, three. "It's the divorce petition, darling. From your dad."

"The what?"

"It means he wants to make it official, our separation. It's just paperwork, that's all, so I don't know why I'm being such an idiot about it." She forces a laugh, pulls a palm across her face.

Lotte is holding the carton of orange juice still. There's a sudden scribble of color across her cheeks and, standing there like that, she looks so young. A memory snatches Grace, of the three of them. They're walking through Regent's Park, just past the place where across the ditch you can see the animals in the zoo. There's snow on the ground and Lotte on Ben's shoulders. Pink spots in the middle of her fat cheeks and her head thrown back, laughing and laughing at something he has just said.

Grace puts a hand on her daughter's arm. "Are you okay?" she asks. "It's horrible for you, all of this, I know. You didn't choose any of it."

"I'm fine," Lotte says, too quickly. Like she's shutting a door.

Beside them the dishwasher beeps and swishes, starting its next cycle. Grace shuffles the papers in her hands, pushes out a breath. And then, before she understands what's happening, Lotte has her arms around her and she's hugging her, gripping her tight. She feels the crush of the documents between them, sharp corners poking into her ribs, and Grace is fighting to hold on to herself because it's so unexpected. This just doesn't happen anymore. Her daughter doesn't hug her like this—she barely touches her most days.

"I'm sorry," she murmurs into Lotte's hair. "I'm sorry we couldn't make it work for you."

"I'm sorry too, Mum," her child says, in a squashed voice that betrays her. And Grace thinks her heart might break.

Grace has no idea how long they stand there like that. But she's like a junkie, hoovering it up, inhaling her child, because she knows this is something slippery, rare. She knows she has to hold the moment tight.

When Lotte pulls back, they aren't quite able to look at each other because there is something too powerful in what has just happened. It doesn't fit the way they are with each other now, and it's like they're afraid to acknowledge it. And Grace hates the fact that she feels this way. She could never have imagined she would be anything other than herself with her child.

Lotte takes a glass from the draining board, pours herself some juice. "Did you ever start watching that season of *Parks and Rec*?" she asks, her back to Grace. Her voice is too casual and Grace has to dig her nails into her palms before she tells her no.

"Okay!" Her daughter spins round. Her hands are on her hips and there's resolve in her eyes. "So tonight we get takeout and we binge the glory that is Leslie Knope . . . Plan?"

And Grace nods because she can't speak. Because who is this astonishing child-woman? How is she the same person who less than a fortnight ago told her head teacher to screw his school?

Then Lotte leans in toward her, kisses her cheek. Soft, swift lips against her skin. And Grace is still trying to process that this has happened because Lotte has not kissed her voluntarily in—she can't remember how long—when the kitchen door clicks shut, and she is gone.

Grace stands for a moment, listens to the tread of her daughter's footsteps on the stairs. "I miss you," she says quietly, into the empty kitchen.

2003

GRACE IS SITTING on the edge of her chair at the doctor's office. She hasn't taken off her coat and she's squeezing her knees together as if that way she might be able to keep everything in. She's been putting this off for weeks—she's already canceled one appointment—and now that she's here, she just wants to leave. The doctor is washing her hands vigorously at the sink. With her sleek dark chignon and thin lips, she reminds Grace, disconcertingly, of her old chemistry teacher.

"So," the doctor says, her back to Grace, "how can I help?"

And Grace starts to tell her about the constant headaches, that she feels nauseated almost all the time but is never actually sick. She doesn't say she's pretty certain it has to do with the job. There's a lot of dumb press coverage still and she feels the pressure of it—she can't pretend she doesn't—and she's expecting to come away with anxiety pills that she probably won't take, maybe something to help her sleep that she will.

The doctor seats herself at her desk so that she's sideways to Grace. She picks up Grace's notes, puts them down again. "Could you be pregnant?" she asks, without looking up.

It's the standard question, the one they always ask off the bat.

"Ha! No." Grace laughs darkly, like, *Chance would be a fine thing.*

If the doctor gets the joke she doesn't acknowledge it. Instead she scribbles aggressively on a pad of headed paper, trying to get the ink of her pen to flow. "Ugh, this damn thing . . ." she says, and then with a glance at Grace, ". . . sorry."

"No, no," Grace smiles, "that's okay."

The doctor abandons the pen, roots around for another in a pot on her desk. "So, no sexual partners at present?"

Grace resists the urge to laugh a second time. "Nope," she says, and shifts in her seat. When are they going to get to the bit about the sleeping tablets? The doctor writes something on her pad and Grace shuffles her feet on the floor, stares straight ahead across the room toward a tall yellow bin marked *Sharps*.

"And how about in the last five or six months? Any sexual partners?"

The doctor eyes Grace's waist as she says it. Grace definitely sees her do this.

And she's all set to tell her no when her mind flashes to the previous September—to the Polyglot convention, and to her lost weekend at the Kerensa Hotel. A clouded, dangerous knowledge uncoils in her as she starts to count backward, moving her fingers minutely on the seat of the chair as she does it. *February, January, December, November, October . . .*

When she's finished she knots her fingers in her lap, looks up at the doctor. Her head feels hot, her tongue fat and dry in her mouth.

"Shit," she murmurs. She can't stop herself.

The doctor places her pen carefully on the desk. There's the smell of antiseptic and ammonia, and Grace feels sick again, the familiar ache around her throat, her jaw.

"But I've definitely . . . there's been blood," she starts to say. "I mean, I'm really irregular anyhow and light, and I've been kind of stressed with work and . . . he withdrew," she finishes limply.

"I think we'd better pop you up onto the bed and examine you."

Grace makes her mind go blank as the doctor stands and moves across the room. Then she drags herself out of her seat, hovers while the doctor draws the curtain around the cubicle and gestures for Grace to enter. She's still in her coat and stumbling out of her trousers, when she hears the doctor pull on a pair of surgical gloves at the other side of the curtain with a snap that sounds like a gunshot.

Now

GRACE IS PUSHING on through the gloopy heat up the hill to the baker's when the little boy comes from nowhere. He's maybe three and he's hurtling down the hill on a red plastic scooter, tacking an erratic line down the pavement. She can see from the shudder of the handlebars and his white-knuckle grip that he is out of control.

"NO!" Her voice comes out crazy, before she's even aware that she's going to shout. There's no parent in sight and the little boy is veering toward the curbstone now. Grace doesn't think twice as she lunges across the pavement, wrenches the child from the scooter. A car horn sounds as the scooter tumbles onto the tarmac inches from the road. The child looks up at her, shocked, and bursts into tears.

"Steady on, Lewis Hamilton!" A woman in a floral dress is running down the hill, her brown ponytail jumping from the top of her head. She takes the child from Grace's arms, gives her a look that says, *Honestly, kids!* "Ssh, ssh, you're okay," she says to the little boy. "This nice lady was just trying to help." She turns to Grace. "He's very good on the brake."

"Sorry, I just . . ." Grace starts, but she can't go on because she's shaken still, and she's already beginning to wonder—a barely formed thought—whether maybe she overreacted.

The woman bends to pick up the scooter from the pavement, all the time talking to her little boy, a stream of words that sound like kisses.

As the pair move off, Grace has the sense that the eyes of the people in the nearby cars are on her. She feels suddenly exposed, like she's ripped off her clothes, her skin. She's so close to the cake shop now—she can almost read the sign outside—but with the heat and the cars there's a pressure in her, like extreme thirst, and she can't stand it. Right next to her is a cobbled passageway, a gap between the buildings that's the side entrance to the pub. She ducks down it. She escapes.

The door to the pub kitchen is open and through it she sees a TV high up in a corner, a man in a jacket and tie on screen, the red news banner running underneath him. The volume's turned up above the noise of the kitchen so that it's blaring out into the passage.

". . . over the coming century, the Met Office Hadley Centre is predicting—and I'm quoting here—'warmer, wetter winters and hotter, drier summers, along with an increase in the frequency and intensity of extremes.' A leading force in the study of climate change, the boffins at the Hadley Centre say that if emissions are not reduced, we can expect severe heat waves, like the one we're currently experiencing, every other year by 2050 . . ."

Grace moves down the passageway until the sound of the TV fades like a steady exhalation. Then she stops, leans up against the wall. The brick is hot through her shirt, like flames up her back, and it's almost comforting. And she's thinking about Lotte. About the bewildering fact that she is sixteen today, and where has the time gone, because she feels like somehow she's missed it—that all she has instead are a handful of old photographs in her mind. And then she's thinking about the toddler on the scooter, remembering the sticky sweet smell of him, the solid feel of his small body in her arms. She pulls her phone from her pocket and she's clicking on iCloud, finding the clip because it's like everything is against her today. She's losing the will to go on and this is her opium, her secret shameful fix.

And here she is! Her little girl. Eighteen months old and sitting on a bench at Burnham Overy Staithe, looking out at the sailing boats. Her hair is sun-bleached and curling, like mad question marks, her fat little legs stuck straight out on the seat. And she's wearing the cherry-red shoes, the ones they kept. There's the clank and rattle of masts and she's pointing. "Is dat one?" she's saying. "Is dat? Is dat?" Because she's looking for seals like the ones they saw at Blakeney Point. Then the little girl gasps, and Grace feels her daughter's joy spread through her, like syrup, even though she knows what is coming, she's anticipating every movement, every nuance. "Mummy! A blutterfy . . ." There's the wind through the microphone so that her small voice is faint, and Grace tenses each muscle in her face as she strains to hear. And her fingers are itching because she wants to reach into the film and touch her lost child. It is unbearable to her that she will never do that again. That her baby—this baby—is lost to her forever.

A text pings onto the screen, obscuring the top of the picture, erasing the sky, part of her child's face, and Grace hits pause as if she's been caught. The message is from Cate, the letters all capped up so that it is shouting at her: GRACE! I'M WORRIED ABOUT YOU. PICK UP YOUR DAMN PHONE!!!!

Four Months Earlier

IT'S BEEN TWENTY minutes since she picked up the call from Northmere Park and Grace is supposed to be at work. Instead she's here, stuck in a queue of traffic stretching back from the Turkish grocery store to the car wash. She's hammering her heel impatiently in the footwell, as a delivery-man with crates of fruit stacked high crosses the road at a pace so slow it would almost be comedic if it wasn't for the shadowy panic in her.

She'd stood on the doorstep on her way out, heart twisting as the attendance officer introduced herself. *Lotte has skipped the last two periods*, she'd said, and the words punched her. *The situation is getting critical now*, the woman added sternly, as though she was head of Special Branch or maybe Leader of the Free World. And Grace gripped her car keys so hard they left a mark across her palm. She had no idea whether she was furious or afraid or both, as the woman started to talk about in-school counseling, an urgent meeting with the head of house, a referral to Child and Adolescent Mental Health Services.

Through the windscreen she sees the deliveryman stop in the middle of the road, redistributing his load.

"Oh, come on." Grace leans over the steering wheel, her jaw clenched tight. She has called work claiming a family crisis and she has no real plan, just that she will drive the streets until she tracks Lotte down. Behind her eyes the words from her daughter's Instagram scroll like they're on ticker tape . . . *Not answering my DMs. I see you I see you I see you . . . don't you dare block me bitch . . .* There's the familiar feeling of shapeless dread in her and she wants to make it stop.

"*Merde!* Come on!" Grace hits the horn, just a light tap but—it's like a punishment—at that precise moment one of the crates crashes to the ground. Fat striped watermelons hit the tarmac and split, spewing pulp and seeds, like internal organs.

Grace loops through Ally Pally and up past the Rec, then cuts back on herself along by the row of shops, the petrol station, until she meets the Broadway. She passes the church on the corner, and she's keeping one eye on the traffic, the other on the people on the street, scanning the shoppers for her daughter's candy-floss hair, an incongruous school uniform, the blazer hooked over her arm in that way she does. Nothing. And then she's on to the road that tracks the edge of Highgate Wood all the way to the tube, an impatient queue of cars behind her because she's doing under twenty.

The traffic lights turn red as she gets to the pub on the corner. Glancing across, she thinks of the three of them sitting at a table in the beer garden. On the bench next to her Lotte is laughing because the lemonade she's drinking is fizzing in her nose, and opposite her Ben lifts his pint to his lips. He's caught the sun and has the sleepy look he gets after the first hit of alcohol, the look she loves. Leaning over the table, she kisses him, tells him he tastes of holidays. "You can't taste of holidays, Mummy," Lotte says.

"Yes, you can," Ben answers, without taking his eyes from Grace's face.

It goes through her mind to call him, wondering if she'd have time before the lights change. Then just as quickly she dispels the idea because she's starting to understand that what she's doing is madness. An impossible quest. The fact is Lotte could be anywhere.

She's waiting in the hallway when Lotte gets back from school. Or, rather, *not* from school. Grace has to lean her shoulder into the wall to steady herself because the relief at seeing the dark shape of her daughter through the frosted glass as she comes up the path is enormous, almost as huge as the anger that follows instantly. There's the swing of the front door, the rush of air, and she's dumping her bag, saying hi like everything is normal. As though she's just back from the abject boredom of double maths.

"Where have you been?" Grace asks, and she can hear that her voice is tight, like she's talking through her teeth.

"What do you mean?" Lotte frowns, as if she doesn't understand the question.

"Don't," Grace says. "Just don't." She's eyeing the chip in the paintwork where the door bangs back on itself because she finds she isn't able to look her daughter full in the face.

Lotte sticks her hands on her hips, blows out a sigh that makes her lips flubber. "So I took a period off, so what?"

Grace is blindsided. If she'd expected anything it wasn't this. Stupidly. It trips her every time, this irrationality, the stubborn illogic. This refusal to back down.

"Everyone does it." Lotte kicks off her shoes, leaves them where they fall. "It's no big deal."

Tipping back her head, Grace tries to count the petals on the ceiling rose before she will allow herself to speak. She knows this is the process— this is how it works. It isn't personal, but it doesn't make it any easier, the slipping away. And it makes no sense because where is she, the sweet, kind child-adult who gorged on pizza and laughter and Netflix just a few nights ago? Curled like a cat against her on the sofa, so close that Grace couldn't have said where her own body stopped and her daughter's began. She should know better but it feels like betrayal.

"What's going on, Lotte? Where were you?"

"Around . . ."

"Around? Are you serious?"

Her daughter shrugs. "You don't have to be so savage about it." She rummages in her school bag, pulling out her water bottle, her makeup bag patterned with goggle-eyed avocados.

"That's not an answer. Who were you with? Were you on your own?"

"Yes." Lotte twists the lid off a lip gloss, starts to apply it with infuriating insouciance. "How does it affect you? I mean, what difference does it make? Look, I told you, it's no big deal. I one hundred percent don't learn anything at school anyway. It's a waste of time." She rolls her eyes, and then, under her breath, "Jesus Christ . . ."

It's all the clichés and Grace balls her hands into fists. She would like to snatch the lip gloss from her daughter. She would like to open her mouth wide and scream.

"It absolutely is a big deal." She wants to list the reasons why, starting with "You are fifteen and no one knew where you were and it's not safe," and ending with "Because you're doing your GCSEs and you will fuck up your life." But there are gaps in her mind where the words should be, and she thinks of the magazine article in her drawer, the bullet-point list of symptoms . . . *difficulty concentrating . . . memory lapses . . .* She only knows that she's too tired for all this, doesn't have the strength to argue with the arrogance, the blind naivete, the unreason. Her daughter is an empty tweet bulldozing through logic and nuance and truth, and there is no comeback for that.

Lotte elbows her way past, almost knocking the picture of the Madonna and Child from the opposite wall. And instead of going into the kitchen to get something to eat, as she normally would, she heads up the stairs toward her room, like they're all done here.

"You always do this, you know that?" Her daughter tips the words over her shoulder.

"Do what? You mean not agreeing with every single thing you say and do? Having an opinion? You know that thing we have? Freedom of speech? Democracy?" She's shouting now—she's done with trying to keep this thing from igniting. "The last time I checked it was all still in place. Just about. And believe it or not this is not all about you. You know what, Lotte? I don't want calls from the attendance officer at school making me feel like I'm a shit mother." She stalls minutely as she swears. Even though she's done it almost deliberately to shock, to try to get through, she still feels the failure of it. She feels winded, she feels scared. She forces herself to lower her voice. "I didn't go into work today because of this, because of you. Do you realize that? I could lose my job. And then what? It's obvious you're unhappy. Talk to me. Tell me. Help me out here. Please. What's with the absences?"

Lotte stops at the top of the stairs. She has her hand on the newel post and she turns to look down at Grace, and there's something in her expression, something Grace doesn't recognize. Panic flares in her gut.

"What's with the absences?" Lotte's voice is a harmonic. "You're asking *me* that? What about your big *absence*, huh?" She flicks her index fingers like knives, putting air quotes around the word. "You left us for—how long was it, Mum? Remind me. I'd have to go some to match it, wouldn't I? We never talk about that, do we?" She pauses, and when she speaks again it's as though she's talking to herself. "We never ever did."

Grace stands, stunned, as her daughter pushes herself off the stairs, disappears down the landing. And as the bedroom door bangs shut she sinks to the floor where she's standing. It's as though the oxygen has been sucked from the hallway. She feels dizzy. What has just happened? Grace is struggling to understand. Her mind is slipping and sliding, trying to reconcile what she knows with what she thought she knew. She can't believe what Lotte has just said to her, because her daughter is right: they have never discussed the time she left, not ever. It's so long ago now and Grace has allowed herself to believe that maybe—*maybe*—Lotte had forgotten.

2003

Welcome to your Orange voicemail. You have two new messages. First new message. Received Monday 24 February at 2:17 p.m. . . .

"... Hi, it's ... Wait ..."

To return the call at your normal call rate press five. To listen to your next call press two ...

"Hey, hi, it's Grace. Grace Adams. From the Polyglot thing? It's been a while, I know, and I guess ... Sorry, I don't really know what I'm trying to say here. I ... just ... Can you call me back? I need to ... It'd be good if you could. My number's ... oh, I can never remember it ... 0795 ... no. I'm going to assume it's come up on your screen. Okay, call me back. Thanks."

To return the call at your normal call rate press five ...

BEN PUTS HIS phone down on the lectern on top of his notes and finds that he's smiling. He can't help it because she is ... What is she? He has no idea. Five months since he last heard from her and she calls like this—out of the blue and with a knot of words that he's trying to make sense of but can't. A message that has made him fizz inside with what? Laughter? He can't figure her out. He can't figure himself out when it comes to her.

The last few students are leaving the lecture hall and he nods but doesn't really see them as they straggle past the front of the stage. And he's weighing up whether to call her back, how long he should leave it, when his phone starts to buzz, jumping a little on top of his notes like an insect is trapped in there. He checks the screen and sees that it's her, it's Grace—she's calling back again already. And, goddamnit, he's nervous—he's like a fourteen-year-old on a first date. Glancing around the room he lets the phone ring once, twice, three times, making sure everyone has left. He doesn't want an audience for this.

He pulls a breath deep into his lungs before he picks up.

"Wow!" he says. "It's TV's Grace Adams."

"Ben, hi," she says, and her voice is serious. He'd expected her to laugh or maybe berate him and he knows immediately that something isn't right. He knows enough about her to understand this.

"So listen," she's saying now, "there's no way to sugarcoat this so I'm just going to come out and say it." She stops.

Ben wonders for a second whether she's been cut off midsentence and the irony is too much for him. Then he hears her clear her throat and he laughs.

"What?" she asks. "What's so funny?"

"Sorry . . . It's just you were really building up to something there and then . . ." He shrugs even though he knows she can't see him.

"I'm pregnant, Ben."

"Oh," he says, after a pause. "Congratulations." But even as the words are coming out of his mouth he knows this isn't the correct response.

There's row after row of empty seats stretching away from him and no natural light, just the artificial glare that hurts his eyes. And Ben feels as if he is taking part in some kind of experimental theater piece—that he's flying loose without any lines. That none of this is real.

"Okay, so it won't mean anything to you, it didn't mean anything to me a week ago, but I'm twenty-two weeks along or thereabouts apparently, and counting back that brings us to . . ." She lets the sentence drop.

Seconds pass, and he's grappling his way into the light. "Oh," he says again, quieter this time. Ben kneads the skin on his forehead, like somehow that might help him wrap his head around what she's telling him. "Corn-wall," he murmurs.

"There's been no one since you so . . ."

She's being so matter of fact about it that it's making him feel like they're discussing the weather, as though they're in for a rainy fortnight ahead and it's a bit of a bummer. She's being too matter of fact, he knows this.

"I'm sure you're probably seeing someone but I wanted to . . . I thought you should know."

There has been someone, yes. There is someone. Lina. They've been hanging out for a couple of months but she'll be in Milan for the next two terms as part of her PhD. He knows he should say something to Grace about it, that now is the moment, but instinct makes him hold back. He doesn't want to tell her.

He shakes his head as though he's trying to clear water from his ears. "How long have you known?"

"Just over a week." She says it with an upward intonation, like it's the punchline to a joke. "It's amazing what you don't see when you don't want to see it."

He remembers then. The two of them pressed up against the college bar. She is all amber hair and eyes sharp with humor, emptying red wine from a bottle into her glass. And there's her voice that's velvet at the edges so it's obvious she's a little drunk . . . *I broke up with my boyfriend a month ago. I don't want children and it turns out that was a deal-breaker . . .*

There's the smell of her in the air around him. The salt and beeswax smell that he has conjured from nowhere like magic.

"You told me you don't want children." He's saying it as much to him-self as to her.

"Yep," she says. "I know."

Silence stretches between them. An almost-calm, except that he can't think straight—his mind is yoyoing, trying to process what she's telling him. Five minutes ago he was giving a lecture, introducing the principles of psycholinguistics to a room full of indifferent students, and now this. He can't even begin to figure out what he wants to ask, what he's supposed to say.

"Well, this is some way to greet an old friend," he tells her at last, and it's lame, he knows it's lame, but he's got nothing else.

"It's not too late," Grace says quietly.

For what? he wants to ask. But he knows. He isn't stupid.

There's her breath on the line. He imagines it escaping from her mouth, snaking into the ether like smoke.

Now

By the time she arrives at the bakery the place has taken on a near-religious significance in her mind. As though she's about to cross the holy threshold of the Blue Mosque or Angkor Wat or the Dome of the Rock after a long pilgrimage. The swinging sign in the street outside hangs motionless and the cakes in the window look as though they're melting in the heat. There's a fondant frog whose eye has slipped and a sweating tower of Bakewell tarts.

The sugary-warm smell blasts her as she enters the shop, and all of a sudden she's starving. She casts an eye around, taking in the Chelsea buns, the custard tarts, the poppy-seed bagels, the Madeira loaf cakes, the sesame sourdoughs, the vanilla slices, the chocolate éclairs, the rosemary focaccias, the cinnamon raisin breads. She feels as if she could sit down in the middle of the floor and eat everything in here, stuff herself with carbohydrates until she feels sick.

"Can I help you?" The woman behind the counter is signaling for her to come over. She has doughy skin that makes her look like one of the pastries she's selling.

"I'm here to pick up an order." Grace smiles. "It's my daughter's sixteenth-birthday cake." She isn't sure why she says this. She can hear the pushy pride in her voice as though she's the kind of woman who has a husband, a cockapoo, membership at the tennis club, an active role in the PTA. As though she's the kind of woman who does this sort of thing, who orders bespoke cakes for special occasions.

"Name, please?" Grace can see the woman's forehead glistening at the hairline where the elastic of her blue nylon hat is digging in.

She gives it and the woman disappears out the back, returns a minute later with a shiny white box. She places it on top of the counter. It's a small box and Grace knows immediately that she has brought out the wrong one. Before she can say anything the woman opens the lid with a flourish.

The cake doesn't even touch the sides of the box. Grace steps a little closer, peers in. There are two tiny figures on top. Tiny. The bronzed woman's bikini is three pink dots of icing, the man's trunks a single green streak. And, yes, there's Lotte's name on the side in gold, as they'd discussed. But the lettering is scarcely bigger than standard handwriting. Minute bottles of suntan oil, hearts, sliders, thongs are scattered across the cake. The size of them means they're clumsily cast with no detail.

It's a big, big cake . . . she hears herself telling Ben, and the voice in her head sounds overblown, self-aggrandizing, desperate. *Two tiers, fluorescent piping, her name in gold icing . . .* Now that it's here in front of her she sees that Lotte's sixteenth-birthday cake, the grand, striking centerpiece she'd imagined—the symbol of her unshakable love for her child—would barely feed five people.

Grace is aware of a queue building up behind her. "It's smaller than I was expecting," she says. "I mean, is this it? Are you sure?"

"It's a *Love Island* cake," the woman replies, like that explains everything. Her hands are resting on the countertop either side of the pristine box. Grace eyes her bitten nails.

"It's really quite small," Grace says. And she can feel something like panic rising in her.

"It's a very good-sized cake." The woman behind the counter draws her lips into a thin line. "It has two tiers."

"It does indeed have two tiers," Grace says, under her breath. Despite herself she has that awkward feeling, as though she's playing in a space that's out of her league, like this woman will be thinking she should have bought her cake up the road at Marks & Spencer. She glances down at the floor, back up again. She is forty-five years old. Forty-fucking-five. How old does she have to get before people start to treat her like she's a grown woman?

"It's handcrafted," the woman continues. "Artisanal."

"Artisanal?" Grace snorts through her nose. "More like invisible!"

"I'm afraid you didn't pay enough for a larger cake." The woman is talking now with an exaggerated patience. "If you want a bigger cake you have to pay more." She points to an éclair gleaming in its ruffled paper case behind the slanted glass counter. "Two pounds fifty," the woman says. Then she points to a gingerbread man, three fat Smarties pressed into its middle. "One pound seventy." Then to a walnut cake. "Five ninety-nine," she says. "Because, you see, it's the whole cake. It serves six." And it's difficult to know whether she's being facetious or not because beneath her elasticated hat her pasty face is a blank.

There's heat at Grace's back and she imagines it's the eyes of the people in the queue behind her. She can feel blood beating against her temples as she turns to look at the show cakes in the window. A four-tier princess cake with glossy pink icing and sparkling edible crystals, a football pitch cake the size of a paving slab complete with two teams. A towering fat chocolate cake built like a Gothic cathedral. Her mind flashes to Lotte, aged two and four and six and ten, her small face lit up in the semidark of their kitchen, giddy-eyed and blowing out her birthday candles. These sumptuous, extravagant cakes in the window are the kind she'd imagined herself showing up with at the party. The kind that would make Lotte glow that way again. A cake that would say everything that needed to be said, that would return them to the way they'd been. Grace pictures the two of them propped up against the pillows in her bed, Lotte's head on her shoulder, and the brilliant, brash colors of *Love Island* on TV.

"I can't look," Lotte's saying, and she's watching through her fingers, because the mahogany-tanned couple on the screen are having a row in their swimsuits about the lie-detector test he's just taken. "And, anyway, how do they know the test is accurate, that he'd be tempted by other women? Mum, I can't bear it. I totally ship these two."

Grace laughs as she peels her daughter's hands from her face. "It's a good word," she says. "'Ship.' It plugs a gap in language. *I want these two to get together*. There's no existing word for that."

"Shush." Lotte adjusts her head, getting comfortable, until she's resting her cheek against the fleshy part beneath Grace's collarbone. "You absolute nerd, Mum."

"That's two hundred pounds, please," the woman behind the counter announces in a twittery tone. A tone that suggests this entire transaction is perfectly reasonable. Jesus Christ, *cuánto*? Grace thinks, and it takes all her strength not to ask the woman in the blue plastic hat what on earth she'd have to pay for a decent-sized cake. Like, would she have to remortgage her house?

Grace pulls her card from her pocket, flinching at the amount on the screen as she punches in her PIN. She can't believe she's doing this, paying this. Everything in her wants to push the cake off the counter, to stamp the gloop and sponge remains into the floor. She watches as the woman snips ribbon from a roll, begins to tie up the box. Then, using the scissors as a blade, she starts to curl the ends. She is taking an implausibly long time to do this, almost like she's doing it on purpose.

When at last the woman is finished, Grace bursts from the shop. She makes it all the way to the crest of the hill before something fells her. She has the cake box clutched in both hands as she folds forward over her knees, winded. She can't believe what is happening to her. Her husband, her daughter, her job—her *jobs*: she has lost them all. And now this joke of a cake. After what she's done it's everything she deserves. It's the icing on the fucking cake.

Four Months Earlier

"WHAT ON EARTH, Ben?"

"Well, hey, hi to you too, Cate." Ben pushes himself up onto one elbow, checks the clock on his bedside table: 6 a.m. "You do know what time it is here, right?"

It's as if he hasn't spoken.

"So I told myself I wouldn't call, I wouldn't interfere . . ." Her voice, which is so like her sister's but different enough that he can tell them apart, is thin on the line. She sounds a little hyped, like maybe she's taken something, although he thought she didn't do that anymore. ". . . but I mean, Jesus H. Christ."

"You mean Sara told you not to call, not to interfere." He grinds a fist into his eye socket. He needs to pee.

"Look, Grace is making out like she doesn't care but she does. Of course she bloody does. You sent the divorce papers through without even discussing it with her. Without even telling her . . ."

"Wait. What?" He sits upright. Suddenly he's wide awake.

"I mean, what was going through your head? You did that for, what, shits and giggles?"

Light is starting to come in around the edges of the blind and there's a thin bright rectangle flickering on the bedroom wall. "She got it already?" He says it as much to himself as to her.

"I know you're angry with her."

"I'm not angry."

There's silence on the line. He wants to bury his head under the pillow, go back to sleep, escape all this. When she starts to talk again her voice has softened.

"I know you're angry, Ben, because of everything . . ."

His stomach twists. And he's willing her not to continue because this is a place they don't go. They never have. At least, not since that one time. Drunk in a downtown bar in LA. How far away that moment seems. How many years ago now? How long after the time that's a blur of words and sounds, smells and images?

"But Grace, she . . ." He hears her make a small sound, like she's zipping herself up. He pictures her there in Los Angeles, sitting out by the night-lit pool. The dusty-citrus smell of the heat, the click and buzz of cicadas, avocados heavy in the trees. "And Lotte," she says at last. "What about Lotte?"

"I'm trying, Cate. Grace won't—"

"Don't be that guy, Ben. Don't be that dad."

"That's not fair." He swings his legs out of the bed and stands. "You know that's not fair."

"She's my niece. I love her, and I love my sister. You did once too, remember? I don't know, it's a wild suggestion but maybe you still do. Either way she needs you. She can't do it alone."

"She's not doing it alone."

"Lotte's pretending it's all fine. That she's all grown-up. But she isn't. She's fifteen, she's a child. And she's been through so much."

The words hang. He won't touch them.

"Your daughter's acting out. You see that, right? Complacency is complicity. Doing something is always better than doing nothing."

You're giving me advice? Ben is thinking but doesn't say. *Like it all went so well for you with Dylan.* She's speaking like one of the pamphlets she brings home from her life-coaching sessions and usually he'd laugh about it—at her, with her—but the fact is he knows she's right. *You've gone in and shut the door, darling,* his mum would have said, if she was alive. A part of him knows he's slowly screwing this whole thing up because he doesn't want to think about it, about any of it. It hurts too much.

"I tried to talk to Grace—"

"And she pushed you away. Tell me something I don't know. Push harder, okay. Break into Alcatraz—I believe in you."

Her voice has a Los Angeles twang now. She would hate it if she knew that. He can imagine the expression on her face if he told her—her eyes rolled back in her head. It is this, he realizes, that makes her sound different from Grace, and he has a sudden memory. Grace in a yellow sundress in a bar in Los Feliz. She's pregnant and poking him in the chest and laughing. *If my sister wasn't gay I'd think you two were having an affair . . .*

Cate is saying something now about parenting and Sara and Dylan, and Ben's mind drifts further. He's thinking about the fate boxes—Lotte's fate boxes—and he can see her like it was yesterday. She's on the patio next to the sandpit and she's blowing bubbles. She's got a little plastic wand and she's concentrating hard, her lips fixed in a small *o* as she blows. And then she's watching the bubbles snatched by the wind, following them with her eyes until they pop. *Daddy,* she says, and she's looking at the bubbles still, not him. *Daddy, you know there's these little boxes coming from your head, and I call them the boxes of life because they disappear one by one when you've done that one thing in your life. They're invisible to us but they're see-through so you can see the pictures inside of your life and really the line of boxes is controlling you. And then when you get to the top and you've only got one more box left—which will be the one which will tell you how you die—then you float all the way up to that last box and then you climb onto the cloud and the cloud is Heaven.*

She was seven years old. He knows this because he can see, through the French windows, her birthday balloons hanging in the kitchen from the week before. And because it was an astonishing thing for a child of that age to say—to outline the fundaments of determinism—and he'd logged it. "Do you really think that?" he'd asked. *No,* she'd told him, shaking her head. *It's just one of my funny stories, but I like thinking about it.* She was like a little white witch, standing there. Heartbreakingly earnest with her fluffy blond hair and Grace's dark, dark eyes, and it had stopped his breath.

"Ben?"

"Yes, right," he murmurs, even though he has no idea what Cate has just said.

"Okay, good."

"So how is Sara?" he asks quickly, because he doesn't want to talk anymore about this. His chest is tight and he wants to get up, down a glass of water, do some stretches, go for a run. He won't sleep again now.

"Sara?" He hears her lips vibrating against the mouthpiece. "Oh, you know, working too hard, pissing me off. The usual domestic bliss . . ."

"Nice." He laughs, and sniffs the air. He can smell that his breath is bad. "And Dylan?"

"Barely working at all, pissing me off. The usual domestic piss . . . sorry, bliss."

They're both laughing now and he has a sudden urge to see her, to get on a plane, to fly out there to their beautiful house at the edge of Griffith Park, beneath the Observatory. To fly back to the way things were before.

2003

She is already seated at a table in the Russian Tea Rooms when he gets there. He sees her through the smoked-glass window, and it's like a force field drops down blocking him—he isn't able to move. She's wearing a jumper the color of grass and her hair is bunched to one side in a Spanish knot. Her gaze is lowered, focused on something at the table, and he can tell that she is oblivious to everything around her.

Beside him, someone coughs and he becomes aware of a middle-aged couple who have the look of regulars, sitting at one of the outdoor tables. They're wearing hats and coats and there's steam blowing from their mouths as well as their coffee cups—and he thinks maybe the cough is pointed, that he's been standing a little too close for a little too long. It's enough to jerk him out of his stasis and he puts a palm to the glass door, pushes it open.

Inside it's dark, the walls and ceiling painted deep crimson. It's a moment before she looks up from the book she's reading, sees him hovering in the doorway. His heart is banging in his chest as he raises his hand in a half wave, picks his way through the tables toward her.

She has a plate of blinis in front of her and she apologizes. "I'm starving," she says. "I couldn't wait, sorry."

She doesn't sound sorry at all and he feels the bounce of it, because under the circumstances only she would open like this.

"Smoked salmon and smetana." She forks a piece into her mouth.

He isn't sure she should be eating it—his brother's wife, Amelia, is pregnant for the fourth time and she is vocal at family gatherings about all the foods she needs to avoid. He's trying not to look at her stomach—he knows instinctively that he should not do this—and his eyes are aching with the effort of it.

"Have one, they're really good."

Ben hesitates before he leans across to kiss her cheek. He's been standing there too long so it's awkward and he misses, grazes her ear with his mouth. She smells different, not how he remembered, like coconut or sun lotion, although it's freezing outside. There's the fishiness of the salmon too and it throws him a little.

"What are you reading?" he asks, as he seats himself opposite her, and he nods at the book that's facedown on the table.

The words they aren't saying spike the air around them.

She turns the book over and he sees it's a dog-eared copy of *La Peste*. She's reading it in the original French.

"I picked it up at the secondhand-book shop across the street." She points over his shoulder out through the café window. "I was early. But also I thought it would give me something to do if you didn't show up. Save me sitting here like an idiot." She shrugs.

With the light on her face he notices for the first time how pale she looks. There are shadows under her eyes, and the skin at the edges of her mouth is crepey, drooping almost. She looks exhausted, he thinks. Sad.

"I'm glad you came." She doesn't look at him as she says it and he almost doesn't catch it.

Ben inhales, exhales. "So you're okay?"

She wipes her mouth with a napkin, places it back on the table before she answers. "I mean, I'm five months pregnant. Unexpectedly." She dips her head to the side, pulls a face. "But apart from that, peachy . . . and I suppose I'm trying to figure out what it means that you're here."

Her tone of voice doesn't match the expression in her eyes. She is scared, he realizes. As scared as he is. "I don't know," he says at last. "I don't know what it means. I'm sorry . . ."

"We should maybe not have been so cavalier with the contraception," she murmurs.

"Right." He slow-nods. "That is a fact."

"I had some bleeding early on and then a couple of months in," she's looking down at her hands, "so it wasn't obvious, you know?" Her eyes find his. "It's perfectly normal in the first trimester, apparently, and . . ." she falters.

There's the strange pull of her. Ben is sure he couldn't look away if he tried. "I felt like . . . I didn't . . . We never really joined up the dots." The words tangle in his throat. "I mean, afterward, so . . ."

Her gaze is the dark sea that day in Cornwall. "So we're making up for it now?"

"I guess something like that."

A woman with curly black hair comes to stand by their table, flips to a fresh page on her order pad. Grace speaks to her in Russian and it's strange to him that he can't understand—it isn't one of his languages and he can make out only the odd word. He tells the woman he's eaten because he isn't hungry, but Grace urges him to pick a cake from behind the counter and he follows the woman across the café. There's a tableau of Red Square painted in oils beneath the till, shelves of exquisitely decorated *matryoshka* dolls eyeing him from the back wall. He points to a layered honey cake, and while the woman carves him a slice he's thinking of the dolls inside the dolls inside the dolls, picturing the smallest ones— the babies—hidden at their wooden mothers' hearts.

He's sitting back down when Grace produces a grainy paper photograph from between the pages of her book. "I didn't know whether you'd want to see it, but this is the photo . . . of the scan . . ." The paper is curling up at the edges. As she holds it out to him he sees that her fingers are trembling a little.

Taking the image from her, he can make out something in the shape of an apostrophe.

"That's the head," she tells him, pointing. "That's an ear, those are feet . . ."

There's the sense that he is leaping from a high cliff into bright emerald waters. It seems impossible that this is their child, that they have done this. It's like a magic trick and there is something so precarious in all of it. Across from him Grace has her hand on her belly. He wonders if she's aware she's holding it there and he finds himself imagining what he might say if, when . . . because she is extraordinary, this woman. He has never met anyone like her—she knocks the breath from him. . . . *The first time*

I saw her she spoke in tongues, he thinks. *The second time, she saved a woman. The third time I saw her she was a television star. The fourth time, she had made you.*

"I watch you on TV sometimes," he says. "On those rock-bottom digestive-dunking afternoons, y'know?" But he's looking at the photograph still and it seizes him from nowhere, a pressure behind his eyes that's about to spill. He has to stop speaking. When he looks up at her, he sees her see. There's the blaze of her cheeks as though she's just come in from the outside—it's the only tell in her, the only way he knows.

"We could split the prize," she says softly. There's the color in her cheeks still, but she's scrunching her lips to one side and there's humor in the tilt of her eyes. "Do you want to come with me?"

And he's smiling at her, remembering the Polyglot convention that seems so long ago now. The silver trophy on the bar, her intelligent eyes liquid with triumph and alcohol. And later the wild insanity of their laughter, the glister of her the moment she knew he would join her, that they would go together.

"What?" she's saying. "Ben?"

There's a loosening around his forehead, his temples.

"Yes," he tells her. "I would like to come with you."

Now

Lotte,

~~I've written so many letters to you in my head and they are all wrong—~~

Dear Lotte,

  Dad says you still don't want to see me. I know you're in pain ~~and I ache for you.~~ No one gives you the answers, you know, when you become a mum. There are a million handbooks and there is no handbook. ~~The truth is we are winging it, all of us, all of the time and—~~

Lotte,

  Remember, "Even monkeys fall from trees"? ~~We used to say it all the time when you were little, our favorite Japanese expression.~~ That everyone messes up sometimes—

Darling Lotte,

  ~~I desperately wanted to be perfect for you, a mother-goddess, but—~~

  Lotte, sweetheart, I love you. I'm sorry. Come home. xxx

GRACE HAS LEFT the high street behind her at last and she's walking at speed along the narrow pavement heading toward Suicide Bridge. All the words from all the letters she started but never finished—never sent—are marching through her mind in time with her steps. Crumpled lined paper—her balled-up, ballsed-up efforts—scattered by the side of her bed among a toppling pile of books, clumped dust, a tube of hydrocortisone ointment, used vaginal suppository plungers, squeezed-out bottles of hand cream, a brush thick-matted with hair, spray-on magnesium that promises well-being but stings like hell, several half-empty blister packs of acetaminophen, curling plastic strips torn from sanitary towels, a stack of out-of-date interiors catalogues, a greasy tin of lavender sleep balm that doesn't work, dirty knickers, picked-off toenails . . . She could go on. It's Young British Artist Tracey Emin's iconic *My Bed* exhibit—except the HRT version. Ben used to tease her for it. *You're disgusting*, he'd tell her, laughing, *an utter slob. What happened to the woman who lined up her Bics like beautiful stationery soldiers, where did she go?* Then he'd press her down onto their bed and . . . Grace stops the thought. Because that was before. That was a long, long time ago.

The sun is at its highest point in the sky. There's the burn of it on her, through her, as she moves along the street. The feeling she is being seared across her scalp, along her shoulders, down the front of her newly liver-spotted chest. The impression she is being cooked alive. She has the cake box under one arm because she's trying, failing, to shade its contents; she doesn't want to think about the melting tarts in the bakery window, the collapsing fondant menagerie.

Grace knows she must speed up now, to make up the time she has lost, but she can feel the skin at the back of her ankle starting to rub raw, the beginning of a blister that's making her wince as she walks. She's wearing *inappropriate footwear*, as she's said to Lotte a thousand times. New train-ers that she hasn't worn in yet—hasn't worn out until now—since she is convinced they are too young for her. Bright white Nikes with flashes of color at the sides, an intricate lace-up system that beguiled her, and wear-ing them, she looks like she thinks she's eighteen, fourteen even, God help her. *Damn, looking very Gen Z there, boomer!* Lotte had declared in her TikTok voice, when she'd barged into the bedroom, caught Grace turning her foot this way and that in front of the full-length mirror. Grace had shriveled where she was standing and held her daughter's reflected gaze. *Tell me the truth, am I too old?* And Lotte had lifted her shoulders, let them drop. Started to dance out of the room, snapping her limbs in time to a private beat. *Um, yes, no, maybe. Just don't wear them in front of my friends, okay?* Then her voice had drifted back as she'd disappeared out onto the landing, *But can I borrow them if you keep them?*

As she comes onto the bridge Grace sees the homeless woman. The pavement is narrow and she's sitting cross-legged, her back pressed against the tall steel bars that have been erected over the stonework to stop people jumping. Grace pats her pocket, reflexively, pointlessly, because she already knows that all she has on her is a twenty-pound note. It's what she grabbed when she abandoned the car and she can't give this woman the only cash she has. She can't give her a *twenty-pound note.*

They are the only two people on the bridge and Grace doesn't know where to look. If she looks at her, the woman will think she's going to give her money. If she doesn't look she will seem a heartless bitch. Grace starts to swivel her eyes from side to side, bizarrely, stiffly, like a shifty eighties Action Man. Sweat slides down the back of her neck. Fixing an apology-smile on her face, a smile she hopes will communicate solidarity, she moves out into the road to pass the woman. *I have a monthly direct debit set up with Shelter*, she wants to blurt.

"Mummy . . ." Lotte's voice is in her ear, a sudden stage whisper. It's nighttime and they're coming through the tunnel by Finsbury Park tube, back from seeing *The Lion King* in town, a birthday treat. Her daughter's slim hand is in hers, Ben just up ahead. The pavement is crammed and they've walked past several homeless people. Lotte is staring at them one after another because she is ten, and tugging on her arm. ". . . Mummy, I just think someone needs to take notice." Grace squeezes her hand, feels shame slide through her, walks on. She hates that her child is witnessing this, wants to protect her from the knowledge that this is a fact of modern society, that it isn't something consigned to bleak history, like Jack the Ripper or the death penalty, because how the hell is she supposed to explain it? How is she supposed to explain away the fact that adults, herself included, allow it to happen? As she's thinking this, Lotte tips up her head. Lights from the cars in the tunnel color her small face red, then white, then red again. Her expression is questioning, perplexed. "Because, I mean, if I was those people," she says, in her sweet high voice, "then I would be pretty angry that no one notices they're there."

Grace stops on the bridge. The woman sitting on the pavement behind her had called out to her as she passed, and Grace had half turned her head, but not enough to look at her. She stares through the spiked bars at the traffic on the road far below. What is she thinking? This woman is someone's daughter. Someone's daughter wearing far too many clothes considering the sunshine blasting down on her. There's a hot rush in her throat as she turns back, hands the note to the woman, who thanks her, tells her to have a nice day.

Now Grace can meet her eyes. Black eyes, the same color as her hair, and long, thin eyebrows that look like pencil markings. She has a red scarf loose around her head, and as Grace walks away, it's like she's hallucinating because the imprint of the woman's face on her retinas starts to morph, becoming the face of the *matryoshka*. Until from nowhere it's there, life-sized on the pavement ahead of her, all glossed wood and staring eyes and a blood-red pout. Then just as quickly the vision recedes and Grace sees instead the wooden doll smashed to pieces on Lotte's bedroom floor. She feels the same black pressure at her chest, hears her daughter's voice in her head, screaming, *We all know what you did.*

Four Months Earlier

IN THE END she'd left the divorce papers at home. It had seemed too confrontational to bring them (although a part of her was tempted). To thrust them at him, like something from a movie, *See, this is what you've done.* Her hand is hovering over the buzzer outside Ben's flat. *Ben's flat.* How strange those two words sound in her head. She has agreed to meet him here, at this unfamiliar all-white modern block that's squeezed into the gap between two Victorian houses. She hasn't seen him for months and never without Lotte as their buffer, but he was insistent in his texts, and she was curious—she wants to see how he lives now, without her. Where Lotte goes every other weekend.

Grace presses the buzzer and almost immediately his voice comes over the intercom.

"Hold on," he says, and the sound of him is a little distorted. "I'm coming down."

He has the upstairs flat, which is split-level, and he owns half of the garden. She knows this because she has quizzed Lotte. She has tried to make it casual but Lotte isn't stupid: she sees straight through her. *Why don't you ask him yourself?*

When Ben opens the door she feels it instantly. A leap in her gut that ambushes her. He's barefoot and wearing a gray T-shirt and jeans, and there's his uncertain smile, the half-laughing eyes. But it's the shape of him that gets her. The way he's standing with one hand on the door frame, his slim, loose build that is both familiar and other—and she's thinking of the black jumper with the holes at the wrists. The one she loved but pretended to hate. And is she ovulating? Because it's like she's twenty-eight years old again, seeing him for the first time.

"Hi," he says. "Thanks for coming, Grace." It's oddly formal, the way he says this, and he stands back to let her go past him.

"No, after you." She holds out the flat of her palm in the direction of the hallway. "I have no idea where I'm going."

Upstairs the flat opens out into a large living space, the whole thing paid for with his parents' money. Out of the proceeds from the sale of their Scottish pile, split four ways between Ben and his three brothers. Well, not entirely. That isn't exactly fair, and she knows it. All the walls are knocked through and everything is white. White kitchen, white floor, white shelving, white paintwork. Her instinct is to make a joke of it, like she doesn't dare touch anything, or "Pass me my sunglasses," but she would feel uncomfortable saying it, too self-conscious or informal. She takes in leather chairs, a mid-century-style sofa, a zinc-topped table. And she's thinking about their furniture back home—the things they've had since he moved in with her to the basement flat in Chalk Farm. Trying to imagine him picking out this new stuff and finding she can't.

"Can I get you something?" Ben is moving through to the kitchen. "Water?"

Grace swallows, suddenly thirsty, and she nods.

He has his back to her, running the tap. Her eyes are drawn to the ridge of his shoulder blades, the pull and release of muscle and tendon that she can see through the material of his T-shirt. She's standing next to the zinc-topped table and her hands find its edge.

"So you want to talk about the divorce?" The word is a shard of glass in her mouth.

"Yes, no . . ." He puts the water on the side, pulls his hands through his hair. "Grace, I didn't think the papers would come through that soon. I don't know what I thought. I wasn't thinking . . ."

She bites down on her lip, like that way she might trap the emotion she doesn't want him to see.

"Are you all right?" Ben is moving toward her and his expression is so serious she almost has to look away. There's a sound like tinnitus in her ears that's maybe real—distant building work, the high-pitched squeal of a drill—or maybe in her head.

"Grace," he says. "I'm sorry, I . . ." And then his hands go either side of her face and she feels herself fall into him. His mouth is on the flesh at her jaw, her neck, her collarbone, and each touch is a shock, like her nerves have pushed through to the surface of her skin. Something slides away in her and she knows she could stop him—knows she should stop him—but she won't: that is the last thing in the world she wants to do.

He has his hands inside her shirt, underneath her bra, and she's fumbling with his belt when he stops, stills her hand. "Not here," he says, and he indicates the three tall windows that make up most of the far wall, and through them the street beyond.

Adrenaline hums through her as he leads her up a short flight of stairs to his bedroom because she doesn't want him to change his mind; she doesn't want to change her mind. He has her wrists in his hands and as they come through the door she presses her body into the back of him, imprinting herself there. And Grace understands that they are scared to lose contact—if they let go the spell might break.

In the room there's the smell of sleep, and the bed is wide and low and unmade. He moves her in front of him, turns her slowly. Then he's pushing his thumbs into the flesh either side of her spine and they come together until their foreheads are touching, their faces so close it blurs her vision.

How long has it been since they've done this? There's the nine months since he left and then before that a year, eighteen months, two years . . . the thought falls away as he unlaces his fingers, pulls her mouth to his.

"You're beautiful." He blows the words into her, she can feel them against her teeth, her tongue. "You're so beautiful I love fucking you . . ."

I love fucking you you're beautiful . . .

There's a pause, a stretched second after he says it before something in her shatters. And then she's pushing herself up and off him, adjusting her shirt, her bra, her knickers that have twisted up around her thigh.

"Grace?" Ben is up on one elbow. His eyes are groggy still, like he's drunk or stoned. "What's wrong? Did I hurt you?"

And she's shaking her head because she isn't able to talk. What would she say? There's the chill of sweat on her body and she is all at once filled with anger so profound that it takes everything in her not to pound her fists against him, to bruise him, to break him. *I love fucking you you're beautiful* . . . The words spin and spin in her because it is all reminding her of a time before, a lost time. There are pictures in her mind that she can't get out—the urgent, transcendent, long-ago sex that turned furious, toxic. As if they were trying to quench their bottomless rage.

"I can't bear that this has happened to us," Ben says then, and it's like he's read her mind.

She's kneeling up on the bed still, and she turns her head so she isn't looking at him because otherwise she knows she'll cry. Across the room there's a door that's half-open and she can see inside an en-suite bathroom, bottle-green towels draped over a rail, a kind she would never buy.

"Are you seeing someone else?" She can't stop the question spilling from her mouth—even though a part of her doesn't want to know. There's a sudden heat through her and she finds she hardly dares move, waiting for him to answer.

"No!" His response is a reflex and he lets out a laugh as though she's said something outlandish. But then his face softens and he starts to shake his head slowly, puzzled. "No, Grace, there's no one else."

"The divorce petition," she blurts. "I thought maybe you had . . . maybe that was why . . ." She feels stupid, vulnerable, unlike herself. Would you tell me if? she wants to ask. Will you tell me when?

Ben is sitting on the side of the bed now, his head in his hands. "Jesus, it's all such a mess," he murmurs.

"Yup." Grace stands and moves toward the bathroom. "We've really screwed it up."

It isn't until she's left Ben's flat and she's walking back down the street headed for the tube that she allows the thought in. The smell of him has stayed on her skin, the clean winter smell that she knows so well. She brings her wrists to her face, inhales him. She sees his eyes locked on hers and at the same time somewhere she can't reach him, feels his hands in the dip of her back and she wants to pretend it isn't true but she can't. The fact is she still loves him; she still loves her husband. She never stopped.

2003

SHE IS LATE. The baby is late. Ten days past her due date, and it feels like an affront to Grace, who now faces *intervention*, the whispered dread of being induced. After all, this baby—this resolute, tenacious blob of cells—was so damn quick to make herself at home here in Grace's uterus. So what's with the coy shtick now? It's Sunday and they should be in the Lansdowne with the papers and a roast, but instead she and Ben and the no-nonsense midwife-acupuncturist are deep in the bowels of UCH. There are electrodes attached to needles that are stuck in her stomach, her feet, her face, and the midwife is running a charge through them, a mounting vibration that is making Grace feel sick. They've been down here for hours, trying to kick-start the contractions, and these skinny needles have been set alight, flicked, and waggled, and Grace thinks she might vomit if it continues much longer.

The midwife looks up to check on her patient. Her dark, bobbed hair, which had been hanging forward over Grace's swollen toes, falls perfectly into place, framing her face.

"You big." She clicks her tongue.

And although she doesn't have much English, Grace hears her loud and clear. Because Grace is huge. She's enormous. If another person asks if she's expecting twins, she will slap them. It's humiliating enough that months before she took maternity leave the producers erected a screen on set—made to look like bookshelves—so that viewers didn't have to witness the showy obscenity of her swelling stomach. The fact that she was no longer a size ten. The shocking evidence that *she has had sex*. Oh, the irony! Given the drooling tabloid coverage that had come before.

"This baby says no." The midwife wags a finger, rolls her eyes, as if the baby not playing ball is somehow a failing on Fat Grace's part.

Ben is hovering at Grace's shoulder and she turns to him. "I feel sick," she says quietly.

He leaps into action. She sees him physically jerk: he has a role. "Sorry." Ben moves toward the midwife. "She's feeling sick?" He mimes the action and bile floods Grace's throat.

Still working the needles, the midwife gestures to the window. Ben fiddles with the catch, pushes on the glass, and a shiver of air moves through the room. But it isn't enough. It's nowhere near enough, and Grace is on the edge now. She's got that heady feeling coming up from her neck through her glands. "I'm going to be sick," she tells Ben.

"I think we need to stop," Ben says loudly, and the midwife glances up, takes a look at Grace. In one swift movement she stands, plucks a needle from the packet beside her, and plants it in the top of Grace's head.

Instantly, everything clears. The sickness is gone, the rising swell in her jaw, across her tongue, has vanished. Her head is fine. Grace is completely fine and she can't believe it—it's like witchcraft.

"All good?" the midwife asks.

"All good." Grace blinks, smiles.

"Sorcery . . ." Ben whispers, and maybe it's something to do with the strange miracle this midwife is performing, but Grace is all at once struck by love for him. Flooded with it, like the weird energy rushing through her chakras. This beautiful man who speaks her language, who understands her. Who understands her in three different languages, no less. *Tú eres mi media naranja*, she thinks. She almost says. *You are the other half of my orange*—my soul mate. She pictures the nerdy adolescent he's described to her, who wallpapered his bedroom with vocab lists he'd written out on A4 sheets, and she wonders for a moment what this baby of theirs will be like. There's so much she doesn't know about Ben, and she knows it's fast—four months since she found him again—but there isn't a doubt in her mind. She's in love with him.

* * *

Walking back across Regent's Park, they vow that once they get home, back to the flat in Chalk Farm, they will try everything they can to get the baby out. Already Grace has had a membrane sweep—the memory sets her teeth on edge—and she's been mainlining raspberry-leaf tea for weeks to loosen the cervix or tone the uterus, she isn't sure which, but she's doing it anyway, throwing everything at it. And now they will have sex, they will eat hot curry, gorge on pineapple, drink castor oil—it will be a smorgasbord of alternative quackery, old wives' tales. They will try it all.

Ben steers her through the front door, across the lounge, and into their basement bedroom the moment they get back. "I mean business, Grace," he says. "Let's do this."

There's the faint smell of damp in there, the Moses basket in the corner that tips her stomach each time she sees it, cellular blankets washed and folded, implausibly small sleepers. Ready. Under the window are the packing boxes from Ben's house—they've been stacked there for weeks now, unopened—and Grace squeezes past them, sits down on the end of the bed. Everything hurts, from her teeth to her stupidly large tits. She's exhausted.

Ben scoops a pile of cushions from the bed onto the floor, comes to sit beside her. "Doggy-style?" He tips his head to one side, shoots up his eyebrows, and they burst out laughing.

"*So* appealing." Grace pokes her tongue into her cheek, pushes him away.

"In fact you are . . ." Taking her hand, he places it in his lap and she feels that he is hard. Grace snorts. "Really?" she says.

"What can I say?" Ben shrugs. "I'd conjugate your verbs any day of the week. The thing is, Grace Adams, you're just too fuckable."

"And you, Ben Kerr, are just too *jayus*." She's trying not to laugh, and when he looks confused, she elucidates. "It's Indonesian. It means someone who tells jokes that are so bloody awful, all you can do is go with it."

Closing his eyes, Ben makes a face like he's blissed out. "God, I love it when you talk untranslatable words to me."

"Sssh." Grace covers his mouth with her hand. "Less of your smut, stranger. She can hear you . . ."

* * *

Ben is in the shower and she's lying on her side on top of the sheets when the first contraction comes. She feels as if someone has reached down inside her abdomen and twisted. Heat spreads from behind her eyes, engulfing her. This is it, she thinks. She knows this is it. When the contraction subsides she puts her hands on the great dome of her stomach, this newly shared space in her body that will soon be hers again. "Are you doing okay in there?" she whispers, and feels her baby shift a little under her fingers. Outside the window, the light is starting to change so that there's a strange tangerine glow in the room. In this moment she doesn't understand how she could ever have thought this was something she didn't want to do. She knows she should be afraid but she isn't because it feels so right. It feels inevitable.

She hears the clunk of the boiler as the water shuts off and then Ben is in the room. His hair is wet and there's a towel around his waist and he smells of apples, newness.

"I think it's starting," she tells him, and she feels her heart pick up as she says it.

He comes toward her, then backs away, like he doesn't know what to do. "Wait," he says. "Hold on, I have something for you . . ."

She hears the sound of a cupboard door opening and shutting, in the lounge or maybe the kitchen, she can't tell which, and then he's back in the bedroom, holding a paper bag.

"It's a *matryoshka*," he tells her, as he hands it over. "A symbol of family and fertility, mothers and daughters and all that stuff, but I'm guessing you know that. I just thought because of the Tea Rooms . . . I wanted to . . ." He trails off, flicks water from where it's dripped from his hair onto his shoulders.

There's tissue paper stuffed into the top of the bag and Grace removes it, pulls out the Russian doll. She is painted in midnight blue and scarlet, emerald and gold, flowers and fruit and vines twisting around her, and her beautiful solemn face is stamped with pink rosy cheeks, dark, curling lashes. There's the hard, cold feel of the glossed wood against Grace's fingers and from nowhere it flashes through her mind that this *matryoshka* might jinx them.

"Thanks," she says, and smiles up at Ben, pressing the thought away until it disappears. A second contraction comes then and she stops, shuts her eyes, waits for it to pass.

"You okay?" He takes her hand, strokes his thumb across her palm. "I mean this is good, isn't it? This was the plan."

Grace raises her eyebrows.

"Well, not exactly *the* plan . . ." Ben laughs.

She cradles her stomach. "I guess you'd better put the bag in the hall. We just need the bottle of water from the fridge. Everything else is packed," she says.

Grace waits for him to leave the room before she screws the *matryoshka* in half. Then she takes out the doll inside, remakes the first doll and lays it on top of the sheet. She does this again and again and again, until she finds the tiny baby at the center, the one that won't crack in half.

Now

THERE ARE TREES across the Heath as far as she can see. Green foliage, like low-hanging clouds, and fat, ancient trunks that would take ten people—arms at full stretch—to encircle them. The sky burns an unyielding blue but she's keeping to the shade. She's up to her knees in long grass, wading through vetch and lady's bedstraw and oxeye daisies and meadow cranesbill, and trying not to think about any ticks that might be lurking. Her trainer is padded out at the back with a paper napkin swiped from an outdoor table at one of the cafés along Swain's Lane, and now that the blister is cushioned there's a blissful freedom in each step she takes. It is as if there are little pockets of oxygenated air beneath her feet, lifting her up, propelling her forward.

The sun has brought out the lovers. They are on the benches and the grassy slopes and in the low branches of trees. And they are here in her path. Grace is looking the other way as she trips on the corner of a spread blanket, nearly drops her cake box onto a couple camouflaged among the meadow plants. She mumbles an apology but the man is lying on top of his girlfriend, and if they notice Grace they don't acknowledge her. She walks on, faster now, despite the wild tangle lashing her ankles, her calves, because she is trying to outmaneuver a memory that is snapping at her. She sees for a moment the raw love bite on her daughter's neck, ineffectually covered with cheap foundation that has turned the flesh orange, the words bright-lit on screen, *imma drag one of my friends to meet him the first time tho . . . you're cute af gonna miss ya . . . This post is unavailable . . .* Lotte down a gloomy side road, her pink hair falling across her face . . . *I see you I see you I see you.* A sound comes from Grace's throat—part cry, part snarl—and she has to shake her head to clear the thoughts.

Something is glinting up ahead by the side of the dusty path. A turquoise flash—a distraction—that makes her think of kingfishers and sea glass. She moves toward it and finds in the dirt a plastic water pistol, a good-sized one. There's an instant crazed elation in her as she picks it up. Her sweating palm is slippery against the outer casing and her mind flicks to the Walt Whitman poem—grease-spotted now, the words faded—that Ben pinned to the fridge when Lotte was maybe four or five. *Why, who makes much of a miracle? As to me I know of nothing else but miracles . . .* One of the ponds is just across the path and Grace almost breaks into a run to reach it. Crouching down, she places the cake box on a brown patch of grass, fills the plastic pistol, watches the water bubble and turn blue-jeweled. The vivid sky above her, the egg-yolk sun, light hitting the pond like flung crystals, all of it is the hope in her as she presses the rubber trigger, dousing her neck, her face, her arms, down the front of her shirt, the top of her scalp. The feel of the cold spray on her skin is indecent. The relief, the release a bright epiphany.

She's refilling the water pistol when she hears someone calling, "*Mummy, look!*" It takes her a second to process that she's heard the words in Japanese. Turning, she sees a little girl standing just across the path from her. She has a thick black fringe that's been cut too short and she's staring at Grace in the guileless way that kids do. Her mother is farther along the path, deep in conversation with a friend.

"*Konnichiwa,*" Grace says.

The little girl continues to stare. She's maybe three, the same age Grace was when her dad took the job with Unilever in Tokyo and they'd moved to Japan for eighteen months. It's the weirdest thing because she has no memories of this time. Or perhaps she does: it's just she isn't sure they weren't constructed years later from a handful of faded photographs. False memories of towering fluoro-bright buildings, verdigris-topped temples, Spaghetti Junction roads like something from the future. But it's the reason she fell in love with language. Even though it was a love born out of a discombobulating fear, an existential crisis.

There'd been the box in the loft they'd found the Christmas she was eleven, the one her dad had brought down to the lounge thinking it was decorations. In it were a bunch of dusty documents, an old cassette tape, her name inked in capitals on the side. When they'd played the tape back she'd heard a young child's voice chattering away in a language she didn't recognize. It was her voice and the nanny's having a conversation in Japanese and she couldn't pick out a single word. *What am I saying?* she'd asked her parents, and they'd laughed and shrugged, and Cate had nodded along to the recording, stroked her chin with her face faux-serious, as though she was following it all. Grace had smiled, too, but she hadn't found it funny. Afterward she'd taken the tape to her bedroom, played it over and over, rewinding it until it squealed because she couldn't come to terms with the fact that she wasn't able to understand herself. She thought that if she just listened long enough, hard enough, maybe she would be able to decipher the code, unlock the mystery, the meaning of the words. She would have given anything to suck the strange sentences out of the cassette player and back onto her tongue because who was she, this person on the tape? This Japanese-speaking version of her who had vanished. And if that person was her, then who was she now? Which was the real Grace?

It was the first language she decided to learn. The moment she knew she never wanted to feel that way again. Out of step with herself. But she hadn't banked on motherhood, on Lotte. On the gulf in language and meaning that has opened up between them. The communication breakdown that makes her feel like her eleven-year-old self, rewinding the tape over and over again.

Grace clears her throat, smiles at the little girl. "I used to live in Japan when I was your age," she tells her. She says it first in English and then, when the girl doesn't reply, in Japanese.

The child is staring at her still when her mother calls her name: Ume, Plum Blossom, a beautiful name. And when she doesn't move, her mother comes and scoops her by the hand. She's eyeing Grace as she does it. It isn't a friendly look and, sitting there at the edge of the pond, Grace feels suddenly self-conscious, exposed, ridiculous. A grown woman squirting herself with a toy water pistol in the middle of Hampstead Heath. The little girl is clutching her mother's hand but she keeps turning back, twisting her small body round to check on the crazy woman with the kid's toy.

Grace waits until the child has gone before she pushes the barrel of the pistol into the center of her forehead. Presses against the skin there so that it hurts. Then she lets the pistol fall to the ground and digs her fingernails into the dirt, fighting to hold on to herself. She misses her daughter. The thought swoops and claims her, and she draws her knees up to her chest, puts her head on her knees. She misses her little girl. Keeping her whole body still, so that no one will know, she begins to cry.

Three Months Earlier

leyla.nicol_ damn sis you do be glowing

        jivan.s Tiktok tik tok tik tok. cute af gonna miss ya

lotteadamskerr_ @jivan.s not going anywhere dw

        jivan.s when u famous

lotteadamskerr_ @jivan.s imma already famous haha

        tbone.vegan That tiny skirt. Those legs. You are indecent.

lotteadamskerr_ @ tbone.vegan lol

        tbone.vegan Wanna meet later usual place?

lotteadamskerr_ @ tbone.vegan yass

        tbone.vegan This post is unavailable

parisxnc ewwwww get a room who is this dude

        leyla.nicol_ @lotteadamskerr_ you do realize this is your public account

parisxnc oof

SHE AND LOTTE are squeezed into the middle of a row in the middle of the school hall. There's a greasy smell of that day's lunches and the deputy head is onstage presenting a slideshow on exam revision technique with his signature catatonic delivery. Grace has not a clue what he's saying: her senses are sharpened and she is surreptitiously surveying the boys in the room. All of them have been forced to come and are sitting slumped next to their parents like they'd rather be anywhere else. Which one of you? she's thinking. Which one? *Wanna meet later usual place . . . fck I want you now dm me babe . . . get a room . . . and when I say come you know what I mean . . . why aren't you in school . . .* The words from Lotte's Instagram—the words she can't unsee—are seeping into her mind like poison.

Many of these kids she's known since Nursery, Reception—since they were three years old, four—except now they are taller than she is, with snappable legs and too-deep voices and peach fuzz and shifting sideways glances, and a diet of on-tap porn running through the core of them. Even so it seems ridiculous that one of them could have written those words. Two rows in front of her there's Louis. Grace remembers the birthday party when he ate his tea sitting under her kitchen table and now there he is, blond hair turned dark and a hanging side fringe that obscures half his face. Could it be him? Across the aisle there's Kwame, the class comic in junior school. She had to look twice to place him. His once-chubby face has grown long and there's a smattering of acne across his cheeks. Is it him? Along from him is Luca—Luca, who has always been a beautiful boy, still is beautiful. Him?

Something's pricking at her, though. Words that won't quite leave her alone, something creepy . . . *Who is this dude?* Whoever he is, she doesn't understand why Lotte's friends don't know him. tbone.vegan. The name alone makes her want to scream. When she'd clicked on it she found a private account and it felt like iron shutters coming down, like she was being barred entry to her daughter's secret life. Her mind shifts from the boys at school—these strange man-children—to the Instagram accounts of Lotte's friends she trawled, searching for she didn't know what, hating herself as she did it. Reading between the lines of what was written there, words, acronyms she struggled to decipher but wanted to understand. It's language after all, her currency. . . . *u have any other qs . . . hahaha ofc . . . imma drag one of my friends to meet him the first time tho . . . so edgy . . . edgy af . . .* The fact is this boy—this man—could be anyone online. A sleazy sexual predator exploiting her child. She shuts down the thought:

she can't bear it. Lotte would not be so stupid. For all the stupid things she's done, Grace knows this: she has drilled it.

Next to her, Lotte raises her hand and Grace glances across. Her daughter is holding her arm high in the air, stretching out of her shoulder and spreading her fingers, like *look at me*. But the deputy head is deep in his gray presentation, gesturing with a laser pointer at a graph beamed wonkily onto the screen behind him, and if he sees her he doesn't show it. A second passes, two, three, and then Lotte clears her throat—an exaggerated, aggressive sound that says, "Excuse me, hello-o." What are you doing? Grace thinks.

Onstage the deputy head clicks onto his next slide. "I'll take questions at the end," he says, without looking in their direction.

"But what's the point?" Her daughter's voice carries across the hall. People in front of them twist in their seats.

Heat floods Grace's neck, her face. "Lotte . . ." she murmurs under her breath, a warning.

"I'm sorry?" The deputy head is looking their way now. He's keeping his voice level but a small, patronizing smile has crept onto his lips. His eyes are two hard marbles.

"What's the point, sir?" Lotte says again. "Revision, GCSEs, all this stress." She waves a hand in the direction of the PowerPoint. "For what? So that we can go to some uni and get into massive debt we'll never pay off? Then move back in with our parents until we're thirty? Take an internship that doesn't pay at all, or a job that won't pay enough for us to ever afford a house and—"

"And then you die." A muffled voice comes from somewhere farther back in the hall, and there's a smattering of laughter.

Two rows in front, Freja has swiveled to look at them. Grace tries to avoid her eye, but it's too late: she's snared her. And she's got that look on her face, the too-concerned look. Grace stares through her, like she hasn't seen her, sets her expression to neutral. Oh, do fuck off, she thinks.

The deputy head has turned back to his presentation. "Moving on," he says. "And I'll be taking *sensible* questions at the end."

There's a stagy cough from the row behind. Grace turns to see her friend Nisha joining her thumbs and forefingers into a heart, communicating solidarity. Next to Nisha, their friend Judith moves her cerise-painted mouth to form the words, *Screw them.* For a vanishing second, Grace wishes Ben were here too, but they have decided to divide these events between them now. She doesn't need an audience assessing the state of their collapsed marriage, other parents smugly congratulating themselves that they are doing better. In fact, it was his turn to come tonight, but he'd texted apologetically to say there'd been a last-minute meeting at work and could she step in, he'd do the next one? In reality, it's mostly Grace who comes along these days—and how quickly they've settled into that cliché. She lives ten minutes away and her work is more flexible; it's easier for her. How is it, she thinks, that in an age when female scientists have found a way to edit the genome, it is still seen as *her* job, the mother's job, to attend these school meetings—to deal with the school admin full stop?

Grace hears the sound of Lotte's chair shunting noisily backward at the same moment as she gets to her feet. And it's as though her daughter is towering above her, above everyone in there—a giant in the room. Then Lotte is pushing her way along the row, past the knees of the still-seated people. Grace sits stunned, mortified, stranded, the beat of her heart in her ears. She considers going after her, instantly dismisses the idea. She shouldn't care what these people think—she was sold the lie that past the age of forty she wouldn't care, that a magic line would be drawn in the sand—but she can't help it, she does. She would like the ground to open up and swallow her. Literally. As in a sinkhole, a sudden earthquake. Anything.

When she gets to the end of the row, Lotte turns toward the back of the hall and begins striding out. Her footsteps resonate around the room as she walks up the central aisle and it makes Grace think of weddings and funerals. There's the sound of people shuffling in their seats to get a better look. She's wearing a skirt that Grace would like to yank down to cover more than just her buttocks, a top that stops well short of her impossibly small waist. The pink dye in her hair is fading and it's scraped up into a high ponytail that's swishing side to side with each step. It is nonchalant hair. They are deliberate steps. She isn't apologizing in her gait, like maybe she's trying to nip out to the toilet unnoticed. Everything about her says, "This is bullshit. I've had it. I'm out of here." Onstage the deputy head falters, then continues. From two rows in front she can feel

Freja's judgy eyes on the side of her face. Grace has a sudden urge to rise in her seat and cheer her daughter on.

"Excuse me, sorry . . . excuse me . . ." The deputy head is taking questions and Grace is squeezing along the row of people, hunched and overapologizing in a spitty stage whisper, like that way she might salvage the reputation of herself and her child. It's been five, maybe ten minutes since Lotte left the room. As she's approaching the swing doors, a teacher peels away from the wall at the back of the hall and comes to hold the door for her. There's the school reception area beyond and Grace spots her daughter instantly, sitting legs crossed and head down, both thumbs working her phone. At the *thwump* of air displaced, Lotte looks up, gets to her feet, and starts to walk out.

"Lotte," Grace hisses, not too loud because the door to the assembly hall hasn't closed completely.

"Lotte's mum?"

The teacher has come in behind her, and now that's it: she's trapped.

Grace stops next to the faceless shop dummy dressed in a Northmere Park uniform. "Yes!" She turns, steeling herself for a lecture about her awful child, her piss-poor parenting. The teacher looks vaguely familiar: she's seen him before at meetings, parents' evenings, but not up close, and she's never spoken to him. He's tall with fair hair and clear, light eyes, and he's wearing a suit but it's contemporary, a tight cut, and his tie is loose. He's wearing it like he's in skinny jeans and a dark T-shirt and it strikes her how attractive he is, how *hot*. Grace screws up the thought, tosses it immediately. Of all the things she should be thinking as a mother right now. *You are so inappropriate*, she hears Lotte's voice in her head.

The teacher introduces himself as Mr. Karlsson. "I'm the music tech guy," he tells her. "I teach Lotte. Do you have just a second?"

There's something in the way he says it. A lazy upward pull around his mouth, the way he is looking at her—looking into her.

Grace is conscious that she isn't quite able to control the set of her face. She makes a show of looking across at the exit after Lotte. He has thrown her off-kilter and she doesn't want him to see it. Staring through the glass doors that have turned black in the dark she wonders if she's imagined it.

"Sorry, yes," she says distractedly. And then, "Listen, please ignore my daughter. She can be a bit of a . . ." She's going to say "twat," but stops herself. He is a teacher, after all. ". . . a bit of an idiot."

Facing him again, she sees that he is faintly amused. He reminds her of someone she knew at university. Or *wanted* to know. A psychology student in the year above. It isn't how he looks, more the way he's holding himself. A relaxed arrogance that she shouldn't find beguiling but—God help the guilty feminist in her—she does. And he is young, she realizes, late twenties at most, more trainee than teacher. The way police officers seem to her these days, drivers, doctors. Or, rather, she is old. She is so old. How ridiculous that she could have thought he might be . . . what? Hitting on her?

He glances up at the strip light that's started to flicker above them, casting a hard jerky glare. "Oh, don't worry, she's got a point," he says. "This culture of tests and targets is out of control. Put in place by a bunch of people who've barely crossed the threshold of a classroom in the past thirty years." He makes a face. "The kids are all under too much pressure, it's no wonder we're in the middle of a mental-health crisis."

It isn't what she expected him to say. He isn't toeing the company line in the way that some teachers do, and she respects him for it. It's disarming. Even though it should annoy her because he's half her age and talking like maybe she doesn't realize all this, as if maybe she needs advice about her own daughter.

"Lotte's a talented musician, and I'm sure she's doing fine in her other subjects, but she's giving herself a hard time right now. I see it in lessons. Others might not agree." He raises his eyebrows and looks pointedly toward the assembly hall, then at the faceless dummy, and they laugh. "So, yeah . . ." He leans back against the wall behind him.

There's an ease about him, a low-key authority that belies his age. A not-so-subtle irreverence—like he's part of the school machine, but also isn't. A real human being. And maybe the truth is she does need advice. Right now, when it comes to Lotte, she feels like she's making it up as she goes along. There's the nagging thought, ever present, that she doesn't have the skill set for it, doesn't know how to parent her own child in this moment.

"You're right." She nods, and for an instant she considers off-loading on him, spewing up her concerns, her fears, because instinct tells her he would reassure her. That he would shrug and make it all go away, like, *Don't sweat it, that's teenagers for you.* After all, it wasn't so long ago for him, he should remember.

Instead, she zips herself up. "Thanks," she tells him, and scrunches her nose. "I probably shouldn't have called her a twat."

"You didn't."

He laughs then, dips his head, and she feels a strange, unnerving desire move through her. And she's laughing too, pulling a face, but what's wrong with her? They have exchanged a handful of sentences, she's been standing here no more than a few minutes, and yet she's feeling something she hasn't felt in she doesn't know how long.

Grace glances once again at the exit. She should be out there catching up with Lotte, finding out what's going on with her daughter, sorting things out. But at the same time she wants to stay. Whatever this is, it feels good, like she's pressed pause on her frenzied mind. She looks back at the teacher. The light flickering above them is making her feel a bit trippy, and maybe she's delusional, perhaps it's all in her head, but there's a pull in the air between them, she's sure of it. She thinks if she stays a moment longer she will take his face in her hands and put her mouth on his beautiful mouth, push her hands up and under his half-tucked shirt.

"I have to go." Her voice comes out too loud and she steps backward, stumbles on her heel. And she feels instantly stupid, as though she's implied he's trying to keep her there.

"Okay, see you around, Lotte's mum," he says, frank eyes on her face. "It was nice to meet you." Then he pushes himself off the wall, crosses the reception area back toward the hall.

2004

GRACE IS WANDERING the corridors of the Big House. It's the first time she's been here, to this extraordinary place where Ben grew up, where his mother still lives. She has had four hours' sleep maximum because the baby is teething, and she is a ghost of a person, floating up and down staircases and in and out of the rooms of this labyrinthine building, like the Gray Lady. The baby is clutched to her breast because now she is asleep. Now. Of course she is. And Grace is trying to find Ben, has no idea where he has gone. She can hear hammering, the distant rev of a drill coming from the grounds. The marquee is being set up beyond the formal gardens, beyond the tennis courts and the rectangular stone pool, in the meadow that stretches all the way to the river, in time for tomorrow evening's rehearsal dinner. Walking the halls of the family seat—the Scottish castle, Ben and his three brothers call it—she feels that she is a visitor in her own life, an interloper in the preparations for her own wedding.

She's coming along the passage by the kitchens when she hears raised voices. Ahead of her is the door to the boot room and beyond that the herb garden, and she moves quietly along the flagstones, hoping she can make it out into the cold slap of the morning before she is noticed.

"Does she ever put the baby down, darling? I mean, how does she go to the loo?"

The voice is coming from the kitchens and it's Ben's mother's—she has known her only a day and she would recognize it anywhere. Low and throaty, like she has a thirty-a-day habit, and the words slurring together

as though she's a little drunk, when in fact she's just leaking her lazy enti-
tlement. Grace stops where she is, cups the baby's head.

"I know she's a baby virgin, but I thought she was going to snatch little
Charlotte out of my arms when I finally got my hands on her yesterday!
She needs to be crawling around, finding her freedom. She's too old for
all that coddling."

"Lotte," she hears Ben say. "Her name's Lotte, not Charlotte."

"She didn't take her eyes off me the entire time. I'm fairly experienced
in that department, Benjamin. What with the four sons."

Grace feels a tightening in her throat. She is unable to move from
where she's standing. She imagines Helena, feet planted self-righteously in
front of the huge butler sink, Le Creuset pans hung from the rafters above.
She pictures her dried-out hair dyed the color of stale honey and set with
so much hairspray it moves in a single piece when she turns her head. A
fitted tweedy jacket worn with navy slacks, slip-on loafers. Pearly-pink nail
polish.

"She's pretty, darling. Quite pretty. Just, you know, it would be nice to
see a bit of personality."

"Are you hearing yourself?" Ben's voice carries out into the passageway. "She was a TV *personality*, Helena. That not good enough for you?"

Is this happening? Grace thinks. Is she really here? Or has she fallen
asleep with the baby in her arms? Maybe she's swimming up to conscious-
ness, about to wake any second now in the oak-paneled bedroom that is
like something out of Agatha Christie and smells of candle wax and Flash.
She shifts her body minutely, soundlessly, because standing there like this,
her hip is starting to seize up. Against her chest the baby sighs in her sleep.

"You do realize this is the mother of your grandchild, right?" Ben is
saying now, and Grace can hear in his voice that he's exasperated. She has
never heard him this way before. "The woman I'm marrying in two days."

The chill of the flagstones is seeping up through the thin soles of her
canvas shoes. She wants to leave, doesn't want to hear any more, but at the
same time she can't move: she doesn't want to alert them to her presence.
Oh, by the way, did I warn you my mother is toxic? Just tune her out. Ben
had winked at her from the driver's seat as they'd driven past the outskirts
of Glasgow the day before. *Remember, the Mayans in southern Mexico and
Honduras use the same word for "in-laws" as they do for "stupidity." Bol,*

Grace thinks now. Stupid in-law. But even so the woman is like a carica-ture of herself. Grace hadn't got across the threshold yesterday before Hel-ena had tossed over her shoulder, "And, darling, who said you wouldn't have lost the baby weight in time? I mean, it's barely noticeable, well done, you. Wipe your feet! Carol's had the whole team polishing *everything*."

In the kitchen Ben's voice is growing louder, angry, and it's so shocking to her because this is not the man she knows. The man she barely knows, admittedly. She starts to do the maths, aware she's trying to distract her-self. There's the five months that doesn't count, and then another four months and now the baby is ten months old, so fourteen months. She has known him fourteen months. That's all. A fraction of her life, yet for most of that it has felt like she's known him always.

". . . and you're trotting around after her like a little sheep. Which is a bit rich considering you barely had a choice about all this in the first place."

Just tune her out . . .

Now Ben is starting to shout and she moves her hands to cover the baby's ears, holding them there lightly. Barely breathing because, however bad this is, she doesn't want her to wake up. That would be worse: the day would be ruined; they would not get her back on track. Grace is patho-logical about sleep or lack of it, she knows this. It's the shapeless gray drag that tracks the edge of her always, the beast that stalks ready to suck her in, down.

". . . my whole life . . ." she hears, ". . . you're a damn snob . . . ashamed to be related to you . . . the damage you wreak . . . I love her . . . you have no idea . . ."

And just as she's thinking that she can't stand here any longer—that they will come out and catch her and then what?—Ben slams through the kitchen door and out into the passage. Both of them start.

"Oh, God," he says, and it must be obvious from her face that she's floored. And she knows she looks out of place standing there because she feels suddenly strange, two-dimensional, like it isn't really her there at all. Only the weight of the baby in her arms tells her she's real.

"I'm sorry." Ben comes toward her, and he looks stricken. He puts his hands on her shoulders, takes them off, pulls his fingers through his hair. It's like he doesn't know what to do with himself, and it's so unlike him, this self-consciousness. "Listen, Grace." He places a palm softly against the baby's back, and he's keeping his voice low because she's sleeping, or maybe because of his mother, who has not followed him out of the kitchen. "Take Lotte," he grapples in his pocket and pulls out the keys, "and get in the car, okay?"

There are huge catering trucks in the driveway. Her car—their car—is parked at the outer edge alongside a thorny wall of rosebush that must be ten feet high. All the words she's overheard are running through her head as she opens the car door, straps the baby in. There's a moment when Lotte's eyes flutter open but then, miraculously, close again. And she's sitting in the driver's seat, her chest slack like she might cry, when she sees in the rearview mirror Ben come out of the front door, bumping two suitcases down the steps between the two stone lions, past the sculpted evergreens in their vast terracotta pots. She's expecting at any moment to see his mother appear behind him, arms aloft, fingernails pointy like a Disney witch's. Grace grips the steering wheel, trying to anchor herself. What are they doing?

The car judders and bounces back on its suspension as Ben opens the boot, pushes in the suitcases. And then he's opening the passenger door, sliding in beside her.

"So how do you feel about eloping?" he says, with a grin. But there is fire in his eyes, fury. His hair is crazier even than usual, as though he has yanked his fingers through it from all angles. Like his fight has been with his styling wax rather than his mother.

She wants to say, *What's going on, Ben?* Instead she asks, "Is this why she didn't come to see Lotte in London, after she was born? I mean, am I the reason?"

Ben turns his body to hers, takes her upper arms, holds her firmly. "It's not you," he says. "It's her."

Grace drops her gaze, feels the swell of tears.

"Seriously, hon." Ben tips up her chin so she's looking at him. "She isn't worth it. She's a professional bitch, okay? It's what she does. It's not really her fault, I don't think. She's the seventh daughter of seven daughters—a final bad fairy, or something. All very Gothic. The point is they didn't want her, she was the wrong sex, and we've all had to live with the fallout. Cycle of violence and all that."

Grace frowns. "Is that true? You never told me that."

"Pretty much." He shrugs. "That, and just a general lack of emotional intelligence that goes with the *breeding*." He puts quotation marks around the words with his intonation.

"Then how are you so normal?"

He shoots up his eyebrows. "Normal? I'm just keeping it together until after you've officially signed up to me. So, how about it?" He waves an arm around him, taking in the catering trucks, the gravel drive, the house. "I mean it, Grace. Screw all this. It isn't us. Let's do it our way. Let's go and get married, just you and me. What's stopping us?"

For the first time she remembers her sister, Sara, Dylan—all of them sleeping off their jet lag somewhere in the guest wing. "I can't leave Cate," she says. Madly. Like, aside from that she's considering it. Is she considering it?

"You *can* leave Cate," he says. "She's more than a match for my bloody mother. I think she might enjoy the battle."

"What about my parents?" She checks the mirror, as though her mum and dad might be coming up the drive, as though they might catch them here like this, even though they're not due to arrive until the next day. "They haven't seen Lotte for three months and she's changed so much. Mum's made this huge deal about the amber bracelet she's bringing for her teething, like we've exchanged ten detailed emails about it, minimum. *The beads on the more expensive one on the internet are double-knotted for safety, Grace,* and *It'll look tasteful with her flower-girl dress* and—"

"I don't care," he tells her, and he yanks at his seat belt, pushes it into the buckle. "You know what? I couldn't care less. They will all of them figure it out. They'll get a slap-up meal out of it, vintage champagne— maybe they'll keep the close-up magician, who knows?" He takes her face in his hands and his palms are hot although it's cold outside. "I want you. Just you. No one else. Well . . . her too, I guess." He jerks his thumb at the sleeping baby in the back of the car. And then his face softens; she feels the release of it in her stomach. It's him again.

"I love you, Grace. I fucking love you. That's all."

"Tell me in Mandarin," she says, and when he starts to answer she shakes her head, smiling, turns the key in the ignition.

It is only as she pulls onto the motorway twenty minutes later that she understands they won't go back. She pictures her wedding dress hanging in the mahogany wardrobe in the room her sister is staying in. So Ben wouldn't see it. Empty hangers and an antique gold key that rattled in its lock. Ivory tulle exploding from a smooth satin bodice that constricted her lungs but would have made her parents cry. She feels a twist of guilt in her gut, punches the thought away. She can sell the dress on eBay.

Grace glances in the rearview mirror at her daughter asleep in the back. Blissfully asleep, her face impossibly pale and peaceful, ethereal, as though she is half in this world, half out. And then she flicks her eyes across to the passenger seat, to her soon-to-be husband, the father of her child. He's drumming his fingers on his knees absentmindedly, in the way that he does. Those long, beautiful fingers. He is so steadfast, she thinks. So honest and loyal and open. She didn't choose him, not exactly, but she would have. She loves him. It scares her to think she almost let him drift away.

Northern soul is on the car stereo and she reaches out a hand, cranks the volume up, just a little, just enough to drown out the doubts. Next to her Ben whoops—quietly, so he won't wake the baby—and they start to laugh at their muted rebellion. A skittish unsteady laughter that feels liberating and dangerous all at once.

Grace presses her foot down on the accelerator, watches the speed dial rise. "Are we doing this?" she asks.

Ben places a hand on her thigh, high up, with intent. She can feel the force of his touch moving through her. "You better believe it, baby," he says.

Now

BEN HAS STRIPPED off his T-shirt and he's standing there half-naked in the kitchen, tipping crisps into bowls. He's worried he's doing this too soon, that in the heat the crisps will start to soften and sweat, that they will be ruined—chewy—by the time Lotte's guests arrive. But he wants to be prepared—he can't leave it all until the last minute. He has his laptop on the kitchen counter, too, because he's been emailing back and forth with one of his PhD students, who's having a minor crisis. And he's just about to type in details of a couple of reference books, sign off with reassuring words, when his phone pings with a number he doesn't recognize.

It's not someone in his contacts but it doesn't look like spam—like someone trying to push him compensation for an accident he didn't have—and he thinks immediately of Grace. His stomach tips. He has been trying to block it temporarily, but in the midst of everything he's juggling, there is Grace. Something has happened to Grace. Or, rather, Grace has happened to something. He has tried to call her back but she hasn't picked up since they spoke maybe an hour ago. Ben peers at the notification. Standing there with his top off he feels suddenly vulnerable, and as he clicks on the message he's steeling himself. Words fill the screen. The message is more like a short essay than a text. A *full-on Mum* text, Lotte would call it.

> Hi Ben, Olivia's mum Freja Harris here! You might
> not remember me, but I'm very active on the PTA
> at Northmere Park (for my sins!). I got your number

from Nisha Kaur, I hope you don't mind. I wasn't sure
whether to send this and I don't want to interfere—I
know things have been very difficult for Grace and you
all—but I'm aware you actively co-parent so I thought I
ought to let you know.

Ben, who has been so hot all day, feels goose bumps crawl across the
back of his neck. He scans the rest of the message.

. . . terribly worried after I bumped into Grace
earlier because she didn't seem herself. The way she
was behaving was very erratic. She was different,
distracted, not quite there, but also—and it isn't easy
to type this—pretty rude, to be honest. Truthfully,
her behavior was alarming. (I should mention I'm six
months into training to be a counselor [second career!],
and if you want my [professional] opinion, I think she
needs help.)

With his free hand Ben starts to ball up the empty crisps packets,
throwing them one by one into the bin. He has no idea why he does this.
He's just aware he needs to be doing something, occupying his hands, his
mind . . . *and, Jesus Christ, it shouldn't be that hard to get a cake from A
to fucking B*, he hears Grace say. *I'm having to walk to you because I think
maybe I've done something stupid, Ben* . . . He has a thousand questions he
would like to ask the woman who has sent this text. But there's the urge in
him to protect Grace, to protect Lotte, to protect them. His whole body is
tense as he hammers out a reply.

Freja. Of course I remember you. Thanks for your text.
I've just this moment spoken to Grace and can assure
you she's absolutely fine. Crossed wires perhaps? Ben

As soon as he's hit send he opens his last message to Grace; he needs to
contact her. *Erratic*, he thinks, as he starts to type, and he's trying to picture where she might be, what she has done. *Alarming . . . Not quite there*.

Grace, I'm trying to get hold of you. Why aren't you
picking up? Where are you? What's going on? I've had
a text from one of your friends. She thinks you need
help?

Ben deletes the last sentence, hovers his hands over the screen; there's tightness behind his eyes. Is she on her way here still? Bringing the demented-sounding cake that she'd described in breathy detail to him over the phone? He wants to tell her not to come, that she'll ruin the party for his daughter, *their* daughter. But how can he? He's anxious and afraid, and he's angry. It's Lotte's day and he doesn't want to be thinking about this.

"Dad!"

Ben starts as if he's done something wrong.

"Ew . . ." His daughter puts up a hand as she comes into the room as though she's shading her face. "What are you doing? Put a shirt on."

She's changed her clothes again and there's a silk scarf tied in her hair now—a swirling seventies pattern of pink and amber and black that he knows in his core, like it's a favorite ornament from a childhood home, and even with her hand up to her face it sends a shock through him. She's holding her fingers up in a peace sign. "Can I have two more people?" she's saying now. "Please. Just two, and then that's all, I promise."

It's Grace's scarf, the one she wore in her hair the day they finally got married. Two years after they'd planned because it turned out you had to book a fortnight in advance to elope spontaneously at Gretna Green. He can see her, standing on the wide, wide steps of Marylebone Register Office wearing a green dress and gold ankle boots, an outsize men's blazer hanging from her shoulders. Laughing with the bewildered couple— tourists from Hong Kong—they'd pulled off the street to bear witness. He sees Lotte, a toddler then, running in circles around a fat Corinthian pillar clutching to her head the policeman's hat she took everywhere with her, slept with each night. He feels the sudden charge in the wood-paneled room where they made their vows and Grace started to cry, surprising them both. How he could have exploded with the love straining at the edges of him. This is the Grace he remembers from the time before. The Grace who vanished. He'd hoped and he'd waited, and now and then there were pieces of her, glimpses, but she never came back, not really.

"Dad?"

Ben shakes his head, brings himself into the room. Lotte is still standing in the doorway. His child, his daughter, to all intents and purposes a woman. There's a glow about her. It's the happiest he's seen her in he can't remember how long. He thinks back to the day—how many weeks ago now?—when he opened the door to find her distraught on his doorstep. Eyes raw, makeup streaked across her cheeks, her weekend bag stuffed full at her feet. How his heart had contracted. And he'd been helpless as she'd moved around the house for days that turned into weeks, like someone had shredded her heart, her soul.

"Can I?" Lotte asks.

His mind is half-in, half-out of the room and he nods at his daughter, *yes*, even though he's unsure of what he's agreed to.

She's on her phone texting immediately but on the landing she stops, turns back, fixes her oil-dark eyes on him. "Please don't be all weird when my friends get here, okay?"

Ben raises his eyebrows at her but he's smiling. Lotte kicks her foot up to her bottom, gives a little bounce.

As soon as she's gone he returns his fingers to the screen, jabs out a final sentence.

> I'm worried about you. Call me, text me, email me,
> whatever. I just want to know you're okay. Do it for
> Lotte, if not for me. B

As he presses send, Ben feels dread scrape across his scalp. He places the phone facedown on the kitchen worktop, rests his forehead on the cool marble. "Where the hell are you, Grace?" he murmurs, as though somehow the words might reach her over the ether. Like that way he might be able to summon her at last.

Three Months Earlier

SHE'S TURNING ONTO her street when she sees him coming toward her. There's a guitar case strapped to his back and he's walking down the middle of the road like he's owning his place in the world. As if he'll take his chances with any traffic—any*one*—that might come along. Her hand goes automatically to her hair that's pulled back into a tight ponytail after the gym; she catches herself doing this and feels instantly ridiculous. He's practically a kid—what does she care what he thinks of her? What does he care how she looks? In all likelihood he won't remember who she is or even that they've met before. And she's just thinking that she'll put her head down and walk on past when he glances across at her, holds up his hand in acknowledgment.

"Lotte's mum, hi," he calls, and there's that same look of faint amusement on his face, like they're sharing a joke about something, she isn't sure what. Then he starts to cut across to the pavement as though he intends to stop and talk to her. There are cars parked bumper to bumper and, with the guitar on his back, he has to turn sideways to squeeze through a gap. Watching him, it strikes her all over again how stupidly beautiful he is. The sculpted length of his neck, the easy way he maneuvers his body, despite the awkward load he's carrying. It's almost laughable, the look of him. Like he's a catalog model or a cartoon heartthrob brought to life, but roughed up at the edges a little to make him seem real, plausible, not unpalatably perfect. She wonders if he realizes this.

"Grace," she corrects him, as he steps up onto the pavement in front of her.

He smiles with his eyes, presses a palm to his chest. "Nate."

The name loops through her mind. She likes it. It's a nice name. It's better than Mr. Karlsson. It suits him.

"It's what most of the students call me, to be honest," he says. "'Sir' doesn't sit so well with me."

She nods, imagining him taking a class full of secondary-school kids. Tuning up instruments, helping them find their way around software, plugging in sound equipment. Loose-limbed and laid-back with them. And maybe it's the thought of him surrounded by all those perfect gravity-defying bodies as she stands there in her Lycra, but Grace has the sudden urge to cover herself. She swings her bag round to the front because she won't be able to suck in her stomach and breathe for the duration of this conversation they are having. She's barely able to suck it in at all these days, the fleshy overhang that encircles her waist—her "waist," she thinks, putting silent air quotes around the word. The midlife skulk and strike of it. She's wishing now that she had extracted her no-show pants from the overstuffed laundry basket that morning, as she'd considered doing. Spritzed them with perfume, worn them anyway. As if that would have made all the difference. As if that way he wouldn't notice her hair threaded with gray above her ears. She knows it's more noticeable scraped up like this: the hair underneath is dark, the contrast starker. She really needs to get her shit together and make an appointment to get her roots done—she always, always leaves it too long, even though it makes her feel a thousand years old like this. It's just that sitting in the hairdresser's lately she can hardly bear to look at herself in the harsh-lit mirror. She can coat on as much mascara as she likes, shade her lips with Chanel, there's no disguising that everything on her face is sloping downward, like it's given up.

Grace inclines her head in the direction Mr. Karlsson—*Nate*—has come from. "Shouldn't you be at school?" she asks. She means it as a joke, as if she's talking to a child, not a teacher, and it isn't her intention—of course it isn't—but she realizes too late that something in her intonation makes it sound as if she's flirting with him. Color flares in her cheeks; she feels the blood spread through the tributary of veins just beneath the surface of her flesh. Her head, the whole of her, feels hot.

"I'm part-time." Nate digs his thumbs through the straps of his guitar case, hitches it higher up his back. She takes in the movements of his hands, his slim, sure fingers. If he's noticed she's blushing he doesn't show it. "And, anyway, it's different. Technically I'm a technician, not a teacher, so there are gaps in my timetable."

"Technically a technician." Grace laughs. "I like that."

He's looking at her like she's speaking in tongues. For a moment she's tempted to do it. To reel something off in Russian or Japanese or Dutch because why not? The whole encounter is starting to feel a little surreal.

Since they're talking jobs, she thinks maybe she'll mention she used to work in TV. She wonders if she can find a subtle way to make the segue. She hates herself for it but she wants him to know that she's an interesting person, who worked an interesting job. A job she valued—loved, even—she has long since realized. A job she still misses.

Someone comes up behind them then, a woman with short hair pushing a bicycle, and the moment is gone. It's the perfect opportunity for her to make her excuses, move off, but instead she steps to one side, they both do. They stand without speaking until the woman has moved past. As if in tacit agreement that their conversation is private, a secret between them. Grace can feel goosebumps starting to creep across her flesh, her body temperature dropping after the sweat she worked up on the treadmill, and she's asking herself why she's still here. She needs to get home and shower.

"So this is your street?"

Even though he has framed it as a question, the thought crosses her mind that he already knows the answer, he has found out somehow where she lives. And when she tells him yes, gesturing up the road toward her house, she can't help thinking that it's no coincidence him showing up like this. It isn't a road you'd necessarily walk down—especially not coming from the school to the shops or the bus. Then just as quickly she is filled with self-loathing. Wrapping her arms around her body she pinches her skin hard, the droopy bit at her triceps, the *bingo wing*. She is a horrible fantasist. Thank God—*thank God*—no one can see inside her head.

As she's thinking this he reaches out, brushes his thumb across her temple.

What is he doing? Her heart speeds up and she's certain he must be able to feel the blood pulsing there, against that soft dent where there's no bone, the place where if you press too hard it could kill you.

"You have a . . ." He trails off, and he's looking at her that way again, the same way he looked at her in the flickering light of the school reception area, the way she has thought about since. Like he's trying to see through to her retinas, searching for something. In the daylight, she can make out a small scar on his cheekbone, white and shiny in the shape of a circumflex. Grace knows she should break the moment. She's thinking about Lotte, about the fact that this man is her teacher. She should step backward away from him but she finds she isn't able to move. She remembers this long-ago feeling, this bright beam of focus illuminating her, and it's intoxicating. He's holding his thumb there too long. He is crossing a boundary—they both are—and it beguiles and unsettles her all at once.

"There." Taking his hand from her face, he presents his thumb where a small leaf is stuck to the pad of skin. He's leaned in toward her to show her and she can smell cigarettes on him, a smell that takes her back to a past life. She would like to bury her nose in the collar of his wool coat, inhale the scent of him. Of her youth.

Behind them a car horn sounds and she jolts, swings round guiltily.

"Grace!"

It's a moment before she recognizes Nisha. Her friend has stopped her car in the middle of the road. She has the window wound down and she's shouting over the sound of the engine.

"Hi! I'm on the hunt for a parking space, but do you have a minute?"

"Totally." Grace nods wildly, smiles too brightly.

"Okay, I'm out of here."

Does she imagine that she feels his breath on her neck as he says it?

He dips his head as she turns back to him. Whatever had burned in his eyes before has gone. "Nice to see you again," he says. And he moves off down the street, his guitar banging lightly against his back.

Grace crosses to Nisha's car.

"Lotte's teacher." She waves a hand, dismissing him. And she's wondering, as her friend cuts the engine, whether she saw anything, whether there was anything *to* see. There's the aftershock of his touch on her skin, she knows that much. The certainty that something passed between them.

Every part of her wants to turn and watch him go, to see if he looks back. Instead she stares at Nisha, at the place on her forehead where her third eye would be. Otherwise she thinks she might give herself away.

"The music guy, I recognize him." Nisha shoots up her eyebrows conspiratorially, like, *Obviously we're too old but you would, wouldn't you?* And Grace feels predatory, cheapened, ashamed. She forces a laugh.

Glancing into the rearview mirror, Nisha checks the road. "I have a ton of stuff to get from the shops but I saw you there and I've been meaning to text. Listen, does Lotte own a tie-dye hoodie?"

It's an odd question to ask, and there's something in the way she says it that makes Grace falter before she replies. "Yes?" She frowns a little.

"Okay, then it was definitely her."

Grace shakes her head, confused.

"Oh, God, I should have called you, Grace, I'm sorry," Nisha says. "Lotte was outside our house last night at two o'clock in the morning."

"Wait. What? I'm not following."

"You know the green space opposite? The bit where people bring their dogs to shit? She was there. Voices travel and I sleep so lightly, and it looked like her but it was pretty dark and it was the middle of the night, I wasn't a hundred percent, not sure enough to phone you . . ."

"But she was at home," Grace says. "In bed."

Nisha pulls a face. "I'm pretty sure. It was her voice, her hair." She pauses. "Her hoodie."

Grace's mind is pinballing from Nisha's words to the night before. Two in the morning? She'd shouted up to Lotte to say goodnight at, what, eleven thirty? And her daughter had called back down with her Instagram voice. If she'd gone out after that Grace would have heard her leave, surely.

"And she was with a guy," Nisha says now. "Like *with* him."

Grace feels her heart pick up. "Who?" She tries to keep her voice even. "Luca? Kwame . . . ?"

"I didn't see. They were there and then they were gone, y'know?" Nisha checks her rearview mirror again. A car has turned onto the road and is coming up behind her. There are parked cars on both sides and the road is too narrow for two cars to pass. "He had his back to me. Wearing a cap, a dark jacket. Not a voice I recognized." She starts the engine and Grace feels a flicker of annoyance—she can't help herself. Would her friend even have texted if they hadn't bumped into each other like this?

"Listen, I have to run," Nisha's eyes are on the rearview mirror, "but call me later, okay? I really want to help." Planting a kiss on her palm, she blows it across the passenger seat and pulls away.

Turning to walk home, Grace feels a tremor start up at the center of her. This isn't Lotte, she thinks. It's not what she does. So why does she believe it? Why does she know that Nisha has not made a mistake? That her child was out in the middle of the night, doing God knows what with God knows who. What is wrong with her? Has she lost her mind? Anything could have happened to her.

Coming in through the gate, she remembers the torn-off scrap of paper she found in Lotte's blazer. *I nearly came just looking at you today . . .* The toxic, secret Instagram chat she can't unsee . . . *that tiny skirt. Those legs. You are indecent . . .* The words scream through her head, and Grace understands finally that she has lost control. That she is gripping fast to her child but she can't hold on. She's nearly sixteen. Grace can't give her time out or put her on the naughty step. Lotte can up and walk out whenever she wants. The truth is, there is no sanction she can make that will stop her doing whatever she wants to do. It has crept up on her, this powerlessness, and pounced. And it is terrifying.

2006

Hey, so let's not leave it so long next time.
   I'm in London again late January.
   We should get more coffee, or something stronger . . . ?

Love, L x

IT'S NEARLY 11:30 p.m. and they've just filed into a pew to the left of the nave—Grace's mum, Anne, her dad, Michael, Grace, and, last, him. Lotte is back at the Adamses' with Cate and Sara, who have refused to come because *Well, religion*, as Cate put it, screwing up her face. Marching ahead through the Christmas-card snow, her arm hooked through Michael's, Grace has not spoken to Ben all the way to the church. Ostentatiously, he feels, as he and Anne followed them. It isn't like her to act this way, and he doesn't know whether it has to do with him or not, or whether some ancient family psychodrama is being played out in her head and he's just collateral damage.

Ben takes the order of service from the seat, lowers himself onto the hard pew. He's relieved not to have to make small talk with Anne anymore. She's always on edge around these kinds of events, anything that involves getting to a certain place on time. There's the smell of dust and floor polish and old ladies' lipstick, and he is stifling the urge to sneeze when Grace turns to him and drops a folded-up pamphlet into his lap, like it's a live grenade.

"You forgot to empty your pockets," she says coldly.

She's wearing his navy wool peacoat, the one he uses for work, retrieved from the boot of the car because she left hers in London, along with the presents for her parents and a chestnut stuffing.

"Thanks, I think?" He frowns, and tries to meet her eyes but she looks away.

Adjusting her scarf, Anne shoots them a look. Over the mumble of the congregation, she's caught the edge in Grace's voice. "You need to turn your ringers off for Mass," she tells them, after a pause.

They could have had Christmas at home just the three of them. At the new house that's not so central but where there's a bath, not just a shower, their own front door. Lotte is three now and starting to understand the magic in it all. And as he unfolds the leaflet in his lap, he's picturing his adorable girl standing at the tree earlier that evening, her soft face illuminated by the boiled-sweet glow of the fairy lights. How he'd held himself still and watched her from the doorway, and understood that he was the luckiest man alive. He isn't really concentrating as he smooths out the paper, clocks that it's the program for the linguistics conference he'd attended the week before. Automatically, he turns it over, sees the words slanting across the back page, written over the print. *Hey, so let's not leave it so long next time . . . we should get more coffee or something stronger?* Despite the cold outside, the chill in the church, Ben feels insanely hot. *Love, L x,* he reads. Shit, he thinks. Fuck. No.

All at once an anticipatory shuffling is spreading through the church like a wave at a football game, some heavy-duty coughing, an excessive clearing of phlegm from throats. As though an invisible signal has been given. Ben wants to clear his throat too. He wants to shout, hear his voice bouncing back off the stone walls: *This isn't what it looks like, Grace.*

"Grace," he whispers.

But she's facing the front and she jerks her shoulder minutely, shrugging him off.

"Grace," he tries again. Anne turns in her seat, wrinkles her forehead.

From outside, the clock begins to chime the half hour. Ben feels his head getting hotter as the priest moves regally across the transept, mounts the steps to the pulpit.

His mind flashes to the week before. To the conference at the Institute of English Studies. He hadn't checked the program of speakers, so when she walked onstage to present her paper it took him by surprise. He'd tracked his finger down the running order and found her name, *Lina Bell, lecturer in sociolinguistics at Newcastle University*. She'd cut her dark hair shorter but other than that she hadn't changed: same large eyes with pupils almost permanently dilated, same constellation of moles across her neck and collarbone. And when she caught his eye midway through, he'd smiled.

"You disappeared," she said, when she came to find him afterward. And she'd snapped her fingers, like he'd pulled off a magic trick. And it's true, he had disappeared. He hadn't seen her since she'd left for Milan— they'd had a Chinese meal out, made love at her flat, and then she'd caught the plane the next morning—and he hadn't been in touch since Grace. "You never replied to my emails." She raised her eyebrows. "You pig. But even so I'm going to ask you to join me for coffee at the place round the corner. The stuff they serve here is awful."

They're standing to sing the first carol now and he tries again, under the cover of the organ music—the bum notes they'd usually be biting their cheeks not to laugh at. "Grace!"

But she flinches when he leans in toward her, moves her body away.

There had been a night when Lotte woke up screaming every single hour—more than one night. One hundred nights it felt like. They fed her, rocked her, soothed her, put her down in her cot, like bomb-disposal experts. Held their breath until her eyes sprang open and the whole cycle began again. They were beside themselves by the end of it, hallucinating, broken. *Secrets of the Baby Whisperer* didn't work. Gina Ford was worse. The first night of sleep training he'd barred the door, face tight, sending his mind away from the screams. But they'd lasted less than three minutes before Grace, screaming herself, had barreled her body into his, gained entry, made it stop. And the relief of it had filled up his lungs with everything he was holding in until he thought they might burst.

Lotte slept in their bed after that. Small arms flung out, her squidgy little body a full stop between them. She still slept in their bed. Carving a lengthening divide down the middle. Once, they'd snatched sex in the downstairs toilet, while Lotte watched CBeebies in the lounge. Fucking desperately up against the tiny sink to the *Teletubbies* soundtrack, Grace insisting they leave the door open a crack so they could hear her, just in case. Another time, they'd done it in the box room they used as a study—four minutes, start to finish—with Lotte strapped into her bouncy chair in the bedroom next door, her chatter growing louder with every passing second. But mostly, these days, they were too tired even for that.

He went with Lina because it felt rude to say no. He went with her because he wanted to. The coffee shop was Italian and cramped and low-lit. They sat at a table in the window and discussed her paper, their respective universities, mutual friends, college, ambitions. An hour went past, more, and when it turned dark outside and they decided they'd order a bottle of red for old times' sake, he knew he was skipping out on the rest of the conference. "Are you happy?" she'd asked him at one point, out of the blue. And he'd hesitated. Only for a fraction of a second but she'd seen it. "Kids," he'd said. "They're amazing, miraculous. But . . . it bleeds you dry, parenting. Don't let anyone tell you different."

They were out in the street, blowing on their fingers and about to go their separate ways when she slipped her hand into his coat pocket and kissed him. He'd smelt the chocolate smell of her perfume, tasted the bitter tannin on her lips stained the color of sin. Is he being honest when he tells himself he didn't kiss her back? Was there a moment? A pause? An intention?

From nowhere, Grace is pushing roughly past him and out into the aisle. Too late he puts out a hand to stop her and he turns to see her headed for the door at the back. Facing front again he stands there, still mouthing the words to "The Coventry Carol," like that way maybe no one will notice. There's the church kneeler hanging in front of him and he would like to plough his fist into it. Christ, what has he done? Why didn't he just tell her? He has nothing to hide. Does he? He has to talk to her, to explain. Ben feels her parents' eyes on him as he scrambles from the pew and follows her out.

It's lighter outside than inside the church because of the snow. An unreal silver light, and he sees her up ahead right away, swamped in his coat and halfway along the church path.

"Grace, it's not what it looks like. I can explain!" In the dead calm of the snowscape his voice booms back at him.

"Are you hearing yourself?" Grace wheels round, skids on her heel, and nearly goes over. "Jesus Christ, all the clichés. *You* are a cliché." She jabs a finger in the air to accentuate her point.

"Lina's an old girlfriend, okay?" He's aware that he's raising his voice but he needs to get her to listen.

Grace pulls a face, like her eyes are going to jump from her head. "Oh, this just gets better."

He's close enough that he can smell the alcohol on her. They've both been drinking steadily all day, but he feels stone-cold sober now. "I didn't tell you about her because it was right before Lotte, and once I'd . . . once you'd . . . It just seemed so small then." He drags a hand across his forehead. "And then I didn't mention seeing her at the conference because . . ." He pauses. Why didn't he? Because Lina tried to kiss him? Because guilt? Because maybe for a moment her desire made him feel good? Because maybe for a split second, longer even, he wanted Lina right back? ". . . because there was nothing really to say."

Grace clutches her hair, like a silent scream, bends forward at the waist so she can better project her words. "Fuck you!" she roars.

Ben stops, stunned. She has never spoken to him like this before. It isn't that she doesn't swear: she loves to swear. She will swear at anyone and anything—her friends, the television, the neighbors' cats—but not like this. Not like she means it. He can see that she's shaking, furious.

"I gave up my job for this," she shouts. "For us. You think I'll ever get back in again? To that stupid white men's club? And now, what, I'm a non-person to you? A fucking baby minder? A *stay-at-home mum*?" She spits the words like they're cyanide.

There's a noise behind them, the heavy sound of the church door opening and falling shut. Ben turns, heart banging in his chest, to see Michael coming up the steps and along the short path toward them. He's wearing a red beanie that's ridden up, exposing the white hair above his ears, and he looks at Ben steadily with their eyes—Grace and Lotte's. He's almost drawn level with them when he slips in the snow. Instinctively, Ben and Grace jerk forward, put out their hands to steady him.

"Are you okay, Dad?" Grace asks.

"We can all hear you in there." His voice is low. "Your mother's mortified."

Ben pictures Anne in the church, fingering the onyx pendant at her neck, pulling her dark pink jacket tight around her.

"Go home, both of you," Michael says now, and Ben hears in the words a trace of the Cheshire accent that isn't usually there. "Before someone calls the police. Go home and sort this out. You're making a show of yourselves." And he turns and moves off down the path, back into the church.

They stand for a second across from each other. The color is high in Grace's cheeks, like she's been slapped. Then she starts to walk away. It's beginning to snow again and wet flakes fleck his face as he slides in the snow trying to keep pace with her.

She's turning onto the pavement and he sees her glance up at the church clock. "Merry Christmas," she murmurs.

"Nothing happened." He has his hand on her shoulder trying to make her look at him. "Nothing at all."

"Get off me." Her voice is a warning.

"What do you want me to do?" He turns his palms to the sky, like he's appealing to a higher force. "Grace? Tell me, I'll do it. I'll call her now if you want?" Snatching the phone from his pocket, he starts to punch in digits. "Look, I'm dialing the number . . . Here I am, this is me doing it . . ."

When she doesn't stop him, he throws his phone down into the snow, steps in front of her to block her path. "My God, Grace, is it not clear how much I love you? I bloody worship you. I mean, isn't it obvious?"

"No," she says, and she's moving round his body. "No, it really isn't."

"What do you want me to say? I'll say it. Grace? I'll swear on Lotte's life." He's keeping pace with her and he feels ridiculous proposing this, like he's a kid about to cut his arm and pledge blood brothers. But even so there's an instant before he does it, a fraction of a second when it crosses his mind that maybe it will jinx them. Because does it count, what happened? Did he cross a line? He covers his heart with his hand, presses hard against the muscle and bone he can feel through his clothes. "I swear on Lotte's life I didn't . . ."

"Sometimes I worry you think I trapped you." She says it so quietly he isn't sure he's heard her right. Her head is down and he has to strain to catch the words.

"That you might feel like you didn't have a free choice." She stops next to a low wall, drags her fingers across the pillowed snow.

"What?" he says, bewildered. "What are you talking about?"

"I'd only known you five minutes," she says, "and then *bam!*" She plunges her fist deep into the snow. When she withdraws her arm, white crystals cling to her sleeve up to the elbow.

Ben shakes his head. Then he laughs. He doesn't know what else to do. He thought he had her mapped. The topography of her mind, her body, inch by inch. But this? He doesn't know about this. They've done everything together. They've talked and talked endlessly about TV and books and politics and people and language and love, and she has never said this before. Not once. Something flares deep in him, the kick of a whisky shot swallowed in one gulp.

"What's wrong with you?" he asks, but he's talking as much to himself as to her. "You and Lotte are the best thing that ever happened to me." He stops, swallows. "But with or without her, I wanted you."

The snow is turning to sleet. Already it's starting to get slushy underfoot, the pristine surface darkening, dirtying. There's the sound of music, singing, coming from the church. In the gap between them, their breath steams the air.

"I will leave you, Ben, if you ever . . ." She lets the sentence hang. Her eyes are bright, snow-lit. "Know that I will leave," she says again. "That's all."

Now

GRACE HAS NO idea where she is. None. It is as if she's sleepwalked out of the wild and into a mahogany and gold gated community of manicured lawns and reinforced front doors. Security cameras dot the corners of each house. Porsches, Lexuses, Teslas are parked in graveled drives. She has been lost in thought—years away—and walking, walking on autopilot, and now she's hit the bottom of a dead-end road where there are tall gates, a sign prohibiting entry, and beyond the gates, a golf course.

Grace takes out her phone and types the street name into Google Maps. Then, pinching her fingers to the screen, she expands the view. She sees immediately that she's nowhere near where she expected to be, and it's all she can do not to sink to the ground where she's standing. She has taken a wrong turn, several wrong turns; she's come a mile in the wrong direction and she must have lost an hour. An *hour*. Maybe more by the time she gets back on track. That's it, she thinks. That is it. Give up, Grace. Go home.

Putting the cake on the pavement, she slumps down next to it. Her heel is sore, two of her toes are numb, and there's a shooting pain in her calf. She can feel a throb in her back that's spreading from her coccyx all the way up her spine; she doesn't know how she will ever get up again. She has her phone in her hand still and she swipes Google Maps shut. Then her thumb finds iCloud and before she can stop herself she's clicked. The video is there. It comes up straight away, starts to play.

"Mummy!" her little girl is saying. "A blutterfy . . ." Eyes fixed on the screen, Grace is mouthing the words ahead of time as if she's urging her on, as though if she doesn't do this her daughter might not say what she knows she's going to say next. "I love it, Mummy! . . . And I love you, Mummy." Now the camera zooms in so that her child's face is drawn toward her. There's her perfect apricot skin, her serious dark eyes, long lashes that look as though they've been dipped in black ink. The camera can't get close enough.

Grace can see from the map that the quickest way back to where she wants to be is to cut across the golf course. She doesn't stop to think. The cake in one hand, she hauls herself up and over the gates, using the Private Property sign as a foothold. There's a moment when she slips, has to grab for one of the molded spikes at the top of the gate and as she does this the cake box gets trapped, squashed between her chest and the metal bars. Two feet on the ground, she checks the damage. The box has crumpled at one edge, just a little, nothing she won't be able to press back into shape, hide under a strand of ribbon.

She's reached the far side of the course when she comes across a set of golf clubs standing in the middle of the path. Abandoned, she thinks. And as she's thinking it she dips a hand into the bag, helps herself to a club. Testing it on the ground she feels her spirits rise. The metal is cool to the touch and it's sturdy. She needs it: she's going to use it as a walking aid to propel her farther and faster to Lotte.

This time she's on the inside—she can go through the gate not over, and she has her hand up to the bolt when the shout comes. Too late, she turns instinctively. There are three golfers a hundred meters or so from her. They look to be in their seventies and they're wearing the pastel colors, the ironed trousers, the detergent-white sun visors of their tribe.

"That's my club!" one of the men shouts. Despite his age, he has a voice like a four-by-four revving at traffic lights. "You're taking my club."

There's a moment, a drawn-out second, when Grace eyes the men on the green, and then she hitches the dented cake box under her arm, hoists the golf club onto her shoulder. Blood throbbing in her veins, she walks through the gate without looking back.

Three Months Earlier

Grace Adams   Yesterday at 7:04

ENOUGH!

To: Ben Kerr

Ben—I can't do this anymore. I'm losing it.

Apparently being out at 2 a.m. on a school night is totally reasonable. Asking who she was with is totally unreasonable and an invasion of her privacy and I am insanely overprotective. The worst of all mothers. ALL her friends say so. Because they are fifteen and therefore the last word on this.

It's your turn to talk to her. I'm done.

HE HAS TAKEN Lotte to the Indian restaurant at the edge of Kilburn. The one she loves—the one they both love—with its emerald-painted walls, wicker maharaja chairs, and the holographic picture of a waterfall that looks from a certain angle as if it's flowing. A neutral space. Across from him she's studying the menu, although he knows she'll order like she always does, the lamb pasanda with pilau rice, garlic naan, and mint raita. And he's thinking about the fear behind the rage in Grace's email. He knows if he let himself he would feel it too. There's been another letter from school, and his daughter is now in the "red zone," whatever that means, but he's having a hard time believing it all. A hard time reconciling the Lotte sitting opposite him with this other Lotte who does not fit the blueprint of his child.

The waiter sets down a Coke and a bottle of Cobra, tucks the drinks tray under his arm, and takes their order. Ben's hand slips on the cool glass as he lifts his beer, swallows a mouthful.

"It's not okay, Lotte," he says, once the waiter has left.

She's sucking the lemon from her Coke and glances up, seems momentarily confused. Then she slow-blinks and flares her nostrils, like she's drawing in strength.

"I know you know that." Ben shifts in his chair and the wicker creaks. "Out that late, I mean."

"Yes, thank you. Mum already gave me the rape lecture. Which obviously was fierce."

He winces at "rape." He winces at her voice rinsed with sarcasm, disdain.

"I don't know who you were with, but Facebook, Instagram, all of that," he says, "you don't know who half these people actually are even if you think you do and—"

"Oh, my God, nobody has Facebook. Only old people." She cuts across him with dazzling teenage logic. "I understand the internet better than you. Just because Mum read one article in the *Guardian* about online grooming. I'm not an idiot."

Her words unseat him. How does she know this is coming from Grace? That she's practically given him a list to get through.

"Dad," Lotte is leaning forward over the table, and her tone is so condescending, it's almost pity, "we've been doing this in PSHE since, like, year seven."

"Okay," he says, because it's probably true that she understands all of this better than he does. He knows she sees it all, dreads to think what she has come across on the social-media platforms she's glued to, they're all glued to. *But even so, you have no idea*, he wants to say. "The thing is, Lotte—"

"Look, it was just a boy from school," she says. "Happy? Are we done? Can we talk about something else now?"

A boy from school. This is more than she has said to Grace. Suddenly he wants to shout, to demand who he is, this boy. And it shocks him, the force of his feelings that seem to have come from nowhere. Under the table he squeezes his hands into fists.

"Lotte . . ."

"Please don't ask me who, Dad, because it's none of your business, and please don't talk to me about consent," she murmurs. "I'm not ten."

There is something off about the way she's talking. Twitchy. She isn't quite meeting his eyes, and her tone is so brittle he has the feeling he could take her words and snap them in two.

He picks up his beer, changes his mind, places it back on the table. "You'd tell me if there was something bothering you—frightening you—wouldn't you? I wouldn't have to ask?"

She looks at him as if he's mad. Her eyes say, "I'm not going to dignify that with an answer," but he can see that her teeth are clenched, that she's holding her jaw tight.

"And skunk, ketamine . . ." Ben ploughs on because, according to Grace, according to the parent network, according to Radio 4, it's a thing already, they're not too young. Some of the kids are doing it. "You know they're psychoactive . . . Ketamine is a horse tranquilizer, you know this, right? You know that if you're out of your mind you aren't able to make sensible calls."

"Jesus." She has her elbows on the table, drops her head into her hands.

He's making a mess of this, he knows. *Out of your mind?* He sounds like his mother. He doesn't want to be having this conversation.

"I have to say this stuff, Lotte."

"Is everything okay?" The waiter has arrived at the table with their food.

Lotte lifts her head from her hands and nods but doesn't smile. There are white marks on her forehead where her fingers have pressed in. They watch in silence as the waiter sets out little metal dishes too hot to touch. The colors, the spices, the heady fragrances, they are edible works of art and Ben realizes how hungry he is.

He waits until they've filled their plates before he tries again. "If you don't tell us anything, we don't know. Do you see that? And if we can't trust you . . ." He lets the sentence hang.

Lotte forks rice and meat into her mouth and chews. "You sound like Mum." She says it like she had higher hopes for him, like she thought he'd do better.

She doesn't respect me, Grace had told him on the phone. *She talks to me like she thinks I'm an idiot. Like there's nothing I could possibly tell her she doesn't already know. It's so arrogant, but the way she does it . . . sometimes it makes me feel like she's got a point. And it's all reserved for me. She doesn't do it to you. I hear her, when you're FaceTiming. It's all cozy bonding over Tessa Violet and Tumblr, or whatever. Memes! I'm just the nagging old bag who doesn't get it . . .*

"How is Mum?" he asks.

Lotte shakes her head, shrugs.

And she brought up the fact that I left, Ben. She's never mentioned it before. The language Grace had used was opaque and it took him a moment, more than that, to grasp what she was talking about. And when he understood finally, he didn't know how to respond. *Okay* . . . he'd said at last. *No, it's not okay,* she'd replied.

Looking at Lotte across the table now, at her hair lying against her cheek, at the dimple that appears beneath one eye when she's concentrating, he's thinking about how she barely broke her stride when it happened. Or maybe they were too busy looking elsewhere to notice. She was just eight, but resilient like kids are, and by the time they looked up—weeks later, months later—she was getting on with her life, seemed to be handling it so well they didn't want to raise it with her. Why would they, if she was doing okay? He knows in his heart that was wrong. Maybe if he was honest with himself he'd admit he knew at the time. Perhaps the truth is he couldn't bear to do what was best for his child because it didn't suit him. Is this the fallout, the damage? Everything that's happening with her now? Is this the start of it?

Ben pulls in a breath, pushes it out slowly. "Lotte, there's something I wanted to talk to you about . . ." he starts to say.

But then from nowhere she lets her fork drop to her plate, puts a hand to her mouth. He sees in her face that she's about to cry. The attitude, the scorn, is gone. Her eyes are a mute scream.

"I wish you'd never split up." The words jolt from her, and she starts to cry. "I miss you, Daddy." She's trying to wipe the tears from her face but they keep coming—her cheeks are slippery with them. "It's wrong without you. It's not like home."

Ben feels his heart splintering as he plucks his napkin from his lap, pushes back his chair, and goes to her. "It's okay," he murmurs, and he takes her hot head in his hands, pulls her in to his chest. "It's okay, darling."

Just like that she's his little girl again. Like she's fallen and cut her knee, or another child has pushed her over in the sandpit. She has not called him "Daddy" in he doesn't know how long, and holding her he feels the loss of it—the loss of *her*—in the pit of him. But he understands, too, with a sudden clarity, something he already knows: that for all her talk, she needs him. And seeing her like this, feeling her loose and broken in his arms, he can't help thinking they're overreacting, Grace and him. That their panic at her secret life online—offline—is just that, *panic*. Because look at her, she's so young still, so innocent, still half in childhood, half out. Kissing the crown of her head, he strokes her hair. "The thing is sweetheart, your mum and I . . ."

But she's shaking her head to tell him to stop. "It doesn't matter," she says, and she pulls herself up and out of his arms, away from him. Wipes her nose with the back of her hand. "Honestly, I'm fine," she says. "I am, I get it."

"Lotte?" The moment is breaking. He wants to snatch it back.

"No," she says. "Please don't."

There's makeup ringing her eyes, smudging her cheekbones like fresh bruises. Like someone has punched her, he thinks. "You have a . . . Your mascara . . ." He makes small moons under his own eyes with his fingers.

She doesn't look at him as she gets up from the table, heads to the toilet. And he's sitting back down when next to her plate her phone pings, lights up with a new notification. She is entitled to her privacy, Ben thinks, drumming his fingers on his thighs. But then something seizes him. Checking over his shoulder, he leans across the table and nudges the phone, angling it toward him so he can read the message.

> **leyla.nicol_** OMG yass *keyboard smash* LOTTEEEEE ur famous bb! cray crayyy u be trending girl! GCSEs lol who needs themmmm with a bod like yours and a shit ton of followers amiright? 70K views and counting!!! hashtaginfluencerrrrrrrr!*!*!

Ben snatches his hand back, like he's touched something sharp. His elbow catches the glass of beer, knocking it over. Amber liquid spreads across the thick white tablecloth. The waiter is at his shoulder before he's had a chance to react, a clutch of paper napkins in his hand, and Ben is apologizing but his mind is elsewhere. He isn't sure what he's just read. A language in half code, a cipher that is foreign to him.

As soon as the waiter is gone, he checks the phone again. The screen has gone dark but he sees the words anyway, stamped somewhere behind his eyes as though he's taken a photograph of them. . . . *with a bod like yours . . . shit ton of followers . . . 70K views . . . influencerrrrr!!!* There's the pungent smell of the food left on the table that's suddenly too strong. The impression that someone has just turned the background music up way too loud in there.

2008

WALKING IN THROUGH the door at Soho House on Greek Street, Grace feels a fraud. And maybe she just imagines it, but the woman at the desk gives her a look like she has the stench of fish fingers and sickly-syrupy kids' medicine about her, as though she should be grabbing her afternoon coffee at a church hall playgroup, not here.

Upstairs, she's shown to her table. It's like dusk in here, everything painted dark, and she has the dislocating sense she's stumbled into Picasso's Blue Period. As she's sliding into the banquette, she spots Marie on the other side of the dining room. It's been five years since they worked together, five years since she's seen her in the flesh, and Marie is looking good—she's looking young, which pretty much amounts to the same thing. She's wearing a navy silk blouse and palazzo pants, her bleached hair chopped into her trademark pixie cut, and she's talking to three women seated at another table. Nodding in Grace's direction, she acknowledges her arrival. Grace makes to get up and join her but Marie holds up a finger. She actually does this. Like, stop. Don't come any closer; I'm into something important here: you'll have to wait. Something inside Grace collapses.

In the end it was the thought of Ben's mother's long-ago words, slicing through the thick stone wall of the Scottish house, that had prompted her to dial Marie's number. . . . *She's pretty, darling . . . just, you know, it would be nice to see a bit of personality . . .* It was spite, basically, that propelled her. Revenge. And Grace is trying to keep that in mind now, sitting there awkwardly, not knowing what to do with her hands, her head, her whole body. She is thirty-four years old but feels twenty-one again, as though she is someone with zero experience waiting to interview for a first job. In this, she understands, she is the antithesis of Marie, who, in the time Grace has been away, has advanced from assistant to executive producer. These two words had been like small stab wounds to Grace's eyes when she'd searched up her former colleague online, found a glossy picture with Marie's title in bold type, an intimidating paragraph detailing her achievements beneath. Glancing around the room Grace pretends to take in the paintings on the walls, like she couldn't be more relaxed, sitting here alone. Like she is simply indulging in a bit of me-time.

Sorry, Marie mouths, crossing the dining room toward her at last. And she rolls her eyes, winds her finger in the air. She's drinking champagne even though it's four o'clock in the afternoon. Grace is aware there was a time when this wouldn't have seemed like something transgressive.

"This is lunch," she tells Grace, as she seats herself in the chair opposite, brings the glass to her lips. "Join me?"

"Why not?" Grace smiles, although the thought of it makes her a little panicky, sickish. She's already asking herself how she'll get through bedtime later.

"So where the heck have you been, stranger?" Marie asks, as she signals to the waitress, points at her glass, and holds up two fingers.

Where has she been? It feels like an existential question. I don't know, she wants to say. Honestly, I have no idea. She'd extended her maternity leave once and then again until she hadn't gone back at all. And now Lotte is five, she's started school. The Sleep is finally—*finally*—sorted. She and Ben have their own bed back. They have sex on Friday nights without fail. Almost without fail. It's not spontaneous but it's something, and it's good, always. Things are good. But recently she's felt as if there's a gap in her, a space, a void. She is starting to feel the itch of resentment toward Ben too. His steady climb up the ranks at work, unimpeded by the arrival of *their* child. The global linguistics conferences he's invited to speak at, the cultural-exchange junkets to international universities.

"I've been focusing on the translations up to now," Grace tells her. She doesn't say that it's soul-destroying work she cranks out at the kitchen table. She doesn't say she would ask for a fraction of the amount she used to be paid just to feel the high-octane rush of TV again. Hell, she'd probably do it for free. That for all the artifice and egos it was a dream job, even though maybe she hadn't known it at the time. She hadn't *hated* all the attention. Some of it—the more toxic elements—yes. But it had been words. Curious, bewitching, rare words and, not to put too fine a point on it, she would do almost anything to spend sanctioned time exclusively in the company of adults again.

The waitress comes and saves her, setting down their drinks. The glass in front of her is tall, slim, cold-frosted, and suddenly there is nothing Grace wants more than to feel the hit of alcohol behind her eyes. "Cheers," she murmurs, taking a gulp.

"And so, what?" Marie raises her eyebrows, her whole face stretches upward. "You're looking to come back to telly?" The way she says it makes Grace feel as though she's putting in an audacious application for the next space mission.

"I'd love to." She smiles too wide, feels the squeak of her incisors against her mouth, which has gone dry.

"Interesting," Marie says, tapping her nails on the side of her glass. "And are you thinking of any more children?"

"I didn't want the one I've got!" The words gurgle from her, a laughing shield. It's her stock response and it's funny because it's both true and also obviously isn't. At least, she finds it funny. Some people don't. But either way it's great for deflecting the many, *many* queries she's getting on this, the nudge-nudge questions people have been asking with increasing regularity since Lotte turned three. The fact is she honestly doesn't know how to reply. They don't talk about it, she and Ben. She doesn't really know why. Maybe it's to do with the fact they were so brutally hijacked by Lotte's arrival, that and their ongoing PTSD from her years of refusing to sleep.

"Okay, Grace, I'm going to be honest with you." Marie pauses. "You kinda missed your moment." She scrunches up her face as if she's tasted something bad.

Grace blinks, swallows.

"But the show? The tabloids loved me. I went down well," she hears herself say.

"That's old currency." Marie shrugs.

Grace nods, forces a smile. There's the creep of blood up her neck. It isn't that she'd expected to jump back in right where she left off, of course she hadn't. But this outright *no*? She hadn't anticipated that either. Pressing her thumb into the prongs of the fork on the table in front of her, she feels the flesh dent. She wonders whether if she presses hard enough she could pierce the skin. She imagines the pain would feel good.

"Also, it will suck you dry." Marie is saying now. "The hours, the intensity. I mean, you forget. Family-friendly it is not."

She shouldn't have come. She's Norma bloody Desmond, a delusional has-been. She has humiliated herself. Marie will tell this tale all over Telly Land. The fact that not-so-*Amazing Grace Adams* hadn't understood she'd forfeited her shot. How soon before she can get up and leave? She just wants to make it stop.

Grace resists the urge to check her watch while they chat briefly about old colleagues—who's left the industry, who's ended up where, and as soon as she thinks she can get away with it she drains her drink, makes her excuses.

As she's getting up from the table, Marie stands too. She's trapped between the chair and the table so that her body is a little bent, and there's an awkwardness in her all of a sudden that Grace has never witnessed before.

"The other day when she fell over, my little girl went to the nanny, not me." Marie is twisting a button at the neck of her blouse as she speaks. "Even though I was standing much closer to her when it happened."

That's all she says. She doesn't put any context around it like where they were, how the child fell, whether there was blood. Quick, simple words, but the color is high in her cheeks.

You have a daughter? Grace wants to ask, because she hadn't known. But she understands it isn't the point.

When their eyes meet something passes between them.

"Ain't no winners in this." Marie twists her mouth to the side.

Grace knows that the woman is gifting her something that is costing her. And maybe it's the afternoon drinking, but before she can stop herself she's moving toward Marie, putting her arms around her, although this isn't something they've ever done. Marie is more an air-kissing kind of woman. There's a beat, and then she feels Marie's fingers press lightly against her ribs. Her skin smells of bergamot and smoke.

"Yup, it's a Gordian knot," Grace murmurs into the top of her shoulder.

Marie lets go, gives her a look, like, *What are you talking about?*

"From the Alexander the Great legend," Grace clarifies. "It's impossible to untangle." And then she turns and leaves, without looking back.

Now

As the day goes on the heat is solidifying and she's thirstier than she's ever been before. Her throat is stripped, her mouth, her lips feel fuzzy with it, swollen. By the time she reaches a newsagent she's having difficulty tamping down the panic—the urge to drink has overtaken her. It's all she can think about and she's in through the door and selecting a bottle of water from the fridge, placing it on the counter with a single-minded focus that's burning as bright as the carcinogenic sunshine outside. She's getting out her card to pay when the man behind the counter points at a sign, written in ballpoint and sellotaped to the till:

Minimum charge on card: £10

"I don't have any cash," Grace tells him. She wants to explain that she gave all her money to the woman on Suicide Bridge. But if she has more words they're stranded in the desert of her mouth.

The man shrugs, shakes his head. He has a thick dark beard, which seems to move a little slower than his chin.

It runs through her mind that in her pocket there's the water pistol she refilled at a dog bowl outside the Spaniards Inn. She wonders if she could put from her mind the grit and dog slobber and dead insects and drink that. Nausea rises in her and she drops her head into her hands right there at the counter.

Someone reaches round her then. She feels the shift in the air and thinks that the man with the beard is moving on to his next customer. There's a light touch on her arm, and when she doesn't react it comes again. Glancing up, she sees a woman standing over her. She's older, with dyed brown hair that's showing gray at the roots, large eyes set far apart in her face. In one movement, the woman places a pound coin in the bearded man's palm and hands Grace the water she tried to buy.

"There you go, love," she says. "You look like you could do with a drink." And then she laughs at the double meaning of what she's just said.

Grace is all set to refuse, but the woman has turned from her already and she's starting to pack her own shopping into a wrinkled Sainsbury's bag, as though there's nothing unusually kind in what she's done. When Grace thanks her, the woman smiles distractedly over her shoulder.

She's sitting on a low wall outside the shop, gulping the water and telling herself she must save some for the rest of her journey, when the woman comes out. The cake box is on one side of her, the golf club leaning up against the wall.

"Let me get a look at your foot there," the woman says, and she's pointing at Grace's heel.

It takes Grace a moment to understand what she's talking about. But when she pivots her ankle she sees straight away that blood has seeped through the paper napkin she has wedged in there. It's spreading across her sock in the shape of a butterfly.

The woman tuts softly. "And here?" she says, indicating Grace's arm.

Grace twists her arm so she can see. Her elbow has been skinned. The raw flesh is bloodied and speckled with dirt. What must this woman think of her?

"You've been in the wars." The woman digs in her handbag, bringing out a packet of tissues. A large plaster.

She has dark skin and a slight accent, she's maybe Turkish, and she's speaking phrases Grace would associate with her granny and there's comfort in it.

"Once a mum, always a mum." The woman waggles the plaster at Grace. And then without asking she seats herself on the wall next to her. It occurs to Grace, as the woman takes her foot in her hand, that maybe she's mad. Either that, or some kind of twenty-first-century fairy godmother who has fallen through the gaps in a story.

"Can I?" the woman asks now. But she doesn't wait for an answer as she eases the shoe from Grace's foot and peels off her sock, then the crimson-shot tissue.

And Grace lets her. Because she is too tired, too relieved to object. And because she's thinking about the little red shoes, size five. She's feeling her daughter's small foot in her hands, toes wriggling as she fastens the silver buckles; she can smell the soft leather. That's when she starts to judder. A throb that starts in her sole and travels up through her heel, her ankle, her calf, her knee, her thigh. She is sure the woman must be able to see her shake.

"I have a daughter about your age," the woman says, as she wets a tissue, dabs at the wound. "Lives in Canada now. And my son, he's a nurse. I've just come from seeing him at the hospital."

It's strange to feel her touch, this woman. But her blunt tenderness, her straightforward compassion loosens something in Grace and she gives in to it. Lets the woman's gentle words drift in and around her. *Once a mum . . .* The phrase loops and comes back to her and she weighs it in her mind.

And then, like she's come unhooked from herself, she's back at the old house, the one up by the station, with the pale green front door. Her mum is in the lounge talking to a friend. It's the first time she's got out of bed in three days, which is a thing she does sometimes. Something frightening and quiet, unspoken. *She's very tired. You're to leave her be,* her dad had told them the first morning she didn't come down. Not looking at them, her and Cate, as he put bread in the toaster, spooned coffee granules into a mug. It's what he always said when it happened. Word for word with no explanation.

The door to the lounge is open a crack, just enough so that twelve-year-old Grace can see the edge of her mum through it. She's sitting forward on the big sofa with her cardigan pulled tight around her, the sky blue one that's soft as clouds, and Jill from down the road is across from her. Grace knows this because she let her mum's friend in earlier, but she can't see her—the gap in the door isn't wide enough. Grace is hardly breathing because her mum is talking quietly and the breath is too loud in her ears. There's a tickle in her throat from the not breathing and she knows that any minute she'll have to cough and then she'll give herself away. She's about to move from the door when she hears her mum say, "I should never have had children." For a moment she thinks she mustn't have heard right. But then her mum says it again. "I should never have had them. It's too hard. I can't do it, I'm failing them. They'll be scarred from all this—they'd be better off without me. If I'd known I'd never have had them, Jill, I wouldn't."

Her mum's friend starts to speak, a low murmuring, but Grace doesn't hear what she says because she takes flight. A force is propelling her body, her legs. For a second she thinks she'll go and find Cate, who'll be in her bedroom listening to her Walkman. Instead, she finds herself running, running down the hall and through the kitchen, out of the back door and into the garden. And she doesn't stop, even when she's reached the end of the alleyway that runs behind the houses on her street, because the words are still banging against the inside of her head and she needs to outrun them.

It's the reason Grace didn't want children, this overheard conversation. She'd made the decision there and then: she would not be like her mother. She was afraid that she, too, would not be able to do it, that maybe it was something passed down, a failing in her family. That maybe she was partly to blame for the struggle, the misery. And afterward she hadn't questioned it, this long-held belief that had grown rigid in her. Not until Lotte.

It used to make her sad when her mum shut herself away in that darkened room. Sad and scared and hopeless. She loved her so much, but she remembers thinking other mothers weren't like that and it felt like a dirty secret, something she couldn't discuss even with her sister. Later, when she understood that her mum couldn't help it, that it was a chemical thing, it felt better in theory but not in the moment. Never in the moment.

And now? Sitting here on the low wall next to this woman—this mother of all mothers with the hands of an angel—she understands that in the end the curse got her, too.

"I'm a terrible mother."

At first Grace isn't sure she's said it out loud. But then the woman stills her hands, nods slowly.

"How old are your children?"

There's a stopped moment, and Grace falters. "Sixteen," she says at last. "My daughter's sixteen today. It's her birthday." She adjusts the cake box on the wall next to her. There's a streak of mud across the top, and she licks her finger, tries to wipe it off. "She's living with her dad." The sentence lets loose from her mouth like a shower of gravel. She can't look at the woman as she says it.

"It's the hardest age." The woman presses the plaster into place, pats her foot to let her know she's done. "Take it from someone who knows. But they come back, you know."

"It's my fault, though." Grace picks up her sock, tries to put it on but can't muster the energy. "I don't remember a time when I didn't feel tired, and there's this dread in me constantly because I have no idea what I'm doing." She closes her eyes briefly, opens them again. She doesn't say that she is heartsick, lonely, that she just wants it to stop. "The thing is, I'm trying to read between the lines all the time and it's exhausting. All the tech—Instagram, Snapchat, whatever. This secret life they live that we know nothing about." She glances up, shrugs her shoulders. "And sometimes I have so much rage it scares me."

The woman smiles, shakes her head. "That's not rage, darling. That's your fear, your grief exploded." She pinches her fingers together, then springs them apart so that her empty hands are stars. "You do the best you can. We all do." She says it like it's a simple fact, like *easy as that*. Then, twisting her mouth a little, she adds, "You won't be a slave to the Change forever, you know. I'm guessing you're already on the road to being set free?" She's exaggerating the words, like she's some kind of TV evangelist. "It's a nightmare right now, yes, but there is hope out the other side and it's a blessed relief. Believe me."

But you don't understand, Grace wants to tell her, as she watches the woman put the tissues back into her bag. Notices her awkward movement, the way she clutches her hip as she pushes herself off the wall.

"You'll need to clean them up when you get home." She's pointing at Grace's ankle, her elbow. Her manner is brisk now like she needs to get on.

"Thank you," Grace murmurs. She wants to say more, but she can't. The kindness has undone her finally.

The woman comes toward her then, takes Grace's face in her hands. Firmly, so that her cheeks feel squashed. Close up like this, there are dazzling amber jewels in her eyes.

"I know you feel like no one sees you," the woman says, and her breath is sweet, like lilac. "I'm here telling you, I see you."

Three Months Earlier

GRACE IS SITTING on a plastic chair in the waiting room and she's agitated. She's been here twenty minutes already, watching for her name to come up on the electronic screen, jerking her head up each time it beeps, signaling that a new patient has been called. She's increasingly convinced that she's fallen off the list somehow, that they've forgotten to input her details. In her hand is the leaflet the receptionist has given her and that she can't believe she's holding. She feels like it's something she should be passing to the old woman sitting across from her with one swollen ankle in a support stocking. And she's only half reading it, skipping the bits she doesn't want to think about—the Hobson's choice of cancer versus cancer as though, really, it has nothing to do with her, when she sees him come in.

Grace stuffs the leaflet under her thighs, sits on it. She's staring straight ahead but the whole of her left side is fizzing as though somehow his nerves have fused with hers across the space between them. And she's wondering whether he can feel it too. She won't—she can't—look across at him; she thinks her body will give her away. It's the first time she's seen him since they met on her street, and her mind flashes again to that place. His thumb at her temple, the small scar on his cheekbone, the smell of cigarettes and wool. The way he studied her face as if he was trying to find something lost, how it had both intoxicated and disquieted her. Sitting there, she feels the heat rise in her.

Out of the corner of her eye, she can see him moving up the queue for Reception, and when she's certain he's moved forward enough that he will have his back to her, she looks up. At the same moment he turns. Instantly she sees that it isn't him, it isn't Nate. The man in the queue isn't even remotely like him—he's a good ten years older for a start. He has a similar build, the same fair hair, but that's where the likeness stops. Grace blinks, looks away. She is delusional. She's like a fourteen-year-old with an inappropriate and embarrassing crush. Except, except . . . the way he touched her, the way he looked at her . . . When the electronic screen beeps she jumps. This time it's her name, *Grace Adams. Room 13.*

The doctor is tapping away at her computer as she comes through the door. She's a few years older than Grace, short hair and a weekend-hiker look to her.

"How can I help?" The woman doesn't stop typing, sighs out the words like it's a bit of an inconvenience Grace being here at all.

Where to start? Grace thinks, as she seats herself awkwardly to the side of the desk. A part of her wants to say, According to my husband— whom I no longer live with—my daughter is TikTok famous, whatever that means, for not wearing very many clothes and mouthing along to songs. Apparently, she's gone viral because she dances illegally on scaffolding, which you can imagine I'm thrilled about. I only know all this because my husband saw a text on her phone calling her an *influencer* with a *hot bod*. She has tens of thousands of followers, which you'd think

I might have known *as her mother*, but I guess I haven't really been in the loop there! And she's seeing a boy she won't let me meet, won't even talk to me about, a boy she may or may not be having sex with. Oh, and two days ago I masturbated thinking about a man who is probably young enough to be my son and who also happens to be my child's teacher. I thought I saw him just now out in the waiting room, but it turns out I imagined it. *Is there a hormone patch for that?*

Always gynecological, Grace thinks, as she stands behind the curtain peeling off her clothes beneath her waist. Always. Why, just for once, couldn't she be in here for an issue with her arm, her foot, her finger? And should she leave her socks on? Does she usually? She decides that she will, then regrets it as soon as she's climbed onto the bed and is lying on the creased paper sheet. Two thin black M&S ankle socks make a mockery of her semi-nakedness, or the other way around, she isn't sure which, just that she's shivery, vulnerable, ridiculous. It goes through her mind that Nate would turn and run if he saw her like this. Either that or he'd stand there and laugh because she's ludicrous. She is old.

"Okaaay." The doctor announces herself with unconvincing heartiness as she swooshes in through the curtain. She adjusts Grace's knees like they're entirely detached from her patient, wrestles with the angle of her lamp.

"It's pretty cold out this morning," Grace finds herself saying.

"And relax," the woman says tightly.

There's the usual feeling of panic while the doctor is examining her, because what might she find? Grace fixes her eyes on the halogen light in the ceiling above, tries not to think about the ocular damage it might cause, attempts to send her mind away. She has not even discussed the whole TikTok thing with Lotte, although it lightly poisons the air between them. She hasn't mentioned again the boy she may or may not be sleeping with. The truth is she has disengaged from her daughter, the same way she has disengaged in recent months from the news. Gradually, gradually she has stopped watching, reading about the ripped-up things that make her angry, fearful, sad. The things that highlight her impotence and erase her, that make her feel her voice has been stolen. And she's ashamed, guilty at this withdrawal on both counts, but it's what she has to do. It's her shield, the only protection she has, because although she knows she should rise above it—she should act her *age*—she is not robust enough to withstand the near-constant assault.

But then there are moments, small blasts of sunshine, when her child is back. "Leyla says you remind her of that actress," Lotte said, the other day, standing behind her in the kitchen as Grace loaded washing into the machine. "The one with the red hair. She was in *Hunger Games* . . . so, you know, it's not all over for you, Mum."

Grace could hear the smile in her voice and she'd bubbled up, pathetically pleased because she knew the actress was considered hot, but mostly because she understood that her daughter was offering herself up. "I was a TV starlet once, of course," Grace had replied, her voice a sigh, as she'd straightened up. "You ruined that."

And Lotte had rolled her eyes at this well-worn joke between them. "Lol," she'd said sarcastically. "But please stop. I knew I should never have mentioned it."

Those times she was perfect. And Grace would have to hold on to herself, stop herself from reaching out to touch her child's perfect skin, to stroke her perfect hair, to kiss the crown of her perfect head, her cheeks, her eyes, the palms of her hands. Sometimes she did it anyway, hiding herself behind a mask of humor, an addict covering her tracks. Hair roughly ruffled, or a cheek pinched too deep, too-long exaggerated kisses on the back of her head. Just so she could touch her child. And Lotte would flinch theatrically, but meaning it, and pull away. "Get off me . . ."

"So." The doctor is snapping off the spot lamp, peeling the rubber gloves from her hands. "It looks as though you may have an autoimmune disorder of the vulva."

Come again? Grace thinks. Because surely that is not a thing. But there's that sick feeling inside as she swings her legs off the bed, searches for her knickers, which she's hidden under her jeans so that the doctor wouldn't see them lying limp on the chair, as if that way she might preserve some dignity in all this.

The doctor is back at her computer when Grace emerges from behind the curtain. She mumbles a Latin word that Grace doesn't catch but assumes is her diagnosis. She opens her mouth to ask the doctor to repeat it—she knows she'd understand the Latin—but the doctor is already talking at her.

"It's basically a condition where your vulva is slowly subsumed by your vagina," the doctor says, swiveling in her chair and clasping her fingers so that her hands form a single fist. "I mean, I don't know what your vagina looked like before," she says slightly crossly, like that's somehow Grace's fault, "but I can see there are some areas where things seem to have adhered and shouldn't have."

Grace feels her pulse kick a little harder but she must have a mystified look on her face because the doctor elucidates.

"It's like your vagina is eating itself."

Grace blinks. Did she just hallucinate that?

"And linked to this condition is a slightly raised chance of contracting cancer, we're talking one percent . . ."

And that's it. She's said the C-word and Grace doesn't hear any more. She's vaguely aware that the doctor is quoting statistics at her, percentages, something about steroids, her age . . . but her mind is swooping in and out of her chest with her breath and she just wants to get out of there. Grace is and isn't in the room as the doctor prints out a prescription and hands it to her, suggests she make an appointment with the women's health team to discuss her other symptoms on the way out. "It might be you'll want to consider HRT," the doctor tells her.

"Thank you," Grace hears herself say, in a stupid singsong voice, as she makes for the door. As though the doctor has passed her a check for a generous amount rather than a prescription for vaginal steroids, a warning that she's a cancer risk. "Thank you," she repeats, as she shuts the door quietly, politely, behind her. Her too-loud shoes squeak on the floor tiles as she makes her way back down the corridor, trying to process what has just happened. She's thinking about her stalling body, about everything she has lost. This condition she apparently has that sounds made up: an autoimmune disorder of the *vulva*. She could almost laugh, except that it's all too, too hard. "Give up, Grace," she murmurs, into the empty echo of the corridor. There's no point. Just give up.

2012

GRACE IS GONE. She's left him a note on the kitchen table and that's how he knows. The first he knows. This is not a note that says *Please get toothpaste* or *Lotte karate pickup 6:15*. The kind of note that seems to belong to a past life. A before. And he is an idiot, because how did he not see this coming? He could have stopped it. But he didn't, and he has no idea how he's supposed to deal with it, how he's supposed to hide his anguish from his eight-year-old daughter, who'll be down for her breakfast at any moment.

He's called Grace's phone ten, maybe twenty times but it's ringing out and now he's sitting here reading the words over and over with that sick feeling inside. *I can't stay . . . I can't breathe in this house . . . Tell Lotte I love her . . . that it isn't her fault . . . this isn't a choice . . .* It's the most she's said to him, the most she has communicated in weeks, these few sentences scribbled on a piece of blue paper taken from Lotte's art drawer. Because Grace is no longer speaking. Except to Lotte. Language, the force between them, their superpower, has evaporated. Shut off overnight so that now there's just silence.

Ben bites down on his lip until there's the sharp rust taste, and he's pulling his fuggy mind through the past twelve hours, trying to unpick them, and he can't. They're sleeping in separate bedrooms and he drank too much again last night, pretty much passed out rather than fell asleep so he didn't hear her get up, didn't hear her leave. *Tell her I'll be back . . .* He is clinging to these words. Of everything she's written, this. Because it means she plans to return, and of course she does because she won't leave Lotte, he knows this. Whatever else she might do she won't do that. He's certain of it. He's pretty sure he's certain.

Behind him there's movement in the air and Lotte wanders in. He hasn't heard her on the stairs, her ninja tread, this new restraint in her that means she appears from nowhere, like a ghost, making him jump. A change he doesn't want to dwell on because it's easier that way, easier to pretend she's doing okay. That because she's a kid, she's in the moment with everything, so he doesn't have to worry, not really. She has her nightie on, the one with the tiny tessellated elephants, and she's so skinny it's like they don't feed her. Straight up and down, head to toe, and legs that look as if they might snap. Her hair is white-blond still—even though everyone said it would have turned brown by now—and it's crazy from sleep, like deranged clouds, so that his heart hurts to look at her.

"Where's Mummy?" she asks, rubbing the sleep from her eyes.

Ben snatches the note from the table, stuffs it into the waistband of his shorts. *Make it okay for her.* The scrawled sentence flashes in front of his eyes and, all of a sudden, he's furious with Grace. The fury is so huge it's like something entirely separate from him, a whole other entity. How? he wants to shout at his wife, wherever the hell she is. How am I supposed to make it okay for her? And, yes, it is a *choice.* You. Have. Made. A. Choice. The words she has written make him want to pick up the chair he's sitting on, hurl it against the wall. He can hear the smashed-up sound of it, see the wood splintering. *Where are you, Grace?*

"Mummy has a work thing," he says. "She had to leave early. And we're going to be late, sleepyhead." He's trying to keep his voice light but the intonation is all wrong, the sentences claggy in his mouth. "We need to get you ready for school quick sticks, madam."

She's asking question after question as he shakes Rice Krispies into a bowl, adds milk, takes a spoon from the drawer. *When is she coming back and who is she with and why didn't she say goodbye?* A rat-a-tat-tat of language that's like a hammer and chisel against his brain. He answers as vaguely as he can: he doesn't want to lie; he doesn't want to alarm her.

"Now, eat," he says, as he sets the bowl on the table, brushes the hair from her face.

Moving over to the counter, he flips up the lid of his laptop. There's the usual avalanche of morning emails and he scans them quickly, searching for something—anything—that might have come from Grace. He's telling himself there's every chance she'll have been in touch already, that she'll have changed her mind, she's already headed home. But there's nothing.

He's about to shut the lid when he notices a message in his junk dated a few days before. *Where were you?* it says in the subject line, and he's about to dismiss it, but then he sees who it's from and something flares in him.

Lina Bell   Tuesday at 8:12

Where were you?

To: Ben Kerr

Hey Ben. Was hoping I might see you at the conference last week. My first in five years and can you please tell me where the heck that time has gone? Anyway, feel cheated as I thought you were on the program?! Drop me a line, let's catch up, okay? I'm down again next month. Lina x

It's the first time he's heard from her in years. Five years, he supposes, going by what she's said in her email. And despite himself, despite everything that's going on, or maybe because of it, Ben's mind is pulled back to the dark Italian café in Bloomsbury. To the hours and hours they'd talked, to the freezing street that smelt of burned coffee and diesel, to the chocolate and tannin taste of her mouth on his. Then his mind spools back further still, and he's picturing the night he first met her at a post-grad social. He remembers strip lighting, warm white wine, limp finger food. And afterward how they'd fucked drunkenly, hopelessly, up against the blocky white humanities building. There was frost on the ground and her bare shoulders where her shirt had come loose. And he'd traced his finger clumsily down her neck, along her collarbone, joining the dots of the moles scattered there.

"Daddy?"

Lotte is staring at him.

"Are you okay?" she asks.

Lotte has put down her spoon and he can see she's hardly eaten. There's a beige sludge smeared around her bowl that makes him nauseous. He pushes Lina from his mind, glances at the clock on the wall. Have a bit more, he wants to say, but he knows she'll shake her head. Grace would insist. Would have insisted. But he doesn't have the energy for the battle. She's so thin, he thinks again. Is she too thin? He makes a mental note to keep an eye on this, to register what she's eating, or rather not eating, because he knows he hasn't been noticing her enough.

"Right." He claps his hands, and he can feel that his mouth is smiling but not his eyes, because he has rocks in him. Gray and weighted and dragging. "Let's do this. Upstairs, clothes on, teeth brushed. I'm timing you. We've got fifteen minutes tops, okay?"

As soon as Lotte has left the room he takes the blue paper from his waistband, smooths it out. And the action must have released Grace's perfume from where she's touched the page, because he catches the scent of her. The coconut and tobacco smell of her face cream that is so familiar he scarcely notices it anymore. A memory slams at him, then. Grace is standing in front of the cooker, her body jackknifed over, and she's ripping at her hair with her hands. "Don't do anything stupid, Grace," he's pleading with her. "Please, Lotte needs you." And then louder, because he can't seem to get her attention and he doesn't dare touch her in this moment they're in: "*I* need you, Grace."

Now

SHE'S GETTING CLOSER. Any minute now she will pop out onto Finchley Road. There's that evening feel to things, an agitation in the air, as she walks past a man in a tight suit locking up an estate agent, a woman with dip-dyed hair scribbling specials on a chalkboard outside a tapas bar. Up ahead, a man with a guitar strapped to his back is coming up the steps from a basement flat. Instantly, Nate Karlsson flashes through her mind. But she shakes her head, dispels the thought.

Grace guesses it's maybe just after six but she's no longer checking the time because she doesn't want to know—and also because her phone is almost out of charge. Down to 2 percent last time she looked and she's trying to save the battery just in case.

The golf club has come into its own. This far into the journey she's leaning her weight on it with each step. She's like one of those smug hikers, swinging their poles as if they're turbocharged. Except she's more of an anti-hiker. A too-slow, lopsided, half-collapsed kind. Her body is a site of pain and her mind . . . She isn't sure where her mind is at; she isn't entirely certain, at this moment, of who she is. There's just the sense that she has passed through several different versions of herself as she has walked, shape-shifting like the fickle city landscape around her.

What has stopped her giving up? Not just today, but before. Before today and after . . . She catches the thought, buries it. Lotte, of course. Her daughter has stopped her. She could never, she would never . . . No matter how bad things get, there is always Lotte.

Turning onto the main road, she decides this is the moment to call Ben. To let him know she's still on her way, just a little further behind schedule than she would have liked, and can he please tell Lotte she hasn't forgotten her. She's mapping these words in her head when her phone starts to vibrate. Juggling the cake box, the golf club, she pulls it from her pocket. She doesn't know the number, it's not someone in her contacts, but she picks up anyway because her instant thought, as it always is, is that it might be something to do with her child.

There's a man's voice at the end of the line, but now that she's on the main road she can't make out what he's saying over the sound of the traffic.

"I can't hear you. Hold on." Grace maneuvers the golf club so that it's clamped between her knees, traps the phone against her shoulder, sticks a finger in the other ear.

"Okay," she says. "Try again. Hello."

"Am I speaking to Mrs. Adams?"

She doesn't recognize the voice.

"Yup," she says. "Yes."

"This is Sergeant Davis. I'm calling from the Metropolitan Police."

Her head goes dizzy.

"Is it my daughter? Has something happened?" The words spurt from her.

"No." The police officer sounds confused. "No, Mrs. Adams, I'm contacting you because I need to ask, are you the owner of a blue Peugeot estate, registration number KV68 TFK?"

Grace closes her eyes, opens them again, tries to steady the jumping in her lungs. The car. It seems days ago now, weeks even, since she switched off the engine, got out, and started to walk. She begins to nod, even though she's aware the man can't see her.

"It is my car, yes," she says at last.

"We found your vehicle abandoned earlier today, Mrs. Adams, and traced your number via the DVLA. Can I ask were you the driver of the car at around midday today?"

"No, I . . ." Grace starts to say. "Well, I suppose technically I was driving, yes, but . . ."

"We have several witnesses who have described a woman in her late forties getting out of the car before leaving it in stationary traffic."

There's a split second when all Grace can think is *late* forties? Because she knows she's having a bad day but she's forty-five, for Christ's sake. Slap-bang in the middle of her forties, nowhere near the end. And anyhow surely—*surely*—she can pass for early forties at the very least. She goes hot with shame. On top of everything else she is failing at aging too.

"I have to tell you, Mrs. Adams, that this is a serious offense and . . ."

"I'm having a miscarriage," she hears herself say. And even as the words are coming out of her mouth she is appalled. She has no idea why she's said it. "I had to leave my car there because I'm losing my . . ." Grace falters, she can't go on. A smile that isn't a smile stretches across her teeth. And then she finds that she's starting to cry as if it's true. As if at that moment, standing in the middle of Finchley Road, six lanes of traffic in front of her, with a golf club gripped between her knees, a bashed-up cake box under one arm, she is bleeding out. Right there in the street. "Sorry," she murmurs. "It's just . . . I'm losing my baby," she tells the officer now. "I've lost my child."

"Okay, Mrs. Adams," the officer on the end of the line is saying and his tone has altered. Even against the noise of the traffic she hears this. He sounds a little abashed, younger somehow. Gentle. "I can hear that you're outside. Can I ask, are you on your own? Is anyone with you?"

"No," she murmurs. "There's no one."

"You sound like maybe you're in trouble, Mrs. Adams. You understand the emergency services are available to you, should you require them? I can get help on its way to you if you let me know where you are."

Panic flares in her. "No," she says too quickly. "I'm . . . My sister lives nearby. I'm almost . . . I don't need help," she finishes. And then she hangs up.

He rings back twice, a third time. Grace stares at the phone, glowing in her palm like a nuclear device.

What has she done? They're not stupid. They'll know. They have CCTV. She has lied to a police officer. That's a crime. She's watched enough *Line of Duty* to know this. Will she be charged? Arrested? Fined? Banned from driving? Will she go to prison? There's the sound of a siren and she casts around. Her hands are shaking and she's remembering the men on the golf course, feels the stolen club digging into her kneecap. Can the police track her via her mobile? She's pretty sure they can do this. Lotte would know. Can they prove she isn't telling the truth about the miscarriage? She can claim temporary insanity. *Is* she insane?

She doesn't want to be here. She doesn't feel safe, and from nowhere she finds herself longing for the soft-furnished domain of her parents' house. The feeling is coming from a place she can't quite locate and it surprises her because she's usually a little on edge whenever she's there, like there's an ever-present danger that teenage Grace will rear up and bite. But it's also the place she went to seek refuge when she needed it most. She can't remember much from that time, but an image comes to her now. There's her dad in his armchair doing the crossword, her mum on the striped sofa with Lotte leaning into her, bare feet tucked up under her skinny bottom, the two of them watching *Strictly Come Dancing* together. Grace has been to fetch a glass of water from the kitchen, and as she comes back into the room she's gripped by the sight of this fusion of her mum and her child; she's remembering how it feels. The taken-for-granted ease of it, the familiar comfort of her mum's warm side against hers.

Grace stares at her mobile, which has stopped ringing at last, sees her face reflected in the black screen. Her eyes are round with fresh knowledge. One overheard conversation. One desperate moment that has lodged inside Grace like the child in her. For the first time she understands why her mum said what she did all those years ago. It was because of the guilt. The same guilt Grace feels. The universal mothering guilt that is surely implanted in the delivery room along with that Pitocin shot. One out, one in. This crazed truth that no matter how hard they try, mothers feel they have failed their kids, that they are not good enough, not quite up to the job. When her mum said she wished she'd never had children, she didn't mean it, Grace thinks. Of course she didn't, and it's like a revelation that should have come years ago.

Passersby turn to stare at her. They're not even trying to hide it, but no one offers help. She isn't crying anymore, but she can feel that her face is printed with tears and she's aware, she's not stupid, that she looks a mess. Her scalp is itchy, her hair sweat-sculpted to her forehead, her cheeks, like she's trekked across El Caminito del Rey rather than walked through north London.

Grace sniffs her armpit. She smells bad. She feels bad. She doesn't want to be here but she knows she has to finish what she's started. *I've gone too far to go back*, she thinks. But it's Ben's voice in her head, not hers.

It was a Wednesday, she remembers that. That and the chemical smell of limescale remover. She's in the bathroom scouring the place because she's on deadline and it seems like the lesser of two evils. When Ben comes in she jumps: this is one of the places in the house they avoid now if the other is there. She knows even before he starts speaking that something is wrong. "I've gone too far to go back, Grace," he says, in a voice that's too controlled, and he can't quite meet her eye. He's wearing the light-blue shirt, unbuttoned at the neck, so she can see the red blotches at the top of his chest that betray him. "Do you understand what I'm saying? It's too late to start again." And maybe it's the fumes from the spray cleaner she's holding but Grace feels her throat tighten because why is he talking like this, in riddles that make no sense, in twisted code? When she tries to speak he cuts across her. "I can't do this anymore. I've found a flat in Swiss Cottage, I get the keys next week . . ." and she barely hears the rest.

In the middle of Finchley Road Grace stops, tips up her head, stares at the hard blue sky. She has gone way, way too far to go back to the beginning.

Two Months Earlier

Northmere Park School
London
N8 6TJ
nps@haringey.sch.uk

Dear Parent or Carer of Lotte Adams Kerr,
The situation with Lotte's attendance and attitude is now critical. Unfortunately they have refused to attend their meetings with their assigned teacher and/or school counselor. In line with school policy we are unable to authorize any absence without a note/notes from a doctor or other authorized professional. These have not been provided.

As previously discussed we have a duty to report the repeated or prolonged absence of any pupil and we are fast moving to a point where external agencies may become involved. Please contact the school as a matter of urgency in the hope that we can resolve this matter before we are forced to take further action.

Yours faithfully,
John Power, Head Teacher

TORN FROM ITS envelope, the letter from the school is on the passenger seat and Grace is reading it in snatched bursts on her way to work—any time the traffic slows, or she's forced to pull in to let another car past. With each sentence there's a falling-away feeling inside. First her chest goes, then her stomach, then behind her eyes, and she's aware she isn't concentrating on the road like she should be.

"What the hell do you want me to do?" she shouts, into the hollow of the car, once she's read to the end. She would like someone please to tell her how she can stop her daughter behaving this way. She can't physically walk her into the school, pin her to her seat, make her stay there. Don't they understand she can't force her? That she is basically powerless?

"Get her in on the anxiety gig," Cate had said, last time they'd spoken on the phone. "Then they can't touch you—they're too terrified. Honestly, do it. Reap all the fringe benefits. You'll get her in the 'panic room' for exams, a special toilet pass, the works . . . although I'm pretty sure there's more kids in those rooms than not these days, the stats are insane, it's a bloody epidemic, so I'm not sure how exactly it's supposed to help . . ." And Grace had laughed, but she'd felt the cold creep of fear because what if? She hasn't a clue what goes on inside Lotte's head these days. Where once she'd been certain, now she is not; now she sees threat everywhere. She removed the old karate belt from Lotte's bedroom the other day, the green one. Just in case. She'd spotted it curled like a snake on the shelf while she was hoovering and an image had slapped her. The thick green material tight around her child's neck, her body dangling horribly. And Grace had cried out loud over the sound of the vacuum cleaner to shunt the thought forcibly from her mind.

She's just passed the old library, its windows pasted over since the council was forced to close it last year, when a car reverses out from a side road in front of her. Grace slams on the brakes. Gestures through the windscreen palms up, like, *What the hell?* but the driver ignores her. Forced to wait, she takes the letter from the car seat, scrunches it until her fingers hurt and launches the ball of paper into the back of the car. And that's when she sees her. Through the passenger window, halfway down the side road that's dark with overhung trees. It takes a moment for her brain to process the fact that it's Lotte. Lotte who should be at school. But it's her, there's no doubt about it. There's her orange backpack, her candy floss hair newly dyed, and she isn't alone. She's pressing her body into someone Grace can't see, who's leaned up against a plane tree, arms around her daughter's waist, legs either side of her.

Behind Grace, a car horn blasts. She tears her eyes from her daughter, sees that the car that pulled out in front of her has gone, and empty road stretches ahead.

"Shit." Revving the engine, she takes her foot off the clutch too quickly and stalls.

The person in the car behind leans on their horn.

Driving off, she glances dangerously over her shoulder—as if that way she might be able to see around the corner or through the dark line of trees to her daughter—and then back at the road, searching frantically for a place to park. The cars are bumper to bumper and she's gone past the Rec and the Catholic church and almost as far as the health center by the time she finds a space, pulls into it. Jumping out of her car, she starts running back down the road she's just driven along. Her bag is banging against her hip, her breath coming in bursts.

By the time she reaches the Rec her shirt has come loose from the waistband of her skirt and her socks have slipped so that her bare heels are rubbing against her boots. Grace decides she'll cut through the playground and the field beyond, to the gap in the trees that will spit her out onto the side road. She runs past a mum and a toddler by the swings, another woman propping up her baby on a bouncy primary-colored elephant. Out in the field, there's a dog walker and a woman in running gear, edging her way along the perimeter.

It's hard to tell how long she's been going, maybe five minutes since she parked, and as she comes through the gap in the trees she feels a stitch in her side, like fingers digging in. There's a row of garages lining the opposite side of the street, the trees on her side casting everything in gloom, and it's deserted. She checks and checks again, although she already knows. Her daughter is gone.

Grace jams her hands on her hips, bends at the waist trying to catch her breath. From nowhere it starts to rain. Fast, fat drops that soak instantly through her clothes, run down her face, the back of her neck. The smell of tar is in her nostrils and water is gathering in new puddles. Pretty soon the rain will have washed the place clean, she thinks, glancing down the street to where her daughter had been. She's too late.

He was not wearing a school uniform. The thought assaults her. From what she could see of him she could make out jeans and bare arms, the short sleeves of a T-shirt. This was not Luca or Kwame or Louis. This was not one of the boys from school, so who? Her mind is all at once flooded with words, images from Lotte's social media accounts. Every article she has ever read about online exploitation and grooming is fighting its way up and out of her memory. And there's something else too, something more that's unsettled her, a feeling of deep unease she can't shake. Inside her head it's like she's on a white-knuckle ride at a dystopian fair—she has no idea what will be coming at her next.

Grace sinks to her haunches in the middle of the street, grips her hair with both hands trying to anchor herself. This is the reason Lotte has been bunking off school. This is who she went to meet in the middle of the night. *That tiny skirt, those legs, you are indecent and when I say come you know what I mean . . .* This stranger is responsible for all the comments Grace can't unsee. He is the reason her daughter has lost her mind. He's the reason she feels as if she's losing Lotte.

Karen Marsden had been waiting to intercept Grace as she'd beeped her way in through the glass double doors at Stanhope Primary, twenty minutes late for work. Now the head teacher is leaning at a slant against her desk. She's wearing a navy skirt suit and fingering the lanyard at her neck in a way that suggests maybe she also works for MI5. Grace is trying to keep a neutral expression on her face. A ridiculously overqualified teaching assistant—a woman in her fifties, who's a Cambridge graduate—is apparently taking her French class.

"I'm afraid there have been complaints from some of the parents, Madame Adams." Karen Marsden looks at a spot just to the left of Grace's head as she says this.

"I'm sorry, what?" Grace refolds her arms across her breasts. She is aware that her shirt is see-through in patches from the rain. Her body temperature is fluctuating wildly and she's sure it must be apparent to the woman standing across from her. A moment ago she was freezing cold, now her face feels like it might be melting. She can feel sweat standing out on her upper lip, her chin; any moment now it will drip onto the industrial-green carpet at her feet.

"The problem being the crying," the head teacher says now. She can't quite meet Grace's eyes as she says it.

"Oh." Grace swallows, and her mind flashes to the magazine article in the chest of drawers in her bedroom. The stock photograph of three women in nylon old-lady slacks and cashmere sweaters who look closer in age to her mum than her—like, if they haven't already booked this year's Saga holiday, they will be doing so imminently. In the picture, one of the women is bravely sob-smiling while being comforted by the other two. *Feelings of sadness/desolation.* Grace pictures the words stamped on the page. *Uncontrollable crying.* She can feel her damp skirt sticking to the backs of her thighs. It's making the flesh there itch.

"Look, I can explain," she says.

She sees for a moment the little girl, Maisie. Her earnest face, legs swinging under her desk in class the week before. The children are holding up pictures they've drawn of their favorite foods, *Le gâteau, le hamburger, les frites* . . . and Grace is naming the shops where they'd buy these foods so that they can chant the words back to her. *La boulangerie, la boucherie, le supermarché.* The children start to talk about Tesco and Waitrose and Aldi and the Co-op, how they hate shopping with their parents. And then Maisie, who has a clear, strong voice for someone so small, fixes her green eyes on Grace and says, "Usually, because it's quite late at night and my mum says the shops are shut, we go to the food bank." She says it straight out like it's a simple fact. It's her contribution to the class conversation. And the other kids nod, like, Oh, okay, that's where your family does their shopping. Then someone calls out that KFC is the *best* and the talk moves on.

But something's swelling in Grace that she can't stop. A feeling that is at once heavy and liquid. The wrongness of it is all at once unbearable to her. "Miss," one of the children is calling, she can't say which one. "Miss, are you okay?" And Grace becomes aware that standing there, holding up a cartoon drawing of a butcher's shop and in charge of a class of thirty children, she's crying. She's crying and she can't stop. It's as though a switch has flicked somewhere in her brain and she can't turn it off. She is completely and utterly out of control. She's a biblical flood. A tsunami. She isn't able even to stutter out an apology, to tell the kids she's okay, really, just give her a minute, because the words drown in her throat. Some of the children are circling her now, touching her arms, her back, looks of concern on their small faces, and someone must have gone to fetch the class teacher because suddenly he's there, looming in front of the Vikings display, an appalled expression in his eyes.

". . . and then there's the issue with your punctuality." Karen Marsden is steepling her fingers at her chest. Her coral nail varnish is chipping off at the edges.

Grace realizes she can't trust her own emotions anymore. She can't trust herself. It's impossible to tell where the perimenopause stops and she begins, and she's asking herself who she would be if it wasn't for these chemical enemies raging through her body, hijacking her mind, who she would be if her self had not come apart from her. She imagines she'd be nailing life, sailing through serenely. Coping at least.

Glancing up, she tries to interject, but the head doesn't seem interested in waiting for her to explain.

". . . but mostly, to be perfectly honest, there's this problem with the budget cuts . . ."

She's putting the rubbish out when she sees Lotte coming up the road toward her. Every muscle in her body tenses. There must be something in the set of her face that alerts her daughter because she stops uneasily the other side of the gate, as if she's deliberately keeping a buffer between them. Grace spots the love bite on her neck straight away. It's poorly concealed in foundation the color of American Tan tights.

"I saw you." She keeps her voice low, aware of the neighbors. "This morning, near the Rec."

Lotte closes her eyes, lets her head fall back.

"What's going on, Lotte?" Grace has one hand on the bin like she's trying to stabilize herself, the other clutching the bag of rubbish that's splitting at the seams. "Who is he? This whole TikTok thing, is it to do with that?"

Lotte doesn't answer.

Grace dumps the bin bag on the path, comes toward her. There's a hum in her mind, like bees swarming. "You're so young, darling. You think

you're not but you are. You don't know the first thing about . . . I just want
to know who he is. Did you meet him online? Is he older than you?"

"Oh, my God, are you hearing yourself?" Lotte smiles incredulously,
as though there's a private joke that Grace wouldn't get because she's too
old, too stupid, too paranoid, too bigoted.

Her eyes flick to her daughter's skirt. It's rolled up at the top, the way
they're not allowed to have it at school, rolled up so high Grace could
swear she can see a flash of knickers at Lotte's crotch.

"Nice." Lotte shakes her head slowly, following Grace's eyeline down to
her skirt and then back up again. "So now you're slut-shaming."

"What? No." She puts a hand on the gate and Lotte steps back.

"Brilliant, this just gets better. You know what? I don't care *lol*. I'm a
teenager, I'm supposed to do this. How do you not get that? I mean, why
did you even have children if you—"

"I lost my job today because of you," Grace says slowly, quietly.

Lotte frowns. Uncertainty flickers across her face. For a split second
she looks eight years old again.

There's a long moment. Grace can hear her own blood in her ears. And
then Lotte turns and walks off down the street.

"Wait," Grace calls. "Lotte!" Why did she say that? She hadn't even
known she was thinking it. Of course it isn't her child's fault that she's
been fired. "I didn't mean it," she shouts. And as her words bounce back
at her, she covers her face with her hands. They are greasy, stinking with
rubbish residue, and she almost gags. Everything she can't say is pressing
against her throat. *Don't you understand? I'm scared to death.*

2012

GRACE IS TRYING not to think about the fact that she's left Lotte in London without saying goodbye. She's trying not to dwell on the fact that Cate is not expecting her. She's felt the low thrum of nausea in the Uber all the way from LAX, and now as she steps from the cab, eyes the square concrete house beyond the security gate, she realizes she has no backup plan, no idea what she will do if her sister isn't there. The familiar dust-and-blue-gum smell catches in her throat as she buzzes the intercom and waits. She knows that her face will be flashing up on the small screen that's fixed to the wall at the bottom of the stairs.

The intercom rings and rings, and she's just starting to panic when there's the crackle of static and then her sister's voice.

"Grace! Oh, my God, wait, I'm right there."

The automatic gate opens slowly and as Grace moves through it and onto the path between tall thirsty grasses, her sister appears at the door. She has a towel wrapped around her head like she's just got out of the shower, shorts and a T-shirt pulled on. There's a moment when their eyes meet and then Cate bolts forward. There is something superhuman in the way she moves because one minute she's on the wide doorstep, the next thing she's at the end of the path throwing her arms around Grace.

"You're exhausted, look at you," Cate says into her hair. Then she grips Grace by her upper arms, studying her face.

And Grace sees tears in her sister's eyes. She sees this and registers surprise—as an intellectual fact rather than an emotion she actually feels.

Because Cate doesn't cry. It's her thing. And yet here she is with the glassy stare of someone who is trying hard to hold on to herself.

"I won't make you talk if you don't want to," Cate says.

Then she blinks, and Grace watches a single tear bloom and tip down her sister's cheek. She makes no move to brush it away—although she must be able to feel the slide of it—as if it hasn't happened.

"And you can stay as long as you want, okay? I love you." Cate says the last three words as if she's dusting off her hands, like, *Let's go*. Then she reaches for Grace's suitcase, starts to wheel it with purpose toward the house.

Walking behind her, Grace feels as though her legs might go from under her. All she wants is to sleep.

Grace is standing in front of the Tesla display in the Griffith Observatory and she has no idea how she got there. There are bolts of sharp white light zigzagging through the tall glass box with a violence that matches the inside of her head. Each new shock of light hurts her eyes and she takes it and takes it and takes it until she can't anymore.

She knows they saw the Hollywood sign on the way up and the memory of it is spinning her out because it makes her feel as if she isn't really here. It makes her feel like she's watching a movie, or maybe she's in a movie, and there you go, this proves it: those nine iconic letters that, close up, look more like a flimsy cardboard cutout. So that she understands she has been tricked.

And then she's running from the building and out through the formal lawns that seem to have been built on top of the world, and she doesn't stop until she gets to an edge that gives out over the whole of Los Angeles. She's vaguely aware of Sara catching up with her, placing a hand on her back, but she doesn't turn. Beneath her, she sees brown hills green-tufted, the downtown skyline, low-rise sprawl, palm trees, a hump of distant mountain. She could squash all of it with pinched fingers. And she teeters there.

Cate has taken indefinite leave. She's brought Grace to Santa Monica and they sit on the steep sand looking out at the water. The ocean is big and gray and wild. It's a different element from the sea at Brighton where they grew up. A world away from that picture-postcard strip that seemed contained, stopped at its edges, like it was caught in a frame. Beside her Cate is reading the Stieg Larsson book Grace has seen lying around the house, pages splayed, and that she's picked up several times. But Grace can no longer read. She's tried but the words jump about on the page. There is sand in her shoes but she won't take them off: she needs to know that at any given moment she'll be ready to up and leave.

After a while the sight of the sea gets too much. It is too indefinite, too infinite. Grace presses the heels of her hands into her eye sockets. She sees bonfires there. Licking, spitting flames that she knows must be the pattern of her irises against the inside of her eyelids, but that she can only think are a manifestation of her desperation, her rage at what has happened.

The guest bathroom is tiled all the way round. Every surface is covered with little orange squares that glint. Grace can't look at herself in the mirror. She averts her eyes when she's cleaning her teeth. *If* she cleans her teeth. And she can't cry. There's something huge, malignant, balled inside her, filling her from the pit of her stomach upward, outward. Something that needs to rupture but won't. Her nephew avoids her: when she walks into the kitchen, the lounge, the den, he walks out. She didn't notice this at first but now she sees it and she doesn't blame him. If she could, she would walk out of any room that she was in.

She's alone in the house for the first time since she's been here. Out by the pool in the wide parched garden. There are the red hills in the distance, a lizard scatting in the grass. Grace is hugging her knees to her chest and listening to the hypnotic suck and pull of the filter system. Although she's hot she won't dip her toes into the water that's right there. She's imagining it, though, the cold blue shock of it. A bone ache that would feel like relief.

A plane flies overhead and written in its wake, in letters that look like blown smoke rings against the cerulean sky, are the words *I love you.* Grace presses the pads of her fingers hard into her upper arms; she feels as if she might be sick. She wonders who the message is from, wonders who it's for. Wonders once the plane has passed, the letters dissipated, if maybe she's imagined it. Lying back on the scrubby grass, she stares at the sun. And even though she knows it's dangerous, she allows herself to remember.

She and Ben are floating at the edge of the pool. They've taken off their clothes because it's after dark and everyone else is in bed. There's her yellow dress balled on the side and the pool lights are on, glowing emerald and violet and magenta and turquoise, their colors drifting. Cate and Sara have been mixing negronis all night so Ben is a little drunk. It's all the more noticeable because, although he doesn't know it, she is sober. His hand is on her stomach, covering the almost-swelling there, and she's wondering whether maybe he's guessed. She hasn't told him yet because it's too early and she isn't certain what he will say. He's talking about *Quantum of Solace*, the film they went to see earlier at the Chinese Theatre, but she isn't following. The words she's been keeping in are colliding on her tongue, and she's opening her mouth to let the secret out when Lotte appears at the gap in the glass doors. She's holding White Lion by one leg and her eyes are slitted with tiredness. "I can't sleep, Mummy," she says, because of the noise of the air-con, and the jet lag, and the strange bed, and now she's too hot. And although it's maybe one in the morning they tell her to jump into the pool with them: that way she can cool off and they'll tire her out.

They take it in turns to swim with her on their backs and pretty soon Lotte has the huge inflatable dolphin out of the pool shed and they're trying and failing to get on and stay on. They are all of them laughing and screaming and shushing, and when Grace dives down underwater, comes back up for air, she is seized by a moment of clarity. There's a fullness in her, like she's been pumped with sunshine, and she can't stop smiling.

Across the water Ben catches her eye. There's Lotte on his shoulders and his hair plastered to his face. *I love you*, he mouths. And for a split second Grace knows that this is the happiest moment of her life.

Now

GRACE HAS DECIDED to jump on the tube. She'd considered doing this hours ago, near to the start of her journey, when she'd known she was maybe twenty minutes up the road from Archway station. But—and it seems laughable now—it had felt like an impossible detour at the time. Compulsively, obsessively, absurdly, she hadn't wanted to waver from the direct path she was on. This time, the red and blue sign was right there on the street, a beacon, a balm to her ruined body that might have been emblazoned with the words *Grace Adams* rather than the name of the station. There's the tick and screech of the tube on the rails, the black dirt underground smell, and she's feeling smug. Like finally, finally she's got something right because this will save her time. She'll be at Swiss Cottage in less than a minute, and from there she's round the corner—she's as good as arrived. There's just this man who's standing a little too close to her; it's a half-empty carriage so there's no reason for him to be this near. She has her face set and she's holding herself tight against the metal pole near the doors, trying to ignore him. She'll be there in seconds.

When she feels something brush against the side of her breast, she jerks around. But the man is looking the other way down the carriage as though he hasn't noticed her. He's older than her with dirty brown hair parted to one side, and he's wearing a loose suit, pointed black shoes. Grace takes a step away, as far as she can without letting go of the pole, repositions her body so that she's facing entirely away from him. Her pulse is going in her neck and she's holding her breath, waiting for the tube to come to a stop in the station because they must surely be almost there, when suddenly he presses into her from behind. She feels the violent shape of his erection forced against her coccyx and her entire body falls into the pit of her stomach. For a snatched second she sees his face above hers, reflected in the dark glass of the door, a look of angry concentration stretched across his features.

Then there's the scream of the electric brakes or maybe it's her, she can't tell which, but she's wheeling round. He is so close to her she can smell something nasty—musty—like garlic or spunk on his breath or in his pores. He is all the men who have ever catcalled her, flashed her, threatened rape, assaulted her, terrified her, diminished her at twelve and twenty-two and forty-two, and before she knows what she's doing, she has slammed her forehead into his face. There's a loud pop and her head seems to bounce back and away. Pain drives a line between her eyes. The man has his hand up to his nose and there's dark blood coming through his fingers, lots of it, so that it's dripping onto the speckled tube floor. Grace becomes aware that the other people in the carriage are twitching in their seats. A couple of them have half risen.

"Are you all right?" she hears someone ask, but she isn't certain whether they are addressing her or the man with the sex-shop breath who's stepped back from her now.

"You fucking bitch," he's saying over and over, still with his hand to his face. "You fucking bitch . . ."

Another man has risen at the end of the carriage, an older man. He points a finger at her. "You need help, love," he shouts angrily.

And then the tube pulls into the station and the doors are sliding open. One foot on the platform, Grace glances from the older man to the other passengers eyeing her covertly. Her throat is dry, lungs bursting in her chest.

She chokes out, "Me? I'm the issue here?"

Two Months Earlier

Northmere Park Presents: The Big Gig
Everyone's favorite annual extravaganza!
There will be: Bands, Bar, Food, Stalls, Raffle. What's not
to love?
ALL welcome!
*Please come and support the school. PTA-run events like
this help plug the gaps in funding cuts.

LOTTE SLAMS INTO the lounge and crosses to the mirror above the fireplace. She's wearing her coat and there's an air of impending doom about her; every action is an aggressive sigh because she's late and she needs to communicate the unfairness of this, despite the fact that it's entirely her fault and she is always late—she's pathologically late—so it should come as no surprise. On the sofa Grace pushes her laptop to one side, and even though she knows it's best not to say anything at all, the words spill out.

"Leyla will wait. Don't get stressed."

"I'm not stressed," Lotte murmurs through her teeth. She's fiddling with her face, trying to blend the makeup at her jaw. And then she widens her eyes, like a howl. "I need to put more foundation on."

"What?" Grace blurts. Because her daughter looks beautiful. Ridiculously, impossibly so, and how can she not see that? "Lotte, you're perfect. Honestly, leave your face alone!"

But Lotte has already left the room, her footsteps thudding up the stairs.

Grace is hovering by the front door, brandishing a ten-pound note, when she comes down several minutes later. Lotte takes the money, thanks her and, as she's pushing her feet into her trainers, Grace notices the hairs on her face thick-coated in makeup. They're standing out from her skin, which is two shades darker than her neck.

"You've put too much on now," she hears herself say. And she doesn't know what is wrong with her because she'd had the thought and consciously stopped it, then said it anyway. And now that's it: she can't unsay it. She knows Lotte is nervous about the night ahead, anxious about the gig—her first-ever live solo dance performance—and she's just made it worse.

Lotte glances up, blinks in sardonic disbelief. "Why would you say that?" Grabbing her bag, she pulls open the door. She doesn't say goodbye and she's on her phone already as she moves down the path, out through the gate.

The light is dipping a little, streaked amber at its edges, and white bulbs are strung up around the stalls. There's the smell of frying onions and chewing gum. Grace has moved away from the group of parents because Ben is here too so it's awkward—she can feel assessing eyes on them—and because she's nervous for Lotte, so she'd rather watch alone. She's had a single beer and she's starting another but there's that tender ache at the base of her skull already, the slightly sick feeling that she knows means she will have a migraine later, or tomorrow, if she drinks it. She's a cheap date these days, she thinks. A cheap bloody boring date. It has crossed her mind that she might see Nate here, on the mixing desk or plugging guitars into amps, checking levels, herding kids. She'd had the thought as she applied lipstick in the bathroom earlier. Switched up the color from neutral to crimson. Blotting her mouth, she'd eyed the bright pigment bleeding into the lines above her top lip, and felt instantly hollowed out.

On the outdoor stage a couple of girls are playing ukuleles, singing something she vaguely recognizes, and they're good, they have sweet voices.

There's a crowd of kids watching and, through the gaps, Grace can see Lotte at the side of the stage, talking to the music teacher, Mr. Somebody. She can't remember his name. It's strange watching her like this, at a remove. She seems different somehow, older, as though she's entirely separate and nothing to do with Grace at all. It's exactly how she felt when she saw her down the side road next to the Rec. Her pink hair, her orange backpack, her body pressed up against . . . who? The exact same delay in recognition that afterward frightened her, made her question her mothering instinct, question her *self*. Will he come to watch her daughter tonight? She casts around, feels her teeth clamp together. There are hundreds of people here: How would she ever know?

A cheer goes up and Grace swivels her head, tightens her grip on the bottle of beer she's holding, because there's Lotte, jumping up onto the stage. She has a mic in her hand and she's looking out into the audience, smiling widely. She's wearing baggy tracksuit bottoms and a white top that stretches across her collarbones and stops just beneath her ribs. Huge hoop earrings that almost scrape her shoulders.

A beat starts up and Lotte holds up her fingers, counting them off *one two three four* . . . Students have rushed to the space in front of the stage and they're whooping and pumping their arms in the air. Then Lotte starts to dance. Tight, complex moves that make her body seem all muscle and sinew and perfect control. And Grace recognizes it. It's the dance that has apparently made her daughter TikTok famous. The one Natasha showed her how to access and that they'd hunched over her phone in the coffee shop on the corner to watch, reading the thousands of comments left there. Lotte is mouthing along to the words now, MC-ing the crowd in between, and they are all of them up and dancing, bodies in sync with her daughter's, eyes fixed front, cultlike. As she moves across the stage, Lotte's limbs carve invisible sculptures. There's something so compelling, so natural, in the rhythm of her, as if the elements up there—the air on her skin, the earth at her feet—have altered their structure. Her pink hair has burst over her shoulders, her face. She is incandescent, and Grace can't take her eyes off her.

"Yes, Lotte!" she yells, and her voice comes out gargled because she is so insanely proud that her stomach is twisted up with it. But there's something else too. She's remembering something she'd forgotten she knew. She feels it bodily and its force shocks her. That giddy up-and-out-of-herself high that comes from the music, the dancing, the intensity, the promise. It's like she can smell it, taste it, and why hasn't she realized before that it is gone? She has had those moments—in bars and clubs and at festivals, parties, she had them a long time ago and she will never have them again. Standing there, Grace hugs her arms around her body. It isn't that she's jealous, not exactly, because it fills her up that her daughter gets to feel this way. But there's a grief in her too, for this thing she hadn't known she'd lost.

Grace is stepping back from the crowd when something makes her turn. And that's when she sees him. Watching her. He's over by one of the outdoor tables, maybe fifteen meters away, and the way he's holding himself, like there's a stillness in him, makes her think he's been looking at her for some time. He's in a black T-shirt and chinos, not the suit she's seen him in before. Her eyes are drawn to his chest, to the taut definition of his arms that she can see are worked out, and it surprises her because it's not what she would have expected from the narrowness of him. He's looking right at her, smiling, and there's laughter in the crease of his forehead, bracketed around his mouth. And maybe the single beer has gone to her head because when she smiles back she can feel in her eyes, in the way she's looking at him, that she's asking a question, or issuing a challenge. Like, *Shall we?* Or, *Come on, then.*

"Hi," he mouths, and she's starting to laugh, she can't help herself, when someone clamps her shoulder.

"Jesus!" Her hand flies to her chest.

Nisha swings around in front of her, taking hold of Grace's face as though she's all set to kiss her. There's the sticky smell of Pimm's on her breath.

"*Your* kid," Nisha says into her ear, over the sound of the music. And then her friend stands back, turns up her palms one mother to another, as if to say, *It's all you, you did this.*

They stand side by side facing the stage, Nisha bumping her hip against Grace's in time with the music. Though she can't let herself look yet, all Grace is thinking about is him. She's imagining him there to the right of her, watching still, and the thought makes her stomach contract.

When she turns at last, it's with the certainty of someone who can feel his gaze on her. Instead, in the place where he was standing, there's a group of children, younger kids sucking lollipops and sticking out their colored tongues. Something that might be panic rises in her and she skates her eyes around the grounds checking the stalls, the bar, the side of the stage, the mixing desk. But it's too late. He's gone.

It's starting to get dark and Grace has had enough. She's made her excuses and she's trying to find Lotte to tell her she's going home. Ben left soon after the performance, he's long gone, so it's no use asking him where their daughter is. She's been twice round the outside space, all the way over to the all-weather pitch, the tennis courts, the drama block, and back. She's tried calling too, texting, and now she's standing by the school gates with the security guard looking her over and she's ready to leave. Although she isn't admitting it to herself, the thought is there, tugging somewhere in the depths of her, that she has been looking for him too, for Nate. She knows this and a part of her feels the shame of it, but there's the drag of disappointment in her that he seems to have disappeared.

Heading home. Grace punches the words into her phone. Text me. I need to know when you want picking up okay? Or let me know who you're walking with. 10 p.m. absolute latest. She's feeling the prickle of fear she always gets when Lotte doesn't answer her calls. The same anxiety that creeps through her gut any time her daughter is out after dark or half past eight. Her thumb is poised on the send button when she stops, adds a yellow heart and You were amazing btw. Because even though she's annoyed Lotte isn't answering—even though she could scream with the irony of it because her daughter's phone is permanently welded to her hand and yet she always does this, she never picks up—there's the glow of earlier still, the overwhelming pride in her.

Halfway along the road to where her car is parked, she decides to cross because the alleyway is coming up on her side of the street, overgrown and dark, and it makes her jumpy. Forty-five years old and she still feels there's a chance she might get dragged down there. She has one foot off the curb when she hears it. A noise that sounds like a gasp or a cry, something stifled, muted. It runs through her head to go and fetch the security guard from the school, but there's the sound again and she knows it would take too long to get there and back. She's just reached the alleyway when the noise comes a third time and she looks down into the blackness of the passage as if she's staring down the barrel of a gun. It will be a fox, she thinks, as she stands there, waiting for her eyes to adjust. Then a sudden movement, a brief flash of light or color, catches in her peripheral vision. And although it feels like everything that follows happens slowly, in fact it's all over in a handful of seconds.

At the end of the alleyway there's a mess of pink hair and the flesh of Lotte's bare back that's long and white in the moonlight. And Grace is about to cry out when she understands that her daughter isn't in trouble. Then something else. Someone else, rising up behind. He has his mouth open, like he's eating something exquisite, his dark T-shirt twisted up around his sculpted torso. And her mind is galloping, galloping because there is something so wrong here but she isn't able to make the neural pathways connect, can't join the dots of what she's seeing.

They are facing each other—he and Grace—and over the top of her child's head their eyes fuse. For a second it strikes her that they are so pale, these eyes, they could almost be see-through. That maybe if she stares hard enough, long enough, she could look through them to the inside of his head to see what he's thinking. The same clear eyes that had watched her watching her daughter less than two hours before.

2012

GRACE IS STANDING on the doorstep of her own home and she knows it intimately and not at all. There's the cracked terracotta pot to the left of the door, straggled with self-seeded columbine. The plaster squirrels squatted at the top of the two flat pillars, thick-coated in decades of graying paint. It's early still and the blinds in the bay window of the lounge are drawn, and she eyes the stain that's the shape of Italy at the edge of the central blind. The one she's vowed a thousand times to get at with Vanish. She lets her head tip back, closes her eyes against the morning light.

It's as though several months, no, several years of her life have fallen away. She isn't sure how long exactly. She's not even close to knowing because time is playing tricks on her. There's just the constant thrum of dread; the feeling she's dropped something important along a roadside somewhere and she can't find it. Like her keys: she can't find them. She doesn't have the keys to her own house and she's wondering if it's too early to ring the bell. She doesn't want to wake Lotte if she's still asleep. It isn't fair on her child, and there's nothing to stop her standing here a little longer even though she's greasy with travel, exhausted and cold. But then she finds she's doing it anyway, poking the little plastic button as if she has no control of herself. In the house the buzzer goes off, a small electric shock.

When she sees his outline through the glass her heart stops. She curls her hands into tight fists. She can hardly breathe. He pulls open the door and they stand there. He's in a crumpled T-shirt and shiny runner's shorts and there's his sleep-shot face. Grace feels something inside her fall in. Now that she's here—now that *he's* here—a part of her wants to turn and run again. She doesn't know if she'll be able to go in. She can't see how.

"Grace." His voice is morning rubble, and he coughs to clear it. There's surprise in the crease between his eyebrows, and something else, which she can't read.

Her throat feels coated. She has barely spoken to another person for the past eighteen hours, save to thank the air steward for her meals and to give her address to the cab driver at Heathrow. And she's about to open her mouth to speak when she sees, through the gap in the door, Lotte appear at the top of the stairs. She's wearing the mint green pajamas that are slightly too short for her and her hair is all matted, as if it hasn't been brushed in weeks. There's a hot patch of pink in the middle of her cheek where she's slept on it. All at once Grace sees her child, sleepy-eyed and snuggled down small under her duvet at bedtime. Across the room, Grace is standing with one hand on the light switch, blowing kisses into the newly dark space. *Catch my kisses*, she's telling her daughter, who's giggling as she reaches out a hand from under the covers, snatching a tight fistful of air.

Grace's body ambushes her. She wants more than anything to run to Lotte but there's a force pinning her arms and legs so that she can't move. Her tongue is a beached fish in her mouth. And she's fighting to say something, to call out to her little girl because she mustn't do this, she can't, not now, it isn't fair on her. But it's like she's trapped in the dream where she's trying to run away from danger but her legs won't work.

"Mummy, you're back!"

Lotte's skinny little arms go up above her head, and then she's racing down the stairs as though she's just won the biggest prize at the fair. The giant fluffy bear that no one ever wins, but that anyway—and the children don't know this—is cheap and highly flammable and would split at its seams within days.

Grace starts to shake. The shaking is coming from a place deep-rooted in her, from her blood or her heart. Before she knows what she's doing she's across the threshold and she has her arms around her little girl who feels so slight, so breakable, it's as if beneath the skin she's made of seashells. There's the smell of her, the shampoo and biscuit smell, and Grace pulls it into her lungs like a life force. Her face against the crown of her child's head is hot and itchy with tears.

"I love you, poppet," she murmurs, but her voice is all jammed up and the words come out slurred like she's drunk.

It's a long time before she lets go but she senses, just before she does, Lotte getting twitchy in her arms. Her daughter's hair is damp and flat where her face has been and she reaches out a hand, trying to dab the place dry. She's aware that the tears are coming still, they keep on coming, entirely out of her control.

"I'm sorry, Mummy," Lotte says, like it's her fault Grace is crying. And although Grace can see she's trying to smile, her eyes are a little too wide, too shiny. This is how she knows that her child is not okay. *Children are resilient*, she hears someone—her mum?—say. But however much she might like to tell herself this, she knows, truthfully, that even though she's trying to hide it, Lotte is shouldering a burden that shouldn't be hers.

"Oh, my goodness, no." Grace shakes her head firmly, takes hold of her daughter's slight shoulders. "You haven't done anything wrong. Nothing at all, darling, okay? Do you understand?" She wipes the tears roughly from her eyes. "Mummy's just overtired and being silly, okay? *Okay?*" Squeezing Lotte's shoulders, she digs her fingers in lightly, tickling her until she starts to laugh, wriggles out from under her grip.

Standing in the shadows of the hall Ben is watching her. He has his hands in his hair and he looks older, she sees now. There are flashes of gray at his temples, deep grooves carved between his nose and mouth. As if he's aged five years in the time since she left. She wonders for the first time how he has managed since she's been away. How he has juggled work and drop-off and pickup and after-school clubs. She wonders if anyone has helped out. It's been five weeks, more or less, since she went. She knows this because Cate has told her. *It's time to go home*, her sister said quietly, kindly, as they sat under the trees at the Trails Café in Griffith Park, drinking iced coffee through bamboo straws.

"Come and see my room, Mummy." Lotte is tugging at her hand now, dancing on the spot where she's standing. "I've got new curtains because the other ones fell down. They're from John Lewis and they have little sloths on them. Come on!"

Grace shutters her mind and allows Lotte to lead her up the stairs. Already her daughter is babbling away as if she'd never left.

She's standing on the upstairs landing outside the door to the bedroom when she hears him come in. The chink of his keys against the china dish, then the empty blast of a long, tired exhalation that travels up through the house. She knows it must be a quarter past nine or thereabouts because that's the time it takes to drop Lotte at school and get back. She's standing where she is because she's afraid to enter the room, and now that he's back a part of her is scared to move. Instinctively, madly, she doesn't want to alert him to her presence. But then there's his tread on the stair, the familiar bouncy offbeat rhythm that feels trodden into her bones.

He stops outside the bathroom as though he doesn't want to come any closer.

"So are you back?" he asks. His face is a mask as he says it.

Grace nods, shifts her weight from one foot to the other.

Silence slides across the landing, around the walls they painted together in Mouse's Back when they first moved in. They don't know how to be around each other anymore: something has broken.

Ben lets out a breath, the same noisy breath she'd heard him make in the hallway. Then he interlaces his fingers at the base of his skull. His elbows are parentheses at either side of his face. There's the stretch of his shoulders and his T-shirt riding up, the dark line of hair between his navel and the top of his running shorts. Gripping the door handle behind her, Grace tries to anchor herself. There's a beat, a gap in the fabric of things.

And then he's coming toward her and there's that look on his face. She knows what this is. She can taste it. Blood thumps against her temple, between her legs.

"I missed you," he tells her, and his voice is soft. It's liquid.

There's the shock of his touch as he reaches out a hand, pushes her hair away from her throat.

"Get off me!" The words tear from her.

She sees a moment of confusion on his face before he wrenches himself away.

She can't look at him. Instead she fixes her gaze on the picture on the wall across the landing. The photograph they'd bought at Lizard Point. There's a string of people—thin, fat, old, young—stretched out across a jade river, bathing under a wide square of cobalt sky. She would like to be there now. If she could click her fingers and go back there she would.

Ben is too close to her still. She can hear the rush of air in and out of his mouth, feel him watching her. "Sorry, I thought . . ." he starts to say. "I didn't . . . Look," he grips her arm, "we need to talk about it."

Grace shakes her head, *no*. She could almost laugh out loud, a hard kick of a laugh, because doesn't he understand? She can't.

"YES, WE FUCKING DO, GRACE!"

There's a moment, a split second, when she thinks he might hit her. Because he has never yelled at her like that before. It's all she can do not to put her hands over her ears to block him out. Beneath her feet she feels the floorboards rise and fall as Ben steps back.

"We need to talk about it," he murmurs, as he moves along the landing away from her.

Hugging her arms around her torso, Grace inhales, exhales.

"Then I'll have to leave." The words are a shrug so that there's no way he can mistake her meaning. "I'll have to go."

Now

MUMMY, YOU'RE BACK! Her child's long-ago voice sounds in her head, so that she almost turns as she comes up to the crossing, as if maybe she's behind her. It's a sign, she thinks, a sign her daughter needs her. Grace glances down at the cake box in her hand. There's blood spattered across the white cardboard so that it has the look of a Jackson Pollock canvas. It's collapsing damply in on itself too, from pond water or sweat, she can't say which. And it occurs to her there is a metaphor in this somewhere, the dilapidated box, her caved-in, estrogen-stripped body. It will be a talking point, she tells herself madly. When she gets there.

At the crossing Grace pauses briefly. There's a car a fair distance away and she steps out because she judges the driver has more than enough time to see her. The car starts to speed up. She's certain of this, it isn't just in her head, and it goes through her mind that over the course of her walk she has been erased, become invisible. Her pulse starts to go as she holds up a hand to indicate stop. But the car is still coming at her. She's too far out in the road now to turn back and everything is speeding up and slowing down all at once as the car screams toward her. It's a scarlet car, the color of a London bus. And it's this more than anything that makes her freeze in the middle of the crossing. She can't move. *Not again*, she's thinking. *Not again.* Suddenly there's the last-minute jerk of brakes as the car skids to a stop, front wheels grazing the painted stripes.

Grace has her hand up to her chest. There's a feeling in her like her heart might be about to burst through her rib cage, splattering blood and bone across the tarmac, the bumper of the red car. And it takes her a moment to realize that the driver is laughing. Staring through the windscreen at him, she's unable to speak. He has a tanned face that looks sundamaged, silver hair, and an expensive suit. Next to him in the passenger seat is a woman who looks too young to be his wife.

After a moment the man revs the engine. She hears the aggressive blast of exhaust, sees the car straining forward, but she's shaking still, she can't move. She shifts her gaze to the woman and they lock eyes for a second, before the woman looks down and away. Next there's the electric buzz of the car window opening, and then the man is leaning out. He isn't laughing anymore.

"Will you shift your fat arse!" he yells, in an accent that makes her think of her mother-in-law.

Grace feels something in her detonate. Calmly, too calmly, she approaches the car, positioning her body—her *fat arse*—so that she's standing right up against the bonnet. She adjusts the cake box in her arm, squeezes the grip of the golf club.

"Go on, shift it," the man says, but his tone is less bullish now, a little unsteady.

Grace scrunches up her nose. "Aw, that's a shame." Her voice sounds saccharine, sweet as Parma violet, but she is radiating rage like lasers from her eyes. It almost frightens her, the force of this fury. She has the feeling it might blast the car away down the street. Nodding in the direction of the car's headlight, she clicks her tongue. "Looks like your headlight's faulty," she tells the driver.

"You what?" He screws his mouth into a sneer, like, *What would you know?*

Grace swings the golf club high above her head as if she's aiming for a shot that's far across the fairway. Then she brings it down with force against the car's headlight. There's a sound like a dull explosion, then the sharp splinter-crunch of glass shattering.

"Fucking hell!" she hears the man shout.

"Yeah," Grace says, lowering the club and leaning her weight on it. "You definitely need to get that looked at." She's standing in front of the car still as if she's got all the time in the world, like maybe she's a mechanic, an expert in the field. When she fixes her eyes on the driver, her face is flat, expressionless. "Oops," she says.

The trembling starts up the moment she walks away. Her hands are small earth tremors, the cake box shuddering in her grip. She sees in her peripheral vision that the woman in the passenger seat has her phone out of the window. She's following Grace with the handset as though she's filming her. Grace pivots on her heel, stares hard into the screen so that she knows she's talking directly to the camera. There's a blaze in her voice when she speaks. "My daughter turns sixteen today and she needs a fucking cake. Nothing and nobody's going to stop me getting this to her—it's as simple as that."

Grace takes a left where the red houses fork, and she's scarcely five buildings along when her legs buckle as though something has knocked hard against the tender bone beneath her kneecaps. Nausea rises in her glands; she knows she won't be able to go a step further. There's a garden wall and she slumps down on it. Spiked foliage from the hedge behind digs into her back as she takes out her phone, clicks on iCloud. She has known that she would do this—somewhere in the gray mess of her cerebral cortex, she has known—from the second she walked away from the car.

Here's the staithe and the clanking masts, her baby's crazy curling hair that's like spun sunshine. Those squidgy legs and the cherry-red shoes not much bigger than her fist. "Is dat one?" her daughter is asking, and she's pointing at the water. "Is dat . . . ? Is dat?" Next, she's blinking her eyes while her mouth goes wide. "Mummy! A blutterfy . . . I love it, Mummy! . . . And I love you, Mummy."

Grace bites her lip as the camera zooms in toward her child's perfect soft face and then, too quickly, out again, away from her. The picture pans across salt marshes and winding tidal creeks, past the bright-colored dinghies stranded on rippled mudflats, to the black and white boathouse where two figures are emerging. One tall and dark, one small and fair, they're headed in the direction of the camera. The child is just ahead of the adult and she's walking carefully, watching her step because she has an ice cream held precariously in each hand. The camera follows them as they move along the track, coming closer and closer. Then, as she starts to edge down the grassy slope, the little girl stumbles and the picture dips and swerves a little. "Oops, are you okay, Lotte?" Grace hears her own voice, and the little girl nods, holds up both ice creams as if they're precious trophies and whatever happens, she will not drop them.

"Bea," Lotte calls, and her voice is so sweet and high it's like anime. "I've got your ice cream. It's strawberry, okay? Oh, no, it's dripping . . ." And she starts to giggle, licking at her wrist. The ice cream tilts at a dangerous angle.

"Be careful, sweetheart," Grace hears herself say. There's the wind against the microphone as the camera swings and then the picture is back on the baby, on Bea.

She's twisted round on the bench, her dark eyes earnest. Her hands held out in front of her are small plump stars. "Yotty!" she calls, as Lotte wanders into the frame.

"Bea, don't drop it," Lotte tells her sister, her eyebrows high as she hands over the ice cream. And she hovers there, a small protector, making sure she's got it.

"Bea, poppet, what do you say to your big sister?" Grace's voice comes again. "Can you say thank you, Bea? Thank you, Lotte." She's talking in the singsong voice and although she can't see herself, she can tell from her tone that she's smiling—she's happy—filled up with the love she sees there. The camera moves in close then, as Lotte leans in to kiss her sister's forehead. There's the clumsy clash of them, of her two daughters, her two beautiful girls, and when Lotte pulls back Bea squeals with joy, waggles her feet crazily in the cherry-red shoes.

Sitting there on the wall in the stagnant heat, Grace feels the escaped wind on her skin, the itch of sea in her hair, the mud-salt taste in her mouth. Tears are running down her face and she realizes she's crying, noisy chokes against the back of her throat—she can't stop them. The unbearable urge comes again and she presses her fingers to the screen. Like that way she might be able to reach into the film and touch her lost child. Her beautiful baby Bea. Just one more time, that's all. It would be enough, she'd settle for that. "Please . . ." she bargains with she doesn't know who. And she thinks that maybe she's said it out loud. "Just once, please," she says again. Because she would give anything in the world to hold her two girls. To kiss their faces and fill her heart, just one last time.

Two Months Earlier

GRACE CAN'T SIT down. The sofa, the chair, even the floor cushions repel her. Each time she tries to sit, to dial things down and give an impression of calm, it's like there are spikes in the furniture warding her off. Something—adrenaline, a higher force—is compelling her to tread the wood floor until she has walked this thing out of herself. In the mirror above the fireplace there's no escaping her reflection, which catches in the glass as she paces. Her fallen face. Lines that she can't see beyond etched like cracks in dry plaster across her forehead, between her eyebrows, around her mouth.

In the darkest corner of the room, Lotte is squeezed up against one arm of the green sofa. She's pulled her arms, her knees, her feet, her head in toward her body making herself as small as possible, as though that way she can kid herself, kid them both, that she isn't really here. And she's been crying. She's still crying. Quietly, steadily, desperately.

The thought of his hands on her daughter. The thought of his hands on her. The thought of his hands on her daughter and then on her. She can't get these images from her head and it makes her want to scream and climb out of her skin.

Fuck.

That's what he said when he saw her. Grace hadn't heard him say it but she'd read the word in the shape of his mouth so that he might as well have yelled it. There'd been a stopped moment. Raw shock. She'd taken in a wildness about him, his fair hair falling forward, spread fingers at her daughter's waist, and standing there on the hard pavement, the only one of them prudishly fully dressed, she'd felt stripped bare. Time had stretched wide as they'd locked eyes, but where she'd expected to see panic she'd seen something else, something hard and brazen in him. Then Lotte half turned toward her, and there'd been the same expression on her face she'd had when she'd been caught aged seven scribbling her name in marker pen on the bathroom wall. And Grace had looked at her child and couldn't speak.

A bright blue hair elastic is lying in the middle of the rug and Grace bends to pick it up, fits it out of habit around her wrist, feels the pinch of the skin there. "Why didn't you tell me?" she says now, because she has to say something and it might as well be this.

Lotte glances up, looks at her with eyes swollen sore as if Grace is mad. She feels mad—she feels as if she is going out of her mind.

There'd been a hasty, sordid scrabbling at the end of the alley, a righting of flesh and bodies and clothes. Feeling like a voyeur, Grace had moved a little way off down the street. Heart thudding against her skull as she'd waited, she tried to convince herself that what she'd seen wasn't what she thought. Laughably, she'd tried to rewrite the images stamped on her mind, because it was inconceivable to her that this man, *this* man, was . . . what? What was he doing with her child?

She'd washed her hands at the kitchen sink as soon as she'd come in through the door. Turning the bar of soap over and over between her palms like maybe that way she could make herself clean again. He hadn't tried to talk to her, just sloped off while her back was turned. "We're not doing this here," she'd murmured to Lotte, as they'd strapped themselves into the car. "We'll talk about it at home."

Grace knots her sore fingers together. Her hands are stinging and pink-shiny from the washing, the skin stretched too tight across the bone. "He's your *teacher*." The word tastes like an expletive on her tongue. "You're fifteen, Lotte. A child. He's breaking the law. Are you getting that?"

"I'm not a child."

Grace smiles but there's no light in it. "By every legal definition . . ." She stops, pulls her fingers through her hair. She is so far out of her depth she has no idea where to start. Should she call Ben? The school? The police?

He has toyed with me. The thought flashes across her mind. *He has toyed with us both.*

Grace thinks back to the meeting at school, the mind-numbing session on GCSE revision technique. How Lotte had stood up and walked out of the school hall, and when she'd followed he'd intercepted her. She remembers their conversation, which had felt like flirtation, over by the faceless shop dummy. How different this image looks now from the way it had seemed at the time. But, then, the pull in the air between them. The urge she'd had to put her mouth on his, push her palms up and underneath his half-tucked shirt. How he must have been laughing at her.

"He has a duty of care to you," she murmurs, but she's talking as much to herself as to her daughter.

All along it was him. The stranger, the predator, the groomer she feared. The lies, the ripped-up trust, all him. He was the man she saw with Lotte near the Rec. He is why she's been skipping school, lashing out, shutting herself off. He was the person Nisha heard her with in the middle of the night. He sent those sleazy messages to her Instagram page, concealing his identity for the cheap, nasty thrill of it. Thoughts Grace doesn't want to think scream through her head. How long has it been going on? Weeks? Months? A *year*? Longer? Has her child been to his home? Has she slept with him? Grace shakes her head but the thoughts won't stop. If she has slept with him, does that make it statutory rape?

Grace feels her stomach rush up to her throat, covers her mouth with her hand. There's a juddering in her that's coming from her feet, all the way up her legs, her body, to the crown of her head. Plucking a cushion from the armchair, she grips it to her, tries to anchor herself.

"I need to call Dad," she says.

On the sofa, Lotte lets go of her knees, jerks her head upright.

"Please, Mum." There's a look on her face like her world has fallen in. "Please don't tell anyone. You don't understand, he *gets* me." She pauses. "He loves me and I love him."

Now that Lotte has started to talk, it's like she's gorging after a fast: she won't stop. Grace bites down on her lip until it feels bruised. She doesn't want to be here, listening to this. She sees for the first time that Lotte has lost one of her hoop earrings, the ones she was wearing onstage. There's a dark streak across her top that might be mud. Her hands are filthy too.

". . . because there was this thing with Ella, a row in class, and I think that's when it happened. She was being a bitch and Sir heard her. He stopped it. He talked to me after. He didn't judge me, he just listened, and that's when we both knew . . ."

Sir, Grace thinks. *Sir*.

". . . and it isn't what you think. He texts me all the time telling me he's never felt like this before, that the age thing doesn't matter because I'm mature for my age and he's told me he can wait until I've left school, until I'm eighteen, and then we can be together and it's difficult because we can't . . . I mean, at school, we have to . . ."

Lotte is forward over her knees now, as though if she can just express the purity, the sanctity of her obsession, she will make Grace understand. Grace digs her nails into the cushion she's holding. She'd like to rip it to shreds with her bare hands. Her child thinks this is love? It's like she's been brainwashed.

". . . and I can't text or call him first in case . . . I mean, it's obvious why not and that's hard. And people have talked behind my back about it and," she glances up, "all that stuff you saw on Instagram, the nasty stuff? That was because there were rumors. They were slut-shaming me but they don't know. They think they do but they don't. And it's been so hard for him, the *ethics* of it." She puts air quotes around the word. "The fact that we shouldn't be doing it, which anyway is so stupid. He thinks about it all, we talk about it a lot, like a *lot*, and . . ."

She is a child. Every word out of her mouth, and Grace is blindsided by her daughter's naivete. Because Grace has been tricked. Tricked by "You don't need to pick me up—I'll get an Uber back," and "Don't worry, I'll get lunch at the Co-op," and "I'll text you when I get there," and, occasionally, "Do you want a cup of tea? I'm putting the kettle on."

"You're fifteen, for God's sake, *fifteen*, and he's what? Twenty-six, twenty-seven? And he's a teacher, a fucking teacher. I mean, what did you think you were doing?"

A thought assaults her and the sentences she hasn't yet spoken stick in her teeth. Is she taking her own humiliation out on her daughter? Lotte is not to blame, she knows this. It's all on him. Setting her hands on her hips, she inhales, exhales, takes hold of herself.

"Listen," she says at last. "The thing is, your hormones . . ."

"*My* hormones! Are you kidding me?" Lotte is all at once up and off the sofa. "What about *your* hormones? You're a mess."

The words slam into her. She lets the cushion she's holding fall from her fingers to the floor. In the street outside a car horn sounds, a long, persistent blast. Through the lounge window Grace sees two cars nose to nose, locked in battle, neither driver willing to reverse down the narrow street. There's the smell of spirits and sweat and Lotte's perfume, the too-sweet blueberry smell.

Grace opens her mouth, shuts it again. Steels herself. "You know when you were four you said to me—" She interrupts herself, glances at Lotte. "You'd started school the month before and I'd just read you your bedtime story. I can't remember now which book. *The Snail and the* bloody *Whale* probably—you insisted on it every night for *months*. Do you remember?" She rolls her eyes. "You held my face like this," Grace clamps her palms to her own cheeks, "and you said—and I remember it word for word—you said, 'Soon I'm going to be a grown-up and I'm going to grow a baby and I'll call it Grace to remind me all about you.'"

Lotte drops her head but Grace can see that something in her face is curving upward. There's light there.

"See? I was a goddess to you, then. What happened to us, Lotte?" She means to laugh, but instead her throat shuts. There's a sudden pressure behind her eyes.

"Promise me, Mum." Lotte tips up her chin. "Promise me you won't tell anyone and I'll stop it, okay? I won't see him anymore."

Standing across from her, Lotte's arms are too straight at her sides, her fists tight-packed. But her voice is soft, her expression open, and Grace knows what this means: she can read the language of her child's body like braille.

"Come here, darling." She cups the back of her head with her hand, pulls her close.

There's the beat of Lotte's sobs against her chest as her daughter collapses into her, and Grace is relieved and broken all at once because Lotte is allowing her in. She belongs to her again. Grace is needed, she has a role, and she's ashamed because, despite everything, a part of her wants this: it feels like coming home. They stand like that for long minutes, and when Grace takes Lotte's face in her hands it is wet with tears. She's crying still. She pulls her sleeve down over her palm, wipes away the tears as best she can.

"You're exhausted." She kisses her forehead. "Let's get you to bed. It'll all look better in the morning."

"Promise me you won't tell anyone."

Searching Lotte's eyes, Grace sees Bea there. Solemn, dark eyes that are almost black, lashes that look ink-dipped. She sees everything unspoken, all the things they never said. She sees dread there too, a wild fear that punches her.

"Mum?"

Grace fixes her gaze somewhere just above her child's brow bone. So that she is and isn't looking at her.

"I promise."

She says it quietly. But as the words spill from her mouth they ring and ring inside her head.

2015

KERR, Helena Deborah Talbot (née Campbell), died peacefully on 18 October 2015, aged 89 years, after a short illness. Helena, seventh daughter of the 12th Baronet of Argyll and widow of the late Patrick Kerr (dec'd 1996), is survived by her four sons, Thomas, James, Oliver, and Benjamin, and ten grandchildren. Funeral at St Margaret's Church, Dalry, on 29 October at 12 noon. Family flowers only. All donations to Marie Curie.

IT's THE WEIGHT of the box on his shoulder that's different. There's a presence this time, something heavy that's digging into his muscle and bone, whereas last time there was absence. Lighter than air, he couldn't feel it, couldn't feel anything as if it wasn't real and he wasn't really there walking down the central aisle of the church with a coffin that was far too small, and with his daughter . . . with his daughter where? Where had she been, their baby Bea? The sweet, giggling-soft fidget of her. It was inconceivable that she was nowhere because how could she just stop?

The music is too loud. Even at the back of the church the distorted notes are deafening, like the organist is trying to reach a congregation twenty miles away, and Ben can smell himself already. An underarm oniony scent mixed in with the Sunday-school smell of the wood against his cheek. A smell that rushed at him from childhood when they lifted the box at Tom's count so that his eyes had filled with tears unexpectedly. They'd told him he didn't have to do it if he didn't feel able. Tom had told him. As the eldest of the brothers, and adhering to all things *Debrett's* just as Helena would have wanted, it had fallen to him. Ben had taken the call at work, excused himself to his students, and stepped out of a tutorial into the windowless corridor. Four years on and his brother still couldn't say his niece's name. "You don't have to if you feel you can't because of . . ." he'd managed.

"Oh, you mean because of Bea," Ben had said, with a breeziness he hadn't felt. And when his brother had cleared his throat at the other end of the line, he'd felt bad.

People are standing in the pews and the place is packed, but he's fixing his eyes on the jeweled light through the stained-glass windows, so that he's barely aware of them as he passes. She was born so fast that even the midwife who'd seen it all before was forced to comment. *Hey, Speedy Gonzales!* she'd told Grace. *You barely gave me a chance to wash my hands.* An hour and a half from start to finish, so that afterward it occurred to him that maybe it was a sign. That maybe she was always going to race through her life, like dog years. She would have been six by now. He tracks her age day by day, of course he does. There's a second when he wakes before he remembers, and then he lives it all over again, an instant of blinding grief. How would she have looked at six? How would she have been? He can only fix his memories of Lotte at that age to the wide-open gap where Bea should have been, and there's a wrongness in it. Like those macabre computer-generated police images that artificially age the faces of children who have disappeared years before. The fact is he will never know how she would have been at ten or fifteen or thirty. She was barely more than a baby.

Ben feels as if the pressure on his shoulder, in his mind, might at any moment pin him to the spot and he shifts his gaze, searching the pews for his wife and child. He wonders if Grace thinks these things too. About Bea. He knows she carries a photograph zipped into the inside pocket of her brown leather bag, he's seen it there, but they don't talk about it still. The truth is, these days they hardly talk at all. Language, his ally, fails him here. I have two daughters, I *had* two daughters. What is the answer?

Could somebody please tell him? Because all this time later he still doesn't know.

His gaze snags on the statue of Christ waxy on the cross at the front of the church, gory palms clotted with blood. And then there's the question he's anticipated, half-formed in a hundred mouths, but that only Cate has broached. During that long night of the soul when he'd been in California for a conference. They'd met in a downtown bar and drunk martinis until they got thrown out, and she'd asked him if they would try for another child. Pointed out carefully, gently, unCate-like that it wasn't too late. "It would have to be an immaculate conception," he'd told her bitterly, although he knew it was as much him as it was her. Because the sex had never come back as the counselor had said it could, *with work*. It still makes him cringe to think of it. That final session of the six they'd had free on the NHS, after spending a year and a half on the waiting list. By then it was all way too late. "Do you blame her?" Cate had asked, fishing an olive from her glass. "I think you do." And when he'd paused minutely before he shook his head, she'd wiped her fingers on her shirt and told him slowly, with drunken clarity, "It was an *accident*, you understand that, right?"

At the metal stand in front of the altar he bends his shaking knees as they lower the oak box onto it. Someone, one of his brothers, squeezes his shoulder from behind but he doesn't turn. In the second pew back, Grace is standing, head bowed. At her side, Lotte is glancing around, eyes glossed with tears. She's small for her age still, scrappy and fair, so that she looks closer to ten than twelve, too young to be here. His wife glances up as he moves in next to her, and there's a blankness in her. She doesn't place a hand on his arm or twist her fingers in his. That kind of intimacy is in the past for them too.

The staff from the nursery school were at the crematorium. Faces shocked, like they'd been cheek-slapped. He doesn't know why he remembers them particularly because there'd been hundreds of people. It had just felt surprising somehow, incongruous, like they should have been safely back at their two-roomed world that smelt of gone-off milk and Play-Doh, zipping up small coats and making castles out of toilet-roll tubes. The room where the service was held was enormous, a modern cathedral. He hadn't got up to speak because he'd known he couldn't, and he hadn't heard a word. But there'd been a moment, right after the appalling mechanical whir of the curtain coming across, when a door banged wide at the far end of the room. Bright white sunshine had blasted in, ripping the place through. A supernatural force that dazzled him and that he'd known was her. He'd wanted with every cell in his body for it to be her.

The vicar is addressing the congregation now, his gray hair side-parted, falling across one eye. Next to Ben on the pew, Lotte is studying the picture of her granny printed on the back of the order of service, a long-ago Helena wearing tennis whites and the same stiff-sculpted hairstyle she'd never updated. They hadn't wanted Lotte to come. They'd agreed on that at least. But Lotte had had other ideas, telling them through tears that if they didn't take her she would make her own way there because she and her granny were close, the closest of all the grandchildren, and everybody knew it. Helena didn't try to hide it. *Thick as bloody thieves*, Grace loves to say—*loved* to say—her eyes dark and slitted. *Helena does it to spite me. It's her revenge.*

They're rising to sing "Jerusalem" when he catches sight of Grace's hands on the hymnbook. The tremble in them, like she's hypothermic. Then it happens so fast, it's as if time has shot forward without him. The slam of her hymnbook hitting the stone floor, her body keeling over, crashing to the ground. Her eyes are closed and her face is pale, removed. She has the look of a deep-sleeping child. Ben drops to a crouch, wrestles her torso half-upright. When this doesn't rouse her he starts to panic. He can't tell if she's breathing. She seems utterly lifeless in his arms. "Grace!" He's trying to keep the fear from his voice because he's aware that Lotte is there, but when she doesn't respond, he says her name louder, more urgently. He pulls her upright and into his body, bracing himself against the dead weight of her, attempting to get her off the floor and onto the bench. "Grace!" Did she knock her head on the way down? On the stone floor as she landed? Is she unconscious? He puts his face next to her mouth, his fingers under her nose, but he can't feel anything, no breath.

He's only vaguely aware of the people starting to crowd around him, that the music has stopped. And then his brother is there, next to him at the end of the pew, and he's saying something, asking if this has happened before. "Grace, talk to me!" His mind has tipped and tilted into that dark, terrifying place and there's a wild panic in him now. Not again, he's thinking, not again. It's as if she has left her body completely and it's going on too long. Way, way too long. "Grace!" He jerks her body again. He doesn't know what to do to make her respond. Fury rises in him because why are they all just standing there, doing nothing? "Call an ambulance," he shouts. And then, to everyone and to no one, "Is she breathing? I don't know if she's breathing." It occurs to him suddenly that maybe she's choked. There were cough sweets in the car and she'd put them in her bag, brought them in with her. He grapples again with her body, ringing his arms beneath her rib cage, starts to do the Heimlich maneuver, but she's too heavy and he can't get any purchase and anyway he has no idea what he's doing. Desperate, he sticks two fingers into her mouth, roots around at the back of her throat. He hears a gargled sound and feels her body go rigid, and then she comes to, choking. Her eyes flare wide and there's a look of disorientation, of fear.

"What happened?" she says, and she's leaning away from him like he's violated her somehow.

"I don't know." He keeps a hand on her arm—he doesn't want to let go. "You were out of it. Did you faint?"

"I don't remember." She casts around. The vicar and half of the congregation are out in the aisle. His father-in-law, Michael, must have appeared at some point because he's standing now at the end of the pew, Ben's three brothers just behind.

"Take as long as you need." The vicar nods in Ben's direction.

"You stopped the show," he whispers to her. He tries to smile, even though his heart is crashing in his lungs. "Did you do it to spite Helena?" He means it as a joke but there's the residue of dread still, and he can't put any energy into it. It doesn't sound funny and Grace doesn't laugh.

"She needs fresh air." Michael has a hand on her elbow. "I'll take her outside." He's talking as if Grace is an infant.

Ben makes to rise, but Michael shakes his head. "Stay," he says, and glances toward the front of the church. "You need to stay." His voice is firm, but he's white around the mouth, perspiration glistening at his hairline, and it gives him away.

Ben moves instinctively to Lotte, who's chewing her lower lip, and he can see she's bursting with everything she's holding in, trying to be brave.

The organist strikes up the first notes of "Jerusalem," and she stands on tiptoe, puts her lips close to his ear so he can feel the tickle of them.

"I thought Mummy was dead," she whispers, and she's half laughing, squirming a little, like it's something stupid and childish and she's embarrassed.

He sets his hands on her shoulders, fixes his eyes on hers. Her face is collapsed with anguish and there's bewilderment in the V of her brow. Who will die next? This is the trauma she lives with. He knows this, although she's never articulated it directly, because the counselor told them it's how it is for bereaved children. This is the dreadful legacy, her inescapable truth.

"It was scary," he tells her, over the sound of the organ, the distracted, discordant voices. "But Mummy's okay, I promise, don't worry." He takes her hand in his, strokes his thumb across her soft knuckles. He will ask her later about Bea. About her and Bea, about what she's thinking, feeling. He must do this. He also knows that he won't because while they were looking the other way for those long months, those years, it has become taboo. Around him the voices are lifting now and he clears his throat, tries to find his place in the hymnbook. *I will not cease from mental fight* . . . But as he starts to sing it's like the music plugs him into a place he doesn't want to go . . . *till we have built Jerusalem*, and Ben finds his voice rupturing across the words, grief for his lost child and for his beautiful, broken Grace surging in him like nausea.

The wake is back at the house and Grace doesn't come. She's been checked over by paramedics, and he feels foolish because she's fine: she fainted. That's the diagnosis. He shouldn't have kept pulling her upright—that was why it went on for so long. Leaving Lotte with her cousins, he's come outside to the vast raised patio that stretches the width of the house because he can't shake another hand, can't hear more vacant platitudes, can't stomach any more skittering eyes that don't quite meet his.

Rain has drenched the garden, the grounds beyond. It's dripped from the gutter and pooled on the slabs at the edge of the house. Behind him the floor-to-ceiling windows are open to let the air in and so that people can step out. In front of him, autumn stretches luminous, unreal. Mustard and beetroot, copper and lime. A little way down the garden there's a beech that might be a money tree studded with newly minted two-pence pieces, and under it he sees Isaac, smoking like a furtive schoolboy.

For the first time that day, Ben smiles involuntarily. He can picture the two of them in the overgrown garden of their house that backed onto the weir. The precious hours they spent sitting on the two plastic chairs that came with the rental, drinking cheap beer in the sunshine.

"Hey, Business," he calls. Isaac is high up in a venture-capital firm now and it's the gift that keeps on giving, this joke, because they manage to see each other only every year or so, these days, and, as far as he's concerned, it stays fresh.

Isaac comes toward him. "Well, this is shit, Student," he says, and Ben laughs. He could kiss him.

"Yup." He nods. "We've been to better parties for sure. Thanks for coming."

Isaac hugs him hard and brief, and lets go. "I'm sorry, man," he says. "Becca sends her love. She wanted to be here but, y'know, the kids . . ." He mimes a yawn. Then he takes a final pull on his cigarette, tramples the butt into the wet grass. "Much more interestingly, guess who I saw last month? A blast from the past . . ."

And Ben understands that they will not be talking about his mother, or about death in general, and feels his shoulders drop in relief at this small distraction. This concealed act of friendship that he knows is the shape of Isaac's condolence. "Who?" He shrugs.

"Lina." Isaac shoots up his eyebrows, like *ta-da*. "She asked after you."

"Oh, okay, nice." Ben swallows. He's conscious of the movement of his Adam's apple in his throat, like it's suddenly much too big for the narrow space in there. "How come?" He can't quite look Isaac in the eye as he says it.

Three years ago now. Three times. That was all, and then he'd put a stop to it. Bad timing, or maybe good timing, he couldn't say. There'd been the email that had arrived the day Grace had left for Los Angeles, the morning he'd found her note. The thing is, it had been too easy. Each time they'd met in the basement wine bar off Great Portland Street, the one with the bare brick walls and marble-topped tables, wedged with coasters so they almost sat straight. Each time they'd drunk too much and wound up back at the same hotel just round the corner, the one that pretended exclusivity but where the sheets smelt stale. Lina didn't know what had happened. That was why he did it. One of the reasons. She didn't know about Bea and he didn't tell her so she wouldn't pity him. He could step outside his life for a suspended moment, and it almost worked for the few hours it lasted. Before the creep of self-loathing that always came. For her he was just him, Ben, the person he had always been. Not (whisper it) the poor dad whose child had died.

Isaac is talking still, about mutual friends, an event at Tate Modern, how he'd recognized her instantly because, well, the Mary Quant hair, the stoner eyes. Something about marriage, divorce, no kids, two horses. A professorship and a part-time boyfriend, who owns a whisky distillery on the Isle of Jura.

There was one phone call Grace had answered, sometime in the middle of it all. He'd been in the shower so he hadn't heard it ring and she'd come into the bathroom, holding the phone in front of her. "Lina?" she'd told him. "The name came up but the connection cut after I answered."

Her tone was neutral and he couldn't make out her expression through the steamed-up glass. Blood had pumped the length of his body. "Oh, right, thanks," he'd said, and he could hear in the echo of the shower that his voice was a little too hearty. "There's the conference thing coming up so . . ." But she'd already left the room, the bathroom door clicking shut behind her. And he'd felt his words sucked, like dirty water, down the plughole as he'd trailed off.

He has almost told her more than once. To jerk her out of herself, to get a reaction, start a dialogue, something. But in the end he has not had the courage for that. Or perhaps the truth is he thinks it would finish her, finish them. Maybe some things are best left unsaid.

"Come on." Ben claps his hands together now, cutting his old housemate off midsentence. "There's free booze inside. Funeral perks." He starts to walk back across the lawn. "Let's get, I dunno . . . What's the best we can hope for under the circumstances?" He shrugs, his palms upward. "Numb?"

Now

GRACE KNOWS SHE needs to get up and off the wall. She knows she's acting like a crazy woman sitting here rerunning the video over and over so that she can play back the words that are already imprinted in her again and again and again. *And I love you, Mummy, and I love you, Mummy, and I love you . . .*

There's a before and there's an after. She remembers standing there in the before, on the pavement down the road from the nursery. Next to a winter-stripped tree erupting through the tarmac, cracks spreading at its edges. And she's talking to the other mother, the one she doesn't know well, they'd only become friends the month before after Grace admired her skirt at pickup. The one with the indigo feathers. It's a little after midday and it's cold but they've stopped because the other mother, Emma, had to tie her lace and now they're stuck there, chatting. Distracted. The girls, zipped into their puffy coats, which restrict the movement of their arms, mill around at first, abandoning their scooters and digging sticks into the hard earth at the bottom of the tree. Grace has one ear on the conversation, one eye on Bea. She wants to tell her to stop what she's doing because the place where they're digging will be sprayed with dog piss—she can smell the musky-sweet ammonia from where she's standing. But she doesn't want to appear uptight in front of this new friend so she bites her lip and says nothing.

The woman has started to talk about her husband, intimate details about difficulties at work, the antidepressants he's on. Grace is flattered the woman is confiding in her like this, but she's oversharing. Even she would not give so much away so soon. They've been standing there now for maybe five minutes and the girls are getting twitchy. When Bea drops her stick and starts to wrestle her scooter up off the pavement with her fat little robot arms, Grace makes a move to go. But Emma puts a hand on her wrist, she's midway through an important point. Bea's hat is askew, falling down over her eyes, its pompom drooping, and Grace leans across to adjust it, pulls it tight over her ears, which look sore in the cold.

The two girls have set off on their scooters, going at a slow pace because they're comparing the shiny streamers attached to their handle-bars. Bea's are gold, Mia's rainbow-colored. Grace wants to call to Bea to tell her to be careful, but Emma is talking still and she doesn't want to butt in and call across her. Mostly she doesn't want to appear neurotic. Is she being overprotective? The other woman could be saying anything—she isn't listening as the girls move farther off down the street. She's nodding half-heartedly, discouragingly, she hopes. Why doesn't Emma call to her child to stop?

The girls are maybe twenty meters from them now. They are daw-dling along slowly still but they've reached the point where the pavement begins to slope gradually toward the main road at the bottom. Grace starts to move off and Emma falls into step. She can see that Bea is using her leg as a brake, dragging it along the pavement. It's important to foster independence, Grace thinks, fighting her instincts. They are encouraged at nursery to button up their own coats, on hot days to put sun cream on their arms themselves. Nobody wants to be a helicopter parent—and look at them, they're fine, taking it steady. Even so, is Emma not seeing this? The girls are not yet two and a half.

Mia is a little ahead of Bea when Grace sees her child plant the leg she's been using as a brake on the back of her scooter, trying to catch up. With the slope of the pavement she picks up speed instantly, flies past her friend.

"Bea, STOP!" The words tear from her.

Bea doesn't turn: either she hasn't heard or she's ignoring her.

Grace is running now because, fuck Emma, her child is too close to the road. "STOP, BEA!" She's struggling to get the words out because the cold air is scorching the back of her throat and she's finding it difficult to breathe. She races past Mia who's looking up at her, surprised. "BEA!" Her daughter is so close to the road now, she will surely stop. They've gone over it a hundred times, the "safe place to wait" that's meters back from the edge of the curb. "STOP!" she shouts. Her eyes are fixed on her child but she registers in her peripheral vision a tall red blur up ahead to the right. Something large and solid, a bus, that's moving at speed. "STOP NOW!" she screams.

Bea turns at last at this final shout, and Grace sees her foot go for the brake at the back of her scooter. *Thank God*, she thinks. "STAY THERE!" But then—and she isn't sure what she's seeing—there's the bundle of Bea's blue coat and it's somersaulting up and over the handlebars of the scooter. Grace hears a shriek behind her, the sound of an adult, not a child, and for a split second she wonders why Emma has chosen this moment finally to cry out.

"Mate, are you all right?" A boy is shifting from foot to foot next to her. A boy-man not much older than Lotte. She has no idea where he has come from: she hadn't noticed him approach. He has an Afro that's dark auburn, and freckles, like scattered asteroids, across his nose, his cheeks, his forehead, and he's holding his headphones away from one ear so he can talk to her.

Grace pulls a hand roughly across her face. It comes away wet.

It's my fault, she thinks. *It's all my fault. I am to blame.*

"I'm fine," she tells him. "Thanks."

She sees his gaze flick to the blood-spattered cake box in her lap, the golf club resting against the wall.

"I just need to speak to my daughter," she murmurs, and she's talking as much to herself as to him.

"Oh, right." He eyes her phone. Then, reaching into his pocket, he thrusts a portable charger toward her. "D'you need this?"

Grace shakes her head. She tries to smile, to thank him, but she can't. There's a pause, a drawn-out moment. Behind her, the hedge smells green and bitter; she can taste it like poison on her tongue.

* * *

After the before and before the after is a diabolical no-man's-land. A Hades. In this place there's someone rocking heel to toe, heel to toe at the side of her, and there's blood, lots of blood, and she knows it's not good. Then time seems to leap forward because she is in an ambulance and there's a siren that she knows is near but sounds faraway in her head. And she can't see her little girl because the people in green uniforms are blocking her view, and she is strapped into her seat at the back of the ambulance, she's been told she must wear the seatbelt and sit here for safety reasons. And they are quietly busy these people, a man and a woman. Too quiet, too busy. *Mummy's here, Bea*, she's saying over and over. *Mummy's right here, don't worry.*

Time distorts again and there are blanks, gaps where the information should be. She's in a hospital corridor and Ben is there and she has no idea who called him, how he has found them here. They aren't being allowed into the place where they're holding her baby, doing whatever it is they're doing to her, and she knows that Bea will be frightened without her there, she isn't good with strangers and this thought above all else is making her frantic. Someone somewhere is screaming and Grace thinks the sound might be coming from her own mouth.

Now she's walking the floor. Up and down, up and down the stained vinyl tiles that smell of antiseptic and sick, like that way she might be able to halt her thoughts. Her ribs are claws, and her teeth are clacking in her head, making a noise so loud it sounds like someone is tap-dancing on her skull. *It'll be okay*, Ben is saying. *It'll be okay, Grace.* But it's cold, terribly cold, she can't get warm, and his words freeze and crack and disappear. And then there's a woman treading too carefully down the corridor toward them. There's a lanyard around her neck and she's fixing her eyes on Grace. And Grace is suddenly outside herself looking in. Watching herself, watching the woman, the doctor, who keeps getting closer and closer, and there's nothing Grace can do to stop her reaching them and she knows, she already knows.

"Well, look after yourself, yeah."

Grace blinks, astonished to find the boy-man with the red Afro still standing there.

He gives a sharp tug on the hem of his T-shirt, raises his eyebrows at her, as if to say *I mean it, take care*, then moves off down the street.

Grace looks down at her hands, up again. Before she knows what she's doing she's calling to him. "Thank you!" She shouts it, so that he'll hear her over his headphones. "For being so kind." Her voice is raw at the edges—she sounds demented.

When he turns there's humor, a question mark in the dip of his brow. "Cheers." He laughs. "I'll tell my mum you said that."

His back to her, he holds up a lighter, thumbs it so that a small flame explodes to life. A sign-off as he walks away.

They'd lit paper lanterns, twenty-nine of them. One for each month of her life. She'd come out through the doors of the long rectangular room with the high ceiling, edged sideways down the grassy bank to the flatter ground below. It was dark so she barely recognized the faces of the people around her, but there was a sense of purpose, of industry, after the terrible stasis of inside. Sandwiches curling like snarls at the buffet, the municipal-looking blue board covered with photographs of her daughter she couldn't look at. Her disbelief as she sat in the chair sprayed gold for wedding functions that here she was, doing this. She'd accepted a glass of wine, sipped it absurdly as though maybe she was at a work do or a birthday celebration, as though life had carried on. She wasn't supposed to drink with the medication she was taking.

Outside, people were shivering in the cold but she couldn't feel anything. Under her fingers the fragile bamboo frame through the paper was her baby's fontanel. She had vomited down herself earlier and she could smell the sour stench coming off her. "I was sick on myself," she whispered to Cate, as her sister handed her a plastic lighter. And Cate hugged her and told her it didn't matter. Standing on the grass, the heels of her boots sinking into the mud, she tried to get the wick to ignite, but it wouldn't take. She tried again and again, with mounting urgency, her thumb growing sore against the metal spark wheel. Around her the smell of paraffin wax as lanterns caught and flew, snatched up by the onyx sky. And Grace felt panic grip her because the voice in her head was getting louder and louder, telling her she had to do it, that this was the most important thing she would ever do. "Dammit, light, fucking thing," she muttered. *This is for Bea. I have to do this for Bea.*

Then Ben was at her shoulder. Taking the lighter from her he snapped one flame after another but still the wick wouldn't catch. She could hear the material of his jacket, rubbing against itself, as she held the useless lantern to her chest where her heart hurt, like someone had pinched the muscle and twisted. Above them the sky burned vivid orange. Paper lanterns soaring one by one so that she was dizzy, vertiginous with it. "I couldn't do it," she kept saying. "It wouldn't work." Until, finally, Ben tried to ease the lantern that would not light from her hands. But she clenched her jaw, gripped tight. Nothing in the world would make her let go.

The boy-man has gone and the sun is starting to dip over Swiss Cottage as Grace heaves herself up and off the wall. Music is coming from an open window, a fast electronic beat, and from a back garden the sound of a dog whining. The air is syrupy still, and between her legs and underneath the band of her bra she can feel that her skin is slippery with sweat. Her ill-fitting shoes are dirt-streaked and sprayed with something amber-colored and sticky. There's a pain deep in her shoulder, a burning sensation through her hip. Tenderness at the balls of her feet, and a muscle spasming in her calf. When she takes a step, the raw blister at her ankle screams—it's as if she has slashed at the flesh there with a knife. The inside of her head goes loose and she pauses to steady herself because she thinks for a moment she might black out. But she is round the corner now, almost there. So close it hurts.

Two Months Earlier

Grace Adams   3:48 a.m.

URGENT Meeting Request

To: John Power

Dear Mr. Power,

I need to discuss urgently a child protection issue involving one of your members of staff in accordance with the Children Act 1989/2004. I can't stress clearly enough the serious nature of my concern. Specifically, it relates to the Sexual Offences Act 2003, according to which, as I'm sure you're aware, it is an offense for an adult to engage in sexual activity with any person in respect of whom they are in a position of trust, whether or not the person consented.

Please contact me to arrange a time for me to come in and meet with you. I am available all day today and would suggest this is a matter that cannot wait.

Many thanks,
Grace Adams

LOTTE IS REFUSING to speak. She's on a chair, hugging her knees to her forehead, and Grace is fighting the urge to tell her to take her feet off the seat. Across from them John Power sets the executive toy on his desk going—it's the kind with the five steel balls that knock together in perpetuity once you start it off. It's bizarre that he does this. The loud *tick tick tick* of it in the quiet room, like it's a clock counting down or maybe up. She wonders if it's something he does to break his students.

"Lotte, it doesn't help the situation if you won't talk to us," the head teacher says now.

The woman with the sharp features glances up. She's sitting to the left of John Power, making assiduous notes, about what Grace can't imagine because Lotte hasn't said anything yet. There's every chance she won't say anything at all. She hasn't even acknowledged that Grace is here. She looked at her face as she came into the room and blankly away, like she didn't exist.

"You're not in trouble." The head teacher puts his elbows on the desk, leans forward. "But obviously I don't have to spell it out to you, Lotte, you're a very bright student. The thing is, if once we look further into this we find that . . ." He trails off. "I mean *obviously* this is an extremely serious matter."

Pressing send in the middle of the night, Grace had felt as though she were lobbing a grenade into the tender heart of her life. Sure enough the call had come a little after 7 a.m., asking her to name her time. Lotte doesn't know this, but John Power has not spoken to the teacher yet. To Nate. That will come next. There was no question of getting the two of them into the room together and she's aware already of a closing of ranks, that this is something to be kept quiet. Despite the seriousness of the allegations—which are not allegations, they are fact, as Grace has pointed out several times already—the same old defensiveness that accompanies these parent-teacher conferences is in play. Grace has been fighting the fire inside since long before they called Lotte out of class. "I saw them with my own eyes," she'd told the head and his sidekick two minutes in, her palms up in protest, the long sleepless night in her tone. "This is not opaque or open to question. There is no question about it." *Promise me you won't tell anyone, Mum. Promise me.* She has played Lotte's words over and over in her mind. Heard the false echo of her own response, the dark stain of her words. *I promise.* It was such a stupid thing to have said but in the moment she had felt she had no choice, even as she knew the lie would come back to get her.

On the other side of the desk John Power seizes the steel balls in his fist, releases them gently. Although the sound has stopped, Grace can hear the tick of them still in her head.

Lotte hasn't moved an inch. She will not speak. She's demonstrating remarkable will—Grace almost admires her for it—and they can't force her to talk. They all know this.

"Lotte?" the head teacher tries again.

All at once she wishes Ben was here. She isn't sure she can do this alone. She hasn't called him yet because she doesn't want to face the thought that she has failed yet again.

John Power straightens in his chair. "I think at this stage we're going to have to consider reconvening." He arches his eyebrows, directs a glance at Grace. "We have everything we need for now, and clearly we'll want to be talking to . . ." he hesitates ". . . to the other parties involved."

Out of the corner of her eye, Grace sees Lotte twitch. The other parties. The man her daughter thinks she loves. The man Grace, idiotically, insanely, was momentarily—more than momentarily—beguiled by. She slams the thought shut.

"Okay." The head steeples his fingers, rests his thumbs against his lips. "We're going to have to ask you to remain at home for a few days, Lotte, while we sort this out." He inclines his head, signaling to the sharp-faced woman whose name and title Grace can't recall. "There's a procedure and we'll have to follow it." He turns to Grace. "And we'll need your full cooperation with that."

How is it that Grace feels as if she is the one on trial? She and her daughter both.

"I will expect to be kept updated," she says tightly.

The sentence is barely out of her mouth before Lotte is up from her chair. Grace rises quickly. They reach the door together. Lotte stops and turns to look at her. It is not the look of a child: it's a look of one woman to another, and Grace's insides drop because she sees hurt there, anguish, but something else too. There's disgust, hatred even.

Behind them the head clears his throat. "I'll be in touch."

As they come out of the office, he's the first thing she sees. She thinks for a moment that maybe she's dreamed him up, because surely, surely, they would not be so stupid as to allow this to happen. They have not even had the sense to wait for them to leave. He's at the other end of the corridor walking toward them. His fair hair is falling across his face, and he's walking in the way he does, like he's a pretty relaxed guy but even so nothing and no one will stand in his path. There's a woman with him, escorting him. The one from the school office with the red glasses and the hijab.

Grace fixes her eyes hard on him but if he's noticed them there at the other end of the corridor he doesn't show it. Rage shoots through her. *Look at me*, she thinks. *Look at me, you bastard.* She would like to grab him by the hair and smack his stupid, sculpted face against the pale mint wall that's streaked dirty with children's fingers.

All at once she has the sense of something breaking loose from the side of her. For a moment she doesn't understand, and then Lotte's racing down the corridor toward him.

"Nate!" The word is grief in her daughter's mouth.

Grace sees his gaze flick toward the woman from the office and then away. A small crease carves the space between his eyebrows so that he's wearing a mystified look. And he's almost smiling, his mouth turned up a little at each corner, like, *Who is this? What is this?* As if whatever it is, it's nothing to do with him.

"Nate, I've got the guitar pick you gave me, I've got it on me right now." Her child's voice rips open the quiet in the corridor. "I keep it here because I made you a promise."

Grace watches, horrified, as Lotte stops, reaches a hand inside her school shirt and pulls the pick from her bra, holds it up, a cheap, plastic trophy.

"And I'm going to teach myself to play, so that when we can be together . . ."

"Lotte!" Grace calls, she can't bear it.

He keeps walking: he will not look at either of them. He's denying them both, erasing them. It is almost biblical, this walk of his down the shabby, strip-lit corridor. He is Peter the Apostle. He is Judas minus the kiss. The kiss was last night, she thinks, and the thought makes her queasy, incensed.

"I know you have to do this, Nate." Her daughter's voice is more urgent now. "I understand."

"Lotte!" she calls again, shouting this time.

Outside one of the art rooms, her daughter draws level with him. There's just the woman from the office between them—separating them—and Lotte hugs her arms around her waist, like otherwise she won't be able to stop herself reaching out and touching him. As if instinctively she knows this is something she mustn't do, that it would be going too far.

"I know you can't acknowledge me." She's walking backward now, stumbling to keep pace with them. "I love you. I'll wait . . . just like we said, okay?"

At this the woman next to him jerks her head back exaggeratedly. She's staring at Lotte with unconcealed distaste, with contempt. Nate looks steadfastly away, his expression neutral, as though he is somewhere else altogether.

And Grace is seized suddenly by this scene. Something like ice slips down her spine. Because her daughter looks like a desperate, naive, crazed little girl. She looks like a fantasist. A liar.

Grace barges into Lotte's room before she has a chance to change her mind. They haven't spoken on the drive home. In the passenger seat Lotte kept her head turned away at an angle so acute it must have hurt her neck. Grace is exhausted and afraid. She would like to run and hide from it all. She doesn't want to speak to her daughter, it's the last thing she wants to do right now, but she is the adult, it's down to her. She knows she can't leave things as they are.

It's the usual mess in there and she steps over a pair of curling tongs as she enters, the cord stretched tight from the socket, like a tripwire. Lotte doesn't look up. She has the drawers of her chest pulled out as though she's searching for something, a tangle of clothes at her feet. Her school tie is yanked loose around her neck and she's knotted her hair up into a bun on top of her head. There's the stale smell of air trapped too long in one place.

"Lotte . . ." Grace begins, but she can't go on. Her child is a familiar stranger, someone far off, unreachable.

From nowhere, a decade and a half falls away. Grace is on the hospital bed at UCH, wrecked and weak but buzzing like she's full still of electric shock from the nerve stimulation machine Ben plugged to her back. After nine dragging months she is holding her baby for the first time. This unknowable being, who's shifted and slipped and jerked inside her, pressed shapes like fleshy aliens with her tiny fists, her feet into Grace's skin. A small, raw person tight-swaddled in a hospital sheet, hair slick with blood and gunk. Dark appraising eyes that peel back Grace's soul as they stare into each other's stripped faces. *So this is you.*

"Lotte . . ." she tries again. *Hello, beautiful,* she'd said to her, over and over in the hospital bed, building them in language. *Hello, beautiful baby girl.*

"Lotte, I had to . . ."

Lotte turns from her, starts to stuff the clothes she's pulled from her drawers into a bag that's on the bed. It's the bright green beach bag, the one they got free from Brent Cross, a cosmetics giveaway.

Grace looks from the bag to her daughter. "What are you doing?"

Lotte pulls her lips into her face so that they disappear. For a moment Grace thinks she won't answer. She sees in her child's punched-out eyes that she has broken her heart.

"I'm going to live with Dad," Lotte says.

At first Grace isn't sure she's heard her right. "What?" she says, and takes a step further into the room.

"You had a choice." Lotte has her hand in the drawer and she pulls out a sweatshirt, the blue one with the yellow Japanese symbols.

Grace can feel the beat of heavy wings against her breastbone. "No, I didn't." She shakes her head, lets out a laugh that isn't a laugh. "I'm your *mum,* Lotte. There was no choice. What he did, it . . ."

"I trusted you." Lotte's voice breaks loud across hers. "I trusted you and you broke your promise. But you know what? It doesn't even surprise me. I doubt it'll surprise anyone because that's the kind of person you are. Who could ever count on you?"

"What? What are you talking about? That's not fair."

Her daughter hacks out a scornful laugh. She's taking things out of the drawer still. Haphazardly, recklessly, dumping them into the bag on the bed.

"Stop it, Lotte! Look at me."

Lotte throws the jeans she's holding onto the bag so that they land with a whip crack. Plants her hands on her hips. Her whole body shudders as she takes a breath in. "Could Bea count on you?" Lotte's voice is a rising scale. "Could she?"

Grace stands stunned. She can't remember the last time Lotte mentioned her sister's name. Not since she was ten, eleven maybe.

Casting madly around, Lotte snatches up the dusty *matryoshka* from her bookshelf and slams it to the floor. Brightly colored wood fractures like shrapnel across the room. Grace feels it bodily. These shattered pieces of her past. She sees for a moment the Tea Rooms in Primrose Hill, the Russian dolls lined up behind the counter, secret babies at their centers.

Lotte thins her eyes so that they are small glinting slits. Her voice, when she speaks, vibrates with quiet rage. "We all know what you did."

Something pops in Grace's brain. Before she knows what she's doing she slaps Lotte hard across the cheek. She feels the weight of her entire arm, her shoulder in her palm, registers her daughter's head snap away and then back.

Lotte puts a hand up to her face. Her expression is cut with shock.

Downstairs in the kitchen Grace sets the tap on hot, holds her trembling hands under the scalding water while she fills the sink. Her heart is beating in her chest like she's had a jump scare. Her hands are on fire. "How dare she?" she's saying under her breath. "How dare she?" In her head a cacophony of too-careful voices. *It was an accident . . . You can't blame yourself . . . not your fault . . . an accident . . .*

She takes a pan from the side, slams it into the sink. She has never hit her child before. Ever. Wrenching the metal scourer from the drying rack, she starts to scrub at a dark ring of burned porridge. Water slops over the edge of the pan, escapes the sink, and soaks her blouse. Grace scrubs harder. "I am a person too," she mutters. "I'm *human*." Banging the pan down on the drying rack, she takes a cereal bowl from the side, plunges it hard into the sink, like she's trying to drown it. Milk clouds the water, spreading like slow smoke.

Two minutes pass, maybe three, before she hears footsteps on the stairs. Grace stills her hands, strains to listen. Out in the hallway there's the sound of Lotte stamping her feet into her shoes. Grace pictures the backs of the crazily expensive wedge-sole trainers trodden down and cracked around the heel—she has told Lotte a thousand times to undo her laces before putting them on. She lifts a mug from the sink, grips the rim, watches the tips of her fingers turn white. In a moment she will be gone.

Go out there and stop her, a voice in her head says. *Grow up. Do your job. Be a mother.* But the tender edge of her fury is with her still. She's had it with biting her lip, keeping the peace, squeezing herself into an ever-shrinking space that dictates what's acceptable for her to say, to do, to be. Let Lotte go if that's what she wants. Let Ben deal with it. Let him try. Let him take his turn. Let the two of them figure out for themselves every little thing Grace does that they don't see.

She hears the click of the latch, and the air in the kitchen is displaced as the front door opens. She holds her breath, like that way maybe the moment won't come. Feels the chill of the air lick her ankles. Then the door clunks shut.

Resting her elbows on the sink, she drops her head. The silence in the house assaults her.

How long does she wait? Moving plates and cups and bowls around, pretending to herself she's occupied. A minute? Five? Ten? She couldn't say. Until the words come at her again. *We all know what you did* . . . and the truth shocks her. Lotte hasn't said anything Grace doesn't already feel. Her only crime is that she has articulated her mother's shame. She has uprooted Grace's dark, dirty, unbearable secret. That she is to blame for what happened to Bea.

Grace pulls her hands dripping from the sink, rushes from the room, along the hallway, and out of the house. She doesn't stop to put on her shoes. Small stones dig into the soles of her feet, stabbing the flesh through her thin socks as she runs down the path. At the gate she looks both ways. The street is empty. She starts to run in one direction, then changes her mind, turns, heads the other way. She's gone maybe twenty meters when she decides this is all wrong. Lotte wouldn't have taken this route. She pulls up short, starts to run again the opposite way. There's a noise blaring in her ears that sounds like a car alarm as she turns the corner onto the next street. The road ahead is empty—there's no one as far as she can see.

Even so, she's halfway down it before she stops. She's too late. Her lungs are bursting and she leans forward over her thighs. It's as if she's learned nothing.

When she straightens up she sees it. A rainbow at the end of the road arcing wide and long. It is beautiful, incongruous. Fat-striped and luminous and she can almost—*almost*—see through the gaps in the houses, the trees, the place on one side where it touches down. There's rain on her face that might be tears and above her a dark sky cracked with white sunshine. As she stands there, another rainbow appears, an echo of the first. A double rainbow. She's never seen one before and she can't tear her eyes away. She would like to suck the exquisite curves of color in through her lips, her teeth, swallow them down.

But as she watches, the rainbow starts to fade and disappear. It's there and then it isn't. Grace knots her fingers, brings her hands to her sternum where it feels like it's burning.

2018

GRACE DOESN'T SEE it coming. Strange as it seems, they have existed in this state of suspended animation for so long now that she hasn't noticed anything amiss.

She's in the bathroom on her knees cleaning the bath when he comes in. She has her sleeve rolled up to her armpit, the limescale spray in her hand, and she glances up briefly. He's wearing his work clothes, the soft blue shirt unbuttoned at the neck, the gray chinos, a thin wool tie worn loose. What has he come in for? The fact of him there, even the smell of him, aggravates her. She waits for him to take whatever it is and leave.

Instead he comes toward her, a look on his face that alerts her. "I thought you had a deadline," he says.

She's amazed he even knows this: he hasn't asked about her work for she can't remember how long. But she knows because of the expression on his face, the way he is plucking at the shirtsleeve at his wrist, the way he can't quite look at her, that this is not what he's come to say. "I do," she says. In fact, she's already a fortnight past her deadline. Why else does he think she has embarked on this deep clean?

He makes a sound without moving his lips, crosses the room to pick up a towel that's fallen from the rail. Folds it clumsily, replaces it. What does he want? Turning back to the bath, Grace points the spray at the plughole and squirts.

Behind her Ben clears his throat. "There's no easy way to say this . . ."

It's all it takes. A single cliché. And Grace feels suddenly as if she has stumbled out of her life and onto a stage set. Too carefully she puts down the limescale spray on the bathmat. Keeps the cleaning cloth clutched in her hand as if somehow it might anchor her.

He's standing awkwardly in front of the sink. She can see the back of him reflected in the mirror, his shoulders curving inward, an ironed-in crease zigzagging the length of his shirt.

"I can't do this anymore," he says.

"Do what?" she finds herself asking stupidly. There's a strange pressure pushing against her temples.

"I've gone too far to go back, Grace. Do you understand what I'm saying?" He grips the sink behind him. "It's too late to start again."

She watches his knuckles turn white as he talks. She understands language but it's as if he's using doublespeak.

"I've found a place in Swiss Cottage. I've sorted a short-term lease while I look for something more permanent. I get the keys next week and I'll be moving in on Tuesday, which means you'll be at work when I . . . go. I'll just be taking my clothes and a few basics to start with—I'm not going to be an arsehole about it, obviously—so I hope the impact will be minimal, and . . ."

His mouth is moving but she isn't hearing the words coming out. This is a man she avoids, someone she barely sees, except for their evening meal, the three of them. And even then there's often a reason to skip it. She struggles to remember the last time they had sex. Or a conversation that has stretched further than "Can you pick up bread on your way home?" No niceties, no fluff. If he comes into a room she tends to leave soon after. He does the same. So she doesn't understand why it feels as though she has been struck in the head with a blunt object.

She nods once he's finished. As though it's nothing out of the ordinary, what he's just said.

"Is there someone else?" she asks. Her tone is neutral, transactional, like she's inquiring whether he remembered to pay the gas bill. But the edge of her left eye betrays her: she feels a twitch start up that she can't control.

He shakes his head, fiddles with the top button of his shirt. That infuriating habit of his that used to charm her. There's a flush spreading across his throat, up his neck.

Suddenly she sees in front of her the man she first met at the Polyglot convention, leaning across the seats in the lecture hall toward her, holes at the wrists of his black sweater, hair going in several different directions at once. Beautiful fingers, long with square nails cut short, taking a pen from her hand. His smile that made her think maybe he was laughing at her with her stationery all lined up, the class swot. How she'd decided almost immediately he was the only normal person there. And then afterward in the student bar, her drunken impetuous invitation, *Do you want to come with me?*

The backs of her hands are starting to sting because of the chemical residue she hasn't washed off. She's on her knees next to the bath still—she doesn't think she'd be able to stand if she wanted to.

"*Was* there someone else, Ben?" Her face is open, she's looking at him frankly, but she is twisting the cleaning cloth she's holding into a blue rope. "Did something happen with you and Lina?"

He drops his head, screws fists into his eye sockets. There's dotted stubble poking through the skin at his jaw, like he hasn't shaved for a couple of days. When he looks up his face is bloodless.

"Grace," he says, and takes a step toward her. "I . . ."

But she holds up a hand to stop him. There'd been the note at Christmas all those years ago, scrawled on the back of the conference program. The phone call she'd answered that time, when his ex-girlfriend's name had come up and the line went dead. Even so he could have lied to her and she would have believed it: she doesn't want it to be true.

She shuts her eyes, opens them slowly. The pain is awful.

"You know what?" she says at last, and her voice is soft. "I would never have done that to you. Even with everything that happened . . ." She hesitates, she can't look at him. "I wouldn't have dreamed of it."

He pulls his hands through his hair, blows out a long breath. "I know," he murmurs.

The smell of the limescale remover is making her head throb, a sicky ache that starts at the base of her skull. She presses her thumb into the muscle there, pushes herself up to standing. If she'd imagined this moment, it wasn't like this. There's no drama. Not in the sense that Lotte and her friends would understand the word. It's just bleak, gray, quiet, sad.

"What about Lotte?" She isn't sure she's spoken out loud. She thinks maybe the words are trapped behind the cage of her teeth.

"I'll tell her," Ben answers. "You can be there or not, it's up to you."

Grace covers her face with her hands. She can feel the thump of her pulse in her fingertips. He will tell her. Because that's what he does. That's what he did before, even though it should have been her. He was the one to tell Lotte when she couldn't. She couldn't even bear to be in the room to witness her eight-year-old heart splinter and break.

Don't do this, she's begging him silently, desperately. No child should have to go through what she's been through. She's lost too much already.

Outside the electronic whir of hedge trimmers starts up, answered by an angry call from the magpie that patrols the back garden. Six years of bereavement. That's how long it has taken them to get to this point. Six short long years.

"Do you think we'd have made it if . . ." she pauses ". . . if Bea hadn't . . ." She can't say it.

Ben tips back his head. Grace can see in the harsh halogen light that his eyes are shining.

"But she did die," he says at last, and he spreads his palms as if he's demonstrating there's nothing there.

They stand for a moment across from each other. Just the two of them, as they were back at the start. Her mind dissolves and she's fifteen years away on a beach in Cornwall. Her flesh is stippled with salt and goose-bumps and her cold mouth is on his. *What are you? Fucking Superwoman?* she hears him say.

Something passes between them then, there in the glossy white bathroom that promised perfection when they'd chosen it from the brochure. The awful knowledge that only they share. And for a second, a stopped instant, she thinks he might come toward her.

Instead he glances up at the clock on the wall. "I'm late." He pats his shirt pocket, like he's checking he's got everything before he leaves. "I just didn't want to tell you with Lotte here," he adds, by way of explanation. "But if you want to talk more later, then obviously . . ." He shrugs. And she sees that he has made up his mind.

Grace takes a breath as if to speak. She wants to ask him to stay. She's going to ask him, to reason with him, because in the end it's come from nowhere, what he's saying. He's caught her unawares, and can they at least have a conversation about it? But she's so damn tired; she's worn to the bone with it all.

She drops her eyes to the floor. "We're out of milk. Can you get some after work?" she murmurs. And she bends to pick up the cleaning spray, releasing him.

After he's gone she makes herself finish scouring the bath before she does it, around the silver taps and in between the tiles, the hinged edge of the glass shower screen. Rinsing out the cloth, she sets it on the radiator to dry. Puts the limescale remover back in the bathroom cupboard. Then she climbs the stairs to the loft.

The door is stiff and she yanks the handle up and to the left, which always shifts it, flicks on the light. She feels for the box pushed to the back of the top shelf and takes it down. Kneeling on the landing she lifts the lid, pushes aside the tissue paper that's yellowed with age now, and takes out the small shoes the color of cherries. She rubs her thumbs over the soft leather, pushes her fingers underneath the straps, the silver buckles that rattle, so that she can stroke the sole that's marked with wear where her baby's feet have touched. Here is the marzipan smell of polish and she's remembering Bea sitting on the blue square cube at the shop on the hill, her face marble with concentration while the assistant fitted the little shoes. She'd stared at her feet as if they were something quite separate from her, flexed them one way, then the other. "They are red ones, Mummy," she'd said. "Look! They are actually very shiny."

Grace places the shoes carefully on the floor, reaches into the box and takes out the tiny candy-striped cardigan. Then she buries her face in the wool, trying to find the scent she knows is long gone. And she sits like that on the landing, vaguely aware that the light through the house is changing, until she hears the key in the lock that means Lotte is home from school.

Now

NOW THAT SHE is here at last, standing on the opposite side of the street from Ben's flat, she can't go in. Somewhere between there and here the sky has tipped into darkness. There's an opal moon illuminating the blocky white building, so that it glows between the red-brick Victorian houses on either side. Music is blaring out from the garden, a fast, pounding beat that's making her heart speed up. The party is in full swing.

Looking down at herself—at the battered, blood-spattered cake box, at the golf club in her hand, the weeping welt at her ankle, the raw scrapes across her arms, a brownish bruise at her wrist—she understands for the first time her own absurdity. The insanity of this quest she has undertaken. She has lost her nerve.

You can't come here, Grace. Ben's voice is in her head. She has known all along that she isn't invited, so why only now—now that she has made it here at last—has it finally hit home that Lotte doesn't want her, that she's not welcome?

A scream comes round the side of the house, followed by laughter. Grace shifts her weight from one leg to the other. Her feet are pulsing hearts, red and meaty and throbbing. Step by ludicrous step the long journey has ripped open the past she's spent years trying to block. What she did, or rather what she didn't do: one dangerous, stupid nondecision that tore up their lives, scattered the pieces of them like ashes.

"*Lotte!*" Someone is calling her daughter's name. That precious word.

There's the echo of it down the street, then a snatched burst of song that morphs into a haphazard "Happy Birthday to You."

A memory comes slamming at Grace. She's coming up the stairs, a pile of clean washing in her hands, and sees Lotte outside Bea's bedroom, peeking through the crack in the door. When Lotte hears her she turns, puts a finger to her lips. "What are you doing?" Grace whispers. "I'm watching Bea," Lotte answers. "She's playing the Queen's Announcement. It's the Queen's important birthday." Grace comes up behind her and inches her head around the door. There's Bea wearing her red dressing gown as a cloak and squatting in the middle of her rug. She has set up an orderly line of twenty or thirty toys—a blue bunny, the Indian sari doll, a little Lego storm trooper, Igglepiggle, the knitted zebra, the orange dinosaur, Lotte's pencil-sharpener owl—all facing a small plastic fairy queen on a toilet-roll throne, and Bea is chattering away, animating them in turn, making them each sing a snatch of "Happy Birthday." Lotte reaches up and puts her hand on Grace's arm. "I like it because she thinks she's alone," she whispers, "and I like knowing what she's doing when she's alone."

Now a second memory comes lurching over the first. Grace is in the garden deadheading roses and Lotte is cross-legged on the lawn eating an apple and watching her. "We were doing about the Hindus at school," she says, in her soft, sweet voice. "About reincarnation and coming back as an animal after you die, and it made me think about people dying." She takes a bite of the apple, crunches for a moment. "About how somewhere in your heart you think about it without knowing." Grace squeezes the shears too quickly, nicks her finger that's pinching the stem, brings it to her mouth and sucks the blood from it. "Don't you, Mummy?" Lotte has come to stand next to her.

Grace wipes her finger on her top, streaking blood across it. "Yes, I expect so," she says briskly. "I don't know much about Hinduism. Right, hold these, poppet, careful with the blade." She passes the shears to Lotte, gathers up the shriveled rose heads with unsteady hands. Her back is bent like she's braced for attack. Because she knows—she is certain—that Lotte is talking about her sister. She's trying to talk about Bea. When she stands, her arms full of rotting flowers and sharp thorns, Lotte is looking at her still. But Grace can't answer. "Okay, I need to get rid of these and get tea on," she says quickly, and heads toward the house. "Do you want to watch some TV?"

Across the road a light goes on in an upstairs room. Grace sees a shadow pass in front of the window. When Lotte looked up at her in the garden and asked for help, she failed her. Unbearable though it was, she should have talked to her then about Bea. She should have forced open her own mouth and spoken the words trapped in her throat. *Yes*, she should have said. *We think about your little sister in our hearts and our minds and in our flesh and muscle and bones. We think about her every day, every moment, of course we do. There is never a time when we aren't thinking about this sad thing that happened to us.* She should not have allowed the silence to bloom and take hold and shroud them all. She could have excavated the words, the devastating lexicon that did not want to be found. She could have rebuilt her family, sentence by painful sentence, illuminated with careful semantics the mute darkness that swallowed them. She could have saved them but instead she let them fall apart. The irony is not lost on Grace. She speaks five languages yet she could not find the vocabulary to articulate her heart sickness, to negotiate their grief.

Before Grace understands what she is doing she is off the curb and across the road. There's the sound of a siren in the distance, the hard beat of bass through her temples as she moves down the path, mounts the single step, jabs at the buzzer on the intercom. *I have lost one child*, she thinks, and she presses the buzzer again, holding her finger there this time, pushing down hard. *I will not lose another.*

When Ben opens the door the music from the garden swells and surges like a dam unplugged. He's in a T-shirt and jeans, bare feet, and he looks tired. "Jesus Christ, Grace." He runs his eyes the length of her body. Not in a sexually interested way, but with an expression on his face that tells her he is appalled, alarmed, concerned, even.

"Nice to see you too, Ben." She raises her voice over the sound of the music, and she executes a small curtsy. "Fuck," she mutters, as she straightens, because her knee has cracked. Pain shoots through her thigh.

Ben is looking at her still, his forehead a frown. "What happened?"

"It's been quite a journey." She lifts her eyebrows. "But now I'm here and I need to see her."

"No," Ben moves forward into the doorframe to block her, although she hasn't made any attempt to pass him. "I mean, look at you, Grace. I won't let you ruin this for her."

"Don't be ridiculous." She laughs, and she hears that it comes out a little crazed. "I'm not coming in, I'll just give her the cake, and there's something I need to say to her, just very quickly, okay, and then, *poof*, I'll be gone." Grace tries to click her fingers but she has the cake box balanced in one hand, the golf club in the other, and she almost drops them both. She has to abandon the attempt.

"Dad! Who is it?"

"Lotte . . ." She means to call out but the sound chokes in her throat. Her stomach pitches. She thinks she might fall down, there, on the door-step.

Ben starts to speak but the sound of the siren comes again, louder this time, a street or so away, and he presses his lips closed. For a stretched moment they stare at each other, old lovers, old adversaries.

"She needs to know I came."

Ben hesitates, and then he stands back, opens the door a little wider as Lotte appears at the top of the stairs behind him.

She's exactly the same and completely different, her beautiful, beautiful girl. Tied around her hair is the silk wedding scarf, the swirls of pink and amber and black that Grace wore when she and Ben got married. *She is wearing her scarf.* She's got on a silver dress that stops near the top of her crazy long legs that even now she's sixteen—*sixteen*—still look as though they might snap. And there's her eyes. Those dark, appraising eyes that are at once familiar and other. To look at her Grace feels she is staring at the sun.

Her heart is going and it's difficult to know whether this is the peri-menopausal thing she gets, the terrifying speeding up, like she's driving full throttle toward the edge of a cliff, or whether it's panic, or fear, or love. How long has it been since she's seen her? Eight weeks, two months. Sixty days. Too long. Beginning her useless CBT count, she attempts to steady herself. She is her mother: she should have tried harder to see her; she should have pushed and pushed and not taken no for an answer.

Grace claps a hand over her mouth and the tears come, cool and silent down her hot, sore face. She can't stop them.

In the gloom of the stairwell Lotte looks from Ben to her. "For God's sake," she says, and there's disgust in the set of her face. "What is wrong with you?" She turns to go.

"I brought you a cake!" Grace yells, like she's some kind of maniac. Of all the things she has to say to her child, *this*? This is what she's got.

"I don't want your fucking cake."

"Lotte, wait!" She takes a step toward the door, the taste of salt on her tongue. "Just give me five minutes. That's all. Then I'll go."

In the doorway Ben twists toward their daughter. "She walked here to see you," he tells her. "Mum *walked*."

Lotte's back is a shield, warding them off. "But my friends . . ." She gestures into the house, toward the garden.

"Please, Lotte," he says.

The siren starts up again, louder now, cutting through the beat of the music. The wail of it makes a line of pain behind Grace's eyes. And there's another sound too, a deafening ringing in her head that she knows has nothing to do with the music or the siren.

Grace scrabbles into action. This is her chance! She starts to pull at the ribbon of the cake box. It's knotted hard so she has to tug and tug and she can only get it half off one corner. Her mind flicks to the pasty-faced woman at the baker's. She did this on purpose, Grace thinks.

Lotte is standing a little behind Ben now, and they are both watching her. The box is bashed-up and collapsing, streaked with dirt and soggy with water damage, and it's making the job harder. Plus, she's all fingers and thumbs because she's trying to open the box with one hand, and she's already holding the golf club. It doesn't occur to her to put the club down; instinct tells her she needs it still, a twisted talisman.

"Just hang on a second." Grace flashes a strained smile, because she's scared that any moment now Lotte will give up on her and go.

"What's the red stuff?" Ben asks, pointing to the blood smeared across the top of the box.

"Jam," Grace snaps, and then quickly flashes another smile at Lotte. She tugs again at the ribbon. Harder this time.

"Bingo!" she says, like this is a word within her vernacular. "Okay." She leans in toward them. She finds that her fingers are trembling as she opens the box with as much of a flourish as she can manage. "*Ta-da*," she shrills.

Inside, the cake is rubble. Grace feels something in her give way. She knew it would be bad, but not this bad. Not this bomb site of a caved-in cake with no survivors.

"I think," she says, pointing into the box. "I think that's Dani Dyer . . ."

Grace can't look up. She doesn't want to see their faces. "So it's had a couple of knocks, but you can see there . . . I'm pretty sure that's the L for Lotte, and those," she jabs a finger, "those are definitely a pair of sliders . . ." She stops, swallows. "There was this whole two-tier thing going on and you can't really see that now but it was fantastic. There was fluorescent piping, gold icing, a swimming pool, bikinis, suntan oil, and . . ."

Lotte isn't saying anything.

"It's a *Love Island* theme," Grace clarifies, in case she isn't getting it. "Super tacky, yes, but very . . ." She trails off; she knows she's ridiculous. As laughable as this ruined cake she has transported all the way from the other side of London.

"The thing is, it's . . . artisanal," she finishes.

Lotte rolls her eyes, sets a foot on the bottom stair. "I don't want you here," she says.

"I should have talked to you!" The words bolt from her.

Her daughter stops, pivots on her heel.

"Yes, you're damn right you should have talked to me." Her voice is low and cracked, like she's trying not to cry. "You should have talked to me and not *them*."

Grace is confused. "What?" she says. "Who?"

"You had no right going behind my back. And you promised me. You stood there and you promised. You *lied*."

Nate. She means Nate. After everything they now know, she's still stuck on that.

"Oh, Lotte," she says quietly, and she glances at Ben. "You weren't the first, you know that, right? Dad told you?" She looks to Ben to confirm this and he nods briefly.

When Lotte doesn't reply, she keeps on: "He'd done it before, at different schools. There were at least three other girls like you. Maybe more, they're trying to find out." She puts the cake down on the doorstep, rises slowly because it feels as though something in her lower back might pop. She wants more than anything to reach out to her daughter with her free hand. Lotte's face is stone. But she's still there, Grace thinks. She hasn't moved. She hasn't left and gone back to her party.

"Listen, darling, just let me . . ."

"'S up, girl?" There's a shout and three of Lotte's friends appear, bunched in behind her on the stairs. They are masked sweatily in makeup, perfumed and giddy-eyed, but they stop as soon as they see Grace, eye her warily like they know this is a thing, they've heard all about what's gone on. She recognizes Leyla and Paris, and there's a girl she doesn't know, who's got fair hair down to her waist, a ring through her septum. Leyla puts a hand on Lotte's shoulder, as though she might need protecting.

Grace wets her lips, runs her tongue over skin that is dry and cracked and sore. "I should have been honest with you," she tells Lotte. She's trying to ignore the trio on the stairs because she doesn't have the luxury of avoiding public shame. She needs to get this fixed before her daughter changes her mind and takes off. "I should have been honest with myself."

Lotte adjusts the scarf in her hair, turns to her friends.

No, Grace thinks. *Please.*

"You guys, go back out," she hears her daughter say. "I'll be there in a minute, okay."

Lotte watches her friends leave before she turns to Grace. When she speaks, she looks just beyond her, as if she can't bear to make eye contact. "You made me look so stupid," she says. "In front of the whole school. Everyone."

"I see that." Grace is picking her words like they might be grenades. "I get how hard it was for you. I do."

Her daughter drops her eyes to the floor. A bonfire smell is coming from one of the gardens.

"I'm just so embarrassed," Lotte whispers. "I thought he . . . I thought we were . . . I feel like such an idiot."

Every part of Grace wants to take her child and hold her. But she stays where she is. She hardly dares move. "You're not an idiot," she says. She wants to say, *That man is a sexual predator and you're a child.*

A round of clapping comes from the garden, followed by a series of whoops. Then someone turns the music up.

"I messed up." Grace can feel the thump of bass in her chest. "I broke a promise and I'm sorry, but I don't feel like this is . . ." she pauses, tries not to spit the word like poison, ". . . about *him*, sweetheart. Not anymore." She moves a little closer to the door, just a fraction. "I let you down," she says. "I've been thinking about it all day, going over and over it. I let you down so badly when you needed me most . . ." Grace stops. There's a burning in her lungs. "This thing that happened to us, to our family, to you . . . I didn't see what was staring me in the face. I never talked to you about Bea."

For the first time since she's got there, Lotte looks at her, really looks into the heart of her, and then she tips her gaze upward. Grace sees that her eyes are glassy.

"I just couldn't." Grace dry-washes her face with her free hand. "And I should have, of course I should. I let you down," she says again. "You were so little. I mean, you were eight, for goodness' sake." She's trying to formulate her thoughts, to dig out the buried words, but the siren she keeps hearing is getting louder and louder.

Grace glances toward the road. There's a blue light circling at the end of the street. A police car moving at speed.

"I told myself you were okay but I know—I *knew*—you weren't . . ." she shouts, over the sound of the siren, because she has to say this.

The sound is deafening now, the blue light coming closer.

"Jesus." Ben grimaces, craning his neck to see. Behind him Lotte presses her hands over her ears.

In Grace's mouth a jumble of words, sentences she wants to let out. But she knows she won't be heard. The car is almost at the house, she'll wait for it to pass. She holds up a finger to signal to Lotte to please stay where she is.

But the patrol car doesn't drive past. Instead, it pulls up in front of the house, parked half-on, half-off the curb. The wailing siren cuts out at last, but the blue light continues to rotate as two police officers—one man, one woman—step from the vehicle. The woman is tall, straight up and down, with a thin face, a wide nose. The man, who's the shorter of the two, looks far too young to be doing the job, like he's playing dress-up.

"Shit," Ben mumbles, "neighbors," and he comes out of the house onto the doorstep. "Is it the noise? Music too loud?" He has his hands up in appeasement. "Not a problem, we can turn it down."

"Mrs. Adams?" the female police officer calls, and Grace swings round in confusion. How does this woman know her name? She moves away from the door, a little way down the path. She isn't sure what this is and she can't focus, but her instinct is to put some distance between herself and her daughter, as if this way she might protect Lotte.

"I need to ask you to remain where you are, Mrs. Adams," the police officer says.

"What's happened, Grace?" Ben's face is bleached of color. "What have you done?"

Grace shakes her head, dismisses him. And she fixes her eyes once again on Lotte. "I told myself you were okay because you seemed fine," she tells her daughter. "You were carrying on pretty much as normal, and even though . . ."

"Is everything all right, Ben?" Grace is aware that a man has appeared in the front garden of the house next door. He's in a pair of shorts and moccasin slippers, and the tops of his arms are pink with sunburn. Across the road, a woman in a checked dress has come out onto the street and she's staring at them.

The shorter officer clears his throat noisily. "We've been getting a number of reports in throughout the day, Mrs. Adams. A vehicle abandoned, theft, violent assault, criminal damage," he ticks off the list on his fingers. "To take a couple of specific cases, we've had a report about an attack on a vehicle here in the Finchley Road area. And separately, but in an incident we believe to be linked, a report of a nine iron stolen in the Hampstead area." He eyes the golf club in Grace's hand. "According to witnesses, a woman fitting your description, Mrs. Adams, was the aggressor in every one of these cases. We've had the patrol car driving around the area since the latest altercation . . ." he pauses ". . . and, well, here you are."

Grace holds up a hand to tell him to wait, turns back to her child. This is her chance and she's not going to blow it. She registers a group of teenagers spilling down the stairs, staring out dazed at the police, the flashing light. ". . . and, Lotte, even though I knew that couldn't be right—the counselor told me, for God's sake—I convinced myself it would be worse to bring it up, to drag you through it all. I thought you were better off getting on with your life. I kidded myself and . . ."

"Can I ask you, madam, to place the golf club on the ground?" The female officer has raised her voice to drown Grace out.

"Because it was me who couldn't face it. I didn't know how to talk to you about it. I didn't know how to talk about it at all. I'm so sorry, Lotte, it's . . ."

"Mrs. Adams, I'll ask you again," Grace hears the woman say. "Place the golf club on the ground."

Grace bares her teeth, inhales through her nose. "All right, Juliet Bravo," she calls over her shoulder. "I just need one second with my daughter, okay?"

When she glances back toward the door, Lotte looks stricken. "I'm scared I'm forgetting her, Mum." She balls her hands into fists and hunches over like she's in pain. "I don't remember how she talked—I can't hear her voice anymore. I can't see the detail of her face."

"Mrs. Adams, I couldn't care less what family drama you've got going on here," the policewoman shouts. "Now I'm going to ask you. One. More. Time."

"And I'm so sorry, Mum, I should never have said what I said to you. That you weren't there for her, for Bea . . ." Her child's voice fractures across her sister's name. "It wasn't your fault." Mascara has smudged across the top of her cheeks, the bridge of her nose. "The thing is, how do you love someone you can't remember, Mum?"

There's the blue light from the patrol car in and out of her eyes and Grace can't stand it any longer. She can't stand here with Lotte breaking apart like this. She makes to move toward her.

"You need to stay where you are. Stand still."

At the sound of the woman's voice, it's too much. Something in Grace explodes. She wheels round and with all the force in her, swings the golf club high above her head. "Will you shut up!" she shouts, and she knows—she feels it in every muscle, every blood cell, every atom of her body—that she has lost all reason.

"WEAPON!" a man's voice shouts.

Before Grace knows what's happening, the female officer has pulled a gun from her belt.

"Fuck," she hears Ben cry.

"I have a Taser here, Mrs. Adams," the woman calls, and there's a new edge to her tone. "I don't want to use it, okay?"

But Grace isn't listening. Something cold and wet is seeping through her clothes to her skin. Has she been shot? She didn't hear a blast. Didn't feel the bullet go in. Is that a thing? That you can be shot without feeling it?

The cold wet thing is running down her leg now and she reaches a hand round to find what it is, where it's coming from, and she feels through her pocket the shape of the water pistol she picked up on the Heath. For a moment she doesn't understand. Then she realizes that it's leaking: the plastic pistol is leaking water all down her. She pushes her hand into her pocket, wrenches it out.

"FIREARM!" she hears someone shout.

A force slams her brain hard against her skull and her legs go from under her. There's the too-loud smack in her head of her jaw hitting concrete and something is pinning her down. She isn't able to move and a drone of bees is swarming, stinging her skin, her scalp, puncturing the ligaments, the bone, shocking her repeatedly. Her eyes have rolled back so far in her head she's trying to see out through the whites, and she thinks that maybe she's grinding her teeth but she can't say for sure because she has lost control of her body, her mind. The pain burning through her is excruciating. Like someone is scraping a knife up her spinal cord. And she is juddering, juddering, juddering, like she's a monkey on a stick being made to dance, and there's bile rising in her. She's going to be sick.

"NO! Stop it. Stop!" She's aware that Lotte is out of the house and running in her direction. "No!" Lotte shrieks again.

"DON'T TOUCH HER!" the police officer yells. "You're at risk of shock."

"What have you done to her?" Lotte is screaming, casting around wildly. "Oh my God oh my God." She wraps her arms around her waist. "Is she going to die? Dad, is she going to die?"

And then Ben is there, holding on to Lotte, and he's talking to the police, and Grace can hear that he's trying to stay calm but there's fear, fury in his voice. "You need to stop," he's telling them. "There's no need for you to be doing that. She isn't a threat to you. She isn't a threat to anyone."

Grace is wrestling with her tongue that's lolling in her mouth, trying, failing to coordinate the muscles that will allow her to speak. *Lotte, listen to me, I'm okay*, she wants to say. *I'm not going to die.*

It isn't stopping, this jolting pain. Screwing her mind into a bloody red thing, it's never going to end. The bees are there still, the knife up her spine, her tongue, her eyes useless in her head. Then, just as she's thinking she can't stand it a moment longer, the shorter police officer is suddenly next to her, fitting her hands into handcuffs, pulling her upright. And Grace becomes aware that the convulsions are easing, her heart is no longer slamming against her tonsils.

The man has hold of her elbow as she looks at Lotte. When she speaks her voice comes out fuzzy, like she's a little drunk. "There's nothing . . ." she tries. Shakes her head, starts again. "There's nothing to . . ." Flexing her fingers behind her back, she feels the handcuffs bite her wrists. Then, in a gallop of language, like that way she might be able to outrun the aftershock, "There's nothing to worry about, I promise, my darling." She gestures with her chin at her battered body, the handcuffs, the police car. "I'll sort this out and we'll speak tomorrow. I know how it looks but, honestly, it's nothing that can't be fixed."

And then Lotte is throwing her arms around her and the police officer is looking the other way, allowing them this. There's the weight of her child against her heart and she would do anything—*anything*—to unbind her wrists so that she could hold her in this moment. Instead she presses her cheek against her beloved daughter's, and she kisses her face once, twice, three times, trying to wipe away the tears there with her own skin.

"I like that scarf on you," Grace murmurs, and she touches her nose to Lotte's to show that what she's saying isn't really what she's saying at all. She can feel her child's fingers pressing into her back. For all her makeup, her piled-up hair, her silver dress that's as short as it can possibly be, for all that she's sixteen years old today, a part of her—a shadow her—is also that baby on Grace's hip, the one with the fat, pink cheeks and the koala grip.

"I miss you, Mum," Lotte whispers. "I want to come home."

Her body hurts as they peel Lotte gently from her, but Grace doesn't care. They could Taser her again and she would still feel like cartwheeling with joy because her daughter misses her.

The blue siren is still spinning, lighting her face in patches as they lead her away toward the police car. Grace screws her body round to face her husband and her child, who are standing together in the middle of the path, watching her go. "I love you, okay?" she blurts, and she finds she's talking as much to Ben as to Lotte.

"Go, Grace!" Ben shouts suddenly, and he pulls up a fist, shakes it. And it is so unexpected, so unlike him, so completely nuts, given the situation, like he's cheering her on in the final meters of a marathon or as she steps into a boxing ring, that despite the handcuffs on her wrists, a police officer at each arm, despite everything, she throws back her head and laughs.

As they cup her head to guide her into the car she realizes that in all of this she's forgotten the single most important thing. Grace jerks her head back and the policewoman swears under her breath.

"Happy birthday, Lotte!" Grace calls. "I'm sorry about the crappy cake and—getting arrested." She feels herself pull a face that reminds her of the grimacing emoji, the one with the rectangle of clenched teeth. She wants more than anything to see her daughter smile, to make her laugh again. "Enjoy your party, okay? That's an order!"

Lotte is leaning into her dad, crying and smiling as Grace is driven away. Looking back, as her daughter's features start to fade, everything in her feels like it's coming loose. She has found her daughter again, but she's losing her too. She is losing her child to adulthood—and, will someone please tell her, where did the last decade go? It strikes her—it's like an epiphany—that she won't ever be the mother of a baby or a toddler or a bright, wide-open primary-school child again. She's done it, it's gone. That part is over. It's as though her life has shot forward while she was looking the other way, and there's a grief in it that wrenches her soul.

Cracked voices come over the radio in the front of the patrol car. The woman next to her sighs. There's the smell of stale smoke coming off her. Turned awkwardly in her seat, Grace keeps watch through the window until Lotte is almost out of sight. She's on the pavement in front of the path now, wiping her face with her hands. But Grace can see that she's okay. That she will be okay. That they will. *So this is you*, she thinks, and she says it under her breath, over and over, as the car turns the corner.

Six Months Later

THEY'RE SITTING ON a bench at the edge of the woods waiting for Grace. Cherry Tree Woods. It doesn't have the ring of a community sentence about it. It sounds more like the setting of an Enid Blyton book. But this is where Grace is serving her time, laying a path. It was Lotte's idea that they should stand in solidarity and mark her first day like this. Lotte has packed their lunch herself, which in itself is a minor miracle because, under normal circumstances, it's as much as she can do to switch on the oven or peel a carrot. She's made peanut-butter sandwiches and bought Bombay mix, Pink Lady apples, a packet of Oreos.

A holly bush at their backs is bright with scarlet berries not yet picked off by the birds. The leaves are a vibrant green, young leaves that are almost soft at the edges where they'll become hard and spiked. Ben can see his breath in the air.

"I'm nervous for her," Lotte says now. "What time is it?"

And although she's only articulating what he's feeling too, he shakes his head. "Don't be," he says. "This is your mum we're talking about. She's been Tasered by the Met. This'll be a doddle for her." He nudges Lotte in the ribs and she rolls her eyes.

They've been sitting there no more than five minutes when she comes toward them, still wearing a fluorescent safety vest. There are twigs in her hair and a streak of dirt across her face.

"So it's me and a bunch of dodgy kids in their twenties," she shouts, the moment she's close enough for them to hear. "Which, as you can imagine, makes me feel great about myself." Kissing Lotte on top of her head, she bumps down onto the bench so that the slats spring down and back. "I'm knackered."

"Nice threads." Ben nods at the vest.

"What—this?" Grace fingers the vinyl carefully, as though it's spun from the finest silk. "I'm hoping you get to keep it at the end."

They eat their lunch sitting in a line, staring out through black winter trees that have the look of strange, skeletal people who are watching them back, listening in. Teasing Lotte about her new boyfriend, who's in the year above her at school—even though it's clear she doesn't want to talk about him. Ben doesn't really want to talk about him either, if he's honest.

When they've finished eating, Lotte stands and takes their rubbish from them, balls it up.

"Who *are* you?" Grace breathes, and Lotte pouts her lips, strikes an Instagram pose that makes her look at least twenty-five.

They watch her as she heads across the muddy dip in search of a bin. A mother, a father, and the quiet burn of love for their child. How many visits have they made to the woods over her long-short lifetime? Hundreds? A thousand? Ben's mind telescopes like time-lapse. There's Lotte in a sling against his chest, eyes fluttering in and out of sleep to the sound of birdsong; high on his shoulders pointing up at the green netted treetops; squatted down at a trunk collecting crisp leaves the color of autumn; polishing roots with her woolly hat making a slide for the fairy people; dizzy on a rope swing hung from a thick mossy branch; arms out and balancing the slippy length of a fallen tree; off in the distance, running, running with her cheeks blown apricot in the wind.

Ben waits until he's certain she's out of earshot before he tells Grace, "I had an email yesterday. The court date's been set."

Next to him she nods, but doesn't say anything.

"Three other girls are willing to testify. All from his previous school. So it's up to Lotte what she wants to do. She won't have to go to court."

Now she looks up. "Good," she says, in a low tone. "That's good."

Her hands are resting on the bench and for a moment he's tempted to interlace his fingers in hers, but they're so far beyond that. The rules of them were rewritten a long time ago.

"How's she doing?" he asks instead. "She seems great."

He's looking at her sideways on and she pushes the hair from her face. She's almost glowing sitting there, clear-eyed and with winter in her skin.

"Yeah, she's fine. She wants to keep going to the grief group, which is really positive. There are free biscuits—usually Bourbons—so it's totally worth the effort." She dips her head like she's taking a bow. "No, it's good, they're good. It makes you feel almost normal, y'know, when you're there? Like you're not the only ones, and we're talking more, the two of us. About Bea, I mean. Not lots, but enough, maybe, for now." She leans forward on the bench. "The thing is, what happens next? Sometimes I think, Am I holding too tight? Do I just let go of everything? Will it all work itself out?"

"Not an option," he tells her, in a cod-American accent. "You can't let go because of *this*." He thumps his chest where his heart is. "It's the deal."

Lotte has stopped a little way off. She has her phone out and she's texting. Ben keeps his eyes on his daughter while he speaks. "But you could start by forgiving yourself."

There's a pause, a held moment. Two pigeons fly at each other above their heads, turf war over a single branch.

Grace squints up into the trees. "But do you forgive me?" she asks quietly.

And it is all there, suddenly, jamming the space between them. Their baby. Their Bea. The accident. Everything that has happened. All of it.

He wants to say, *Of course I do*, but maybe because he knows in his heart that now is the moment—he knows things need to change, that they need to start to move on, to really move on—he waits before he answers. He stops. He thinks. Because something is tugging at him, a dark, toxic guilt. Something he's known all along in the root of him.

"Shit, Grace," he says slowly. And then he drops his head into his hands because he isn't able to look at her. "I think I blamed you."

He feels a movement underneath him as Grace shifts position on the bench.

"I thought so," she says softly.

There's an agony in him when he looks up, faces her.

Her eyes are too bright as she smiles at him, but it's a true smile, he knows this.

"Thank you," she says. "For allowing me that. Otherwise . . ." She shrugs, and he can see she's trying to make a joke of it, this thing that is as far from a joke as it can be. "Otherwise I'm just paranoid."

She nudges her shoulder into his then, and he's floored by her kindness.

"Not now, though," he hears himself tell her. He hadn't known he was going to say it until he does. But as the words slip from him, he realizes it's gone. This black thing he's carried without knowing. It isn't in him any longer.

He feels the familiar shape of her hand covering his, briefly, like a shadow from the past drifting through, and then she stands. And there's the sense something has lifted, just a little.

He tilts his chin toward the sky. "Even monkeys fall from trees, Grace," he says. It's her favorite Japanese expression, he knows.

She eyes the treetops. "Nobody's perfect," she agrees.

"Our kid comes damn close, though." He makes a sucking sound through his teeth.

"Yup, that's true," she says.

He's about to add something more, something half-formed and trite to do with life and failure and no regrets. But when they glance at each other, a fast, private exchange, he understands that she already knows.

"Okay, I need to get back to it." She brushes crumbs from her front onto the loamy floor of the wood. "Lotte!" she calls. "Lunch was amazing. I'll see you later, okay?" She blows a kiss across the muddy dip and Lotte glances up from her phone, reaches out a hand and snatches at thin air, closes her hand into a fist, as though she's catching something. And in that instant Ben sees his daughter, small and sleep-fluffy, her duvet pulled up to her chin. She has one small hand stuck out from under the covers and she's catching Grace's kisses as they switch off the light at bedtime.

"Thanks for coming today." Grace swings round to face him. Standing there in her safety vest, with her bird's-nest hair, she looks ridiculous and wonderful. "Maybe next time I'll make like Naomi Campbell and do it in my stilettos." She tips out her hip in a catwalk pose, and he knows she's said it to break the moment.

As she moves off, he lifts his arm in a half wave. "Catch up soon," he calls after her.

The cold has bitten through to his thighs and he can feel the muscles in his legs seizing up as he gets to his feet. Lotte saunters over to him, her phone still in her hand. He puts his arm around her, pulls her in close, and she lets him.

"She's pretty fierce, your mum," he says.

Lotte laughs. "You think?"

The sky punctures from nowhere as they walk away. Hail like small rocks lands in their hair, on their faces, settles for a moment on the ground before it vanishes, leaving dark spots behind. Lotte starts to run toward the car but Ben turns back, just to check.

She's a bright slash of orange way across the clearing. Spade in hand, she's shoveling grit from a sack that's leaning against a tree. Laying it down, patting it firm, building a new path. As he watches, she moves forward a small step, repeats the process, shoring up the edges when the grit spills from the sides. Then she does the same again and again. Working steadily, methodically, purposefully.

Acknowledgments

The idea for this book was inspired by the 1993 film *Falling Down*, written by Ebbe Roe Smith. And by the glorious bundle of women in my life.

Not least Hellie Ogden, agent, guru, champion, and all-round brilliant woman. Thank you for your endless support, I've learned so much from you. My incredible editors, Jess Leeke in the UK, who had me at hello, and who poured her soul into these pages; and in the US, Amy Einhorn, Book Goddess. Thank you both for your passion, generosity, humor, and insight, and for sharing your vast experience. I feel so lucky Grace found you. Huge thanks also to everyone at Henry Holt, especially Caitlin Mulrooney-Lyski, Caroline Zancan, Caitlin O'Shaughnessy, Julia Ortiz, Molly Bloom, Meryl Levavi, Laura Flavin, Alyssa Weinberg, Pat Eisemann, Chris Sergio, Nicolette Seeback Ruggiero, Jason Reigal, Janel Brown, Leela Gebo, Jane Haxby, and Jonathan Bush. And to all at Penguin Michael Joseph, especially Louise Moore, who rooted for Grace from the start, Maddy Woodfield, Clare Parker, Ella Watkins, Jen Harlow, Jen Breslin, Eloise Austin, Kate Elliott, Nick Lowndes, Hazel Orme, Lee Motley, and Kate Dehler. Thanks too to Chantal Noel, Jane Kirby, and the fabulous foreign rights team. And to everyone at Janklow and Nesbit, especially Ma'suma Amiri and Emily Randle.

Thank you to my friends—complete poppets you all—for listening, reading, advising, and whooping, especially Sarah Morell, Vardit Shalet, Sarah Minchin, Hilary Tailor, Lou Wheatley, Roz Hutchison, Andy Baker, Hannah Newman, Tim Minchin, Fi Gold. Thank you, Dai Fujikura,

Didier De Raeck, Cristian Vogel, Fedor Stepanenko, Carla Santana Hernandez, Mathias Schaffhäuser, Walter Morel for excellent swearing in foreign languages.

Thank you, Mum—mother of all mothers—for always bringing the love. Thank you, Cath and Jules, for blind loyalty and cheerleading, THE best sisters bar none. We have climbed every mountain together, followed every rainbow (hell, yeah, that's a stellar *Sound of Music* reference shoehorned in, you're welcome). Thank you to Dad—who, at least, knew he was in these acknowledgments—for reading *Travelling to* (bloody) *Tripiti* on repeat. I'm sorry you didn't get to finish *Paradise Lost*. And thank you to Jeannie, for telling the most perfect stories. Eternally grateful for my sprawling family, my safety net—Dodwells, Baineses, Donaldsons, Morels, Warrens, Ursells, Beggs, Flowers. Thank you, you gorgeous, gorgeous people.

Thank you Cassia, Ione, and Lucia, my beautiful kick-ass girls. This book is really an accidental love letter to you. Thank you, Si, my orange-half. For living and breathing many, *many* thousands of words, and for wizard-like patience start to finish. There's no one I'd rather be walking the journey with.

About the Author

Fran Littlewood has an MA in creative writing from Royal Holloway, University of London. Before her MA, she worked as a journalist, including a stint at *The Times*. She lives in London with her husband and their three daughters. *Amazing Grace Adams* is her debut novel.